TIME

OF

MIRACLES

WRITINGS FROM AN UNBOUND EUROPE

■

BORISLAV PEKIĆ

THE TIME OF MIRACLES

Translated by Lovett F. Edwards

NORTHWESTERN UNIVERSITY PRESS

EVANSTON, ILLINOIS

Northwestern University Press
Evanston, Illinois 60208-4210

Published 1994

Printed in the United States of America

ISBN 0-8101-1117-9

Library of Congress Cataloging-in-Publication Data

Pekić, Borislav, 1930 –
[Vreme cuda. English]
The time of miracles / Borislav Pekić ; translated by Lovett F. Edwards.
p. cm. — (Writings from an unbound Europe)
Originally published: New York : Harcourt Brace Jovanovich, c1976.
ISBN 0-8101-1117-9 (pbk.)
I. Edwards, Lovett Fielding. II. Title. III. Series.
PG1419.26.E5V713 1994
891.73'44—dc20

93-45889
CIP

The paper used in this publication meets the minimum requirements of the American National Standard for Information Sciences—Permanence of Paper for Printed Library Materials, ANSI Z39.48-1984.

To my friends

RADOSLAV PAVLOVIĆ
PRVOSLAV JOVANOVIĆ
DORDJE MILINKOVIĆ

Contents

Foreword

> To every thing there is a season, and a time to every purpose under the heaven: a time to be born, and a time to die; a time to break down, and a time to build up; a time to weep, and a time to laugh; a time to get, and a time to lose; a time to keep silence, and a time to speak; a time to love, and a time to hate; a time of war, and a time of peace. One generation cometh: but the earth abideth for ever. The wind goeth toward the south, and turneth about unto the north; it whirleth about continually, and the wind returneth again according to his circuits. All the rivers run into the sea; yet the sea is not full; unto the place from whence the rivers come, thither they return again. The thing that hath been, it is that which shall be; and that which is done is that which shall be done: and there is no new thing under the sun.
>
> Ecclesiastes 3:1

IN THE BEGINNING God created the heaven and the earth. And God said: "Let there be light." And there was light.

And there was evening and there was morning. And the world was. The first day.

And God created man in his image: male and female.

There was evening and there was morning. And there was man. The sixth day.

And the first man sinned the first sin and was driven from paradise, God's garden planted eastward in Eden. And Cain and Abel were born. And Cain killed Abel in the field. There was morning and there was evening. And there was crime. Who knows on which day.

Foreword

And God as a compensation and a consolation gave Seth. And Seth begat Enos. Then men began to call upon the name of the Lord in the tents. And Enos lived ninety years and died, and his descendant Noah the son of Lamech lived nine times ninety years and died, leaving to his tribe as a heritage a memorial which recalled to them as a warning the forty days of the flood, and three sons of differing skins: Shem, Ham and Japhet.

And there was evening and there was morning. And there was punishment. Who knows on which day.

A descendant of the blessed Shem married the rich herdsman Abraham the son of Terah, Abraham the forefather of his people, who traveling from Ur of the Chaldees into Canaan, once again heard the forgotten voice of the God of Adam: "Get thee out of thy country and from thy kindred, and from thy father's house, unto a land which I shall shew thee. And I will make of thee a great nation." Abraham obeyed and hastened on the mountain of Moriah to conclude an eternal alliance with God.

And there was evening and there was morning. And there was the Testament. Who knows on which day.

In Canaan, Isaac was born to Abraham, father of the people of Israel. And Isaac begat the hairy Esau, who was the ancestor of Edom, and Jacob, who was to be called Israel. And Jacob begat, some by his wife and some by his concubine: Reuben, Simeon, Levi, Judah, Issachar, Zebulon, Benjamin, Dan, Gad, Naphthali, Asher and the wretched Joseph, who led his brethren into the province of Goshen in the land of Khem, those twelve who were the ancestors of the twelve tribes of Israel. That was the time of the first captivity. And when they built with forced labor the cities of Pithom and Rameses, there was born of the tribe of Levi Moses the son of Abraham, who, led by a pillar of fire—by the God of Abraham, the God of Isaac and the God of Jacob—brought his people out of Egyptian slavery in the days which are still today called Exodus. And to him, the Lawgiver, God spoke in a voice of thunder: "I am He Who Was, He Who Is and He Who Will Be. I am thy Lord God and thou shalt have no other gods before me!" Invisible and formless, God burned in a thorn bush in the midst of Horeb, but although burning it was not consumed nor could there be any doubt of his holy Word, nor of his power to command the respect of the chosen people.

And there was evening and there was morning. And there was Law. Who knows on which day.

And when, with the benevolent help of heavenly frogs, lice and locusts, the people of Israel at last took courage to begin their miserable wanderings to their home, and when the distrustful halted to look upon it, Moses went up into the invisible presence of God on the mountain of Nebo, and behold: the land before the Hebrew people and before the eyes of the dying Lawgiver was Canaan, the Promised Land.

Eretz Israel, which Jehovah gave as a possession to his favored people, lazily stretched between the rust-colored caverns of Idumaea and the gray plateau of Aram, between the fertile Jordan basin and the Mediterranean, from the dense, low heavens to the rolling land of yellow groves, yellow caverns and yellow fields under the plow. Why he chose the tribes of the Hebrews upon whom to pour out his almighty favor he himself couldn't explain, and the misfortunes which accompanied them from that time on wherever they went seemed to bear witness that the most powerful of friends is also the greatest bearer of evil. Led out of Noah's stock, thrown into Egyptian slavery and drawn from that as raw suet is thrown on the fire to clarify it, the people of Israel were to be sent into Canaan with the unambiguous promise that, after they had subjugated it, they would find their peace in that country.

They didn't.

They would be scattered to the four corners of the world as the indestructible ash of some very ancient primal myth of suffering, a myth whose episodes were still to be enumerated and whose end still isn't known.

Israel, by good fortune, wasn't condemned to lifelong suffering. The prophets, the angry interpreters of the gods, prophesied a better fate: "Hear, O Israel," they said, "God, who gave you his adopted son Moses to free you from captivity of the body, will give you his only-begotten son to free you from sin, the bondage of the soul. And he will not be one of those false saviors which all peoples have at all times. His kingdom will not be of this but of that world, and in his hands he will not hold a sword but an olive branch!"

It must have been that the Israelites, spoiled by God's favors, didn't hold greatly to empty promises, and fighting in the meantime with their neighbors, the unbelievers, demanded something more definite, some bodily, irrevocable sign of heavenly favor.

Instructed by the Lord God, the prophet Isaiah said to them: "Hear ye now, O house of David; it is a small thing for you to weary men, but will ye weary my God also? Therefore the Lord himself will give you a sign; Behold, a virgin shall conceive, and bear a son, and shall call his name Emmanuel."

And the prophet Isaiah again spoke: "He is despised and rejected of men; a man of sorrows, and acquainted with grief; and we hid as it were our faces from him; he was despised, and we esteemed him not. Surely he hath borne our griefs, and carried our sorrows; yet we did esteem him stricken, smitten of God, and afflicted. But he was wounded for our transgressions, he was bruised for our iniquities; the chastisement of our peace was upon him; and with his stripes we are healed."

And Israel sacrificed fat sacrifices, burned precious offerings, prayed the appointed prayers, all in expectation of that incomparable savior whom John the Baptist in Aenon near to Salim foretold, saying: "Prepare ye the way of the Lord; make his paths straight!"

And behold, the Scripture was fulfilled.

He came during the reign of Octavian Augustus.

This is the true story about him, his teaching and his disciples, his miracles and his passion. This is the true tale of how his new kingdom above all kingdoms was born.

And it was evening and it was morning. And it was Joshua ben Joseph, Jesus the Nazarene, Savior of the world.

Who knows on which day, every day.

THE TIME OF MIRACLES

Now when John had heard in the prison the works of Christ, he sent two of his disciples and said unto him, Art thou he that should come, or do we look for another? Jesus answered and said unto them, Go and shew John again those things which ye do hear and see: The blind receive their sight, and the lame walk, the lepers are cleansed, and the deaf hear, the dead are raised up, and the poor have the gospel preached to them. And blessed is he, whosoever shall not be offended in me.

Matthew 11:2–6

Miracle at Cana

> Jesus saith unto them, Fill the waterpots with water. And they filled them up to the brim. And he saith unto them, Draw out now, and bear unto the governor of the feast. And they bare it. When the ruler of the feast had tasted the water that was made wine, and knew not whence it was, he called the bridegroom, and saith unto him, Every man at the beginning doth set forth good wine; and when men have well drunk, then that which is worse; but thou hast kept the good wine until now. This beginning of miracles did Jesus in Cana of Galilee, and manifested forth his glory; and his disciples believed on him.
>
> John 2:7–11

FROM SIMON, son of Jona, by the Lord's will Peter, apostle and servant of Our Lord Jesus Christ, to all bishops, archdeacons, deacons and elders of all those who have accepted with us the one and only true faith—to the Jews, the Romans, the Corinthians, the Ephesians, the Philippians, the Colossians, the Thessalonians, as well as to all the newcomers: Blessing and the peace of God our Father and of the Lord Jesus Christ.

May this testament find you, wherever you may be, of generous and not wooden heart, of thirsting and not sated soul and with ears open to the word of truth.

This address to all the elders of the Christian communities is from Simon Peter, son of Jona from Bethsaida of Gennesaret whom the Savior named Cephas and changed into the firm rock on which he based his Church. To the glory of the Father, and of the Son and of the Holy Ghost. Amen.

The Time of Miracles

You ask me to visit you, you call for me because I am indispensable to you; indispensable to Corinth, indispensable to Salonica, imperative to Jerusalem, and Rome which doesn't know God can't do without me.

Deceivers! Blasphemers! Hypocrites! Haven't you learned yet that nothing is indispensable except faith and nothing is irreplaceable except faith. Neither doctrines nor teachers. Neither prayer nor the Creed nor believers. Only faith.

Do you mean to tell me that you don't know where I am, that you don't know that I'm rotting in a Roman prison and that tomorrow at dawn they'll crucify me on a cross from which the flesh of your brothers in Christ is already falling? Hypocrites! Blasphemers! Deceivers!

But what are you to Peter when you have no faith; when you're only waiting for my third death rattle to be announced *Urbi et Orbi* before falling like a pestilence upon the Lord's heritage, dividing what is written to be indivisible, violating what was given as inviolable, destroying what was offered as indestructible.

When no single believer or leader of the devout Christian community is convinced that only Peter's sacrifice preserved our faith, and that Peter alone, that foundation stone of the Church able to crush men, was enabled even *in continuo* to preserve all that was worthy and faithful among them, in order that they should live longer, ceaselessly divesting themselves of merit and renouncing their faith.

What are you to me, dear brothers in Christ, if I can no longer enjoy your devotion, even though it may still call to me in some loyal heart, which doesn't dare beat freely when I'm no longer there to record it, when I'm no longer there as a consecrated bell to ring out thunderously the uncertain beatings of your wavering hearts at the gate of true life. No one knows how to halt nature, saying: Now that's enough, stop, get back within your monstrous limitations, into your soulless nothingness.

But all these incessant beatings, sowing among you and those dearest to you fear, suffering and martyrdom, will be as nails of doom driven into my back.

Miracle at Cana

What are you to me, my brothers in Christ, if the hour has come for me to ask myself whether I was right. Within my cell, where even the daylight throws the arrow-shaped shadow of the cross, there's no one to answer me.

If I'm unsure whether I'll be a saint or an outcast in the dreams and books and on the lips of those who'll come after me (and what if no one comes after me?) to smash, profane and dishonor their dead idols, and their sons who'll collect the scattered fragments so as to prostrate themselves once again before their renewed brilliance.

What are you to me, my brothers in Christ, when my trowel—despite your eulogies and reproaches, your apotheoses and anathemas—has built a world in which I'd like to live not as a builder but as a beneficiary, as a subject not a ruler, as a fisherman of Gennesaret and not a Roman saint.

And when, after death has swept away all ugly details and leveled all casual roughnesses and clumsy shortcomings, I stand before the colossal contours of my work: the Church and its mason, one dependent on the other, one for the other, one in the other.

You, I hear, complain that many of our worthy brothers have suffered because of Peter's zealous haste to carry out the commands of his God. Are a few thousand Christians worth more to you than Christianity, a few dozen churchwardens more important than Holy Church?

I say to you, when the praises of God are sung beneath the protecting arches of the Church, not one of you shall recall the builder, the mason, the ikon carver and the craftsman who died in building it. Not one of those Zachariahs consumed by the flames, those Nahors broken on the wheel, those Jonahs cast into prison, those Joshuas torn asunder, those Japhets hanged by the balls before the city guardhouse, will call upon me to assume responsibility. Will those Christians called upon to bear witness to God demand from me an account of their sufferings? Can we who are dead make accusations at the Last Judgment? Can we?

Could the people of Israel have been brought out of Egypt, if God hadn't sent thirst, hunger and pestilence to assist them? Thirst, hunger and pestilence—are they blessings? How could the Moabites and Ammonites have come into being, had not Lot's daughters conceived by their own father? Is incest a virtue? Could the respected patriarch Jacob have become the ancestor of Israel if, wrapped in goatskin like Esau, he hadn't wheedled from the sightless Isaac the blessing intended for his shaggy first-born brother? Is a lie truth?

How could the guilty and the innocent have been separated in Sodom and Gomorrah, so that the sinners were consumed by fire and the innocent blessed with the cool streams of paradise? Is injustice good? Wasn't it from original sin that this world was created, when a drop of bitterness was squeezed from the apple of Eden, that drop which is now oversweet to all things living? Is innocence sin? Who today regards Moses, Lot's daughters, Jacob, Adam and the living God as guilty because they made use of the tools of sin so that sin itself should be rooted out?

Do you dare then to spit upon Peter?

For Peter as well as the Church bequeaths you a sharpened sword with which you'll defend yourself from paganism, heresy, schism and faintheartedness. Even as our most blessed Savior left us a testament to spread the gospel among all peoples, so I, the heir to his power on earth, hand down to all leaders of the churches, and above all to the bishop of Rome, and to those who till the last day sit upon the throne of Peter, this charge and testament.

This won't be the sermon of the Savior, for words have an effect proportionate to him who utters them and to those who hear them, and what am I compared with the golden-tongued Son of God, or you compared with his golden-eared listeners?

And it won't be one of the miracles which he performed, loosing the tongues of the mute, restoring the mad to their senses, the dead to life; for by untangling tongues what will you get but a mob of babblers, that is to say betrayers; by raising the lame to their feet what will you get but a horde of fast runners, that is to say persecutors; by giving sight to the sightless you'll get only the curious, that is to say spies; by bringing the dead to life you'll get more sinners, that is to say enemies. Give up such miracles, my brothers in Christ!

For such miracles converted only those upon whom they were wrought, and left the onlookers afraid of God rather than trusting in him.

Therefore your devoted pastor Peter bequeaths to you a special miracle which, though it took place before our eyes, didn't promise anything special; yet doubt turned to certainty that there was no defense against his spells and that every lack of faith was powerless before him. That was the miracle at Cana in Galilee. And this is how it happened.

On the third day after my coming to the Lord, there was a great heat and we were cooling our feet at Gennesaret, in vague expectation that something would happen to shorten the time of the study of his sermons. For we were his first disciples, and though until that afternoon we'd learned little except to keep out of the way of Herodians, Pharisees and Sadducees, we felt honored that we, so poor and ill-clothed, had been chosen from among so many notable Israelites to preach the gospel of the kingdom of God.

My brother Andrew and I had been chosen, along with Judas ben Simon, known as Iscariot—may his name be damned to the end of time because he betrayed Our Lord for thirty pieces of silver to the leaders so they could crucify him (they said that it was written and that for the world to be saved from sin, what was written had to be carried out to the last letter, which was true, but it wasn't written who'd do it, so every soul was free to choose, and we chose life, loyalty and love, and he death, betrayal and hatred). Also Philip, a washer of the dead from Bethsaida; the twin sons of Zebedee from Capernaum, whom the Teacher called Boanerges (which means sons of thunder) because of the likeness of their fists to summer thunder; and a certain Nathaniel from Cana of Galilee.

This Nathaniel joined us out of simple curiosity; he thought nothing good could come from the Savior's Nazareth, famous for its harlotry, and he joined us only to be convinced. That was what Nathaniel said, but others, surprised at his concern for public morals, said that he'd come to find new friends; all his old friends, from Rama to Hebron, had been crucified on crosses. For Nathaniel was a bandit.

But I tell you, noble elders of the communities, that those crosses, in plan, material and construction, were the same as those Roman crosses from which hang the bloody remains of our brothers. Though the crosses are old, those who bear the crosses are new; just men have replaced the sinners. Therefore, made equal in pain, separated in the memories from what they leave behind them, made equal in the outcome but separated in the reasons for their torments, just men hang on the crosses alongside sinners, bandits among the saints, and criminals among the virtuous.

No words pass among them; the guilty won't plead with the innocent to intercede for them, nor will the innocent defend the guilty. For it will never happen again that the guilty will say to the innocent: Remember me when you come into your kingdom! Nor will it ever happen again that the innocent will say to the guilty: In truth I tell you that today you will be with me in paradise!

I say to you: See who Nathaniel was and see that you have no such men among you, but root them out as tares among the harvests of the true faith.

That Nathaniel saw us as we passed by the fig tree under which he was resting, and waited till we returned from the God-fearing solitude in which we'd come to know the truth, then approached Philip and asked him about the Teacher and his teaching.

Philip was able to tell him little of the teaching, for the light of the sermons hadn't yet cleared away the darkness of his very simple soul, but he said the Teacher was indeed the one whose coming had been vouched for by the prophets, the Son of God who by his suffering would redeem the world from the sin of our first ancestors. He told him also that the Teacher was called Jesus, that he was one of the sons of the carpenter Joseph of Nazareth and some woman called Mary, but that these facts, at first sight so commonplace, were quite different in their higher significance.

For Jesus Christ, our Lord and Teacher, was begotten by Jehovah in a short angelic annunciation even before Mary was espoused by Joseph, so that the person of the Savior might be considered half-divine and half-human, divine in the half begotten by God, human in the half conceived in a woman. That dual origin had produced an ambiguous offspring, neither God nor man but something between the two, which certainly looked like a man and was God, and which sometimes had the qualities of God though he was only a man.

Nathaniel was amazed and said: "Take me to this man so I too can serve him; if the union of heaven and earth has found in him its most perfect form, why should I look for someone else who'll disappoint me?" So Philip brought him.

When these two met, the most upright and the guiltiest, the Messiah pronounced Nathaniel a true Israelite in whom there was no guile, and Nathaniel without hesitation acknowledged him to be the Son of God and his Master. No one else was present at this meeting.

It wasn't clear what advantages resulted from this understanding, unless by his choice of an outlaw the Rabbi intended to confirm the Pharisees' accusation that he surrounded himself with publicans, sinners, whoremongers and criminals, while Nathaniel—who remained among us under the false name of Bartholomew—may have got the mistaken idea that he'd joined a promising company of bandits.

I tell you this so you may see who Nathaniel was and find out if there's anyone like him among you and smash him like a clay pot. For they're a disaster to the Church, sowers of doubt and reapers of unbelief, and they pillage our hearts, wishing to corrupt us and to wrest us from God. You'll see.

So there we were beside Gennesaret, seven of us with the Teacher, and we waited for him to tell us something, but the Son of God remained silent, unlike that talkative preacher from above. Then Nathaniel said that Halil, a rich man from Cana in Galilee, was marrying his son to a girl from Jericho, and that we could all go there if we had nothing better to do than yawn and prepare ourselves for the heavenly kingdom by exercising our jaws.

And when we told the Messiah of the wedding, Philip rebuked us: "How can we go there uninvited? Is there a custom in Israel that men should come uninvited on that day?"

Judas said to him: "Look, the lamb is hungry and thirsty.

Who dares to leave him bleating before the locked fold and not deserve the anger of his father? Let's do some miracle at Cana. It's time for one."

When we set out we still didn't know that Cana in Galilee would be the beginning of the miracles which the Savior would perform in the service of his adopted Father, for it wasn't until after Cana that he began to visit uninvited, to reply unbidden, to teach unasked and to save without being entreated.

And all because, dear brethren in Christ, he realized, saddened and angry, that the world he had to save had no idea of its awesome pains and felt no need of healing. For the yoke of Rome was heavier than the intangible yoke of sin. It was grievous for Israel to welcome the arrogant pagan might, to pay tribute to insatiable Caesar and carry out forced labor on his all-conquering roads, which crisscrossed the kingdom of David in search of new provinces and fresh human quarries of slaves. But it was still harder for Israel to perceive those secret ills of the spirit which gnawed at individuals and tribes, and only sporadically took the ugly forms of paralysis, leprosy and madness.

Could our Savior wait to begin his mission from God till those by whose transformation his mission should be accomplished invited him? Did he dare knock gently when he should have broken down the door, beg humbly when only command would have served? For God had ordained that the world be cleansed of sin, and had given the world to the Savior for his lifetime so that what he bound on earth would be bound in heaven, and what he loosed on earth would be loosed in heaven.

With the assurance of the higher summons we could disregard the lower one; uninvited by the host Halil but guided by the Lord, we came to Cana of Galilee and found ourselves outside the rich man's house. No one invited us in, but among so many guests it was hard to tell who'd been invited and who hadn't. Since it was God's command that we go there, we considered that we'd been invited. I, Simon, son of Jona, first gatekeeper of the Church, confirm that the noble Halil summoned us and that every other interpretation of our presence at Cana is the work of Satan!

We spent a considerable time eating the meat of young kids and drinking wine, for we were very hungry since not one of the seven of us had worked for gain, but had lived as the birds of heaven, which neither sow nor reap but even so manage to live. So we ate and drank heartily, since God had set the table for us.

Then Mary came, the mother of our Jesus, and he showed no respect for her but pretended not to see her. By this indifference he showed us that he saw in her only the bodily intermediary of the higher intention of his Heavenly Father, some kind of chance cauldron in which his mighty seed had been boiling. In his far-reaching wisdom didn't he wish to set a standard for all those who should be chosen for great deeds, that each one so transformed might say without shame or regret even as he'd said to us: "Forsake your father and your mother and come with me, even as I have left my father and my mother and have followed the Lord"?

Pretending not to notice his ill will, his mother approached him to blame him for the shame he was bringing on the house of David by drinking.

And Jesus said: "Woman, what have I to do with thee? Mine hour is not yet come, but pour wine for me and my friends for we have come in the name of the Lord."

And the confirmed drunkard Nathaniel added: "Who is ruler over the whole world and therefore, I hope, is ruler also of the grape."

Then his mother, not without the malice of the sober, told him that there was no wine left, though it was only the second day that we had honored the house of Halil by our presence, and only the fourth day of the marriage at Cana.

And Judas was angry—at the start he was still virtuous, though unbearable in his virtue—because he didn't like anything begun in the name of God and the Scriptures to be interrupted, and he pronounced a curse:

"May it go hard for you, O Galilee, of the brood of vipers! May it go hard for you, unbelieving Cana, which dries the throat of the Son of God! From your vineyards, O harlot among the lands of Canaan, may only water flow!"

Then, as if recalling something, he stopped grumbling—for he'd been grumbling more out of respect for the faith than from any access of anger—and he whispered something in the ear of the Teacher, pointing to six stone jars which served for the custom of ablution. The Teacher commanded the servants to fill them to the brim with water. Each jar held up to three buckets of rainwater for the cattle.

When the servants had done as ordered, the Messiah sent the first jar to the best man to taste it, and the best man, to the consternation of all of us who knew the origin of the liquid, praised the bridegroom because, contrary to custom, he'd left the best wine to the end of the feast. Then, when the wine had been served to the guests, they drank it and it went to their heads as if it had been the best Samarian wine. And they gave great thanks to the Lord, bowed before his son and believed in him.

Of all the wedding guests, he who bowed the most deeply and humbly was a man of Cyrene, by name Simon, son of Eliezer, who'd ridden to Cana from Jerusalem with Rufus, his first-born son, and who, unwavering in the faith, was to bear the Savior's cross to Golgotha and thus be the first among us to reach paradise. You'll see.

That was before all those present collapsed on the floor. Then John the son of Zebedee was surprised and asked: "Rabbi, did you make wine of this water, so that all men have become drunk?"

Jesus said to him: "Taste and say!"

Then the sons of Zebedee, accustomed to doing everything together, tasted that miraculous wine, became drunk at once and like all the men of Cana, have remained drunk ever since. As for Nathaniel, or Bartholomew, he remarked maliciously that he thought the wine was a trifle watered, as if a bit of rainwater had remained at the bottom of each jar which the miracle hadn't reached.

Judas got angry and said to the meek Teacher: "If the heavenly wine is too weak for him, ask him what other wine will be strong enough? And is there any wine that will topple him?"

When asked, Nathaniel said: "There isn't, Lord!"

Then Judas said that this man Nathaniel must be cursed if the miracle which had been wrought was to survive, for if this first one were denied then no other would be acknowledged, nor would all that was written in the Scriptures concerning the miracles of the Son of God be fulfilled.

So Jesus placed a curse on him: "So be it. You'll be granted the haven of paradise but you'll live in filth; they'll bring you sweetmeats and it'll seem to you you're eating carrion; they'll array you in velvet and you'll think you're wearing rags; they'll shower love on you and you'll feel you're being beaten!"

"I tell you," Judas said again, "he who doesn't get drunk on this water will never see paradise!"

And I tell you, dear brothers in Christ, such a man will never see God face to face. For he'll never bathe in the mists of unconditional faith as in the wine of Cana, nor rejoice in God's shadow when it passes across pitiful everyday faces and darkening them, lights up the horizon with incredible visions of a sinless and eternally beautiful future.

I say this to you so you may know who Nathaniel was and see if there are any such men among you, so you may weed them out from the garden of the true faith. For they'll cause scandal among you, tempt you and give you false signs, leading you into the service of the devil, just as they themselves have served him from the beginning of the world. Intoxicated by the devil's wine, they don't know God's but believe it to be water.

After the wedding guests had drunk their fill and fallen under the tables, glorifying the new kingdom which, if no more, assured them first-class drinks, Judas decided it was time for the two of us to taste some. Until then we'd been anxious that all should be according to the Scriptures, paying no attention to ourselves.

So they brought him a mug of the miraculous water; without thinking, he sucked up a mouthful, then spat it out, cursing: "What is this, Simon, you withered fig tree, you rock of rocks?"

"Wine, brother in Christ," I said humbly.

And Judas asked: "What sort of devilish wine?"

I replied that it was the wine which, at his command a little earlier, the Messiah had created from water, and from which the whole world had become drunk.

He placed me before him and said: "Well, Simon, my barren vine, this is just dirty water. But for the chosen and the upright, what's wine to sinners can be nothing more than water. And what's wine to the chosen and the upright, let it be as unattainable to sinners as the Book of Life at the time of the last reading."

I asked him: "What should I do?"

And he said: "Go to the first wineshop and buy some real wine, but see that they don't draw it from the bottom of the barrel. And hurry, Simon, so I can refresh myself, for tomorrow the miracle continues which the Most Blessed began today, changing the water into wine."

When I returned with the wine, he tasted it and said: "This is wine and that was water."

So we drank till the third day after our arrival, and to the seventh day of the marriage at Cana in Galilee.

Simon, son of Jona of Bethsaida of Gennesaret, whom the Savior called Peter or Cephas, whom he turned to the rock upon which he built his magnificent Church, bears witness to this, and leaves it to the Christian elders as a first testament of the faith and a heritage.

To the glory of the Father, and of the Son and of the Holy Ghost. Amen.

Miracle at Jabneel

And, behold, there came a leper and worshipped him, saying: Lord, if thou wilt, thou canst make me clean. And Jesus put forth his hand, and touched him, saying: I will; be thou clean. And immediately his leprosy was cleansed. And Jesus saith unto him: See thou tell no man; but go thy way, shew thyself to the priest, and offer the gift that Moses commanded, for a testimony unto them.

Matthew 8:2–4

TO THE SOUTHWEST of the lake of Gennesaret, between the sluices of Tiberias and the wilderness of Tabor (Gjebel-el-Tura), the dried-up riverbed Jabtel, like a siege trench amid its mane of scorched grasses, riddled by the lairs of snakes and peppered by ratholes, formed the municipal boundary between Old and New Jabneel. But whereas Old Jabneel preened itself in the sweet-smelling slough of the Jordan oasis and the fertile silt of its tributaries—a wet nurse watered by twelve wells consecrated to Adonai, cooled by the dense shade of palms and lulled to sleep by the murmur of the sunlit breezes—New Jabneel was a wretched place surrounded by filth, barren clay, mire and stunted reeds. Uncertain whether to fear the desert's smothering sands or its twin villages that overwhelmed it with disgusting terror with official curses, the riverbed seemed to have surrendered to the ultimate feeling of doom, from generation to generation withdrawing more and more irretrievably into the dead landscape where only the listless shadows of kites and vultures cruised.

New Jabneel, which was a leper settlement, was called "The Unclean" in accord with the Law, and strangers knew that the other Jabneel, a favorite of the God of Jacob, was also called "The Clean."

Founded very long ago, at the time of the battles of Gideon the Judge, Jabneel had grown up as twin villages, but each according to its own image, its own testament and customs, its own destiny and fortunes, on one side leprous and unclean, on the other healthy and clean, without the right but also the inclination to work together. Such twin settlements existed throughout Galilee, Samaria and Judaea, from Idumaea to Syria, from the Mediterranean to the Dead Sea, wherever the twelve sons of Jacob, ancestors of the future twelve tribes of Israel, had sown their seed from the times of the Lawgiver Moses, who on the first day of the second month of the second year after the Exodus, obsessed by the Lord or by the irresistible summons of his own ruling ambition, expelled all lepers from his tents and everyone who had an issue and whoever had been defiled, whether they were among the numbered men or unnumbered women, children or beasts. To the cleansing fire he consigned all curtains, woven stuffs, robes and yarns infected by the disease, and mercilessly razed to the ground all habitations of those who were ill, and destroyed all their public and religious objects, no matter how precious, so that they didn't spread the plague and by their shame humiliate those whom the whim of the Creator, thanks to the intervention of Abraham's son, chose for his vanguard. Ill-tempered like so many single men, Moses the Lawgiver was a pedant as well who prescribed all the Levitical procedure for the diagnosis of leprosy, and handed over its implementation to the priests of the line of Aaron. He gave strict orders that those marked by his finger should go in rags and bareheaded so that God's punishment be displayed in universal ill fame, but with covered mouth and announcing constantly, whenever they passed within a stone's throw of any clean person or tent, "Unclean! One who is unclean is passing here!" For the chosen were few and so why waste them.

In New Jabneel lived the leper woman Egla, married to Uriah of the tribe of Zebulon, an unclean washer of the dead, and we mention Old Jabneel because her former, clean, husband Jeroboam, a newcomer or a refugee from Sidon, held the office of town crier there.

Egla had never forgotten the golden-tongued Jeroboam, though she got on well with the strong, simple giant Uriah, partly because the Lord had separated them both from his chosen community and thus directed them to one another, and partly because advanced leprosy, like any chronic illness, had perverted the hitherto unawakened body of the plowman's son and had forced his newborn lustful fantasies, concentrated and unexpectedly abundant and not divided among many wives and concubines, on the only one available. Egla found enjoyment in Uriah even when, during the summer pestilence, he would crawl exhausted out of the mortuary and caress her with movements—similar to those he used in rubbing corpses—that he enlivened by ribald remarks about clients whose families were bad risks.

In her innocent heart Egla was frightened, yet excited. Despair, the most enduring element of her Old Jabneel memories, provided her delirium with ever fresh and more impressive images of torment, and that delirium aroused still more unbearable scenes, and opened fresh wells of enjoyment, until pain became transformed into a continual enchantment. For it was not possible to suffer without being excited by suffering when she recalled Jeroboam's smooth, freshly washed white skin, instead of Uriah's, which was rasping as the bark of a centuries-old cedar and sprinkled with sparse, graying bristles. Naturally, not because those hairs irritated her, for their prickling stimulated amorous ardor, but because she supposed that her dearest Jeroboam would have enjoyed just as passionately on his loins the prickling of her hair, made sharp and stiff by her illness.

These stimulating images encompassed Egla's bodily passion. Her spiritual passion yearned for Jeroboam's baritone, for that voice deep and clear as the sound of the ram's horn by which the caravans understood one another—a voice that no longer served to arouse her sexual desires, or to issue household commands or chant the psalms of David on the days of the feast of Passover, but rather to anger the people of Old Jabneel with fresh obligations to the Roman bloodsuckers and their heavenly protector. That voice, which Jeroboam released like a sweet bird at dusk, lured Egla out of Uriah's house without fear of scandal, for her husband was busily washing and combing the corpses; it drew her to the Jabtel ravine where, cowering in the hot weeds like a driven beast, she waited to catch the golden falcon of Jeroboam's words, which grew louder or weaker, advanced or retreated, soared or sank deep down, depending at which crossroads he was shouting the instructions of his masters. Naturally, she was unable to see him, still less to touch him. The Law forbade them to even talk to each other. But to her fettered spirit his bodiless voice was a sufficient password, just as the incomprehensible thunderings of God's speech are sufficient for the true believer to interpret with eager heart those words of the supreme will which have not been uttered. However, these words were uttered. They were words addressed to her only. Not all, naturally, but the best among them, those which came from Jeroboam himself and not the decrees of the Emperor or the tetrarch. They were the result of an agreement, of which more will be said shortly, by which Jeroboam, taking advantage of his public position for private ends, interwove news for Egla among the commands for taxes, tithes and summons to forced labor. This is what had happened:

One morning, not a month after Jeroboam had brought his chosen bride into his parents' tent, Egla had felt an itching under her right breast. Painless, and even to some extent pleasant, like a soft breath of wind locked in her bosom, it had vanished by the evening, but upon returning the following day, had even more rudely stung her skin, moist and soft as a marsh flower. Then appeared the first pimples, the color of cinnamon and topped with rough crusts. Saying nothing to her husband, she washed herself in running water, and when Jeroboam came back from work and called her to their mutual enjoyment, she excused herself by saying she had a headache. But the bathing didn't cleanse her and her headache couldn't serve forever as an excuse, so Egla, with a heavy heart but without losing her composure, showed Jeroboam the eczema which had in the meantime reached her other breast. The linen cloth with which she had covered her breasts was also infected, except that on the weave, instead of being fiery red, the infection was the purplish color of rotten fruit.

Hiding his darkest suspicions from his wife, Jeroboam advised her to say nothing to anyone, especially relatives, neighbors and friends, until they learned what were the ultimate aims of that heavenly visitation on her skin. It might be, he said, as much a favorable as an unfavorable omen; a misfortune which might affect anyone, doubtless a warning or a punishment of dissatisfied divinity, but sometimes also a forerunner of some great honor. For the ways of the Lord are mysterious. On many occasions, he said, Hashem, in order to conceal his real intentions, threw a curse of misfortune on a man and—while those closest to him, led astray by the Creator's jest and hoping to follow his divine will, continued to throw stones at the man so marked—he unexpectedly granted him a prophetic or some other lucrative talent.

In order to forestall this evil variant of the divine visitation—as far as human worthlessness made it possible—every night, instead of sharing caresses, they prayed together devotedly to Adonai to forgive them if they had sinned, or if in the carelessness of the fortunate they had brought down upon themselves the divine wrath. But alas, the forgotten sin was, it seemed, unforgivable. Either Jehovah didn't wish to explain himself clearly or wavered between two opposing meanings to which Egla's illness must be imputed. In any case, God remained as deaf as a stone.

"Perhaps he really is deaf!" said Jeroboam.

"How can a god be deaf?" Egla replied in wonder.

"God can do anything," explained Jeroboam, "and since he is almighty, what is to prevent him from being deaf? All opposites, which among us are skillfully divided, are contained in him, so that to one his ear is keen and to another deaf. If he is really God then he must at the same time be long-sighted and blind, keen of hearing and deaf, active and paralyzed. And I think that in the same way he must both exist and not exist. Those are principles on which are created his omnipresence and his omnipotence, two equal axes of his divine nature."

These complex dogmas didn't affect Egla. Common sense spoke this to her: if God is both long-sighted and blind, he must, to be whole, be both at the same time, and then he could be neither one nor the other. What then, in the name of Sarah's barrenness, must he be?

Jeroboam scolded his wife for absent-mindedness, which was evident even in her household tasks, and for which he had not reproached her till now.

"You yourself," he said, "don't recall your offense. Perhaps your forgetfulness irritates him, as I must confess it irritates me."

"Yes, yes," said Egla scornfully, "you men always stick together."

"Don't be silly, woman!" Jeroboam yelled. "If he's everything, then God can't be man only, but also woman! Isn't the Hittite Great Mother bearded, and doesn't her divine partner have breasts such as you have, though naturally not as nice? Hasn't the sacred Ishtar Alilat a whacking great beard of which even Moses might be envious? I don't defend our Adonai as a male, but as an orderly man who puts all things, even all sins, in their right place, where he can find them when he needs them."

And Jeroboam quoted the edifying example of his mother Malchis, who had a special reminder for every sin in the form of palm sticks of various shapes, so that she always selected the appropriate prayer for forgiveness.

"Ha, your mother!" Egla mocked. "So it's because of her that there's no patch of shade from Hazor to Rama!"

Fortunately Jeroboam didn't hear her; he was searching for other possible excuses for divine indolence. "Perhaps he's busy with more important tasks."

"There's no task more important than my skin."

"Perhaps he's tired and not up to anything."

"Does a mother dare to get tired?" Egla asked soberly. "It isn't enough to give birth to a child; you must also care for it."

At the same time she thought of the world which Jehovah

created of his own free will and with the help of a single magic word.

"Perhaps he doesn't know Hebrew?"

"Doesn't Adonai rule over the Israelites? How could the Lord not know the language of his servants?"

"For God's sake, woman," Jeroboam burst out, "the Romans rule over the Promised Land without knowing its language!"

Every night they argued bitterly between their litanies, which had become repetitious, for so much time had passed since that morning when, leaning over the well, Egla had for the first time felt the heavenly itch. And for her it was much worse, not only because of the blooming skin which by this time no balm from Horzin, Cana, Nain or Tiberias as far as Jabneel could heal, but because, with the instinct of an unfulfilled woman, she understood that her Jeroboam was drawing away from her. On one occasion when, panting like mules, they had ended the last of their useless supplications, Egla noticed that her husband's prayer mat was a foot farther from hers than on the previous evening. As soon as he had thrown himself on the bed about to snore, she had said to him:

"Jeroboam, my lord and husband, instead of wasting our time bowing down, let's talk with open hearts. Why pretend that Adonai is well inclined to me, though I have no idea how I have incurred his displeasure, except that when panting in your fervent embrace I called upon him and, because I wanted him to share my joy, not knowing what I was saying I took his name in vain, and in my words of love expressed the simplicity of, I must say, our mutual fever. May I remind you that I shouted out other oaths as well, which in their glorious essence were no less dignified than His hymns and which, in the light of day, one regards as curses. What has been done cannot be undone. It's not up to us but to Adonai to worry about my supposed offense, which he has already regarded as a reason for such a disgusting sentence!"

"You hate our God, Egla!" said Jeroboam, more astounded then frightened.

"I hate him," the sick woman confessed brazenly. "Couldn't

he have transformed me into a pillar of salt like Lot's wife who, bless her, paid no heed to his prohibitions and preferred to be accursed and salted rather than uninformed? Couldn't he have struck me with one of his thunderbolts which wiped out the dancers around the Golden Calf, or simply closed my womb as he did with Abraham's Sarah and so many fertile women throughout Canaan? My every limb is at the disposal of his insatiable love of justice. Instead of destroying my skin, couldn't he have used me for all the proofs which a corrupt, unbounded imagination nurtured by omnipotence could plan in its fearful loneliness?"

And Jeroboam implored:

"Don't blaspheme, my dearest. Don't provoke greater punishment."

"A lot Egla cares about such nonsense!"

"Hashem, don't listen to her!" wailed Jeroboam. He was no coward, but he wasn't sure that from such an immeasurable distance their Judge would be able to distinguish his voice from the voice of his wife, a sinner.

"Every woman who values her dignity would reply that way, and I tell you, Jeroboam, that the dignity of the most wretched woman, who stems directly from the Great Mother, Creator of all things, even if she squanders it on clients in a brothel, is greater than the dignity of the greatest man-god—male. But that wasn't what I had in mind. Let's talk about ourselves."

Jeroboam assumed a cautious attitude: "About us? What is there between us?"

"Nothing, and that's what worries me."

"But Egla, my dove, I love you!"

"I know," she replied vaguely, "and that's my greatest worry. If you didn't love me you could stay with me and watch with indifference how, according to some divine project, I disintegrate, and how, fulfilling some inhuman misson, I am transformed into a monster in the image of that very will which allotted me this fate, and you could leave me often without oil and bread, clothes and pleasure. But Jeroboam, my love and my lord, as you are beyond all measure devoted to me, you will not endure that process of transformation with a single one of your tender senses, and one night, when your prayer mat moves all the way to the door, you'll wrap yourself in it and run away."

"As Adonai is my witness, I'll never leave you!"

"Don't speak to me of Adonai!" shrieked Egla. "He has shown what he can do. Look!" She uncovered her breasts.

"Let's wail to other gods, but first be good and cover your breasts," her husband proposed, turning his head away. "They say that Cybele is inclined to spite those who share the heavens with her. Would a good sacrifice, let's say a ram without blemish from your father's flock, be enough to bribe her?"

"Cybele is a woman. I don't want to be indebted to women."

"All right. But Ammon-Ra is a man and he holds the whole world under his eye, the sun, like a disc. If we turn to him, perhaps we'll win him over."

But Egla would not place any trust in a cowardly god who had lost his independence, and who was held captive in Rome together with his degraded semidivine followers, to beg on his hind legs before Jupiter Capitolinus.

That reason was convincing enough to urge Jeroboam to ask his wife: "What do you think, my dearest, of the Roman gods that I mentioned? If those vulgar people rule the world, surely it's only because their god is a more resourceful protector than any other."

Egla rejected this sober proposal with scorn. "I'd rather die than be cured by some barbarian in woolly pants. And I don't want to plead with anyone. I hate all gods—ah, if only you knew how much I hate them. So tomorrow, Jeroboam, take me to Ismai, the servant of your God, and let that be the end."

Jeroboam, who was drowsy, agreed, and promised that the next day the priest Ismai would examine her wherever the eye can see, and cleanse or brand her according to the Law. To tell the truth, no love could preserve Jeroboam's knees from the callouses deposited by so many increasingly complex and worn penetential prayers, and no conjugal devotion could so blind him that he couldn't foresee in the transformation of Egla's breasts what his wife would look like in a month or in a year.

The next day they appeared before the rabbi, saying: "We think there's leprosy in her flesh and in her clothing." Ismai called upon Egla to undress, which she did with the obstinacy of a cripple in whom the disgust of the public arouses self-respect, and without compassion or disgust he conscientiously examined the woman's illness and infected garments and, after finding that her hairs had not whitened, shut her up for seven days, her and her infected garments separately. After seven days he inspected the sick woman and her clothes even more carefully, and found that the infection had spread in the weave; he ceremoniously declared it unclean and burned it with living fire, but the woman, on whom he didn't notice any change, he sent back into quarantine for yet another seven days. Only when, at the end of the second week, he saw that her hairs had whitened and that the swellings had spread to her armpit, did he say—praise be to Jehovah from whom all things spring, and to whom all things return—that it was acute leprosy and that Egla was unclean.

They were not surprised. Dejected but knowing where they now stood, they breathed a sigh of relief. Jeroboam went to the market to buy for his wife the little copper bells which according to the Law she now had to wear, and to jingle in order to tell the healthy of her leprosy. Egla, returning home, ripped her outer garments, took off her shoes, uncovered her head, covered her mouth, packed up her bedding and her personal clothes and that same evening, without saying farewell to her neighbors or her relatives and accompanied only by her grieving husband, made her way to New Jabneel.

The air was black as a forest. Only the rustling of the gritty dust shaken from the desert weeds was heard. Two or three stars seemed like some illegible inscription on a darkened reliquary. At the tenth Roman stade from the settlement, the gravel began to squeak under Jeroboam's shoes.

Egla knew that Jeroboam was weeping. The leper woman

too would have wailed, had the sky been clear enough to see once more in the rays of the moonlight her husband's face: the imperial profile from a silver coin which every night she had warmed between her palms. Fortunately it was as dark as under the earth. When they reached the Jabtel stream and it was time to part, Jeroboam finally spoke:

"Egla, my soul, you know I am the town crier and every evening I go around Jabneel to tell the people what they must do and pay, to whom they must bow the knee and what the tetrarch's charity will bestow on them, from which we all live, though many die as well. If you come to this ravine and the wind is favorable, you'll hear me. Between the imperial decrees I'll insert my heart, which belongs to you alone."

Now Egla too was saddened. "Jeroboam, my bunch of flowers who rested between my breasts, Egla will come to listen to you every evening. It tears my soul that I won't be able to see you, but I implore you by all our memories not to forget sometimes to tell me the Jabneel gossip."

Thus they stood in the darkness, cold as water. Jeroboam imagined himself resting in the moist trough between Egla's festering breasts and breathing in their heavy smell—which for the crier's subtle sexuality was an unbearably disturbing image.

"May God grant that you become clean again!" he said, just as a few sluggish beams of moonlight lit up his handsome dark face.

Egla screamed. "Don't mention gods to me!"

No longer able to endure the inaccessible closeness of the man who was taken from her through their carelessness, she leaped barefoot into the ravine and fled toward New Jabneel to begin her unclean life. Distressed and desolate as the stormy arch of Shebat, Jeroboam went his way to Old Jabneel to continue his clean one.

And now, since everything has been said about Egla and her first husband Jeroboam of Sidon, we must—though it's of less importance to our story—pay some attention to her second husband Uriah of the tribe of Zebulon.

Uriah ibn Miam was an old settler of unclean Jabneel.

Declared a leper according to all the rules of the Levites in his former homeland around the lake of Semechoritis, he had settled in the neighborhood before his future bride Egla. As he was not disgusted by anything save the prospect of breaking his back tearing fruits from the barren soil, he had agreed to become a washer of the dead, the person who would, for a wage, replace the sorrowing relatives in the preparation of bodies for their final settlement of accounts with Jehovah. His craft turned out to be lucrative. His hands were full of work, or rather of corpses, especially in the months of Marchesvan and Kislev in the rainy season, when he became the most sought-after craftsman in the town. He was neither famous nor wealthy, but the adopting of a profession which couldn't run dry of raw materials—for every man must die even as he must piss or breathe—assured his future. Hence Uriah's godless serenity, his constant but disloyal optimism, his colorful, far-reaching oaths which summarized all his earthly experience, and above all his fickle nonchalance in his relations with heaven.

Uriah simply didn't take the struggle with God seriously. If there was any doubt that there had been a serious charge against him, the proof was that he had been sentenced, and this proof was that his living flesh was falling from his bones without pain. Despite everything he looked on "his little lepress"—an expression which he used in the same way as healthy men refer to their "little wife" or "little house"—more as a supplementary but certainly rather exceptional decoration of his own skin, than as a condemnation whose far-reaching aim was to prepare for some future posthumous troubles. He would usually say: "Even if he really intends to have further dealings with Uriah, how will God know I'm a leper? For when I go up there, I won't bring my skin with me!" His rationalism pleased the penal colony, consoling the sufferers with the hope that suffering, like everything else in nature, has its own end, not subject to God. He was popular as a sort of prophet, but an unconventional prophet whose preaching, defying official teaching, released sinners from the conviction that their behavior had brought upon them an inexhaustible source of misfortune.

He became acquainted with the newcomer Egla at the sheep-killing during the Passover festival. The testamentary ceremonial was respected at New as well as Old Jabneel. The branded ones didn't accept that only the harsher aspects of their faith should apply to them and obstinately continued to celebrate all the good ones. What did they care whether this was pleasing to God or annoyed him? They didn't enjoy being lepers.

Their similarity of views concerning the judgment of Adonai brought them together, though Uriah's views were based on indifference and Egla's on hatred; their refusal to accept the imputed sin united them, though Uriah regarded this as a fact of life and rejected it as a crime, while Egla denied it in any form. They were provoked by the feeling of unjustified abandonment, and the pale around them brought them into temporary alliance, which didn't offend Egla's memories of Jeroboam or humiliate Uriah's dignity as a secondary husband. Let's add to that another, a practical reason: both were freed from worries about their daily bread. Each assumed the part of labor assigned them at the expulsion eastward in Eden. Uriah earned for both and Egla cooked for both.

Let's add, to keep the balance, that the clumsy washer of the dead was a handsome youth—naturally in the manner appropriate to lepers, for his illness had already passed into the so-called "leonine stage" in which his rough features had become magnified to kingly proportions, giving him the appearance of an inflated devil-may-care fellow—and with that we have enumerated the more decisive reasons for Egla's attraction to him. And if we admit that she had only just tasted the first fruits of her sentence, and that she was—once again from a leper's viewpoint—the most sexually attractive young woman in New Jabneel, we have added the final reason for Uriah's decision. They fell in love.

From that time there passed three years of the Lord. Nothing in that time changed in New Jabneel except that fresh lepers came—convinced that their misfortune was a divine oversight, an error in the distribution of divine benevolence, and that they would be cleansed and leave—and that the old settlers died off, since there was no other means of escape. All that time Egla loved Uriah, in no way diminishing her love for Jeroboam, and loved her husband from Sidon without in any way depriving her lover from Zebulon. Though to the one she gave her nights and a great part of her days, and to the other only that part shortly before nightfall, this disproportion didn't influence the equalization of her love. What's more, Uriah's presence actually prevented Egla from forgetting Jeroboam, whose power still remained in his sonorous voice, which every evening hovered over the Jabtel like the downy wing of a bird.

This was the real beginning of the tale of the miracle at Jabneel.

One dry evening of Elul in the eleventh year of the reign of the Emperor Tiberius Caesar Augustus, this unfortunate woman was once again in the Jabtel ravine. Jeroboam hadn't yet begun to cry his news. The dusk rained down over the lethargy of the desert in which, from an ocher distance, the bristling ramparts of Old Jabneel gleamed like the whitened ribs of a sacrificed bull. The shadowy cypresses along the Ramah road looked like a melancholy procession of pilgrims and penitents.

Wretched Egla, she thought, you have never felt so oppressed, as taut as a lute string, except perhaps that morning when you recognized on your breasts the hideous imprint of God's finger. This moment was the calm before the storm, as if her tight-stretched body would at any moment snap.

Then she was relieved: Jeroboam began to cry the news, first from the poverty-stricken northern suburb, sounding thin as a cymbal at its first whisper; then nearer and clearer—the crier must have been standing near the village hall or the pound for fattening the sacrificial rams; then still nearer, in front of the little synagogue, his silken voice buzzing like the rubbing of the clapper in the hollow of a bell, wailing, roaring and rustling like David's playing when one by one he subjugated the evil spirits of King Saul; then loudly raging in an explosion of still more incomprehensible orders and decrees which clanged and clashed in the monotony of the crier's chant, thundered with the boom of rolling syllables or died away in long-drawn wailing, dragging out word after word, now piercing as an awl, now enigmatically diffused; now—Egla strained her ears to hear—in front of Ruwin's shop, now in the alley by the poorhouse, now above the deserted market place, now crushed by the hundred-fold thudding of the hammers before the doors of Elimelech's smithy, until like an unendurable storm it forced its way to the southern guard posts and poured down upon Egla in ornate official phrases:

"To all citizens of Jabneel, of both the upper and the lower town, of the four suburbs and of the commune of Jabneel greeting from the Most Gracious King of Galilee and Peraea, Herod Antipas the Tetrarch. Let it be known that we are concerned and in fatherly anger that the tithe due to Caesar is being paid sluggishly, that the state taxes are being evaded by subterfuges unworthy of true believers, that those who are under an obligation to provide labor are avoiding their responsibilities. We have also noticed that our subjects do not obey the Testament of Our Father; that priests are bribed not to expel the unclean from among them, that they look through their fingers at the incestuous and those who waste their seed, and not only benevolently protect adulterers but lead them to whoredom by their own example; and that the very people do not show us respect but call us 'Edomite vagabond,' 'palace toady' and other highly treasonable insults which encourage them to revolt against the Lord's anointed and shed the blood of the faithful. But desiring that Israel remain the favorite of He Who Is, who has consecrated it to himself and his aims, Herod, Tetrarch of Galilee and Peraea, gives order that he who does not pay to the people what belongs to the people shall be scourged and then crucified, and his property be forfeit; he who does not pay to God what is God's, in blasphemy and lawlessness, let his tongue be torn out, let him be castrated, let him be quartered and his filthy entrails scattered to the four winds, except the east; he who does not pay to Caesar what is Caesar's let him suffer all those punishments hereafter written—let his property be forfeit, let his skin be shaven from him with a razor, his tongue torn out, his eyes burned out in daylight, his ears cut off in the midst of the market place and ground on a block, his limbs crushed and broken by mallets, and then let him be castrated, quartered and his entrails thrown anywhere except to the east, and let all those who escape this punishment be crucified for three days and that you, my dear one, are like a company of horses in Pharaoh's chariots, your cheeks comely with rows of jewels, your neck with chains of gold, and your hair like a flock of goats which pasture on the hills of Gilead; your lips are as a thread of scarlet, your neck is like the tower of David built for an armory where a thousand bucklers hang, your two breasts are like two young roes which feed among the lilies, your lips drip as the honeycomb, my bride, honey and milk are under your tongue and the smell of your garments is like the smell of Lebanon; you are a closed garden, my sister, my bride, a spring shut up, a fountain sealed, my little dove in the clefts of the rock, in the secret places of the heights, let me see your face, let me hear your voice, for your face is divine and your voice sweet, and this also your king orders to the people of Old Jabneel: we have heard a report of a crafty troublemaker, a schismatic and apostate, Jesus of Nazareth who, declaring himself to be the Son of God and King of the Jews, has laid greedy hands on God's inheritance, absolving the lawless, cleansing the lepers, raising the dead, making whole the maimed and therefore binding those who are loosed in heaven and loosing those who are bound in heaven, blaspheming, seducing, luring and desecrating (for who dares to raise up again one whom Adonai's will has numbered and set aside and my club has struck on the neck), therefore we proclaim to any who may know him that it is Caesar's will that this usurper in the interests of public order and security be denounced to the nearest guard post, and whoever remains deaf to this instruction let him be slain as an accomplice, for you are as lovely, my dear one, as Tersa, and not as your sister Asya who, still unbetrothed, was seduced by a certain deserter from the Gabriel legion who was chased, unsuccessfully however, to the seacoast of Syria—you are comely as Jerusalem, terrible as an army with banners, your navel is like a round goblet with liquor, your belly is like a heap of wheat set about with lilies, your neck is like a tower of ivory, your eyes like fishpools in Heshbon by the gate of Bath-rabbim, your nose is as the tower of Lebanon which looks toward Damascus, how fair and how pleasant, O love, for delights, O sister of Jaira, who, the filthy scoundrel, is now in the town jail for stealing my goats, your stature is like a palm tree and your breasts are clusters of grapes, and for its part the Municipal Council advises that you bring for taxes: five punnets of figs out of a basket for every male person, but not rotten or wormy; a log of oil for every person, male or female, from a pitcher, not rancid; a sack of wheat from the threshing floor for every male child among the Jabneel families, but not as in the last collection mixed with cockles, dung and sand; an omer of wine from the barrel for every numbered person, but not as sour as vinegar; and one young heifer from the fold for every family, but with its legs not maimed, and not barren or covered with mange in place of hair, my little dove in the crannies of the rock, in the secret places of the heights, for your voice is sweet and your face more than divine!"

Three times repeated, the long-drawn wail of the ram's horn signified that the crier had ended his duty. Every sound died away, only the wind moaned with a brittle rustling of crumpled parchment. Enthralled by Jeroboam's voice, whose last echoes faded away among the rocky crevasses, the reptiles, scraping their dried stomachs, crawled into their stony lairs to sleep. Dappled by the last rays of the setting sun, the sand was cooling. Patches of darkness rose out of the soil as if, all around, a multitude of geysers was making ready to spout into the heavens.

When Jeroboam ended, Egla remained standing with her face turned toward the southern ramparts of Jabneel. Suddenly she was seized with dizziness, the painful awareness of a sufferer spinning in a world which, like a giant wheel of confusing scenes, is turning round its own fixed axis, round the massive gates of Jabneel. She hovered among the leaping, oval reflections which burst into fireworks, singeing her and forcing her to spin still faster, whirling and swaying like a drugged dancer in the Eleusinian mysteries, swung by her own weight and suicidal fever, first on her feet until she collapsed sobbing, then on her knees until she fell into the dust, scraping her limbs on the rock, scratching her face with her nails and whimpering like a young animal in its death throes, swallowing sand moist with tears, mucus, sweat and urine. She was spinning incredibly fast, now on her head, now on her heels, now with belly in the air, now on her stomach with legs and head raised, contorted into a snake-like ball of limbs which all at once unwound with lightning speed, madly striking the earth only at the next moment, condensed into a shrieking ball of bleeding flesh which—ricocheting from the rocks, crashing from the cliffs, torn by twigs and stabbed by thorns and stung by the desert nettles—rolled along the frontier between clean and unclean without approaching anyone from Jabneel.

At daybreak some men in dusty traveling cloaks were descending from the hills of Naphthali—not merchants, for they had no mules or donkeys—and their torches flickering and glowing in the dew lit up Egla's battered body. One of them, a reddish, small-boned man with a warm, frank face, thought that the woman was weeping. Gathering the folds of his chiton around his knees, he knelt down beside Egla.

"Why are you grieving, sister?" he asked with a rasping, authoritative voice in the gurgling dialect of Upper Galilee.

"Are you God, stranger, that you must know everything?" retorted Egla.

Why didn't he go his way and leave her alone a little longer before she dragged herself back to the leper colony, while the broken echoes of Jeroboam's psalm still resounded through her body like the melodious breaking of a costly bowl?

"I am," said the red-haired man calmly, as if to be God was the most common accomplishment in Canaan, and to make the acquaintance of the All-Highest in the desert more commonplace than to meet pack donkeys on the Zion road. "I am Jesus of Nazareth."

Curled up like a ball, with her cheek on the ground, which

was gradually acquiring warmth and light, Egla could see only the intruder's shabby sandals. Was he that rebel, she asked herself, regarding whom the tetrarch had issued his warning, and whom her beloved Jeroboam had called the looser of the bound and the binder of the loose? And she said questioningly:

"Then you must already know what you ask."

"I don't. The shepherd knows all the ills that torment his flock, but even he—such is the composition of the flock—can't guess which illness makes any single sheep whimper."

Egla heard one of his companions say: "Let's go, Rabbi. Dawn is breaking. A guard might come."

To which the red-haired man replied: "Didn't you keep telling me all the way that, as long as the heavens and the earth stand, not even the smallest jot or tittle of the Law will be accomplished until everything is fulfilled, and didn't you keep telling me the whole journey long: it is written that you will heal some wretched person. If I'm not mistaken, that person is lying here before us. What do you want now?"

"It is written that you'll heal a wretched person upon leaving Capernaum, and as we all know, we have come from Hazor."

"Judas, son of Simon," said the Nazarene ill-humoredly, "once and for all I tell you that the time isn't far distant when it will be revealed to you: he has done it because it was written. And you do this, but not everything that is written. You'll be told: do it again and if you do it again you'll be contrary to the Scriptures. You'll be told: do it again and do it seven times, seventy-seven times and seven times seventy-seven times, until your Testament is fulfilled. For if a single word of the Testament is not fulfilled, it's as if not one has been fulfilled. I don't know what you'll do then."

"I will do it," Jehuda said dryly.

"How important is it for the future of the world whether we heal her on leaving Capernaum or Hazor? Are you ill, sister?"

What is Uriah doing now, Egla was thinking to herself. Perhaps he has gathered the neighbors and they are searching all around the settlement in panic that she has crossed the frontier between clean and unclean and, having forgotten to warn the passers-by of her illness with her little bells, has fallen, shattered by their stones. Perhaps he is sitting on the threshold, chewing his rye bread dipped in goat's milk and waiting for me to come back without worrying at all. He was able to hold himself back from trying to influence events, even when they didn't stem directly from God.

"Are you paralyzed?"

Perhaps he was slightly surprised but in no way horrified, angered or depressed—Uriah never gave way to well-defined moods; perhaps he was listening to the first cautious gossip of the lepers who had seen her, in his absence, on the road toward Jabtel, and who could base their possible doubts only on the coincidence of the crier's announcement and Egla's evening walk.

"Are you barren?"

Disturbed by the persistence of the stranger, Egla denied this misfortune.

"You speak, so you aren't dumb," observed the traveler in perplexity. "You hear me, so you aren't deaf. Can you see me, sister?"

"No," replied Egla, and once again heard the dry, expressionless voice of the man they called Jehuda, a voice that sounded like the crackling of twigs.

"I don't pretend to be a sage, Rabbi, or want to set myself up conceitedly as an expert on prophecy, but in the interests of the true faith and of the salvation of the entire universe, I must warn you that, despite this whore drunkenly blubbering and rolling about in ditches, no miracle has been forecast for the blind between Hazor and Capernaum, but across there"—Jehuda pointed to the southeast—"in the Land of the Gergesenes, two madmen are waiting for you to drive the demons out of them into a herd of swine now peacefully rooting in the earth beside the highway."

Suddenly Egla felt sorry for the little Nazarene and his zeal, which had met with no response from his nasty fellow travelers. More to spite Judas, who had called her a whore—she in whom Adonai had taken a personal if vengeful interest, thus inadvertently acknowledging her—than to gain any advantage for herself out of a situation that promised nothing, she said:

"I'm not a whore, Jehuda, nor am I blind, that you should be so concerned. I don't see you because I'm not looking at you, and I'm not looking at you because I have no desire to see you. Neither you nor anyone else."

"You speak rudely but soberly," said the Nazarene, "therefore you aren't mad. Let the turbid Jordan bear me away if I can guess why you're unhappy!"

"The turbid Jordan will bear us all away, Rabbi," broke in a voice which Egla now heard for the first time, "if we wait around for the trumpet to announce the dawn for the third time, calling on the guard to open the gates of Jabneel."

Suddenly the little traveler burst out:

"Go away, Cephas! Get out! Everyone get out! I want to talk with this woman alone. Why are you going away? Did I say to get out? If I told you to get out, I wanted you to stay. If I said go far away, I expected that you'd come very close. If I ordered you not to budge, I wanted you to leave. If I wanted you to come closer, I expected you to go far away, you numbskulls, you shameless ignoramuses, you morons, who will never learn that under what has been said ripens what is unsaid, which you should follow; that behind what is done lies what has not been done, which you should do for me. In the improbable it is possible that you will save me and then you will have thrones in the kingdom which I announce. Now approach so that you're still far away and hear what will not be said." He turned to the woman. "What's your name?"

"Egla."

"Forgive me for annoying you, Egla," the stranger went on tenderly, "and don't find fault with my friends. They are born men."

"And you?" asked Egla, awaiting one of those answers which would define with precision the nature and extent of his madness.

He sighed. "That's a complex matter, I admit. But I'll try to explain why your role is essential and irreplaceable. Bearing in mind the long-term aim of saving the world, God begat me so I could die as a man, and a man I am insofar as it's possible, so that, at suitable moments which numerous prophets have specified, I can become God. And so, being now God now man, then again God and again man and never, if I'm not mistaken, in any scrambled state satisfying both principles at the same time—and because, in the course of these transformations, nothing changes either on me or in me except my effect upon things, and even that I can realize only through you and others like you—because of all this, I never know what I am or when, until, having wrought some miracle, I again usurp my divine nature. When I'm temporarily man or feeling pain, I realize that I'm in my human guise, although before I was temporarily God. However, thanks to my apostle Judas who, being mainly interested in my higher sphere of action, continually reminds me of my social obligations, I know what I must be." And he added in confidence: "I must become God, Egla!"

"Is that so?" she sighed, straining to remain friendly. Though her experience of higher powers had not been happy, she couldn't free herself from sympathy for this fragile but fervent preacher of good deeds, whose imagined power overburdened him with so many duties. "And you've been so nice to me."

"Really?" he said, touched. How moved he was by this vague praise, he whom they had showered with epithets more murderous than the mallets with which they clubbed bullocks to death. "That is pleasant to me as a man, but insufficient as the Son of man, but even that half-attraction permits me to seek something more of you and to await with certainty till I shall obtain it."

"Well, what is it you want?"

"I want you to tell me why you're so unhappy."

"What will you do if I tell you?"

"Nothing against your will, but if you agree, I'll try to help you."

She squirmed but after a short pause asked sharply: "Whom will you help—me or yourself?"

"You understand quickly—devilishly quickly for a . . ."

"A harlot."

"No, I wanted to say that for a dying woman who has met God only in an unpleasant form of personal misfortune, you understand quickly the difficulties of so exceptional a situation. Let's say that it will be of help to both of us."

Having proposed a fair exchange of good deeds, he remained silent, awaiting a reply. Sensing that he expected some form of cooperation which would cost her nothing, and thinking that kind and indulgent behavior toward an unfortunate whom Adonai had punished even more harshly than herself might be accepted and recorded as a payment for a sin committed long ago, she decided not to disappoint this crazy youth who, kneeling meekly above her, smelled of the freshness of the forests of Naphthali he had recently left, the forest scents mingled with the dry dust of the road; and who—the devil alone knew why—hoped to cure an illness which all the healers of Galilee had washed their hands of, and all the doctors she had visited were powerless to do anything about. For a while she found enjoyment in that impossible dream: wasn't this meeting a part of that illusion still to be played which for years she had indulged by going to the Jabtel to listen to Jeroboam's all-too-sweet voice? Then the small red-haired seer would continue with his band to Capernaum, rubbing his hands in satisfaction that by his conceit of almighty power he had added one more exploit, and she would remain as leprous as before, alone with the fragments of a brief dream on their common, tiny rubbish heap. But, she thought, wasn't even that shattering of illusion—like the dispersal of clouds of smoke over ashes—the end of one of her illusory lives at Jabtel? Hadn't she already so many times come back from her dreaming to reality, to the knotty hands of Maim's leprous son, worn out and urgently real, as she would awake after the Galilean's departure?

That was decisive: the coincidence of this lie with all those which until then had maintained her in her unreality. But before she gave way, either from rancor or from the need to shock him, she demanded that he whom they called Jehuda or Judas should approach, so that he too could hear her short confession:

"What I am confessing I do for you, noble sir"—still without raising her head, Egla touched the preacher's sandal—"and as for your fellow traveler who confuses womanhood with whoredom, I wouldn't confide even my lies to him. The fact is, however, that I live with Uriah, who sees to the dead in New Jabneel, and I love Jeroboam, the municipal crier of Old Jabneel. But the truth wouldn't be complete if I didn't mention my liking for Uriah. Perhaps I would, and could, have a hundred husbands and be above reproach, nor would any one of them be able to complain of my insensitivity, for even as you don't know when you're God and when you're man, so I too don't know when I'm in Jeroboam's heart and when in Uriah's, until I feel pain because of the presence or absence of one of them. Right now I'm grieving because I miss Jeroboam." In choosing whether Jeroboam should become plague-stricken and come to her or she be cleansed so that she might return to him, remaining true to all that senseless abracadabra, Egla foresaw complications should both her husbands live in the same settlement, and so decided on her own cleansing. She concluded: "If I were cleansed I'd return to Jeroboam."

"Didn't I say this woman is a harlot!" Jehuda shouted fiercely. "She accepts salvation only to put horns on her husband."

Then the Nazarene began: "There is no reason not worthy of salvation, Judas son of Simon! I say to you, when your time comes, place on the scales your reasons and the reasons of this woman, and you'll see." Then he turned to Egla: "Do you believe, woman?"

And bearing in mind the prologue which promised a positive reply, he was astonished and almost hurt when she stated calmly:

"No."

Unembarrassed, he pretended not to understand and tried once more: "Not at all? Are you sure?"

"Not at all," said Egla, innocently enjoying her outburst of malice but troubled by a feeling that the man they called Jehuda shared her satisfaction.

"You should obey the prophecies," Jehuda said. "They say nothing of healing a leper in the region of Tiberias, but rather in the neighborhood of Capernaum."

"No matter," said the wonder-worker, "or so much the better. If she believed, what would we have gained from this miracle? She would go on believing, cleansed certainly, but not converted. She would differ from this filthy form only in her new appearance, her envelope of skin so to speak, while her soul remained untouched and unmoved by the shock of realization. This way she'll be in labor to be born again as a lamb of God, and her future faith will be sealed sevenfold by shame at her former lack of faith."

After this solemn preamble which none of those present contested, he placed his left hand on the back of Egla's head and with his right hand pressed his heart as if to establish some significant contact between heaven and body. After some time in this exhausting position, uttering dissonant and unintelligible sounds, he took his hands from Egla's head and his heart, leaped up in haste, shook off the dust and sand from his mantle, and making signs to his disciples to gather round him, went on down the Jabtel without addressing a single word of greeting, advice or excuse to the woman. But even if he had said farewell with some encouraging advice which might induce her to renew her neglected ties with God-punishment—now that she recognized him in the more approachable shape of God-forgiveness—or if he had said it with some conventional phrase, she wouldn't have heard him. With her cheek on a stone covered with manna, the nourishment of Israel, facing the clear spring which flowed toward the horizon as into a transparent shoal, Egla at first took part almost indifferently in the intangible but continual change which was being effected in her rotting body and in the fibers of her rotting clothes. Though she was unable to follow this metamorphosis from stage to stage, at first curious, then bewildered and finally more stunned than exalted, she found in the quick fermentation of her flesh only the finished product of that supernatural reproduction of the new, in fact original, appearance of her skin, which now was smooth where before it had been furrowed, gleaming where before it had been murky, delicate where before it had been tough as leather, clear where before it had been scabby, the leonine excrescences and fissures growing smooth and level, even as the earth settles down after the destruction wrought by a catastrophic earthquake. Confused and unable to remember anything, she was the first witness of the rebirth of her own beauty.

Egla looked at her arms in disbelief—after all that she had gone through, even merciful act, of God's providence aroused disgust in her—but she was forced to admit that her skin was perfectly clear, as of a virgin slave newly arrived at the brothel. Tenderly stroking it, she was convinced that its flowery softness had returned with that trace of moisture which lustful male lips require; she pinched herself and found that thanks to the scrupulousness of the magician or his knowledge of anatomy, it was sufficiently firm to spring back under her fingers. Still disbelieving, and being methodical, she subjected it to the test of her other senses. The investigation was satisfactory; her skin smelled like a mown meadow, but with that slight aroma of sweat which makes the skin real, and when she licked it she discerned the salty taste of almonds which have just lost their bitterness.

Praise be to Hashem, she was clean again!

Like a lover she began to kiss and bite her newly changed skin. At first she did it with barbarous veneration, as if by so doing she was kissing the magic in it and therefore the magician himself, and then with uncontrollable animal madness, both innocent and sinful, for she knew that soon this restored skin would wrap itself like a cloak about her husband's body. There was not a trace of vulgar selfishness in her self-adoration, yet as a foretaste of her enjoyment there was at the same time a sinful self-satisfaction similar to masturbation. Dizziness seized her, an excited awareness that she was turning in a world which itself was whirling round the massive gates of Jabneel like a giant wheel of sunbeams round a fixed axis, to break and quiver into leaping oval reflections which burst into fireworks, singeing her and forcing her to spin still faster, whirling and swaying like a drugged dancer in the Eleusinian mysteries, swung by her own lightness and fever of renascence, at first in the place of her last night's suffering which in no gesture nor in any essential feeling differed from her present satisfaction, in the cradle of miracle over which Adonai had announced his forgiveness by the tongue of a wanderer with a rusty red beard; and then her tighter and tighter crazed circles of joy brought her ever closer to the outskirts of clean Jabneel, ever nearer to the dream which twelve hours after the hour of its announcement still resounded in her ears with the roaring summons of Jeroboam's horn.

As she ran toward Jabneel, inflamed by her faith in the God of her fathers which had been canceled by the punishment of leprosy and reborn through her gratitude for her restored health, she shouted joyfully and sincerely: "Our Father, which art in heaven, hallowed be Thy name," and added joyously: "Jeroboam, who art on earth, may I kiss thy face," and then said, "Thy kingdom come," and then, "Thy will be done on earth as it is in heaven," and "Thy will be done on earth, in bed and board," "Give us this day our daily bread," "Give me this day my daily kiss," "And forgive us our debts as we forgive our debtors," "And do not forgive me the debts of my absence as I will not forgive them to you," and prayed sincerely: "Lead us not into temptation but deliver us from evil," and just as sincerely: "Lead me into temptation without delivering me from the sweetness of evil," and then repeated what equally referred to heaven and earth, to God and her husband: "For Thine is the kingdom, the power and the glory for ever and ever. Amen."

The peasants who, burdened with clay waterpots and baskets of reeds, were hurrying back from the Jabneel market, heard Egla calling shamelessly upon He Who Is thought she was mad, and stepped off the path respectfully to make way for her. And the path was the one from which, accompanied by the unhappy Jeroboam, she had stepped across the frontier of the unclean.

To avoid the explanations which the official regulations

would demand of her, Egla intended to slip in between the tax collector's post and the guardhouse, but when she reached the southern gate it was clear to her that this would be impossible, or at any rate very difficult. Fearing that pointless tricks might delay her meeting with Jeroboam, she presented herself, pure as the dawn and fresh as running water, to the excise officer. A braggart, a stiff-necked dandy whom she didn't know, he was surrounded by a shouting, threatening, swearing and imploring crowd of smelly camel drivers and muleteers, traveling peddlers and smugglers offering him bribes, and Galilean peasant women with leaky baskets on their heads.

The official—his name was Jefta—left the line at his post and turned to Egla. With ambiguous words he expressed surprise at not seeing what goods Egla was bringing into the town, and with enterprising hands showed an active interest in her womanly charms, and when she protested—more because she was in a hurry than from any repulsion—and asked him what he was doing, he stated officially that it was his task to assess the value of goods, and since she had brought nothing into Jabneel except her matchless beauty he must assess whatever he could. The Galileans sniggered obsequiously in the hope that the official, noticing this, would reward them when he apportioned their tax.

Without taking his active hands from Egla, Jefta asked her where she was hurrying. "I swear by my night experiences, your goods aren't sold by daylight anywhere in the world."

"I sell nothing, officer," Egla replied sharply, but she was flattered. Jefta was the first man who, after God, had recognized her recovery.

Egla explained that she was the wife of the town crier Jeroboam, and that after a long stay with her husband's relatives in Dan—near Caesarea Philippi—she was now coming home. But a townsman named Jerkoam, one of those busybodies who always step in at wrong moments, said that he knew Jeroboam and that his wife, who was called Egla, had long since been expelled from the camp as unclean.

"Why are you lying, woman?" asked the excise official,

whom Egla's self-confident attitude had offended. "And you, Jerkoam, you swindler, don't try to profit by the mess you have created by not paying your dues!"

"I'm not lying, I'm the woman you speak of, I'm Egla, the wife of Jeroboam."

"But that Egla was leprous!" shouted Jerkoam.

She looked up at the heavens, then said blissfully: "She was leprous, but she met the young God and was cleansed by holding his hand."

"You were leprous?" The official was dumbfounded and leaped backward so suddenly that he found himself in the middle of the mob, which made way for him uneasily, leaving Egla in an empty circle of unbelieving eyes and hesitant bodies.

"She was leprous?" the mob murmured in astonishment.

"I was, but didn't I tell you that He Who Is has once more accepted me as one of his flock? Look!" Egla called out to them, and uncovering her breasts—of which as God's creation she no longer had reason to feel ashamed—she showed a clean bosom to the four corners of the world, displaying it a little longer toward the east to give that quarter a greater satisfaction.

Paying no attention to the evidence, Jefta withdrew a few feet more, frantically wringing his hands, which had touched her clothes, as if washing away some inconspicuous but extraordinarily disgusting filth, and stretched them out toward the newcomer.

"No, you can't enter the town, woman! Go back where you came from and don't upset the honest citizens of Jabneel—and you, Lamech, get into line and pay your tax. If this woman is leprous you aren't, and neither is your money!"

Egla couldn't understand why she should upset the honest citizens of Jabneel when here, before their eyes, was the living proof of the indulgent fatherly care which their common God rendered to them by her healing. But, realizing that such heavenly arguments would find no echo among the listeners, she decided to try earthly ones: she reminded them that Jeroboam had powerful protectors in the Town Council and that, generally speaking, he was very influential because, she said, he who devotedly announced the imperial decrees could not help absorbing some small part of the imperial power inherent in them. Could they, therefore, justify themselves before him when he heard how they had treated his wife?

"Who are you not to acknowledge the decisions of the God of our fathers?" shrieked Egla.

"I acknowledge every decision of his which is in accordance with the regulations of my duties as town excise officer," said Jefta mildly, "but there is nothing in them about leprosy, only about figs, oil, wine and other merchandise. Your case is for the captain of the city guard. Amri, you half-caste"—the official pointed to a swarthy peasant with a clay jug in his hands who was trying to slip away—"go get him at once. Naturally first you will pay your toll to enter the town. And you, woman"—he turned to Egla—"leper or not, stay where you are. Touch nothing. Don't get close to anyone. Even if you've been healed, who knows how conscientiously that was done?"

"God sees all, officer!" said Egla with restraint. Her renewed faith again upheld her.

"But he isn't in danger because he doesn't have to touch anything. Be thankful that I haven't asked you to cover your mouth as the Law requires."

In the meantime the courtyard of the tax collector's post emptied completely; a small number of the visitors paid Jefta the toll quickly without the usual haggling, and vanished into the bluish shadows of the suburban hovels, while a larger number suddenly decided that it was too late for any serious marketing anyway and returned to the Jabtel commune.

Amri rushed back without the captain.

"When I told him what it was about," the half-caste reported breathlessly, "the captain complained about his rheumatism. He greets you warmly and leaves everything to the civil authorities and, as he put it, to your esteemed self."

It can't be said that Jefta was overjoyed. He sent Amri to the priest Ismai, and to be sure that the rabbi would come, he gave orders that any excuse be reported at once to the town authorities as an unparalleled violation of the obligations of a Levite.

"Tell that shabby old nag," he ordered Amri, "that leprosy has always fallen into his line of duty, and if, because of his advanced years, he's forgotten this, let him skim through the pages of the book called Vaikro or Leviticus."

Indifferent to all these arguments, discussions and negotiations, Egla sat on a worn stone used for tethering mules, and ran her fingers through her hair. Aware that every move from the outside into the camp, from the unclean into the clean state and the other way round (the former was, naturally, only an ideal possibility) required certain formalities—a ceremony of absolution which confirmed that the community had first expelled the transgressor and then accepted him back again—she awaited the priest confidently. As soon as Ismai had examined her and established that she had been healed, and had drawn up an official document to confirm it, she would be freed even from the memory of sin and her fellow citizens would no longer have any reason to avoid her.

At long last Ismai came.

He recognized her at once but his dignity wouldn't permit him to admit it, or so Egla thought. When the former leper fell at his feet, less from respect than because the elderly Levite was the first citizen of Jabneel whom she had met after her miraculous healing, he stepped back a few paces saying gruffly that her restoration to health was indubitable as a physical fact, since he could see it with his own eyes, but for her spiritual health the conventional bodily shell was not conclusive. Didn't the infidel soothsayers of the false god Jupiter, he said, open the most thoroughbred of rams, in whose entrails—though they deserved no better—they found a liver as stinking and rotten as stale cheese? Restoration to health was not automatic, and cleansing might only be a prelude to it, or more accurately merely of service to it as light is of service to the sun to warm us. And for the complete transformation of Egla's body, that incidental not to say superfluous shell, he demanded a cleansing ceremony based on Moses' instructions as dictated to him on Sinai by the Lord

God himself. Only by those ceremonies, Ismai explained, could he even *post factum* legalize the facts, and only then assure the reality and give it the force of law which would serve at the same time as a worthy confirmation of the true divine intentions. For they were not only frequently far from clear—the priests were there in order to interpret them—but also in accordance with the rules they were deliberately mysterious so as to also express his omnipotence.

It was the profound and elaborate speech of a distinguished hierophant. The excise official, Jefta, who had followed him at a safe distance, suspected that he'd heard precisely the same speech on other occasions and in quite different circumstances. However, Ismai's theological hair-splitting was of no interest to Egla, who asked if, after the ceremony and the sacrifies it entailed, she would be officially clean.

Ismai replied vaguely that in matters involving or originating in sin there was no complete certainty.

"You were leprous, Egla, and though we allow ourselves to believe that by God alone knows what miracle you are no longer so, we are not bound—in fact it would be blasphemous and harmful if we were to forestall God's plans—to believe that you will not be so again. Therefore follow after me," the Levite called. "I said after me and not with me, woman, for not even those of the seed of Aaron are immune to leprosy. Furthermore, I have young grandchildren."

So Ismai went ahead and Egla followed at a respectful distance. Walking behind the old man, who was hopping along like a rabbit avoiding the pools of dust, she felt for the first time since dawn a certain weakness in her limbs, as if what she avoided calling discouragement was preventing her feet from treading freely and confidently the route to the synagogue, and her lovely head from rising proudly. Perhaps that numbness was the result of a fatigue which would vanish as soon as she came near Jeroboam. In any case she decided that she would submit without complaint to all the requirements of her cleansing, the last and most serious obstacle between her and her husband.

On the porch of the synagogue, in a businesslike manner

and without hesitation, Ismai informed Egla that the ceremony about to take place, though aimed primarily at spiritual cleansing from a predominantly bodily punishment, nonetheless demanded certain material items which were expensive: sparrows, flour, a lamb, for example. Did Egla have money to pay for them?

Egla admitted that she had none, but promised that the expense of the ceremony would be settled by Jeroboam as soon as he heard of her return.

"Then we will put that sum to his account, directly below the expenses which he already owes me for the last Hanukkah festival," said the Levite, and gave his assistants the necessary instructions. "You must admit that I'm showing a great deal of trust in you, for nothing is known yet of Jeroboam's decision regarding you. And when I add that I'm saving you the trouble of obtaining sacrificial victims and will supply you with sparrows, a lamb and a sheep from the synagogue store at a price only a little higher than the market rate, I consider that I've done all a priest could be expected to do in face of such contradictory decisions of his higher authority."

And I do this, he added to himself, with repulsion, for though it flatters me that I'm the first to welcome back into society one who's been expelled, I doubt even so if there's any general remedy as absolute as the disease, or any cure which, though it destroys the evil, also makes its germs harmless.

"The seed ripens," Ismai said aloud, "and who other than the All-Highest knows if it will germinate anew to destroy us?"

"What are you muttering about, honored sir?" asked Egla.

"Nothing, woman, or at any rate nothing that concerns you," Ismai replied grumpily, and with cantors and assistants busied himself with his professional duties.

"Will it last long?" Egla asked, trying to make a guess from the extent of his preparations.

"No, not very. We could, indeed, proceed in accordance with the shortened procedure which Moses provided for the indigent, but that would be insulting to the wife of a municipal official. We will take advantage only of the concession which the Holy Sanhedrin approved during your absence, canceling the seven days of quarantine and ablutions by which the ceremony was ended in former times."

"Then get on with it. Do what you want, but do it quickly!"

After giving orders that two live clean sparrows be brought from the store (which, according to custom, were released so that Egla could catch them without help, which she did easily, for the sparrows were tame and had been trained for religious purposes), along with cedar wood, scarlet and hyssop, an earthenware vessel worn by excessive use, two lambs without blemish and a yearling ewe, three tenths of an ephah of white flour mingled with oil and a separate log of oil, Ismai—continually warning Egla not to approach him—got down to the details of the ceremony.

"Listen to me," he said before beginning, "it isn't good when the person being cleansed doesn't know why this is being done, thinking falsely that even without all these tricks he is healthy, even as conversely it's sometimes good that the condemned man doesn't know what he's accused of lest he defend himself even more obstinately, and thus deservedly arouse greater anger and a more severe punishment. In order to defend us, the Lord doesn't inform us of the reasons for his severe judgments, which we don't discover until our dying day, thankful that he's made it impossible for us to hate him and thereby inevitably compel him to more intense punishments. In their executions wise rulers take him as an example, and those they sentence die in torment, it's true, but curious and not resentful. Even ordinary people in everyday mutual contact don't tell one another the real reasons for their bad moods and hostile behavior. I assume that this has happened to you also, and that the Lord has granted you his highest mercy so you won't know why he banished you."

"Yes," Egla agreed, "my husband Jeroboam and I cudgeled our brains for a long time, but couldn't understand."

"So much the better. That confirms that I was right when I said that ignorance is the best defense against punishment, perhaps even more efficacious than prayer, for petitions cannot be disregarded, but ignorance is silent." Ismai waved Egla farther away from him. "I beg you, lady, don't breathe in my face, or if you must, then put your hand over your mouth. You probably ask: How can I know why I should repent when I don't know why I should repent? And I answer: You don't repent for what you've done but because you realize that you must have done something. The ceremony of cleansing proves your guilt, for if you weren't guilty you wouldn't need to be cleansed. The longer a ceremony, and the more complex and public—some of them, as you know, have been transformed into joyful popular holidays—the greater the sin of the guilty, and the more loathsome and irrefutable. That's why you're being cleansed: because of others and not because of yourself."

"All right, all right, that doesn't bother me, but it does bother me that you are dawdling. I'm in a hurry, Ismai!"

"I'll be done soon," said the priest. "I want to stress that every return and not yours alone is crowned by a corresponding ceremony, which is in proportion to the crime. When the prodigal son returns to the parental home, his father whips him before the feast of welcome—a ritual in every way reminiscent of a birth celebration. From then on he'll no longer believe him, but in all else he'll be loyal to his son. When the repentant adulteress returns to her husband he'll first perform the ritual of forgiveness, which includes a good thrashing. From then on he will be required to respect her, but not to leave her alone with other men."

"Why are you telling me all this?"

"Because, woman, you shouldn't overestimate the power of cleansing, however effective and commensurate with the sincerity of your repentance. I'll cleanse you according to the Law, which I must do because it's my duty, and because it's my conviction that you are indeed healthy, but don't expect me to come into contact with you or share the same air with you longer than my Levitical duty requires."

Then hastily, even offhandedly, Ismai went on with the ceremony. One sparrow was slaughtered over the running water of a stream which flowed beneath the synagogue and its blood collected in the earthenware bowl, in which he immersed the surviving sparrow, the chip of cedar, the hyssop and the scarlet. Then, freeing the living sparrow in the portico (where the Levitical assistants caught it again so it could be used in other cleansings), he sprinkled the former leper seven times with the blood of the slaughtered sparrow and declared her clean.

At first irritated by the slow pace of the procedure, Egla soon surrendered to it ecstatically; she dared not regard anything which came from the Lord, the healer, as boring or repulsive. When Ismai ordered her, she took off her clothes and leaped into the gurgling stream, according to Old Testament custom, to wash both herself and her now healthy garments. The gentle, tickling current reminded her of Jeroboam's hands, only a hundredfold, and the slapping of the little ripples, the smarting of the drops dashed from the main stream, led her neglected body to a frivolous and unruly joy. Instead of the sacred lustration producing a modest, God-fearing and reverent acceptance austerely concentrated on the rinsing away of the rash of lawlessness, instead of identifying herself with her cast-off unclean skin which she had symbolically sloughed, rubbing it with a sponge and drenching it with water, Egla giggled, shrieked, splashed and in a wholly impermissible manner found enjoyment in the sacrificial act. An uninformed observer might have believed that he was witnessing the dissolute gamboling of a bather in a public bath of some city of the West.

Ismai didn't reprove her or call her to order. His passionless little eyes followed the rhythms of the sacred ablutions.

"What are you doing?" she asked him.

"I search for God," said the Levite professionally, "to see if any sign of leprosy remains which his mercy might have overlooked."

When the second part of the cleansing was over, Ismai ordered that two lambs be brought, one as a sacrifice for the offense and the second for the sin. He slaughtered the first lamb, whose carcass by custom belonged to him and which he sent to his house, and with its still warm blood he anointed the tip of Egla's right ear and the thumb of her right hand and the great toe of her right foot. Then he sparingly poured some oil into the palm of his left hand, dipped his finger in the oil and with it made three rapid, consecutive, obligatory ritual movements: seven times he sprinkled the air incarnated by He Who Is and with the rest of the oil gently anointed all the parts of Egla's body, including her head. Finally he brought the sin-sacrifice (the second lamb) and slaughtered the burnt offering (the ewe), and solemnly proclaimed that as far as the Sinaitic rites were concerned, Jeroboam's wife was healthy.

The grateful Egla wanted to kiss his hand, but Ismai drew it back quickly, telling her to leave him as soon as possible so that he could devote himself to his prayers to God, who, to all appearances, was nervously expecting him. Since nothing remained for her to do in the synagogue and her whole being craved Jeroboam, she rushed into the street singing hymns to the Lord.

"Here, O Only One, your heaven is different, more luminous and more alive, more present and more variegated"—as if it were not that same inaccessible heaven to which she had turned so hopelessly from the threshold of Uriah's house—"your air is more silken, more generous, more healthy and more unobtrusive than that of New Jabneel, in which one drowns as if under water! What shade these dense, luxurious and unmoving shadows afford, whereas the wavering shadows of the leper colony are short because of the hovels or because of the immensity of the curse! The swallows of your flock, paying no heed to the colony of the convicted, fly over it to build their nests under the eaves of clean Jabneel. The dust of the streets is less dusty, the camels' dung less stinking and even the corpses, that everyday sight in the Promised Land, here afford an almost enchanting picture of death. The clanging is more resonant, the murmurs more rustling, the day more bright, and that glittering light, the diversion and pastime of the superstitious and the warning to the night owls, more radiant.

"O Almighty God, the world—that heap of confused objects, beings and events, originating from one of your unintentional cries (perhaps, when you were walking, you stubbed your toe on something hard)—is wonderful in the way it forgives and welcomes a former leper despite some of your omens!"

Those omens she had always thought intended for someone else, applied to her in error and hurriedly, mercilessly and clumsily interpreted to her disadvantage. Even so, the world from which she had been uprooted and this one in which she had been planted were one and the same, or at least two similar, twin worlds within arm's reach of one another, under one shell of sky, under the cruising of the same flocks, in the cauldron of the same air, in the shade of similar shadows and in the echoes of identical sounds.

The shops in front of which she passed on her way home were shut. This was strange. As far as she could remember—in Unclean Jabneel all the popular customs were cherished—there was no festival that day. Furthermore, hadn't the peasants been driving their mules to market? Hadn't the tax collector's post been working? Hadn't Ismai, overoccupied with ceremonies and services, been able to devote all his attention to her case alone? Hadn't the dogs been loosed that were now freely roaming the streets, more freely than she liked, which wasn't permitted at the time of national festivals? The citizens she'd met at the southern gate had all been in everyday clothes; the houses, even the richest, had no decorations or garlands; and in the synagogue whence she was returning from, there had been no sign of preparations for any religious service.

As she was passing Elimelech's smithy, where she didn't hear the beating of hammers, the competing yells of apprentices or the filing of nervous hooves before shoeing, she saw the master smith in conversation with an old woman whom she recognized as the midwife Fuva. Many citizens of Old Jabneel, among them Egla herself, had Fuva's skillful hands to thank that they had been born without blemish. She was also respected because she bore the name of that famous

Egyptian midwife Fuva, who according to tradition, despite Pharaoh's express command for the extermination of all the newborn males of Jacob's blood, saved the majority, among them Moses, whom she shut up in an ark of bulrushes daubed with pitch and thrown into the reeds of the Nile. Since the legendary Fuva was to a certain extent a second mother to Moses, this Fuva was also known as "the second mother" and her sons' devotion showered upon her.

Though she was in a hurry, Egla couldn't resist greeting the woman who had taken such an active part in her first birth but so far from her when, in the uncomfortable trough of the Jabtel, as on the bare mat of a beggar, she had been born a second time. She leaned over a stake fence and called them both by name. Though Egla thought that they looked in her direction—with elderly people one never knows—they didn't respond but hurried into the house. Egla smiled compassionately: Poor old things! Egla couldn't expect anything from Fuva at her age, and Elimelech had obviously gone deaf.

She was now in front of her house. She stole up to the door with the childish idea of surprising her husband. Unfortunately the door was barred, so she had to give up her surprise. A bronze knocker in the form of the crier's horn was attached by a chain to the door, bearing witness to the owner's occupation. It was the only new detail; otherwise nothing had changed.

She struck the knocker on the door. No answer. Perhaps, thought Egla, Jeroboam was out, or had gone on a visit to his brother in Sidon. But that was unlikely. Hadn't she heard his voice only the night before? It was still too early for the municipal crier to have gone on his rounds, which began when the last rays of the setting sun lit up the portals of the Council Hall.

Egla walked around the house and stopped next to a rectangular hole in the unhewn Ephraim stone which served as a window. It was a narrow opening, not more than two feet across, offering a glimpse of a smooth, well-trodden clay floor, the end of a sofa with comfortable, striped rush cushions, above which hung a folded mosquito net; a candlestick set into the wall with a burning wick on a tripod of cedar—the most precious jewel of her dowry; and Jeroboam's crier's instrument, made of a ram's horn with an inscription burnt into the ebony handle, from which he was never parted, whether he was on duty or not. If the horn was there, then its owner must be, too, the woman concluded, and she called him by name, then by his nickname and then by the love names with which she had expressed in his embrace the chaste gratitude of her body. Some time passed before a hoarse, unreal, wavering half-voice asked who was calling from the window.

"Jeroboam, my husband and master, it's your darling, your Egla!" she cried out, forcing her trembling heart through her teeth with every word she spoke. Mown down by the sickle of her voice, now surely he would fling the doors wide open and embrace the morning she had brought wrapped around her new-found body; he would strike the sistrum and the kettledrums to announce the holiday of blood, their limbs and bodies would mingle as the sacrificial flour with the sacrificial oil, their words of love would intertwine like the mating of vipers and their eyes would flow into the warm, translucent depths of an ocean of enjoyment.

"Don't mock me, woman, whoever you are," said the quavering voice. "My wife, at discord with God, is long since dead."

"She has made her peace with God, Jeroboam! Don't you know your Egla's voice?"

"Since when have the dead spoken?"

"Don't you hear your Egla's footsteps?"

"Since when can the dead walk?"

There was something repulsively insincere, timidly fearful in that half-voice, which only the night before had been idolatrously singing of her hair as a flock of goats on the hills of Gilead, and had compared her nose to the tower of Lebanon looking toward Damascus. Egla left the window so as not to look at the ram's horn any longer, for she felt that she was speaking not to her husband but to some automaton whose voice escaped as if to mock them both. She flung herself at the door, but hanging there was the miniature of the great unresponsive horn.

"Have you brought a message from the gates of the dead?"

"I bring myself, you fool!" Infuriated, Egla rushed at the door again, her fists pounding on the wood. "Jeroboam, in the Lord's name, don't make an idiot of yourself. Open this accursed door before the neighbors gather to congratulate us. Jeroboam, Jeroboam!" shrieked Egla. "What are you doing? Egla is at your gates! Your Egla! Your dove from the crannies of the rocks!"

By the stir in the house Egla could tell that Jeroboam was hesitating, his hand on the latch, but instead of raising it and opening the door he said with deep concern:

"Do I hear the knocker rattling? I implore you, by Adonai, don't touch the bolt or anything else on the door. Don't touch the wood, the iron, the horn, the chain—have I mentioned it all? Move away! I can't afford yet another cleansing of the house. Couldn't you stand over there by the barn so we can talk like normal people?"

"So you knew all the time who was at the door," whispered Egla, and for the second time since the mysterious healing—the first time was when she was following Ismai to the synagogue—she felt her confidence weakening.

"Jerkoam saw you at the tax collector's post," Jeroboam's voice explained, "and hastened to inform me."

"And you barred the door to me as to an adulteress?"

"Don't be touchy, Egla! I barred the door not to Egla, not to my beloved wife, but to her sinful double who in defiance of the Law returns from the place of atonement whose name I don't dare mention. Do you know that leprosy and its inner sin-content are infectious? Do you want me too to be infected?"

So he doesn't know I'm healthy again, sobbed Egla. How hot-tempered and unjust she had been, accusing him of indifference, and all because he had been misinformed. How could he have known what miracle took place in the Jabtel ravine?

"But I'm no longer leprous, Jeroboam! God has healed me, the priest has examined me conscientiously, carrying out all the requirements of the rite of cleansing. I've bathed in running water and bought the sacrificial victims, for which you'll receive a bill from Ismai."

"All right, I'll pay the bill, but how can I be sure that you have really recovered by God's mercy and that there's no danger of infection if you look at me or touch me?"

"Look!" She moved away from the door and opened her dress like some flying shell from which gushed the trembling light of her bosom. "Look, my lord and husband, there is no trace of leprosy on me. I'm as pure as the tears of Jeremiah, who wept for the captivity of Israel. Look, look, Jeroboam, and speak!"

It seems that in some way, perhaps through some uncaulked hole in the door, Jeroboam could see his wife, because he agreed unwillingly that there was no trace of the disease on her skin and that, by the external signs alone, she was wholly free of the plague.

"But what about your inner being, my Egla," he said, almost hostile. "What about your inner organs, which the priest Ismai couldn't examine? What about your liver, your kidneys, your bladder? What about your heart, your circulation and especially your brain which, enclosed like an egg, may still contain the murderous germs of leprosy?"

Egla couldn't contradict him. The state of her entrails was truly unknown to her. She could only repeat stubbornly that she had been cured by a young man who repesented himself as the Son of God, and that she was convinced that he had done so in the most flawless manner.

"I won't contest the good intentions of this youth, whether he is of divine origin or not," said Jeroboam humbly, "but leprosy is a deep-rooted evil which, like sin, doesn't remain on the surface but penetrates the very marrow of the bones and sometimes even the mind. Ismai has admitted that superficial leprosy isn't as dangerous as internal leprosy, for man can notice it in time and obtain the little bells that give warning. Furthermore, thanks to the lions, foxes, dogs and other beasts into which are turned those whose names I don't dare mention, we are accustomed to endure external leprosy, but we know nothing of the internal leprosy to which the living water of cleansing doesn't penetrate, and which the consecrated blood of the lamb doesn't reach when it falls upon the fingers or the lobe of the ear. That's what Ismai says, and he certainly knows more of these mysteries than anyone in Jabneel"—Jeroboam's voice grew timidly angry—"and you haven't come here to destroy me, have you?"

At this point something reassuring had to be said, so she swore she had no intention of bringing any evil on him. What was more, she had undertaken nothing serious to ensure the return of God's liking for her. Was she to blame that the god of Abraham, of Isaac and of Jacob, moved and won over by her suffering, had sent his envoy-son with all the signs of amnesty? Nor had she compelled him: on the contrary she had behaved insolently and mocked his pretentious promises, taking him to be some traveling charlatan trying to extract money from her for a few drops of colored water which served now against baldness and sterility, now to wipe away leprosy, neutralize every spell or defend against the evil eye. So she had mocked him, even after she had agreed to his senseless play-acting, telling him her story in the expectation that when she asked for help he would offer her some of his magical remedies, tell her a pack of lies about their tested efficacy and in the end ask for a fee. She had relaxed in that jest only when he had begun to exaggerate, saying that he was the Son of Man who was hastening to become God or something like that, and so they had bargained until without any scented water the miracle happened before her very eyes, after which the stranger had taken his hands from her and gone his way. Not even then had she believed herself healed, but had attacked her own flesh and only after exhaustive checks had become convinced that there really had been a miracle.

"Egla, Egla!" cried Jeroboam. His voice sounded as wooden as the barred door through which it reached his wife. "I expected that you'd spare me an explanation, which would have been unnecessary had you listened to me more carefully instead of chitchatting about sons of god—a blasphemy I haven't heard for a long time—and scented waters of wandering quacks. Now I have no choice. But before I begin, promise that you'll listen to me without malice. That's the least I can expect after what you've done to me with your illness."

"Speak," Egla called to him, "but be quick, because I have an evil premonition which the uproar I hear now in the town only increases."

"All right, but that's not all. I want you to know that I adore you and that I'll always love you whatever has happened and however this day turns out," said Jeroboam. She felt that, squatting behind the barred door, he was choosing sincere words which wouldn't finish her off completely, and she was thankful more for his concern about her than for his continued love. "When, may his will be done, Hashem threw a spell over your lovely skin and you had to move to New Jabneel, I stayed to struggle with your memory, to which I paid daily homage in the words of the psalms of the blessed Solomon, and against the memories which your sinful illness had left in the souls of our imperiled fellow citizens."

You, my darling, Egla remembered, are like a company of horses in Pharaoh's chariots, your neck is like the tower of David built for an armory, where a thousand bucklers hang, your lips, O my spouse, drip as the honeycomb; honey and milk are under your tongue.

"I suffered a lot," Jeroboam went on, "but though I don't say you were in anything like paradise, at least you were among your own people, among those whose name I can't even mention, you were so to speak at home, while I lived my life as if cut in two; my soul was profitless beside you in New Jabneel and my body was dragging along here in Old Jabneel, serving the tetrarch. Needless to say, they called me 'the leper's darling' or 'the unclean husband' or 'the accompanist (almost the accomplice) of sin,' though we didn't see each other and I was no longer in any way your husband."

My dear, she thought, you are comely as Jerusalem, terrible as an army with banners, your navel is like a round goblet with liquor, your belly is like a heap of wheat set about with lilies.

"They suspected that I too was a bit leprous because I had been your husband. I didn't blame them. I knew that leprosy need not attack the skin but can find its nest in the heart of some organ, and that it first is revealed as an innocent cold in which no one would recognize God's punishment. My friends fell away from me and they tolerated me in the Council only because they could find no other crier with so penetrating a voice; my employment doesn't demand direct contact with the townsfolk but is carried out at a safe distance, and even if I were a secret leper, I couldn't transmit my leprosy to Caesar's ordinances: I don't have to apply them, only to make them public. But don't imagine that was my only misfortune. Shortly after you left, anonymous letters began to reach Ismai. They said our house was near death and that the mortar, which due to its age was beginning to flake off, was an evidence of the angry fever with which you were infected. Do I hear you muttering outside? You have no right to blame our neighbors, because it has happened more than once that leprosy directed against some specific sinner spread at lightning speed to all his clothes, to his possessions and to the rooms in which he lived, and then, as if leaping from man to man, poisoned with its scabs the neighboring houses as well, until it infected the entire town."

Your eyes, Egla remembered, are like the fishpools in Heshbon by the gate of Beth-rabbim.

"I tell you this so that, understanding their justifiable fear, you may understand mine also," said Jeroboam. "I've submitted to inspections by Ismai, and the house, in the presence of qualified witnesses, has been inspected from attic to cellar several times at the regulation interval of seven days. But nothing evil was found. Thanks to the lapse of time during which no signs of leprosy appeared on me or any of my things, and not to the confidence which the people had in Ismai, I dared once more to mix freely with them and to achieve spiritual peace."

"Peace without me?" asked Egla.

"Peace with my memory of you, but I confess, under the circumstances, without you. Had I had any evil thoughts I could have given you a bill of divorcement, for I would only be following the divine commandment. How many have done that when their wives have been expelled from the camp!"

My little dove in the crannies of the rocks, thought Egla, in the secret places of the heights, let me see your face, let me hear your voice, for your voice is sweet and your face divine.

"Jeroboam, does that mean that you won't open the door to me?" asked Egla.

"I dare not, Egla," wailed her husband, and it was painful to hear him. "I dare not, my love. I fear leprosy. By Adonai, go back to your own and I will, as before, every dusk call down blessings upon you between the imperial and the municipal decrees."

"But I'm not leprous, Jeroboam!" shrieked Egla. "Ismai inspected me as naked as the day I was born! I'm yours again, not theirs!"

But her husband was unmoved. "Ismai's eyes don't even see the sacrifice he slaughters, and what's more, he is open to bribes as he fears for his old age. How can you guarantee that you didn't bribe him to overlook some minute trace of the disease?"

"Perhaps I might be able to live somewhere near you—not with you but near you," Egla pleaded. "Perhaps, temporarily, I could find a place by the stock pens until people see that I'm clean and no danger threatens them. I wouldn't approach you, only look at you; I wouldn't even look at you if you're afraid. I'd only squat motionless and wait until the people have trust in me."

Jeroboam didn't reply.

Egla didn't wait for her husband's reply. Her gaze was now fixed on the streams of citizens approaching Jeroboam's house from different directions. The one coming from the direction of the Council Hall was led by the smith Elimelech, and alongside him limped the "second mother," Fuva. In the nearest stream Egla recognized her nephew Mahir, who was employed at the pound of the sacrificial rams. She felt ashamed that the townsmen, ready to celebrate the miraculous healing which would bring fame to Jabneel and to the whole province of Galilee, would find her before the locked doors of her own house. How could she explain Jeroboam's behavior and turn their righteousness against him? Did she dare say Jeroboam didn't recognize the divine miracle and rejected its value as healing?

A quick glance at the noisy procession approaching across the bridge and led by Jerkoam and the excise officer Jefta convinced her that she wouldn't be able to explain. That mass of threatening limbs would more likely pick up stones than offer prayers. Those faces were not the peaceful faces of friends coming to exalt her healer-God, but hard faces of executioners hurrying to settle their accounts with that God.

The third procession was accompanied by a swarm of children brazenly collecting stones on the road. At their head strode a rabbi with a youthful face, armed with a shepherd's staff tipped with lead. The rest of the citizens were armed with cudgels, hoes and slings. Huge dogs with slavering jaws darted and yelped between their legs.

All the strength with which the young God had filled Egla by the touch of his hand ebbed from her; her trust in the lasting virtue of the divine action—and she considered herself the outcome of such an action—was being butchered at every step of his howling mob with countless blots for faces, this mob of inhuman flexibility that was approaching her with feverish leaps and bounds, and within which every murderer acted like a precise cog in a single animal-like organism.

"Jeroboam," she screamed, "they're coming for me! They're bringing sticks and stones and dogs. Jeroboam, by the divine mercy, open the door!"

Elimelech's mob, Jefta's mob and the rabble led by the rabbi pressed on like three waterfalls in a foaming torrent of curses aimed at Egla.

"Jeroboam," wailed Egla, "they're getting closer! They're shouting: 'Hang the bells on her!' and 'Wipe out the unclean one!' and their dogs are leaping at me. Their eyes are cold as ice. They won't spare me. Jeroboam, in the name of the Lord, open the door!"

Those advancing on Egla were for the most part hungry,

dirty and ragged laborers, but there were also among them cultivated and well-fed persons in Damascus silks of woven gold, escorted by their house servants, and even some borne on litters in the Roman fashion, who bounced up and down on their seats as if prodded by red-hot tridents. There were cripples who, trampled by the sandals of the crowd, crawled on their mats, like snails in their slimy shells, and imbeciles who advanced in packs, the blind tied by leashes to mangy curs which, trod on, yelped in fury. In front of the tavern the clean-shaven soldiers of the Roman garrison toasted this barbarian spectacle in which their feeling of superiority didn't allow them to take part. There were also mothers with children at the breast, who looked ready to throw their children in the dust when they knelt down to pick up a stone of vengeance; and the devout, whose fury was sacred, and fifteen-year-olds whose fury was as innocent as a schoolboy joke on the playing fields; dignitaries whose stones were cast for them by special servants known as "throwers"; ragpickers, potters, coopers, wheelwrights, carpenters, tinkers, smiths, weavers, goldsmiths, cordwainers and other craftsmen; idlers, hired hands, clerks, innkeepers, Levites, ox-herds, thieves, town councilors, whores, actors, peasants, usurers, matrons, free-thinkers and teachers—all mobilized by the Law into a fearless mob which rolled toward Egla, who was screaming before the closed door of Jeroboam's house.

"Jeroboam, they're almost here! Their dogs are rushing at me with open jaws! Jeroboam, by the divine mercy, open the door!"

Only when the first stone, thrown by the weak hand of a cripple or a young child, bounced alongside her, did she turn to the rabble.

"I'm clean, brothers," she screamed hoarsely, revealing her breasts, "I'm clean!"

The arrogant word hurled at the crowd was cast back as a perverted echo: "Unclean! Unclean!"

The stones were now falling as thick as hail. Since the crowd couldn't make up its mind to advance closer and use the hoes and staves, Egla decided to leap the fence and get into the open fields before her retreat was cut off. They didn't hinder her flight because they didn't want to desecrate the town by a stoning, but only to drive her out and finish the job in the wastelands.

The people of Old Jabneel drove Egla to the boundary of the unclean. Only the most daring had courage to throw stones across it; the sinner was now under the protection of her sin and could be allowed to go in peace where the ancient canons permitted her.

And she went.

The people of Old Jabneel looked with God-fearing satisfaction as she was lost to sight on the road to the leper settlement.

Disturbed by the uproar, the men of New Jabneel gathered under their leaders, "Rhinoceros" Azail and Jonadab "the Fox," on the open space in front of the colony, with the terrified newcomers in the forefront. They had armed themselves with sharpened stakes and lead-tipped cudgels. The old settlers, however, believed that no massacre threatened them. Hadn't Jehovah poured down enough rain for the harvests to bear as never before? Hadn't this summer's plague bypassed the chosen people? Hadn't the Romans recalled the evil regent and appointed a new one of whom so little was known that even the lepers feared no danger from his malice? What was even more crucial—so the old settlers said—was that "Herod's evil," the disease from which the tetrarch suffered, had recently taken a milder form. It was natural that he had decimated them in the sixth year of the reign of the Emperor Tiberius, but then not only had the harvest failed but also the tetrarch's bladder pains had demanded a revenge on the sinners as a possible or even probable cause of the national misfortune. Now everything was once more as it should be: Canaan flourished. And where the clean rejoice, the unclean have nothing to fear.

That forecast came true when only one woman appeared on the desolate horizon. By her clothes they recognized her as Uriah's wife Egla, whom they had sought all night in vain, only her clothes appeared more splendid than those of the leper woman, which could have been due to the position of the sun. The woman was walking briskly as if relieved of too heavy a burden, and many thought that she was singing, though not all were agreed on that. Perhaps some bird in the Jabtel ravine was warbling.

As the unknown woman advanced, the lepers' faces grew increasingly worried, and the astounded Azail began to doubt that the woman approaching them was Egla, wife of Uriah, or if she was, then something terrible must have happened to her. Some thought that she was Egla, who had grown ugly overnight and whose features by some terrible action had lost the regal appearance of a leprous face; others swore that it was not Uriah's wife but her twin sister (despite the fact that Egla had no twin sister); a third group, among whom was Azail, believed that it was an unknown and healthy newcomer who only resembled their Egla.

"Why, Azail," the woman said, "don't you know Egla, Uriah's wife?"

The lepers murmured among themselves and the elder grew angry: "I don't deny that, though uglier, you resemble the wife of our washer of the dead, but what do you mean by that deceptive likeness? Our Egla is a leper and you are clean!"

Egla smiled with an inner radiance, the smile of deathbed relief. It was good that—despite the honest will of the young and handsome God-man, and the miracle and the ceremony of absolution by which it was made lawful—there was no hope for lepers, no healing, no return. Leprosy was incurable; and that too was good. Only from that morning on could she live completely outside the camp, as the testaments commanded, and not with a heart which beat on the frontier between two towns. This, she thought, is my third birth.

"What do you want, woman?"

"My bells," said Egla, "my bells which I lost and which, according to the Law, I must wear about my neck or on my clothes."

The lepers raised their hands to heaven as if listening to a sacrilege. Azail frowned. Though they hadn't been especially friendly, Egla felt a longing to caress his dear, swollen face, but the elder stepped back in terror:

"Have you gone out of your mind? Can't you see I'm unclean?"

"What does that matter to you? I'm unclean too," said Egla triumphantly. "Come on, get me some new bells! I want to hang them upon me so that everyone will know I'm a leper!"

Jonadab rejected this demand: the bells belonged only to the unclean and, along with the disease, they made them different from the clean. From the time of Moses those bells were the emblem of their plague-stricken community and only real lepers could wear them round their necks, and not those who had been healed, those who for any fashionable reason wanted to jingle them. He didn't say that Egla had never been a leper; everyone knew that she had been. However, to all it was equally evident that she had been healed and that she no longer belonged to New but to Old Jabneel. Surely Egla herself could see what she looked like?

Egla replied excitedly that she was clean only externally and that within her nothing had changed, that the finger of the God-man had not been able to touch her internal organs or the consecrated blood of the lamb penetrate through her ear, and that not only was she leprous to the greatest degree but that she felt so. What more did he want?

"Ismai of Old Jabneel teaches the inner leprosy is more leprous than superficial leprosy!" she shouted.

"What Ismai teaches is valid for Old Jabneel, but this is New," said Azail. "Here our own teaching is valid. From the times of Sinai we have administered ourselves according to the external signs of God's judgment upon men, garments or houses; we scorn everything internal as suspicious, uncertain and unstable, and scorn everything which could be either this way or that. For us the absence of even the most minute trace of leprosy upon you is conclusive—your entrails do not interest us—and we forbid you to carry the bells which are in some way sacred. You no longer belong to us! Go to them to whom God's mercy has restored you!"

Then Jonadab spoke: if Egla could show them even a single

mark, scab, rash or scar as a proof of leprosy, they would embrace her without prejudice as a wayward sister. Could Egla do that? Obviously, she couldn't. Therefore she must leave them. Clean and unclean, said Jonadab, had nothing in common except the sin which, in the form of a narrow one-way bridge, the Creator had raised between them. Even as the clean had a horror of lepers, so too with reason and justice the lepers had a horror of the clean.

Egla pleaded that she might say farewell to Uriah before she was expelled. And she hastened to the mortuary in the hope that Uriah would help her and bring her leper brothers to their senses, that he would understand her inner uncleanliness and her lack of danger to any in the penal colony. The mob followed her at a distance.

The mortuary in which Uriah ben Miam worked was an ordinary courtyard with gray stone walls around it. A bamboo roof covered only a part of it, and there were slabs for the corpses, and cauldrons in which the oil for anointing smoked.

Uriah showed no astonishment at Egla's changed appearance. He didn't even interrupt his work to offer her a conjugal kiss. He said that he had already heard what had happened, and that he didn't reproach her for going away stealthily and ingratiating herself with God and inducing him to show her his mercy and that he was pleased she'd come to bid him farewell before she left.

"To hell with that! Where am I to go?" Egla burst out, and added that she had no intention of going anywhere. She was unclean. The people of Old Jabneel had convinced her of that. She felt like that with all her body and soul, and her place was here among the lepers. She hadn't come to say farewell but to beg him to intervene for her with the elders: Azail and Jonadab should allow her to stay at least until they were convinced of her irreproachable leprosy. Also, they should return her bells.

Uriah was anointing the naked body of a dead man with a scrap of goatskin in the shape of a mitten, before sewing him into a linen shroud and handing him over to his relatives waiting in the courtyard. He didn't reply.

"But you love me," sobbed Egla, "you must help me to win them over."

Uriah replied that he hadn't fallen in love with her, but with the real Egla, the leprous Egla, with whom she had nothing in common except a vague resemblance such as eternally changing lava has to lifeless, monotonous stone. She was now a completely new woman, but even if he admitted that she was a new, authentic and healthy Egla, in her present form she didn't please him at all. Ugly and colorless, she was sinfully different from him and from everyone else in the community. To be honest, she even disgusted him. No, Uriah said, he didn't want to be harsh, but she had forced him to by her incomprehensible behavior. Couldn't she see that the two of them were now like tinder and water? Who could light tinder by holding it under water?

"But what am I to do, Uriah?" asked Egla wearily.

Uriah advised her to go back to her own people, meaning the people of Old Jabneel, but when Egla told him that they had rejected her cleansing, for which the people of New Jabneel now accused her, and that they would only expel her again, Uriah admitted that he didn't know where she should go.

"No," said Egla, "I have nowhere to go, I have to stay in the settlement whatever happens."

"You won't stay in the settlement," said Uriah. "They won't permit it. Azail and Jonadab will force you to go. That's the Law."

"I don't care about the Law. I have nowhere to go."

"Why should the camp care? We're only keeping the Testament," replied Uriah.

"I don't care about testaments!" shouted Egla.

"Jonadab and Azail look after our interests before God. You will go," concluded Uriah.

"I don't care about gods and I won't go," said Egla lifelessly. "I'll sit here in the courtyard and no one will be able to move me from my country, from my unclean country."

"Don't defile a country which isn't yours," shouted Uriah in fury. "Your country is there, across the Jabtel. Come, get out, go your way!"

"I'll sit right here," screamed Egla, "and your Azail will have to give me back my bells!"

Egla sat down on the ground and crossed her legs.

"All right, but don't say I didn't warn you."

He left the mortuary. The mob outside murmured. Egla sat in the middle of the courtyard and all she saw were the white and disproportionately large feet of the dead men on the slabs, like the roots of some wild plant. Behind them the oil smoked.

Did that young God-man know what had happened to her? Surely he didn't remember the woman whom he had seen fleetingly in a bad light and in a distorted form. She wasn't resentful, for he had done what he could; there had been a miracle and she was healthy. But if he knew so well what would happen to him, if he knew that some transfiguration was imminent for him, then he who had made such a mess of it must have known that stoning awaited her.

And why had the God-man decided to heal her if he knew what awaited her, thanks to his healing? And he must have known, or else he wouldn't have been a God-man.

She couldn't sit there any longer, because the stones were falling nearer and nearer.

What was it that the tetrarch's announcement had said? "Who dares to raise up again one whom Adonai's will has numbered and set aside and my club has struck on the neck." Had he even wished to contest the will of God the Father? As far as he was concerned, Egla thought bitterly, he had succeeded, but the vengeance for that defiance had fallen on her head. Certainly there was no accord beween Father and Son.

Egla stumbled under the hail of stones and rushed toward the opening in the walls surrounding the mortuary. She was half blinded by blood, but still in control of her senses. The lepers leaped after her, yelling. Only once she stopped to reason with them.

"I am unclean, brothers!" she shrieked. "I am unclean!"

But all that came back to her was a fragmentary echo of her pleading, transformed into a curse: "Clean! Clean!"

Then for the third time since that morning her courage

failed her and she rushed toward the path leading out of the settlement. Fearing she would change her mind, the lepers showered her with stones as far as the ravine of the Jabtel, where the most inveterate of the bigots from Old Jabneel were still on guard to make sure that, under cover of night, she wouldn't make another attempt to sneak into the town, bringing misfortune to them and their children. To prevent her from crossing the frontier of the unclean, they awaited her with a shower of stones which they had been collecting since noon. So she was forced to flee along the rough course of the ravine to the desolate no-man's land, attacked by stones from both sides, until both sides got tired and went back to their homes, content that on that day they had upheld the Testament. It would be better for the harvests than any prayer.

Finally the tortured Egla fell on a heap of stones which remained there after the stoning. Later, when she had recovered, she built a little house with those stones and—nourishing herself on nettles, carrion and the eggs of snakes—settled there at the bottom of the ravine, which from that day on was called "Egla's land," and her hovel "Egla's house."

Some years later, two travelers in the garb of pilgrims were making their way down the dry channel of the Jabtel. One of them was a red-haired little man with a hangdog expression, whose eyes were dulled like those of a man condemned to life imprisonment. The other was carrying a bag, and in his eyes was a flame of faith. They came upon the sleeping Egla stretched out like a lizard on the sun-warmed stone.

"A few years ago, Rabbi," said the younger, "if you remember, somewhere about here in the neighborhood of Jabneel, perhaps in this very place, you healed a young leper woman."

The older traveler, the one with eyes like a prisoner's, replied heedlessly: "No, Andrew, I don't remember."

"You did. Thanks to Judas, I remember very well everything concerned with the prophecies. Judas Iscariot tried to prevent you, for none of the prophets had mentioned any miracle in this desolate place, but you did it anyway. Would you like to try again?"

Jesus Christ looked at him defensively: "Why? There's nothing the matter with this woman except that she's old, very old. By the torments which await me in the Holy City, I've never seen an older woman."

"Perhaps she'd like to be young and live her life out again, Rabbi," said the apostle, "even though, I admit, the prophets don't say anything about rejuvenation."

"Don't speak of it, Andrew, son of Jonah! The Lamb of God who, as you see, is going to Jerusalem to his death, and this old woman who is awaiting her death here, will meet again very soon before my Father. Should I deny her that pleasure?"

And they went on their way toward the Holy City of Jerusalem.

Miracle at Jerusalem

> And he was casting out a devil, and it was dumb. And it came to pass, when the devil was gone out, the dumb spake; and the people wondered.
>
> Luke 11:14

THE INDEX FINGER of Valerius Gratus, adorned by a scarab from the land of Khem, gently pointed out the contours of the buildings of Jerusalem, which like dark cliffs hovered in the bluish haze of the west. The finger moved rapidly, without resting longer than necessary for the recalled governor of the province of Judaea to pronounce the right name.

Alongside him, on the porch of the Pretorium, stood the new procurator, just arrived from Rome. His name was Pontius Pilate. His pasty face, not yet tanned by the Mediterranean sun, was hangdog and ill-humored, and the boredom with which he listened to his informant had scarcely a trace of courtesy. However, he was exhausted by the sea voyage from Ostia to Jaffa and by the uncomfortable ride from Jaffa, but it was damnable that, for reasons of state, a rheumatic gentleman in the fifth decade of his life had to get a cramp in his backside in order to display proverbial Roman endurance before these insignificant scraps of the empire. Furthermore, the ostentatious holy places which had alternated along his journey with equally ostentatious dunghills had left a crushing impression on him.

Has this city a sewerage system? he wondered, while the attentive Gratus was telling him the life history of a prophet who had given his name to a synagogue. This deadly way of life, made up of misery and wretchedness, of chosen curses and doglike submissive supplications to some second-rate god or other, instead of impressing the newcomer with its Oriental picturesqueness, almost made him vomit.

Where do they wash? he wondered, half-listening to the precise description of the city fortifications, whose protection Gratus hoped his successor would never have to rely upon.

Where do they exercise? he thought, following the finger of the ex-governor. In fact he was thinking of his Rome, of the chill north wind which clashed with the sea breezes from Ostia, of the fresh rains which peppered the soft banks of the Tiber, of the age-old humps of the sacred hills. He thought of the solid buildings whose significance had been strictly ordained by the Senate and not by the fickle and superstitious imagination of simpletons, of the temples where gods fashioned in the image of man held court, so manlike that one could bargain with them or lie in bed with their divine consorts. He thought of the overseers of his Campanian estate who swindled him outrageously, of the thumbs turned down in the arena, the shattering crash of the chariots at the crucial turn, the rattling of the dice on the marble tables. He thought of his treatise *The Complete Husbandman,* in which he had dared to contradict Terentius Varro, and which remained hopelessly unfinished on his massage-couch. He thought of how his childbearing wife would stand this land of Judaea, which stank of incense, camel dung, carrion and disgusting spices, and whose very horizon was a meadow overgrown by parched weeds. Above all he thought of the Caesar Tiberius who had honored him with command over the province of Judaea, or rather had expelled him from Rome to spend the most productive years of his life among superstitious savages who could not even put a form to their god. Oh, he thought angrily, to hell with the governorship, to hell with Caesar, to hell with beautiful Judaea!

"Look, most honored Pontius," said Valerius Gratus, indicating with his nail the Holy City—the Upper City overlooking the valley of Hinnom, and Acra overlooking the valley of Kidron. "These geographical ignoramuses whom you will now administer believe that the gate of hell is somewhere in this vicinity, which is not a bad thing in that it is always before their eyes." He shifted his finger a little to the left. "And those delapidated hovels, huddled together like sheep frightened by the Roman wolf, are Moriah, a sort of old Jerusalem center, but an unsuccessful copy of our Forum. The house of the most wise Solomon was there at one time, and also the house of his father David, that damn fool, a rat and a cheat, who wrote a book of dirges grieving for God, as our Catullus grieved for Claudia. Anyhow, his people believed him, so why wouldn't God be tricked, too? I expect that God couldn't be more sensible than the people he took under his protection, and that their intellectuals are clever to the degree their god is. I think that peoples have the gods they deserve and that gods choose the peoples whose traits best correspond to their own. What do you think?"

Pilate was thinking of nothing at all. He was holding a handkerchief to his nose as if the stink of the dung heaps of the Judaean hamlets was still in his nostrils. The absence of even the simplest thought was so obvious on his brow that Gratus hastened to proceed.

"A little to the right are the Temple and the Council Hall. Your temporary host, or rather your guest, resides in that palace over there, but I'll speak of him when I have the unpleasant task of briefing you on the political situation you're inheriting."

"I'm much obliged to you, most noble Gratus," said the new governor without much enthusiasm. I can see that you've cooked me a fine broth, he thought, and that you'll serve it to me for breakfast. If there's a revolt or a revolution, my first dispatch to the Palatine will be worthy of the mood of its sender.

"Will you do me the honor of allowing me to accompany you when you inspect these buildings more closely?" asked Gratus.

Pontius Pilate had no intention of inspecting them even from a distance, let alone more closely, either now or—if possible—ever, but he didn't want to insult his predecessor. He expressed a restrained satisfaction at the proposal, and after Pilate's slaves had thrown over his shoulders a linen mantle with a hood to protect his face, the pair of senior Roman officials went out arm in arm into the sweltering Jerusalem dawn.

"This street, which will lead us to the Temple," explained Gratus, "is called 'the Roman street' if used by our countrymen, and 'the Jewish street' in the language of the natives, but its real name ought to be 'the street of the beggars.' It's the favorite meeting place and promenade of the vagabonds who live by alms. Look, noble Pilate, the sight is not particularly attractive, but it conjures up the East more vividly than any description you might send to Rome in the form of a dispatch."

Crippled beggars were dozing on both sides of the street. Under the shadows of the misty dawn they looked like a line of trees desolated by storm. They were motionless as pictures in a dream that ends before it has ever begun. They looked like neglected lattices from which the paint was peeling; inexplicable freaks of mother earth; mechanical dolls not wound up, from some senseless world in which children played with monstrous toys.

"I wouldn't allow them to beg in the presence of the governor, honorable Valerius," Pilate remarked dryly. Till then he had refrained from any comment on Gratus's concessions on ruling, but the superior smile in Gratus's otherwise flattering behavior irritated him. Does this fattened, peach-fed, scented fop with his Oriental habits think I have just come out of the egg, and cannot see the miserable state of the province handed over to my administration? By all the gods, he does!

"What would you do, if that isn't already an official secret?" Gratus asked, making no attempt to conceal the mockery beneath his professional curiosity.

"I'd order the legionaries to disperse them."

"You'd be making a mistake, my distinguished friend," Gratus went on defensively. Beneath his bulging eyelids, tinted in the Oriental manner, he looked at his successor: a typical upstart, he thought, already behaving like a new broom in a house from which the old one has not been removed, already hatching stupid plans for turning everything upside down, and for introducing in this magnificent but natural chaos some silly military order. By Jupiter, he thought, the hungry and the unfortunate mar the regimental proportions and crude mold of his ideal state; if he can't manage to clothe, fatten and entertain them, he'd rather exterminate them than allow them to pollute his untroubled statesman's dream. I bet, thought Gratus, smiling politely, that he is accusing me of negligence and is comparing me, to my disadvantage, with those crazy fellows in the first chapter of *The Complete Husbandman.* Well, my dear Pontius, the well-being of even the tiniest province is not like a beet root which is simply uprooted from the soil, and to rule here in the East isn't like sowing in a furrow straight as an arrow which the plow has made in your famous farmers' handbook. He continued amiably: "Yes, you'd be making a serious mistake. Nothing enables us to enjoy life more than a glance at a man who suffers in that same life. That is, I dare say, the personal benefit which a healthy man extracts from a sick one. The public benefit is merely an accessory. These cripples allow us to be merciful for a few coppers, instead of straining our generosity for a new aqueduct which would cost us who knows how many gold talents. You, I understand, are writing a book on practical husbandry, so you must understand the basic difference between gold and copper, especially if one gives them away. When you have settled down here, dear Pilate"—and that, he thought with a sweet smile, will never happen to that blockhead of an imperialist with a plowshare instead of a face—"you'll realize that ten half-Jews are pleasanter company than one whole Jew. These cripples, who look as if their own god had punished them in our name and at our request, are the most loyal subjects of the Protectorate. I recommend them to your especial favor, governor!"

Pilate remarked that he would bear that in mind. Essentially, the state (he hoped that the attentive reader would perceive that in his treatise on the administration of the stables) was an estate, only larger and more profitable. He would have to throw some coppers to one or two of those beggars, so that their importunate countrymen wouldn't later demand that he petition the Emperor for the construction of some new harbor.

"Shall I introduce you to one of them?" Gratus proposed.

"Couldn't you postpone that, honored Valerius?" The thought that at every awakening his first glance would fall upon this foaming wave of monstrosities, which broke on the solid ramparts of the Pretorium as on the firm bows of some stray Roman trireme, aroused a real seasickness in Pontius Pilate. "I've eaten nothing since yesterday, and I don't believe that a closer acquaintance with one of your protégés would awaken my appetite."

"But today they've had the honor of becoming your subjects," said Gratus.

"I'm enchanted," Pilate replied.

They pulled their hoods across their faces and made their way through the avenue of beggars which swayed toward the roadway as if driven by the wind blowing from all four quarters of Jerusalem; through that jungle of mendicity, imploring, complaining, petitioning, and the impenetrable thicket of voices of all shades, tones and tongues: loud and throaty, asthmatic, nasal, stuttering, clattering, slimy, whining and hissing; voices that sounded like the velvety hooting of owls, the rustling of sand, the shriek of a hurricane, the gurgling of blocked springs, the sizzling of branches and the sputtering of embers stirred up by a poker; voices dark, ringing, muffled, slippery, silken, piercing and penetrating; voices which thudded like hammers, bored like awls, cut like sickles, rasped like files, buzzed like saws and tore the hearing to shreds like the eyeteeth of wolves.

Valerius Gratus strolled on lazily, paying no attention to the crush of the tormented, but Pilate several times was on the verge of bursting out in howls so that, deafened by his own voice, he might drown out all the others.

"Let's choose someone who isn't too talkative and boring," said the old hand, "and among the Zion beggars that could only be Mesezeveilo, known as the Mute. He was born dumb and begs in front of Amonach's tavern."

Protected by his hood, Pilate's astonished gaze ranged over the length of that double wall of despair in which mutilations were evident in all their aspects, mutually complementing one another, one misfortune perfected by the next one even more unfortunate. Alongside the blind, with faces like insensitive masks forming a smooth, impenetrable stone parapet, the deaf-mutes staggered with restless twistings, like fish in an aquarium, that hermetically sealed world of silence where everything unfolds soundlessly as in the deepest dream. Next to them were the possessed, some faces turned blissfully to the consoling brilliance of a private paradise, others grimacing, howling, whimpering, twisting about or making senseless leaps, but most often pouring out disconnected words. The maimed were the most numerous and the most varied: from the legless, who looked like stumps on their cut-off buttocks, and the armless, those bare trees without branches, to the beggars whose absence of one arm seemed balanced by the lack of the opposite leg, down to the paralytics who, despite the possession of all their limbs, slobbered powerlessly on the carpets of their own living wounds. Pilate differentiated the one-eyed, the one-armed, the one-legged and the earless (the noseless didn't count). He saw those who were at the same time one-armed and earless, one-legged and one-armed, earless and one-legged, one-eyed and earless. He saw the eyeless who had had their ears cut off because of their offenses; the armless whose tongues had been torn out; the legless deprived of their noses; the blind, the deaf, and those from whom the blood continually flowed as from a tiny tap.

"Ye Gods," swore Pilate as he dragged himself across the cobbles, "only the lepers are missing!"

Already they were in front of Amonach's tavern. Not far from the door stood Mesezeveilo, a stocky Ishmaelite overgrown with gray hair and dressed in rags. In a deformed hand he was holding an earthenware bowl with which, by clinking coins in it, he hoped to arouse the generosity of passers-by. With the other hand he leaned on a thick staff. From his dumb lips, as if from a well almost dry, gurgled fragmentary sounds that expressed his feelings and thoughts.

Valerius Gratus turned to him. "Hey, Mesezeveilo! How's business this morning?"

The mute recognized the procurator of Judaea and fell

prone, his cheeks shining as if washed by an invisible sponge. When the Roman called on him to stand, the cripple's uncoordinated movements accompanied by inarticulate grunts could only be interpreted as dissatisfaction with the poor receipts from his obvious misery. As proof he shook the bowl, in which a single coin clinked feebly.

Gratus smiled. "What does that mean? Have your compatriots all gone bankrupt out of fear of the new governor? Should he be concerned whether he'll collect the monies due to Caesar in good time?" Then he peered into the bowl. "Look, *Quadrant Bon Eventus,* minted by the divine Augustus. Take care of it, Mesezeveilo, for as the inscription on the back says, it brings good luck."

This Gratus's crazy, thought Pilate, upset by the unstatesmanlike intimacy between a Roman noble and a Jewish ragamuffin. The East has turned his head. It mightn't be a bad idea to include this shameful incident, with the excuse that he was concerned about the noble Valerius, in one of his future dispatches to Rome. He would give it the name of one of those ill-tempered illnesses with which the East avenges itself on Westerners when they reside there too long. What a revenge for this morning! He could picture Caesar stripping the former procurator of Judaea of all his honors, on the pretext that he wished to free him from the burden of state service, and then sending him into the interior to convalesce —the official euphemism for banishment—where, administering an estate no larger than the Roman sewer, he would have time enough to remember Pilate and realize the advantage of genuine welcome over hypocritical politeness.

In the meantime Gratus was asking the mute: "By this coin I can see that a Roman has passed by here. Am I right?"

Mesezeveilo jumped up and down, squeaking, as a sign of agreement.

"Are you a favorite of my legionaries?"

Mesezeveilo again leaped up and squeaked an affirmative reply.

"And you," Gratus then asked him, "do you like us Romans?"

Mesezeveilo jumped up, raised his staff and, squeaking like a rat, pointed alternately to heaven and earth. Fearing he might not be understood, he repeated the same convulsive movements until Valerius Gratus translated to Pilate:

"He wants to say that his attachment to Rome is as great as the distance between heaven and earth; and even though I believe all Orientals exaggerate, he deserves a copper."

He dropped one in the cripple's bowl. The copper coin clinked and Mesezeveilo, as if some giant had kicked him, went on bounding up and down on the pavement. Wheezing and hissing, alternately he drove his staff now into the ground and pointed it at the heavens; his face shone with a fire of gratitude, while he thought: My Jehovah will come down, my Jehovah will plunge down from above to save the sons of Israel; very short is the way between heaven and earth and my Jehovah will leap across it; he is a great leaper across the worlds, the first rider in the saddle of the planets; and you'll have no time to burrow in the earth, nor to hide under the iron shield of death, for my Jehovah will find the Roman bloodsuckers, monsters, filth, godless idolators, cursed by heaven and earth. A curse on you Romans—he leaped enthusiastically, pointing now to heaven and now to earth—on earth and in heaven, under the earth and under the heavens!

"Do you hear him?" Gratus asked the new governor.

"No," Pilate admitted. Was this puffed-up hyper-Oriental trying to make a fool of him by some fairground trick so that, when the story went round of how Pilate had been taken in, all Rome would admire him and laugh at Pilate? Firmly resolved to cut short this unworthy game meant to compromise his reputation, he repeated harshly: "No, I didn't hear him. Did you, honored Gratus?"

Once again defeat. To his amazement the reply of the retiring official had an insulting significance:

"I? Naturally, I didn't hear him. How can one hear someone who is dumb? I meant did you understand him? Were you able to interpret his eloquent movements?"

"No," said Pilate curtly.

"Then let me explain them to you. Though I'm a foreigner and a member of the occupying forces, a long residence among the Jews has let me understand their feelings even when not expressed in any well-known language. When his staff points to the heavens it expresses a summons and doesn't have the sense which it often has in life; it means that Mesezeveilo is evoking his god. Since immediately after that the staff pointed at us, he was pointing out to his god the objects of his earthly gratitude. In short, he prays to God to compensate us for the gift which we have tossed in his bowl. And the more times he repeats those movements, the more sincere his prayer and the greater the expectation of its being granted."

"Excellent," said Pilate. He was a trifle reassured. The subtlety of the explanation showed its trustworthiness: Gratus was not mocking him. Perhaps he shouldn't send that letter to Rome after all.

All this time the cripple never stopped leaping up and down. He muttered unintelligible distorted syllables and was thinking: Fall from heaven, O Jehovah, and on the earth smash the Romans like the lice you once sent to Egypt as a warning, then wiped out as an absolution. Slaughter, O Lord, all tyrants with heavenly thunderbolts and earthly cleavers, so that their bleeding stumps drag along the ground and flap in the skies as a lesson to those who have been torturing us for ages past. This one especially, this one especially, he repeated, thrusting his staff toward Valerius Gratus.

"That poor devil would give his life for me," said Gratus as they walked away, "but since I'm leaving, accept him freely in my name if you ever have need of him."

"I'll hold both you and him to that," said Pilate.

"There you are, governor of Judaea," Gratus concluded. "That's the real East!"

Mesezeveilo didn't calm down until after the two dignitaries had vanished into the winding streets of Tyropoeon. He hated Gratus more than any other Roman, for he saw him every morning as the former procurator opened the window of the Pretorium to the daylight, exhausted from orgies.

Gratus was so unbearably good to him—from time to time he would throw him an asper or two—that he had to hate him even more deeply if he wanted to cancel his beneficence but not lose his money.

Then there emerged from Amonach's tavern Esau ben Korei, a well-to-do idler who spent most of his time—all the time when he was not sober—in the private rooms of brothels and gambling houses. He was tipsy, not drunk but tipsy. Mesezeveilo knew him well and again expressed his feelings by toadying leaps, bows and grunts.

"Catch it, mute!" said Esau, slurring his words, and threw him a coin which missed the bowl.

Mesezeveilo picked it up, swearing at the overamiable face: May your arm wither, may they always overtrump you, may you never be able to raise the cup to your lips!

Esau said: "Last night two Tyrians skinned me alive at backgammon. My purse is as dry as the Sinai desert and my stomach turned by Amonach's slops; one could sour a cabbage in them. Do you think the dice were loaded?"

Mesezeveilo grunted sympathetically, pointing to heaven and earth, and thought to himself: My Jehovah will make you as empty as the heavens and will cover you with despair like the waterlogged soil; he's great with the dice, he's a mighty swindler, my Jehovah; he'll strip your clothes from you as the wind scatters the clouds—those garments of the sky; Jehovah will drain you so you'll be like a bowl thrown on the rubbish heap. Jehovah will suck your blood into his dry throat, and thus emptied you'll be as heavy as the land and as barren as the heavens. My Lord will fatten you with a curse like a field plowed with manure. He'll smother you with sentences and punishments till you're full of misery, as heavy as the earth and as empty as the skies!

"Don't be a fool, mute!" said Esau. "Those damn dice weren't as light as the skies or as heavy as the earth. By the Ark of the Covenant, they were good dice, but this time they were against me."

And Esau staggered off home.

Mesezeveilo took Esau's coin out of the bowl, examined it

carefully front and back, then bit it: it was of real brass, with the face of one of those beardless emperors. Coming from the son of Korei, it might well have been counterfeit.

So passed the first dead hour of the morning. Mesezeveilo spent it cursing all his mendicant competitors, setting his Jehovah and all the gods whose names he could remember on them until he spied a wholesale grain merchant from Syria hurrying to open his office, throwing worried glances at the skies of Tammuz, which were as dry as a thatched roof.

Bowing to him with servile respect, he thought: here comes a fattened boar, a sack of tares, a barren vine from the vineyard of my Lord! Come on, take a spill, you Syrian good-for-nothing, you insatiable beast. My Lord will blind your eyes and the rich man will stumble and be dragged in the dust. My Lord will break the neck of the usurer, snap his thin neck like a reed in the hands of the Omnipotent, or over the knees of the Omnipotent, he thought, rattling his bowl and humbly watching the merchant, who was coming nearer while gazing at the sky. Come on, stumble, fall, burst open like a rotten sack so that wheat for Mesezeveilo flows out, so that the mute can eat his fill, so that his God can dance with a full belly! Come on, come on, come on!

As was his custom, the Syrian passed in front of the cripple. The stammering and snarling, and the clinking of the beggar's bowl, reminded the merchant of the water spirits whose rain dance he had seen during a business trip to Media. So he shouted to Mesezeveilo:

"The Medes say that the dumb can induce rain to fall, and the good God knows that I'll go bankrupt if it doesn't rain soon. So hey, you, whatever your name is, jump, dance, ask for rain, and if your prayer is answered I'll give you half a shekel. Here's a grosh to get by on!"

Zealously, energetically, Mesezeveilo began to jump up and down, puffing and luring the rain for the benefit of the rich man, thinking: The fine rain will not fall, my Jehovah won't let it; the taps of heaven are sealed (his staff stabbed the heavens), there will be no fine rain on the earth (his staff stabbed the ground), my great Economist won't allow it (he drew patterns in the sky and in the dust). The heavens will dry up (the staff again stabbed the heavens) and will become as tiny as a fist; the day will shrink like a shock of parched Syrian wheat and his plow lands (a stab at the earth) will expire from thirst in the hands of the devil!

Mesezeveilo entreated, spitting: Here is your fine rain, evildoer. The gods will send you a cloudburst—grow your wheat under turbid spit!

He went on jumping about until the merchant had gone his way. Then with his heel he ground out the spit as if a harvest for the Syrian might spring from it.

The next passers-by were two provincials dressed like Galilean peasants. Mesezeveilo rattled his bowl and bowed just enough to accord with the modest appearance and undoubtedly shallow purses of the two travelers. He didn't do this from cupidity, but from habit. He didn't spare a single anathema for such worthless persons.

The elder of the two wanted to pass by, but the younger held him back: "Give to the poor, Rabbi, for theirs is the kingdom of heaven."

The elder one answered impatiently: "A short while ago, when I asked for a contribution for expenses, didn't you say you didn't have a penny in your purse, Judas?"

"I'm not thinking of money, Teacher, for it's written: 'I will sing unto the Lord for all his mercies,' and whatever is written must take place. I'm thinking of the treasure for which his soul yearns."

Mesezeveilo's bow grew deeper as he calculated whether that "treasure" would be a copper or a brass asper—on which I'd spit, he thought, because all those who pretend to be generous usually give a bit of junky tin that won't buy an oka of wine. Or might they give a smaller bronze coin, perhaps two bronze coins, one each? They're taking their time thinking it over, the selfish sons of bitches. I hope my Jehcvah takes just as long in choosing the torments to strike them with, unless of course they give a whole sesterce, though with only a half sesterce they could avoid more than half the curses. Since he never stopped making up curses, his overstrained thoughts flowed in two channels: an upper one in which he reckoned, assessed and guessed, and a lower one in which he swore, cursed and reprimanded. Finally it occurred to him that these disguised millionaires might throw into his bowl a whole silver coin, one of those with the snout of some king on it (but why were they waiting so long? Jehovah, wipe them out—but not before they decide) or even a whole gold piece, if anything like that existed outside fairy tales.

Mesezeveilo shut his eyes. He heard the elder traveler say Ephphatha, a summons for something to open—a purse, probably—and felt the gentle touch of fingers on his lips, heard the sound of coughing, and then nothing more.

When he opened his eyes those two had gone and in the bowl, which without a thought in his head he kept shaking, there was no more than before: the quadrant of good luck, the coin from Esau and the governor's copper.

Pontius Pilate returned from Moriah without Valerius Gratus, who had been delayed at a goldsmith's. He stood in front of Amonach's tavern and smiled amicably at the mute. He had seen the strange behavior of the two Galileans and the cripple's disappointment. Here was a chance, he thought, to recruit a reliable dependent and thus do the fatherland a first official service. He chose from his purse a fairly large silver dinar bearing the head of Agrippa and dropped it in the beggar's bowl.

"What do you say to that one, friend?" he asked.

Mesezeveilo was silent.

"Come, speak freely."

Then something improbable happened that so perplexed the governor of Judaea that from then on he regarded all Orientals—rulers or criminals, slaves or nobles—as incomprehensible and, from a Roman viewpoint, irresponsible. Something happened which like a magnet drew all the beggars on the pavement and the guard from in front of the Pretorium—something which even the astonished Mesezeveilo couldn't understand, though he had had his doubts about the two Galilean peasants, and which he couldn't prevent, however much he tried not to say what he thought, and prayed that Jehovah take him under his special protection: the tongue tied since birth, twisted even in his mother's womb, was completely loosened. Gaily, provocatively, derisively, he proclaimed his most secret thoughts, silent till then, in a pure, resounding voice which hovered above the squares, above the roofs of the houses, above the synagogues, above the entire Holy City, like the outcry of the chosen people responding to the revolutionary war cry of the Lord of Hosts.

"So you ask what I have to say, Roman?" Mesezeveilo burst out as if his lungs were a smith's bellows. "I say: Down with Rome! I say: Down with the Emperor Tiberius! Down with the procurator of Judaea! Let us kill the Roman usurers! Let us cast down the gods of the Palatine! Take up the sword, O Israel! To the flames, O Israel! Hurraaah!" he yelled, eyes rolling in astonishment and panic, in preposterous efforts not to think of anything so he would yelp out nothing. He was in deadly fear, like a beast before slaughter, but he couldn't stop abusing and vilifying Rome and the Roman regime until by Pilate's order the guards took him away, first to interrogate him as was the regulation, then to scourge him and finally to crucify him.

Pilate was no longer smiling. He bent down and picked up from the dust the *Quadrant Bon Eventus,* or good-luck coin, which the mute had dropped while struggling with the legionaries. First he blew on it, then cleansed it on the sleeve of his mantle. Putting it in his purse, and with supernatural revelation on his face, he said to Gratus, who had now caught up with him:

"You were right, noble Valerius! The East is strange beyond belief."

Miracle at Siloam

And as Jesus passed by, he saw a man which was blind from his birth. He spat on the ground, and made clay of the spittle, and he anointed the eyes of the blind man with the clay, and said unto him: Go, wash in the pool of Siloam. He went his way therefore, and washed, and came seeing.

John 9:1, 6–7

BARTIMAEUS, son of Timaeus, closed his eyes swollen by the summer heat; he didn't dare to move from his rush mat where the Savior had left him, still less to push out from this secure raft into the open sea of alien, distorted and threatening objects which pounded his newborn sight like waves. He stopped looking as soon as the wonder-working spit had dried on his cheeks, and he had to rely on his unerring ears to confirm where the stranger had gone to after healing him so offhandedly and without questions. The cheering of the Jews convinced him that the Galilean was a descendant of David, overloaded with mercy as the mules with ore from the Ephraim mines, and that he was still running through Siloam, spitting on cripples chosen at random for salvation.

And he shouted: "Hosannah to the son of David!" while devoutly shaking his stomach in front of his nose. Astounded by that stomach's bubblelike appearance, he firmly closed his eyes.

In the pool, beside which he used to spread out his reed mat every morning except Saturday (on the Sabbath even the miracle-working mercy took a rest), the turbid holy water was splashing. The cripples tried to dip at least some part of their mutilated bodies into the mud gently touched by the angel's wing, before it subsided once again into an impotent, smelly marsh.

Ever since you got to know him, thought Bartimaeus—and you've known him since you first came to his pool—that son of a bitch of an angel has always been in a rush. As if he were working for the tax collectors and not for God! Before flying away he just barely moistened his wing, so that the healing ripple stirred only once or twice and the healing eddy only once, creating the holy ring of duckweed into which the cripples jumped shrieking. Those little waves and whirlpools were too weak and trivial for anything other than the removal of corns; the corns would fall off, but arms would stay withered, tongues tied in knots, eyes darkened. The sick man must be lucky as hell to find himself in the pool at the moment of the angel's descent. A split second later, without wetting his feet, he could walk across the heads of his nearest and dearest as if they were logs in a rotting pontoon. You couldn't see the water for bodies, and even when you did it was choking, lathering and sizzling among dark and bloated torsos.

What a stomach! Bartimaeus, son of Timaeus, was astounded. Did he have to travel all the way from Jericho to Siloam to be scared by his own belly button? But your belly button isn't the whole world, you Egyptian ass! The rest of the world must be far more beautiful. Jehovah wasn't as blind as you when he created it.

He opened his left eye and quickly closed it again. A huge, slimy worm was crawling up the bank of the pool, wriggling his way up, his pointed chin stabbing into the mud like a mountaineer's ice ax: Vakvuki, the lame cripple, was pulling himself out of the consecrated water. For God's sake, thought Bartimaeus, were my eyes restored just so I could look at that lousy Vakvuki? But Vakvuki was not the only man in the world, nor the only object upon which the son of Timaeus must waste his newfound eyes; he was curious, but also wanted to be grateful. Surely other people would be more attractive.

Closing his eyes again, he decided, not without a sense of

shame, to ask Vakvuki to leave the tomb which the two of them had shared unselfishly. While blind, he hadn't cared what his roommate looked like, but now, out of respect for sight and for him who had restored it, he didn't dare expose it to this superfluous and repulsive reject of what must be a more perfect world. He would, indeed, lose his best friend, but what was that in comparison with his restored sight!

He felt much better with his eyes closed, as if he saw better that way and without looking could give form to the objects among which he would live, without fear that they would disillusion him or offend him by their clumsiness. It must be, he thought, that under the protection of this advantage God himself walked the earth he had created from nothing; that God felt like a man blind from birth, who in his creations didn't have to follow any examples, laws or prohibitions.

No one, he thought, ever blamed you, Bartimaeus, because the light you created in your dark world was not radiant, because it in no way resembled this dazzling haze and blinding light for the light which he had known was in summer the burning wind, the black scorching sun, the day that warms without illuminating; and in winter the black icicles, the frosty blackness of the blizzard, the day that chills without illuminating. No one reproached you that all the ingredients of your world were black, and that they moved or remained motionless in black space under the black glow of the sun and under the cold black skies. No one reproached you because everything in your world was without edges, tops, angles but nonetheless rasping as scales, wrinkled like palm-tree bark. No one reproached you because the faces in that black world, themselves black, never had a beginning or an end but were interwoven in black unanimity and formlessness, yet even so maintained their own imaginary dark boundaries. No one had ever reproached him that the black distances he covered had no measure except the measure of his strides; that the objects among which he moved had no shape other than that shaped by his own quasi-divine fingers; and that the events in which he took part made no sense until he had adjusted them to the strange, black, subtle and comprehensible dimensions of his own black world.

For in his separate world, in that black sphere beyond all natural laws, which resembled the distorted face of an authentic world reflected in a black mirror, everything fitted like a puzzle, everything moved as if oiled, repeating the images from that shining, doubled world.

So he felt much more secure with his eyes closed. The stone garlands of the portico, which had oppressed him when he looked at them, now hung flabbily in the dark uncertainty of his memory; the cripples whose evil appearance had frightened him disappeared in tame, black traps which he had forged for them; the light again became a black heat, and his self-will the only measure of distance. Nothing threatened him, everything retreated neatly into its own black indifference and into the passionless distance of that moment when Bartimaeus, son of Timaeus, the blind man from Jericho, sneaked back into a world where he alone existed, its creator and autocrat, amid the obedient black objects which he, independent as God, had construed without emulating any of them.

You got your eyes so you could see, he thought as he lay beside the pool, in which now only the imbeciles were lingering, sticking out of the mud like saplings struck by lightning. You shouldn't blame eyes for seeing everything they light upon; no eyes have ever created lunatics. The lunatics always stayed in the water longest, and had the most faith in that son of a bitch of an angel, who didn't fly down every day but only when it suited him or he had nothing better to do. All right, thought Bartimaeus, obviously this isn't a matter of eyes alone. The fault isn't with my eyes alone, either. It wasn't enough to spit on my eyes; the world those eyes see should also have been spat upon. But for so much spit one Savior isn't enough. Not even a thousand!

This time Bartimaeus half opened his right eye, hoping, like every man unused to seeing, that it would have better luck than the left. He saw two knees with holes full of pus like the eyes of two evil little beasts. He swore: "Miniyamin—you damn Samaritan bastard, you bloody son of a bitch!" Bartimaeus threw a rock at the paralytic, who didn't move. I don't have to look at Miniyamin, he thought, and as his eyes wandered they fell on the possessed Ananias, tearing out his hair while blood as dark as a bull's dripped from his head.

"Adonai, Adonai," Bartimaeus prayed, "why are these bastards spoiling my sleep?"

When Miniyamin asked him how he liked the world at first glance, he snapped, "Fuck off!" and turned his back on him.

You must get used to it, Bartimaeus, son of Timaeus, he said to himself, you must begin with the unimportant, safe things that you know through your fingers: this beggar's mat, for instance, which was your cradle and will be your death bed. (The mat was as gray as the skin of a dead rat.) You didn't think it so awful before. You thought it was clean and it was, until you saw it. You thought it was beautiful and it was, until you saw it. You made it filthy with your eyes—with your own stubborn, conceited, untrained eyes. After all, he consoled himself, how does the appearance of a beggar's mat compare with your ability to see it?

He turned on his side. Sprawled on the smooth surface of the holy water, hanging on to floats shaped like necks of imaginary monsters, the last of the lunatics, still waiting for the absent-minded angel, looked like nests of water birds in the halcyon days. He was forced to look at the pool and at the shaggy heads of the idiots. They were happily rubbing themselves with the mud, even though the angel had long since flown away and not a ripple was raised except by their own hands, indefatigable in hope.

"Fuck it!" groaned Bartimaeus, vomiting under that same sun under which he had begun to see.

And he got up and ran until he banged his forehead against a wall: forgetting he could see, he had kept his eyes closed. When he opened them again, he saw before him a slaughter-house yard sprinkled with sand, on which emaciated bulls were falling under the blows of bloody mallets.

He began to run again. At last he could rejoice as he saw a procession hurrying toward him—something worth having eyes to see. It was made up of Nubian slaves, tall, healthy giants with copper rings in their ears, carrying on their shoulders the litter of some Roman dignitary. Bartimaeus didn't know what to admire more: the supple trot of the bearers, the glittering brilliance of the carved litter or the firm body of the official reclining on multicolored leather cushions. But strangely enough, he didn't wonder at any of these things. On the contrary, as he imagined himself on a nobleman's litter, he felt upset because he couldn't have what he saw. Damn you! he swore at his new eyes, futile and envious. Why do you make even beauty seem disgusting?

The rest of the birthday of his eyes he spent in the tomb where he lived, convinced that in its darkness the temptation to open his eyes wouldn't harm him much. But when his eyes had become accustomed to the darkness, in which he could no longer see what he wanted but only what was forced upon him, Bartimaeus realized that he had imagined his dead landlord, with whom he shared the tomb, as much more pleasant than he was. The blind Bartimaeus hadn't been superstitious and hadn't believed that souls dawdled around their former bodies longer than was necessary for those bodies to decompose (the disintegration of that in which they had so believed in life couldn't encourage them to delay further), but the Bartimaeus who could see was no longer so sure about that. He gathered his rags together in haste, left the tomb where he had lived happily for years and found himself in the street without a roof over his head. He consoled himself with the thought that now he could at least see how unfortunate he was and what dangers threatened him.

He hoped to avoid the misfortunes which had befallen him through his salvation by refusing to recognize it, by simply seeking no advantage from it and continuing to live as when he had been happily blind. But the following night, lying with Josavea, a whore visited only by the blind and an occasional lunatic, Bartimaeus found that he was condemned to look so long as he had eyes to see. He surveyed Josavea dispassionately and for the first time since he had come to Siloam he found her ugly. You silly nitwit, he raged, you always thought she was pretty! But you didn't have eyes then. Now you do, but you've lost your love. He ran from the brothel, proving to the woman that sight can rob a man of his virility.

Wandering frantically through Siloam, he looked with curiosity at every object, then turned from it with disgust. He anticipated every day with hope and said farewell to it with oaths; dusk angered him even more, for then he tried unsuccessfully to recapture the complete night of the unseeing. In this hysterical mood he met a Galilean who was a follower of Jesus of Nazareth. He accosted him, hoping that those who had restored his eyes would know what he should do with them.

"With their help," said Matthew, "you'll see your God."

And Bartimaeus replied: "I've already seen my own God, but how do I see our common God?"

"Isn't he in everything around you? Wherever you look you can see his mighty works. Our God lives in everything, even in the smallest pebble, flower and object."

Bartimaeus was silent, wondering why God, to whom all things were accessible, chose the ugliest in which to reside.

"What is it you want, my friend?" asked Matthew. "For whatever you want you can get."

"Nothing, nothing at all!" Bartimaeus shouted in order to forestall any fresh favor, for what had been granted him caused him enough trouble. "You've done enough for me. I was blind and now I can see. What else do I need?"

"Who among sinners, says our Judas Iscariot, knows when and what he may need? So hurry up and ask, since he who made you whole will be with us only a while longer, and then will go to him who sent him. Then, our Judas says, we will look for him but won't find him, and we won't be able to go where he is."

Bartimaeus fled without looking back.

Next day, in a panic that he might meet the wonder-worker and become exposed to some fresh mercy, he set out for Jerusalem.

But first he made a bandage for his eyes. Mercy had been done, a miracle had been wrought—the beggar said to his friends—"but it's up to me, not God, whether I use the eyes restored to me. So far I haven't seen anything worth looking at. I'll wait and save my sight for better times. I'll wait so I don't spoil it before I find things worth looking at, or until such things find me."

However, that evening an outcry from the square of the Sanhedrin aroused his curiosity and made him take off the bandage. He saw the procurator's guard taking the mute Mesezeveilo from the column of shame. Sentenced for insulting the Roman majesty, he had already been whipped. All that now remained was for him to be crucified. Approaching the column of shame, Bartimaeus smelled the stink of oil.

"How could you have insulted the Roman majesty?" he asked. "I thought you were dumb."

"I was," replied Mesezeveilo, groaning, "but that son of a bitch of a prophet from Nazareth untied my tongue."

"Bravo!" said Bartimaeus. "That one doesn't waste time."

"When I was dumb," the beggar went on, "at least I could think what I liked. But the minute I uttered my first word in this hell of a life, the procurator's soldiers thrashed me."

"What did you say?"

"Nothing much. Only what I'd always thought but couldn't put in words. I said: Down with Rome!"

And that was all he said, for he was taken off to the hill of Golgotha.

For days Bartimaeus, son of Timaeus, the beggar from Jericho on the Jordan, prowled around Zion hoping to come across something that would make it worth his while to open wide his newly healed eyes. But he didn't find it—as if all shapes had turned their ugly undersides to spite his eyes, as if the whole capital conspired against his restored sense, showing the worst and most repellent sights.

Then he remembered that Jerusalem wasn't the only city of Israel, and that the objects for which men were given eyes to see were perhaps in some other place: Capernaum, Samaria, Hebron or even his native Jericho—a conscientious man should visit all of them before condemning this earth. Perhaps Galilee, Samaria and Judaea, perhaps Edom, the deserts of Arabia, Syria or the settlements of the Phoenician coastland were full of secret scenes waiting to unfold only for him—scenes created only that Bartimaeus, son of Timaeus, might pluck up courage for his suspicious and disillusioned eyes. But when, not finding what he sought, he returned to Jerusalem one dusty day in the month of Sivan, he said without conviction that the Promised Land was luckily not the only land on earth, that perhaps in distant kingdoms by the Nile or the Indus some important sight was awaiting him that would make having eyes worthwhile.

And he went to look for it.

On the day following his return from his travels about the world, Bartimaeus was brought into the Council Hall, and the son of Timaeus stood before the leaders of Beth Din Hagadol, Annas and Caiaphas.

"What's your name, my good man?" asked the Av Beth Din, or father of the court.

"Bartimaeus, son of Timaeus, honored sir."

"Where do you come from?"

"From Jericho, sir!"

"How long have you been blind?"

"From birth, sir! Hashem was merciful to me."

"And who healed you?"

"Jesus the Nazarene, known as Christ," replied Bartimaeus gruffly. "He made clay, anointed my eyes with it and told me to go to the pool of Siloam and wash. And when I went and washed, I could see."

Then the religious leaders asked: "What do you have to say about this man who opened your eyes?"

Bartimaeus was silent; why should he bother such learned gentlemen with his petty misfortunes?

"What do you think about your Savior, Bartimaeus?" they repeated.

Bartimaeus was again silent, and it wasn't until they asked him a third time that he said angrily:

"I hope I'll meet him again, sirs!"

"Where is he?" the high priest Caiaphas asked slyly.

"I'd like to know that myself."

The Pharisees and the Jewish leaders shouted that this fellow was sinful, and that his desire to meet the Nazarene again showed that he believed in him and in his heretical teaching. And they grew still more angry when he yelled:

"I was blind, wasn't I, and then I saw!"

"And are you a disciple of his that you defend him so?"

"I am."

"He blasphemes!" shouted Annas.

"Let's throw him out of the Council Hall," Caiaphas urged.

"Whip him! Whip him!" yelled the priests and the Beth Din Hagadol.

Bartimaeus submitted calmly to the guard summoned to take him to the column of shame. On his way out of the Council Hall he stumbled at the threshold and fell.

"Are you blind, you ox?" snapped the guard, poking him with his spear.

"Sure as hell, I am, my son! What did you expect?" said the beggar. Opening his eyes, he showed the Pharisees, instead of pupils, two black holes like cold doorways to some mysterious black world.

"But you told us that your so-called Messiah opened them," Caiaphas said in astonishment.

"He did open them, sir, but since I found nothing to look at, I closed them again. I poked them out, to make quite sure. In this epidemic of salvation an honest man must protect himself." Bartimaeus smiled. "Didn't I tell you I'd become his disciple? I saved myself."

Closing his empty eye sockets, he went out peacefully. The tapping of the staff with which Bartimaeus, son of Timaeus, marked his last journey echoed for a while under the arches of the Council Hall.

Miracle at Gadara

And when he was come to the other side into the country of the Gergesenes, there met him two possessed with devils, coming out of the tombs, exceeding fierce, so that no man might pass by that way. And, behold, they cried out, saying, What have we to do with thee, Jesus, thou Son of God? Art thou come hither to torment us before the time?

Matthew 8:28–29

THEY WERE both naked. Ananias was a shaggy rawboned giant with a flattened skull and a face from which the foolish, angelic smile of a child never vanished. His companion in lunacy, Legion—so called because he was inhabited by at least a thousand demons—was his bodily reverse, a parody: Ananias's features reflected in a concave mirror, pointed like a thorn; a disorderly, gnarled face never without a look of irrational excitement. Sometimes their smiles were evil, sometimes blissful, but never in accord with their real mood; with a sweet smile they would throw stones at passers-by, or with the cruelest of smiles they would allow them to pass in peace along the imperial road from Gadara to Jabneel in Galilee that ran beside the city graveyard. There was even more uncertainty about their names. For the most part Ananias didn't acknowledge his own name, but believed that he was called Legion and his fellow lunatic, Ananias, and behaved accordingly; while Legion alternated between one thing and another, even sometimes thinking that he was Ananias and that the name of his friend was Eliphelet. Fortunately, neither these uncertain names nor their arbitrary nicknames played any role in their exemplary friendship.

Ananias most often thought he was a cavalry general in the army of Judas Maccabaeus, less often the burning bush out of which God revealed himself to Moses for the first time. Legion, more modest, usually claimed to be an experienced gardener or a peddler, and only once behaved like a gnarled Samaritan fig tree breaking under the weight of its fruit. Furthermore, in the choice of professions Legion respected certain identities ignored by Ananias, recognizing that there was greater kinship between a fruit tree and a fruitgrower than between a cavalry hero and a tuft of desert grass, however greatly honored by God.

Thus, although each knew what the other was, he didn't know the other well, because most often they understood the same ideas in completely different ways, and had different ideas most often about the same events. For Legion, every Maccabaean officer was a potter who mends pots (a Maccabaean general could perhaps do this better than others), and Ananias welcomed in the enterprising imaginary gardener the incomprehensible boatman of the Gennesaret ferry. Such too was the case with the bronze chains which were forged around their ankles and joined them, allowing the two men only the standard separation of a few paces; Ananias haughtily stated that they were imperial orders granted for heroic conduct in the war of liberation, while for the peace-loving Legion they were golden bracelets which he had obtained for both of them from a grateful empress, perhaps the wife of that very emperor for whom Ananias had fought, and for whom he tended the fig trees. Since they remained constant in their beliefs, the origin of the chains remained one of the countless ineradicable differences between them, differences which had poor prospects of ever being resolved but that in no way made their alliance more difficult.

In fact they had different concepts about the world in which they were mad. Sometimes they feared that they weren't living in the same world, sometimes they believed that each was living in his own distinct, independent, tightly sealed-off world where no one else had admission. In truth, though they had to occupy the same territory at the same time and to make use of the same facts, the worlds of Ananias and Legion were very different, contradictory and inconsistent. There was a crazy tolerance between those two worlds, and since the two madmen had discovered it, let them be forgiven; there was a world of difference between them, but madmen understand one another, so let them be forgiven; freedom to live in such worlds was dangerous, but the madmen took advantage of it, so let them be forgiven. It was sinful to remodel nature, but the lunatics did so, making of it something which God had not intended, so let them be forgiven.

How otherwise could it have happened that, as Ananias and Legion were squatting on the top of the tomb and looking at Gadara, they spoke in this way:

Ananias (excitedly): "Look how the caves have turned blue in the blue sunlight, and how the blue warriors of the Jews in their blue armor are charging up the hill shouting war cries in blue voices! I only ask, where am I? I should be leading them but, alas, I don't see myself, I'm nowhere!"

Legion (in disbelief): "I hear voices, but they're as green as grass and don't come from armed mountaineers but from green rats leaping nimbly over a waterfall turned green in the green sun. And you, my friend, aren't there because you're here, mending pots."

Ananias (irritably): "If I were here, they'd all be slaughtered. But here's a sword and you're alive. So I must be there!"

Legion (resignedly): "By Hashem, I must have made a mistake. I thought I was talking to you."

They were looking at Gadara, a city in the land of the Gergesenes, a trading center which to its people had always seemed more or less the same, in the way that different descriptions of the same object differ only negligibly.

When they were in a good mood they thought "that other" was different, and only when they were angry did they find "that other" unbearable. Since the world, at least that face of it turned toward each individual, doesn't depend on capricious will or play its independent game, but is adjusted—or if you prefer, obligingly disguised—according to each eye, Ananias and Legion were rarely so depressed that they wished to change the twofold character of the world to their own advantage by force. That happend only when there were temporary misunderstandings about the dimensions of the space they occupied.

Skilled in warlike exploits, Ananias would sometimes climb up on the tomb in which they lived, and Legion, loafing amid his imaginary gardens a few feet away, would shout in pain and swear: "Ananias, you bastard, why did you step on my corns?" In fact, they were never clear about the size, extent and position of their own bodies. In such circumstances Legion would display an inordinate amount of self-control. He would ask his friend politely not to push: there was plenty of room for both in the graveyard, so would he please get away from the bed on which Legion was lying.

"I'm not stepping on you," Ananias would say indignantly but with restraint. "I'm not walking on the bed but clinging to a tall tree, holding on to a branch, looking out over a wide expanse to spy the enemies of Israel." Patiently refuting his proofs, Legion would break down Ananias's world to clear a space for his own. "You are not clinging to any tree but to the polished tip of a very picturesque synagogue."

"What synagogue? That's a tree!" Ananias would get angry. "Anyway, it's not a tree, it's a hundred-year-old sea gull."

Then Legion would try to convince his friend that the sea gull, even if a thousand years old, was an ordinary fig tree, a little fig tree burdened by its false resemblance to a tree.

But such misunderstandings were rare and didn't diminish their attachment to each other.

They lived among the little hills not far from Gadara, and though they couldn't agree on how to designate their residence (Legion preferred "property," Ananias "bivouac"), they lived together in a comfortable tomb from which they had expelled the dead owner. The dead man had to share the floor with the desert rats, and the fragile lichen covering the stone, but that didn't bother the friends.

As for the tomb itself, that was different. Legion had a personal theory about the origin and character of their banishment.

"Look," he would say warmly, "how nice, how lavish is the house we've inherited from our late father, Salmon."

"How could our father leave it to the two of us, if we aren't brothers?" Ananias asked.

"Why aren't we, if we have no father?"

Then Ananias would give his version: "This is the deserted catacomb of the palace in which the Emperor Balak, the scourge of Israel, holds us prisoner."

"Don't talk nonsense, brother! We aren't anybody's prisoners."

Ananias didn't give up. "He holds us prisoner because we aren't prisoners."

Neither irrevocable decisions nor complicated compromises were necessary: Legion slept under the honored roof of his father Salmon, while in the same tomb the odious roof of Balak's imperial residence sheltered Ananias from the rain.

There were many magic differences in that one world out of which they had fashioned two, in that ancient, threadbare picture which they had split into two new ones, invisible and unique.

One sultry afternoon, when an unexpected rainstorm of the month of Ab had washed away the stench of carrion, they were squatting among the scattered and eroded hills. Covered with dust from the roads, they were throwing stones at a mark to pass the time, which even in their reasonably ordered worlds was obviously useless. The aim of the game was for each to hit his teammate in the eye, but it was a difficult game because they hadn't agreed where the pupil of that eye was located: one was aiming at his partner's leg, the other at his partner's forehead. Whenever one succeeded, both would squeal with satisfaction.

Not far away, in the shade by the grassy crossroads, a herd of swine was feeding. Ananias believed them to be thoroughbred horses, whereas Legion thought they were more like two-hump camels. While they were throwing their stones with varying success, they talked about the attractive possibility of riding them into Gadara, regardless of whether they were stallions or camels, because when all was said and done they could ride equally well on either.

"Can't you see they're shod?" said Ananias. "Since when have camels been shod?"

"I can't say if it's a custom in Gadara, but the Galileans from the far side of Jordan shoe their camels," said Legion. "They hang bunches of myrrh on their tails."

"But that isn't shoeing, idiot!"

"What the hell is it, then?"

"Saddling. Shoeing is when they pull out their teeth to stop them from biting."

Legion wouldn't admit defeat: "But those animals haven't lost their teeth!"

"Of course not, if you look at their mouths. You've got to look at their hooves."

"In any case," said Legion, "shod or unshod, they're camels, and two-hump camels at that!"

"Shod or unshod," said Ananias, "they're stallions, and racing stallions at that!"

"But stallions aren't horses," shouted Legion, pleased to have caught his friend in an error.

"Who said they were? Did *I?* I only say they're stallions from some famous stud."

"Listen, Ananias, does it matter? You'll ride on a stallion and I'll ride on a camel. The only thing that matters is that we catch the animal so we don't have to go on foot."

After a moment's hesitation, Ananias agreed: "Good. That's right."

"What's right?"

"What you suggested."

"I didn't suggest anything."

"Good," agreed Ananias. "Then what you didn't suggest is right."

"So that's what we'll do," said Legion.

Ananias was the better marksman and the eye he aimed at was nearer the head than the eye Legion was aiming at, but

Legion was the more cunning: by choosing smaller stones, almost pebbles, which were better suited to his physical inferiority, he acquired a certain advantage. After a few hours both were streaming with bloody sweat which cooled them pleasurably in the stifling heat of the month of Ab.

Finally Ananias proposed that they stop playing. He was concerned about his new clothes, which he had just made by rolling in the thin mud left by the morning downpour. Legion agreed. He reckoned that when they reached Gadara his friend would lend him some of his filthiness so he too could dress more decently. Moreover, according to Ananias's authoritative interpretation, that suit was a general's uniform in which he had fought under Judas Maccabaeus against the Syrian tyrant Apollonius. Legion was a confirmed civilian who had a great respect for adventurers and warriors; though for him Ananias wasn't a soldier but a mender of pots, even so something of that respect rubbed off on him.

It was dusk and the shadows over the distant ravine of the Yarmuk were dying away in sullen yellowness when the two friends came out on the imperial road, which was white as snow and deserted. On the barren land before them a lone beggar was driving a billy goat.

Ananias shouted: "Here comes the Emperor Balak against Israel! Let's go harry him and win fame for centuries to come."

"That's Balaam, the priest," replied Legion. "Why should we bother him? Why should we harm a friend of Israel?"

"That's Balak the villain, who tramples us under his feet. Can't you see in his hand the red-hot scepter he oppresses all Moab with, and a slave in chains in front of him?"

"What you see is the priestly staff of the virtuous Balaam, who's driving a bull for a sacrifice of atonement."

"That's Balak. We must kill him," said Ananias.

"It's Balaam. We must leave him alone," said Legion.

Finally Ananias proposed the wise compromise habitual between them: "It would be best if I kill Balak and you allow Balaam to pass in peace."

"That's fair," Legion agreed.

But the beggar didn't reach them. Seeing the madmen coming out of the graves, he drove the billy goat across the fields to avoid them.

"There goes Balak, Israel's foe," said Ananias.

"There goes Balaam, Israel's defender," said Legion.

Once again the imperial road was empty, running smoothly between two deep ditches that were like wrinkles worn by care. To the north a few tamarisks strained toward the lowering sky, and in the east, which was cold without the sun, the bushes scattered over the monotonous landscape resembled a pack of jackals, dark and silent, sniffing the wind. To the south a thicket of sycamores stood like a bunch of abandoned Roman crosses, and over the lake of Gennesaret a whistling sound quavered: the horn warning passengers that the ferry was leaving for Tiberias.

From Gadara a traveler in the coarse clothes of a pilgrim was approaching. At first he didn't notice the two friends. Perhaps, as a stranger in the land of the Gergesenes, he didn't know that the graveyard was inhabited by maniacs. When Ananias leaped out of the ditch, the traveler stepped back in consternation and turned to run away, but Legion skillfully cut off his retreat. The traveler pulled himself together but his heart, split into a thousand tiny hearts, was thumping under his skin everywhere except where it should have thumped.

Ananias wove a close circle around the traveler, then asked: "Where are you hurrying, soldier?"

"To Tiberias, sir," answered the traveler. Though he was not a soldier, he wasn't about to deny it. "I'm running to catch the next ferry."

"Why are you walking in the river? Why don't you use the imperial road like all honest people?"

The traveler was confused. In his own opinion he was indeed walking on the road, but noticing Ananias—naked, monstrous and savagely confident, his filthy body blocking the horizon—he judged it too risky to contradict him.

"Well," he explained humbly, "I thought I'd reach the lake by a short cut."

"Or avoid paying the toll, you rascal?" Ananias burst out,

and struck him on his cheek, leaving a gash down the middle.

The traveler spoke softly: No, he wasn't evading his obligations for using the imperial right of way (render unto Caesar the things that are Caesar's, and to God the things that are God's), but he was a stranger and didn't know the customs of the place; if the noble gentleman who was a guardian of the road—though living in the water and not on the land—would tell him what to do to avoid misunderstandings, he would be grateful and follow the instructions at once.

The traveler had made his apology and explanation only so as to reach the lake and to get out of the way of the madmen. Even so it left a favorable impression on Ananias. Being a soldier, Ananias scorned glib eloquence but at the same time, deprived of its advantages, felt for masters of words a certain concealed admiration. So he pushed the traveler into the ditch, where Legion was loafing about enjoying the sweet scent of imaginary roses, and said:

"This road will lead you to Tiberias."

Hoping that he would now be left in peace, the traveler slid on down into the ditch, but before he could extricate himself from the mud he landed in face down. Legion's fist struck him on the neck.

"Why are you trampling the garden I planted with such care, you bastard?" Normally reserved, Legion became angry and aggressive if anyone neglected to marvel at his rose garden or trampled the vegetables along the borders. "Why are you ruining my work?"

The stranger fidgeted in the mud. Peering alternately at Ananias watching from the edge of the trench, and at Legion squatting in front of him, he did his best to make some sense of his impossible and constantly changing circumstances.

"That man up there told me the road to Gennesaret passes this way."

"This isn't a road, idiot!" Legion shouted. "This is a private estate. And I'm Eliphelet, the owner of these wonderful gardens."

"Is that so?" said the traveler in wonder. "They're very beautiful."

Hastily he crawled up out of the ditch, but Ananias kicked him right back in.

"Where are you going, wretch? Into the river? You want to drown?"

Gathering his clothes around his skinny knees, the traveler sat down in the mud. He seemed powerless. He chewed the mud without daring to spit it out again. Who could tell what this mire meant to these lunatics, what wealth might be hidden in it, what visions it might preserve, what worlds were in danger of being ground by incautious teeth? His lips forced from his numbed spirit a strange question: "O Lord, am I to die in a Gadarene ditch?"

"Do you see, brother," Legion wailed to Ananias, "what this blockhead has done to my garden?"

"He's a pest who doesn't care where he treads. On the other hand, why did you plant rosebushes on the imperial road? People have to walk somewhere!"

"They can walk on the road."

"But this *is* the road."

"The road is what you're standing on, and this is my garden, my blessed, fertile garden," said Legion.

"The garden is what you're cultivating illegally," said Ananias, "and I'm standing in the river. I've waded in up to my waist and I don't dare go any farther. I'm afraid of the whirlpools and rapids."

Legion wavered. He didn't dare let his one ally drown, even in a river he couldn't see. "Very well, even though I don't see it, I don't say there's no river where you're standing. I only meant that water can also serve as a road. Let him take a bird and fly over."

Dragging his legs as if walking in water, Ananias moved close to the ditch. "I wouldn't want him to drown. If you drive him out of your garden, he'll plunge into the torrent, which is deep here. Let him cross your property to the ford."

"He might destroy my vegetables."

"Take him by the hand and lead him, Legion. That way you won't harm the plants."

Legion looked thoughtfully at his companion, then at the traveler, who went on muttering prayers. "Come to think of it, the vegetables haven't sprouted yet, and I don't know the way."

"Surely you know where you planted them!"

"How can I? They haven't even begun to sprout!"

"That's awkward," Ananias conceded. "Then we'll have to kill him."

The traveler peered apathetically at his large white hands, on which the mud was drying like a big dark flower. The trembling of his lips was the only sign that he had heard them and understood. He quickened his invocations to God. The litanies competed with one another like well-trained hunting dogs: "O Lord, didn't you choose me to serve you, to complete your work and liberate your world? Whose city is this that doesn't know God and that your prophets haven't foreseen? I haven't reached the end yet, Lord. Don't let them kill me before my time, and don't let those kill me who weren't born to do it!"

"What's your name, soldier?"

"Joshua. Joshua ben Joseph."

"A Moabite?"

"No, sir. I'm a Nazarene, a carpenter from Nazareth in Galilee."

Legion said sorrowfully, "Well, it looks like we must strangle Joshua, the Nazarene carpenter."

"You're a warrior of Balak, Joshua," Ananias agreed sadly. "We'll have to strangle you."

"But I'm not," said the traveler. "I'm a warrior of God."

"Then we must strangle Joshua, the warrior of God," Legion said, "unless you carry him across the river on your shoulders."

"Why me? Why not you?"

"Because I don't see the river."

"It's deep, devilish deep, and there's no ford." Ananias hesitated, pointing to a bend of the road winding like a snake through the countryside. "Look! That whirlpool is bottomless—we'll both be drowned."

Legion shaded his eyes and gazed in the direction indicated; a black wind dispersed a dusty murk over the fields. "You're right, Ananias. No one could leap over such an abyss with someone on his shoulders. We'll have to kill him."

The man called Jesus the Nazarene was standing in the ditch, and his quivering, anxious eyes followed every movement of the two lunatics. Perhaps, while keeping an eye on them, he was considering the very limited chances of flight; perhaps his weak body was preparing for defense; perhaps he was making every effort to find a new and feasible pretext to delay or even avoid death; or perhaps he was simply trusting to some miracle of help from Gadara, which he would know to be the response of him whom he had always relied on. But the road was empty; not a chance that anyone would come. The heavens gave no sign of life, still less of favor. Everything was mute, closed off, indifferent.

"We'll have to kill you, soldier," Ananias informed him.

"Why?" asked Jesus.

"Because you've been sent to torture us and kill us, the captives of the Emperor Balak."

The traveler showed no sign of resistance. He awaited his execution, plunged in the mud like a thin, brittle plant, conscious of his inability to defend himself, of his transience in the wind which, if unchecked, could tear him out of mother earth even before the time set by the prophets. He went on muttering prayers: "Help me, help me now, O heavenly Father; my time has not yet come and my days are not yet numbered. Save me, Father, for the sake of your intention and the original sin which I'll bear upon myself. Save me, O Lord of Hosts!"

"Let's finish him off before his father collects his kinsmen to hunt us down," Legion said quickly.

Ananias added: "And before he comes with his armies."

But it was too late. As Ananias slid down into the ditch and Legion strode toward the traveler, Jesus raised his hands to a black and seemingly expressionless heaven, and turning toward the swine in the field called upon them in the name of the Lord to accept everything expelled from these men.

Greatly disturbed, the swine grunted and turned their snouts toward the ditch.

At first Ananias and Legion felt no significant change. Nothing visible passed from them to the herd, nothing new entered into them, yet something strange was happening. First a dizziness assailed them, a cobwebby weakness of the senses which didn't sweep the world aside but temporarily transformed it, distorted it as if under a thick lens, remodeled it into a new harmonious whole made up of old misused fragments collected together in a strange way—followed by a painful haze which, moving immovable objects, changed their significance by finding a new place for them in the order of things (as changing the position of a dynamic word alters the whole sense of a sentence), or which, while leaving objects in their old positions, transformed them forcibly, converting hills into houses, houses into tombs, tombs into fish, fish into tears and tears into golden, foaming billows. Flabbergasted rather than frightened, the lunatics took part in the birth of a common truth from which they had been dissociated—I would say they had evaded it, had the choice been theirs—and from which they had created two completely opposite worlds. Unable to resist—how could they know what awaited them—they took part in the travail of the first day, the child-birth of the centuries, whose chaos only God remembered. What had taken place in seven days now took place again in a single instant, faster than the beat of a frightened heart. For these two alone, the birth pangs of genesis were repeated, but what was established before them was disastrous, and what at last hardened before them, like an image in a shattered mirror whose pieces are reassembled in a smooth, clear surface, was horrifying. Legion's flowery garden, in which he had invested so much labor, was dispersed into a marshy channel, in the midst of which the three of them stood like three muddy pillars, smelling of swill; Ananias's swift, turbulent torrent hardened into the imperial road, its dust swirling as far as the horizon. The blue grottoes and green cascades of former manic universes were no longer visible where the jag-toothed ramparts of fortified Gadara now displayed their colorless shadow. Having wavered between the merchant's villa inherited from Salmon and the imperial residence of the

Moabite Balak, their dwelling place was transformed into an ugly tomb surrounded by heaps of grayish earthy deposits. Ananias was no longer the famous participant in the victory over the Syrian tyrant Apollonius, nor was Legion the landowner whose hobby was grafting roses. They were naked, shaggy, filthy vagabonds bound together by a chain. Before them in the ditch no longer shivered Balak's mercenary whom they had to kill, but a fragile, little, reddish man covered with mud. Farther off in the pasture their stallions and camels, which had been ruminating peacefully in expectation of being ridden, were now a herd of maddened swine rushing toward the ravine.

Ananias peered dejectedly at the landscape. He didn't recognize it, but he had seen it in a dream, though not so distorted and repulsive.

"Look, Jesus, the hills are all upside down!" he said.

"The hills stand as they always have," Jesus replied. He spoke in an unfriendly tone, because he was in a hurry. He had an appointment with Judas, and hadn't yet recovered from his fright, though not for a moment of that dreadful encounter had he worried about himself, but only about the mission of salvation entrusted to him. "They stand exactly as my Father established them on the first day, just as they appear to everyone."

"Judas—teacher, friend, brother, my son and my father," wailed the traveler, "have I said what I must say, what is written in the Scriptures? Have I asked for everything which you told me my Creator needs for his garden?"

"Where *is* my garden?" asked Legion, turning around.

"And where is my river?" asked Ananias, turning around.

All around them the dry plain gave off a dusty stench. All around them, with the insecurity of a newborn child, breathed a brand-new world.

Jesus said, "There is no garden except God's garden. There is no river except God's river. Everything else is from the devil."

It sounded like a curse, not a courteous explanation. Refusing to believe it, Legion went on wailing:

"But my garden was *here!*"

"From the devil."

"And my river!" wailed Ananias.

"From the devil."

The world now appeared desolate, worn, deserted. It looked like a picture from which the rain has washed the colors, like an event which nature has deprived of significance. Every scent had evaporated, every sound had been stifled, every movement turned to stone. And that wasn't all. What brought them to final despair was the realization that this world, in addition to all its other shortcomings, was now the same for both of them, whereupon suddenly it became too small. They still didn't realize the consequences of this, but they knew—because now they had their reason and were no longer mad—that in one way or another there must be consequences. There they were in the same world, to whose definite realities they must submit if they wished to survive (though at that moment they didn't really care). Never again would they be happy in their own realities, like little gods among their own works. Never again could they be generals, gardeners, potters, ferrymen, emperors or prophets, sailors or artists —not to mention pebbles or winds. In a word, nothing would ever be their own again and, though they didn't know where all this would lead, they were depressed.

Legion finally plucked up courage to ask the wonder-worker what had happened to the devil who had made a beautiful flower garden out of a stinking ditch for him, and a clear river out of the dusty road for his friend.

Not without divine malice, Jesus pointed to the swine which, one after another, were plunging into the ravine.

"Your devils are dying."

Our devils are dying, thought Ananias, our devilish worlds are dying, our verdant gardens are dying, our rushing rapids, our green and blue voices in the twilight, our camels and horses are dying forever, the luxurious halls of Salmon are destroyed, and the airless dungeons of Balak. And Legion thought: The road is a road; the ditch is a ditch; the tomb is a tomb; and the swine are swine.

And because he was of a gentle nature and inclined to forgive all that he had suffered through their madness, Jesus told them: "You were mad and I have cured you."

And Legion asked meekly: "Is that something we should be grateful for?"

He got no reply. The wonder-worker was already on his way to the ferry which would take him from the Decapolis to the tetrarchy of Galilee.

Ananias and Legion remained squatting in the ditch. The night swept among the harsh contours of the newborn world and they could think more calmly of their situation. They didn't dare talk much, for they were rational now and chatter was not appropriate.

At last, pointing toward the darkening northeast, Ananias asked in a voice which didn't sound like his own: "What do you see there?"

"I see the city of Gadara," Legion replied.

"I see it, too," said Ananias gloomily. "And over there?"

"The lake of Gennesaret reflected in the sky."

"I see it, too. Perhaps there's hope in the west. What do you see to the west, Legion?"

"Hills. And you?"

"The same." Ananias almost burst into tears.

Taking advantage of the last chance to restore something of the magic independence, Legion asked: "What kind of hills?"

"Black hills. I hope they're red to you. They are, aren't they, Legion?"

"No, they're black to me, too. For both our sakes I'd like them to be red, but they aren't. They're damnably black."

"O wonder-worker, destroyer, demolisher of worlds!" cursed Ananias.

"O murderer, torturer, inhuman beast," Legion swore.

"Why didn't we strangle you?"

"Why did we let you go?"

Damn you, Jesus the Nazarene, Son of God! thought both, not finding anathemas strong enough for their hatred, nor lamentations for their despair.

"Let's find some decent clothes and get rid of this chain," said Ananias dully. "We'll go crazy if we continue thinking like this."

Ananias's left leg was chained to Legion's right by a chain which allowed them scarcely five paces of movement.

"Come," said Legion, "let's go to Gadara."

"I don't want to go to Gadara. I'm taking the ferry to Capernaum."

"What's wrong with Gadara?"

"I don't say anything's wrong with Gadara. Only that I'd like to go to Capernaum."

"Go, then. What's keeping you?"

The sand crackled in the desert. They remained silent and annoyed. Then Legion began talking in a harsh, hostile voice:

"The world has suddenly changed. This place was more beautiful before and you were less obstinate."

"Get out, if you don't like it!"

"I will, as soon as we get rid of this chain."

"Then let's go to Capernaum. I know a smith there who'll separate us, no questions asked."

"Why Capernaum? There are smiths in Gadara, too, right here under our noses."

"Because I don't want to go to Gadara," said Ananias.

"And I won't go to Capernaum," said Legion.

"To hell with your Gadara!"

"To hell with your Capernaum!"

They fell silent again, listening to the silence under the starry skies.

"You're crazy," said Ananias.

"I really must have been, to have lived with you for so long."

"And me too, to have put up with it."

That was the first time they mentioned their past disorders. They squatted in the mud, angry and very rational. Though their memory was vague and superficial, they thought almost at the same instant how this misunderstanding would have ended had they still been living, not together, in one world, but each separately in his own. Ananias would have said,

"I'm going this way," and Legion would have said, "I'm going that way," but then, still bickering and squabbling, they would have gone together in no matter what direction, thinking naturally that each was going in his own, one toward Gadara, the other toward Capernaum. For in their lost worlds directions were not as clearly defined as directions in this world, but allowed a man to go to the right in order to arrive on the left, to climb up in order to go down, to fall in order to rise. In the end they'd go off arm in arm to different places, but in one direction which by some marvel contained all directions, so that they would finally and at the same time enter both towns while their five-pace chain clinked behind them. Now that was no longer possible.

Pausing, Ananias said, "I'm going to Capernaum."

"And I to Gadara," said Legion, also pausing.

The next day when the swineherds brought the inquisitive Gadarenes to show them the swine the demons had entered, the two friends were lying in the ditch, beaten to death with the iron chain which had united them for years. One body was turned toward Gadara and the other toward Capernaum, but due to their disfigurement it was hard to tell them apart. Legion was dead already; Ananias was breathing his last, gazing without understanding at the citizens swarming around them. Before approaching, the citizens threw stones at the bodies to make sure both were dead. Then they moved quite close.

Miracle at Magdala

And it came to pass afterward, that he went
throughout every city and village, preaching and
shewing the glad tidings of the kingdom of God:
and the twelve were with him, and certain women,
which had been healed of evil spirits and infirmities,
Mary called Magdalene, out of whom went seven
devils, and Joanna the wife of Chuza, Herod's
steward, and Susanna, and many others, which
ministered unto him of their substance.

Luke 8:1–3

A DULL SIGH reached her from the throats of the mob in the square, as if some gigantic door were swinging open in a draft, and immediately afterward other, individual sighs responded to that single voice, reverberating around the solid walls of Magdala like the smashed, fragmentary echoes of a great summons, once again united in a spontaneous murmur of approval.

The Savior was preaching.

He is developing one of his favorite parables again, the woman thought, wondering if some day she too would be only a successful parable without a tangible body, but with the reputation of a fervent and edifying legend. She didn't hear the divine orator in her heart. It was that way whenever she stood near him; all other voices would remain, but his would fade away in the murmur from which she was unable to pick out a single word.

Except once.

Only once, long ago, when she had felt for the Nazarene nothing but curiosity mingled with compassion. Afterward everything was different and the possibility of a meeting drained away her courage. With the courage to approach him disappeared her ability to hear him. And with her ability to hear him she lost the courage to approach him.

This, of course, had been when she first followed him from Jerusalem. At the beginning. During a fatiguing journey which had led them from the frontier of the Syrian province to Idumaea, from the Dead Sea to the living sea at the foot of Mount Carmel, through the length and breadth of the Promised Land, when they were testing its readiness to accept God's only-begotten Son in the undignified guise of a village carpenter, she had recovered that courage. Following him with other women of similar destiny, she had learned how to approach the wonder-worker. It was best to be helpful to him on the road and to follow him persistently. Under certain circumstances—usually at the end of a sermon, if he needed a more striking proof of his mission than the routine proverbs—it was enough to be at hand. Under other circumstances one had to implore him, nag him, beg him. In all cases, however, an indispensable condition for the working of miracles was the expression of absolute faith in Jesus' kinship with Jehovah. Wherever that faith was sustained with sufficient fervor, aid appeared without delay and a miracle would take place; wherever it was absent—because of prejudice, education, knowledge of the Torah or the inborn suspicion of those who imagine they can compete in omnipotence with the gods—aid was refused and there was no miracle.

However, despite the miracles which didn't take place, those which succeeded were enough to restore to her wavering self-confidence. From a distance, it's true, but in circumstances which left no room for doubt, she had seen how Christ's healing spit opened the eyes of Bartimaeus, son of Timaeus, and how the tongue of the Jerusalem mute Meseze-veilo had been loosed by his command. She had seen the dead hastening from their graves with their coffins on their backs; lunatics restored to reason; a paralytic able again to stand on his legs; and a leper at the gates of Gilgal sloughing his blotched skin like a snake.

Mary Magdalene didn't know if all these sufferers had met him by chance or if they had sought out the divine endowment. However, that was irrelevant to the magnificence of the miracles themselves. What prospects of success does a sick man have in not wishing to become healthy, if the act of healing has a higher aim than health itself—if primarily it displays a union of supernatural forces, and only incidentally brings an advantage to the chance beneficiary? Just as the art of medicine doesn't advance in order to heal, though by healing it achieves its primary purpose, so also wonder-working as the highest form of medicine exhausts its basic aim in the advancement of miracles, those direct links with the Creator, and not in the effect of the miracle on this or that individual.

Before these miracles she had thought that Jesus the Nazarene was unapproachable. Now she knew that he presented no personal barrier; the barriers were all inside her.

In all fairness it must be said that the personal appearance of the prophet from Nazareth was no motive for her indecision. He was of small stature, tiny in the circle of his manly Galilean disciples. His long garments couldn't conceal his extreme thinness, but by hanging on him as on a hanger, stressed it. To tell the truth, there was no divine magnetism about his person. His voice was without resonance or modulation, and when raised in excitement or anger sounded unpleasant. And if his speeches, which lacked subtlety and were delivered in the vulgar dialect of Upper Galilee, were of divine origin, the only proof was that you couldn't understand them.

In any case, Mary now knew how to overcome her indecision and would approach him at a suitable moment. If no occasion arose in her native Magdala, she would lie in wait for him at Hazor, Ramah, Mizpah, Gischala, Ephraim or Bethel. If necessary, she would accompany him to the ends of the world. She would be unyielding, obstinate, insolently persevering, wise as a dove, cunning as a serpent. If crowded out, she would elbow her way to him; if he hurried she would run after him; if he slept she would waken him, fall at his feet, and before uttering her petition, wash them with her tears and wipe them with her hair—caresses which at one time had been paid for as if they were a kiss of heaven.

Then, come what may.

That Susanna was in the same predicament didn't help. Another person's misfortune only increased her own, like a mirror in which her own was disastrously multiplied. Nor did Joanna's example, though her husband had taken her back into his house. Joanna had sinned but was not a sinner: Sin hadn't totally overcome her; her body hadn't been consumed by the fire in which she had taken enjoyment, unaware it had been kindled in hell. Sin had just barely scorched Joanna, wife of Chuza, for she had only warmed herself at it, more inquisitive because of her unhappy marital experience than carried away by passion for the other. (That woman, therefore, was an ordinary adulteress, whom the Evangelists later included by error in the whorish company of Susanna and Mary Magdalene. We are doing our best here, without regard for the harm that could result from it, to tell the real lives of these Israelite harlots, who suddenly and despite the prophecies became saints. If we succeed in describing how reformed they felt in their cleansed state, we will correct those errors without any reflection on their perpetrators.)

The enigmatic presence of Elkan also did little to brighten the mood of our women, though he approached them rarely and never closer than several paces. Elkan had come with them from Jerusalem, but not one of the women could tell if the cripple was accompanying them or Christ. That he was a simpleton, in fact an idiot from birth, and, furthermore, lame in both legs—so that when walking he squirmed as if his feet were twisted—favored the hypothesis that Elkan was following the Savior to entreat him to heal his legs and his reason. However, not once during their journeys had he tried to approach him. On the contrary, whenever the Savior looked at him, Elkan would run for dear life. The hypothesis that he came for the sake of the women was strengthened by the attention which he paid to them. He would bring each of them a gift, something which his darkened mind considered valuable: a handful of pebbles, a bundle of dried grass, fresh cow dung, and for special occasions a dead mouse. He would carefully lay them on a stone near the women, shuffle quickly away to some hidden corner and wait for their reaction. Angry and unhappy, the women responded with stones and curses. He paid no attention to the curses, perhaps because he was also a deaf-mute, and collected the stones for a new gift on some later occasion.

Obviously Mary Magdalene could expect no help from anyone.

Will he ever finish that sermon? she asked herself, waiting on the porch of a deserted house. Would she succeed in pushing through to him? And if she did, would she be able to explain what she wanted as clearly as she hoped? Would Jesus of Nazareth agree to help her?

The last part of her plan, its climax, was the most uncertain. Mary realized that help, if granted her, would be to some extent antinatural, that it would differ heretically from the Messianic message of the ancient writings, and that this concession—for what is such a gesture but a concession to the already defeated demons of sin?—would in a flash set aside everything which in the covenant of Abraham had been worked out in detail with Jehovah, with the collaboration of countless generations of Israelites. Alas, a new miracle would disqualify not only the preceding one—to hell with it!—but all the earlier miracles which had begun with the wedding at Cana in Galilee.

Obviously Mary of Magdala (El Medjel in the speech of the nomads) was not instructed in the highest purpose of miracles, in the mystic, almost sacrificial, sense of wonder-working. At first it might seem comical that a professional whore should fanatically probe matters that had hitherto divided theologians, learned men and doctors of the Temple. However, her future depended on a knowledge of miracles and miracle-working. She had thought of them before as amusing pastimes appropriate to her sex, education and origin, but after what had happened to her as will be related here, she thought that such knowledge might benefit her in dealing with the Savior, so she decided to learn their history and to understand their function over and above their literal application. (It was hard to assume, for example, that the significance of the miraculous opening of Sarah's womb was exhausted by the birth of a mere brat, even though that brat had become Jacob's father; or that God had consumed Sodom with fire merely to teach a lesson to Lot's companions as a punishment for feminine curiosity.) Thus Mary Magdalene, though self-taught, knew that as far back as the times of Abraham similar religious miracles had taken place. Was not the prophet Jonah, through God's intervention, swallowed by a voracious fish similar to a whale, and after three days and three nights in its slimy liver, spewed out again onto dry land? Had not the three holy children, Shadrach, Mesach, and Abednego, walked through the seven-times-heated furnace at Susa in the presence of Nebuchadnezzar? Had not the fingers which God had broken off from his invisible hand told the Emperor Belshazzar that the days of his empire were numbered? Though regulated and inscribed in the Holy Scriptures, didn't all these miracles have a strictly limited purpose: to aid this or that Israelite, to recall to reason this or that self-willed ruler of an alien tribe, and above all to preserve the faith of the chosen people whenever it might waver?

Concerning the Hebrew people, the reader should be aware that there was no other nation in whose affairs God interfered so often, or which so abundantly abused that intervention. The religion of the Israelites was accompanied by a lack of definite obligation about what had been agreed with him at any time. For it was hard to foresee with any certainty when that alliance with God, which had to be glorified and confirmed by elaborate ceremonies, might be temporarily broken off and replaced by punitive deluges, hostile invasions, plagues of locusts or epidemics of barrenness. On neither side, it seems, was there any irrevocable obligation guaranteeing stability between Jehovah and his chosen people; that relationship was more like a concubinage where intolerance and passion alternated. The aim of the miracles, then, was to cheer up the chosen people following some murderous onslaught or massacre provoked by their sudden break with heaven. The Old Testament miracles were outward signs of divine attention, not symptoms of God's actual participation in the lives of men, whereas the New Testament miracles were an inalienable part of that essential transformation which the prophets had promised and laymen called the salvation of the world.

Mary was conscious of the difference in nature and significance between Christ's wonder-working and the insignificant miracles—not to call them tricks—wrought by divine emissaries before him. She was aware of the difficulty which their incompatibility would cause when she stood before the Lord and presented her extraordinary petition. But she had no choice.

"Will he be done soon?" Susanna asked. She was crouching in a mildewed corner with her hands crossed over her swollen stomach. "I can hardly stand."

At the foot of the deserted courtyard, Elkan was scratching about in the earth like a bird with broken legs, digging up fresh offerings for the women.

Really, Mary thought, Susanna looked pretty ill. The long walk and the uncertainty of its aim had worn her out. Together with a certain Asha from Sidon, a witless and bewildered creature accompanied by her mother, Mary looked after Susanna as best she could. She brought water and food which the sick woman could scarcely take. The hardest thing was that Susanna wouldn't cooperate. It was as if she were happy she would die—and they all knew how—before she saw the light of the Savior's countenance. Not one of the women understood her behavior. Susanna had gone with the Christians to see that face and regain her health by that sight, like a salutary anointing with balm. But she had exhausted all her strength in that wearisome journey and vain expectation, and no longer cared whether she would recover or be snuffed out—they all knew how—in some ditch in Magdala.

Mary took good care of her, partly because she was kindhearted and partly because she hoped their joint misfortunes would make a greater impression on the wonder-worker.

Though of the same nature and origin, Susanna's affliction was more obvious than hers. In the sluggishness of her swollen body, in the distortion of her face, in her senseless acts and the complete absence of personal hygiene, her affliction had assumed that malign form which every evil attains when it can no longer be checked except by a miracle.

"I hope he'll be done soon," Mary replied, "if they don't wear him out with heckling."

"I don't see any Levite near him," said Asha. "Perhaps today they'll leave him alone."

"There's always some wise man to nag at him," said Mary. " 'Teacher, why don't you fast as Moses said? Teacher, why do you always speak in parables, as if to put children to sleep and not to awaken men? Why do you perform miracles on the Sabbath? Should I pay taxes to Caesar? Should I respect my parents? How can I win eternal life? Will other peoples be granted the same salvation?' "

"Shut up," yelled Asha, "or I'll scream!"

"Scream away, child," her mother said. "Perhaps you'll feel better."

Questions, questions, questions, Mary thought, first endless sermons and then endless questions. After the stories, explanations. Then interpretation of symbols. Signs. Examples from life. Then new stories arising out of the old, to corroborate them. Then fresh questions. Explanations, interpretations, signs, examples. All this time, she thought, we poor wretches hang about in a muddy ditch, or under leaking eaves which soak us to the skin or give no shade, in some strange courtyard where the dogs growl at us. We wait in fear so we won't miss again that unannounced meeting with God which we dread as much as we want it. The crowd gradually disperses. Their comments reach you along with the thud of their feet. Grumblings, praises, hypocritical piety to save their skins:

"If he really is God, why is he roaming the earth?"

"Couldn't his heavenly Father have given him better clothes when he sent him to us?"

"Damned if I know. I never ask anything."

"Hey, Joseph, did you hear him? An olive branch! Not enough to drive the flies away, let alone the Romans!"

"Could be a special branch. Like the rod Moses used to open a fountain in the rock."

"To tell the truth, fellows, there was something in it."

"Shit!"

"He has a point, I tell you."

"Shit, I say."

"What are you thinking about, Jovila, old friend?"

"I wonder what he meant when he said to his disciples, 'Unto you it is given to know the mysteries of the kingdom of God, but to others in parables, that seeing they might not see, and hearing they might not understand.' Why is he telling us stories if he doesn't want to teach us?"

"Perhaps he wants us to think with our own heads?"

"But what does he mean, 'Blessed are the poor in spirit, for theirs is the kingdom of heaven'? Does he want to teach me to think first and then drive me down into hell?"

"They say he's of the line of David and a king."

"You know, Rahilo, he's not my idea of a king."

"Who is, then?"

"Our tetrarch, Antipas. A handsome fellow!"

"But this fellow's striking, too. He has a lovely face."

"Why did you slap me, idiot?"

"So you can turn the other cheek."

"Don't mock, fellows!"

"Get going, you old fool, beat it!"

You can't see Christ, she thought, when he's surrounded by disciples, walled in by those first bricks of the new faith. Among them he's in thorny armor, in the shell which conceals the pearl. From their commotion, you know when they're getting ready to leave. You know it's high time you left your hiding place. Other women are also coming out, like big rats with hot, fiery eyes. But some hare-brained listener always goes back and asks the wonder-worker some farfetched question. You're lucky if he's answered with a monosyllable. More likely there's an explanation he doesn't understand. Then a fresh parable in obscure language turns a word into a fairy tale. Then an example—one or maybe several. Only then, satisfied at last, does the listener go on his way. Then the women rush out of their temporary refuge and try to reach the Messiah. Hopeless: before him rises the impenetrable wall of his disciples, that twelve-headed bodyguard of God, unbribable, pitiless, implacable.

In her mind Mary Magdalene saw again the hysterical Asha rolling at the feet of the sons of Zebedee, who kicked her away; her massive mother—though she had nothing to ask for herself—plowing her way through that dense New Testament flesh; Susanna, kneeling in entreaty, wailing incessantly as she wrestled with strong, hairy hands that pushed her away from the Lord.

Then suddenly the living shell around the Messiah had dispersed and the women had dared to step into it. But it was empty: there was no pearl in the oyster. The weak, sweaty, blood-stained women had squatted in the stifling dust raised by the apostles' feet. They had squatted hopelessly on the road like birds in time of drought, their mouths wide open, looking in the direction in which the disciples were quickly disappearing. For where they went, he went: the balm for all their suffering. Once again they had risen in a flock like listless birds, and as if by some dark instinct of preservation, followed the Christ.

That's how it was at Emmaus, at Theboue and Gebat-Saul, thought Mary, at Upper and Lower Beth-horon and at Timnath. There was no city, no field, no hamlet, no homestead where things had been any different.

"I think the crowd's breaking up," she said. "Come on, Asha, help Susanna stand up and we'll go to him."

"I can't," Susanna whimpered. "I can't move."

"Get up. Do you want us to miss him again?"

Asha grabbed the sick woman by the shoulders and braced herself to lift her.

"Don't touch me," Susanna sobbed. "I'm heavy as a rock."

"She's heavy as a corpse!" said Asha.

Asha's mother kicked Susanna. "Get up, you bitch!"

But Susanna didn't budge. She was no longer whining in a

needle-thin voice, but with huge hands gripped her stomach, which seemed to be swelling. Staring expressionless at the stony bosses on the wall opposite, she looked like a burst sack of dung spilling out its filth.

Mary Magdalene first looked at the thinning crowd on the Magdala square and then at Susanna, whom Asha and her mother were trying to get on her feet. Whenever they raised her halfway she collapsed again. She lay there in her dark red rags like a huge drop of clotted blood.

"We'll have to leave her here," said Mary, who vowed to herself that if she ever reached the wonder-worker she would speak to him about her. "We must look for the Son of God among his Galileans. If we find him it'll be as if Susanna herself had found him, and we won't have mistreated her needlessly."

Asha and her mother could hardly wait to leave the sick woman, who stank abominably. The three of them hurried across the square, colliding with the chattering citizens of Magdala. As they rushed toward the open space around the well, where the prophet had been speaking, some people asked:

"Isn't that the only daughter of Nahor, who ran off to Jerusalem after rolling in the hay with half of Magdala, and wanting to do as much with the other half?"

Or: "Isn't that the Jerusalem whore they nicknamed the 'worker bee' because she worked like a bee at her trade?"

Or: "Look, that bed penny Mary Magdalene is back, trying to pass for a silver coin!"

But none threw a stone or insulted her in any way.

Evil first affects the soul, so that bodily license is only a mechanical and neutral go-between without the tangible characteristics of leprosy, blindness, dumbness or paralysis. Such evildoing remains exclusively in God's competence and under his strict surveillance. And the word "strict" is used here more to describe the general ruthlessness of divinity than to define divinity's real relationship to licentiousness as an evil, or to lust as the sin from which licentiousness derives. It is evident that such a tolerant attitude toward whoredom was no proof of God's indifference, or of readiness to view with indulgence the bodily immorality of men. God, in fact, postponed his vengeance for purely practical reasons. There were many evils more dangerous than bought-and-paid-for sex; however repulsively such sex distorts love, it is at least its approximate reflection, without real content but with a recollection of its presence. By contrast, what beauty is there in theft, blasphemy and lies? Of what noble feeling is murder the corrupted image? Of what virtuous face is hypocrisy the distorted and monstrous reflection? From the divine standpoint, therefore, prostitution could wait for punishment until the Last Judgment, when it would be justly weighed. Naturally, in cases where whole cities, districts or peoples were infected by this vice—we have only to recall Sodom and Gomorrah—revenge would be immediate; but so long as that vice was practiced by only a few dozen whores and a handful of transgressors of compulsive individuals, vengeance would be delayed. Were it not for venereal disease and a few cases of stoning—where we see the hand of human, not divine, justice—one might conclude wrongly that lust was a privileged sin in the Promised Land.

That was why Mary Magdalene reached the well on the square unhindered. But she didn't find the Savior there—not even an apostle. Leaning on the wellhead, two citizens were squabbling: one insisted that Jesus of Nazareth was indeed the Son of God who would heal the wounds of the world, whereas the other claimed that he was a crafty and deceitful imposter who should be expelled from the town. Mary asked if they knew where the Galilean was, he who a short time before had been preaching at that spot. They answered that they didn't know and that the prophet's disciples could best tell her. Since the disciples weren't around either, they pointed out a stranger—if she looked toward the bazaar, she would see him alone in front of Jonathan's shop—who had come to Magdala to join the Christians (as those who confessed the new faith called themselves), and who ought to know.

Mary thanked them. Followed by Asha and her mother, she

decided to approach the stranger. When she weighed up her prospects of winning him over, they seemed favorable. The stranger's expensive though not luxurious garments confirmed her feeling that he hadn't yet officially joined the Christians: had he done so, he would be wearing the coarse hempen homespun in which Christ's disciples and even Christ himself were clothed. This allowed her to hope that he didn't know what troubled her and wouldn't ruthlessly drive her away like the other apostles. Besides, knowing that the Savior wrought miracles which gave the world an advance payment of salvation, so to speak, he might be willing to help them, for that was his Christian duty, and also would promote his own cause: he would show himself to his new master as a defender of the unfortunate and the wretched. When she finally stood before him she felt a little flustered.

The stranger was looking at a Damascus bracelet displaying its diamond bulge in the shop of Jonathan the goldsmith. Though his wrists trembled slightly, his calm, disinterested gaze didn't betray his anxiety that, once he had joined the Lord, he would have to give up all the lovely things he was used to.

Mary hoped to draw his attention without irritating him by her intrusion. She signalled Asha and her mother to stop a few paces away, then she herself barely touched the stranger's cloak, whose Judaean cut recalled the spirit of its Hellenic model. He turned around and looked vaguely at the three wretched women as if unaware of their presence.

"Don't be annoyed, sir, if we interrupt your thoughts, which are no doubt turned to God."

Judging by his dress he was a Jew, by its quality an aristocrat, and by the casualness of his behavior a well-brought-up and educated man. Therefore she spoke in the distinguished Hebrew which, though learned and practiced in the Jerusalem brothels, was no less usable than the Hebrew learned at the tables of the noblest Sadducees.

"I and my relatives"—what the devil else was she to say: I and these two whores?—"must talk urgently with Jesus of Nazareth. We were directed to you as a person who might take us to him."

The stranger cast one more glance at the bracelet, then turned to Mary Magdalene. Afraid that her impudence might have angered him, she hastened to introduce herself. She said her name was Mary and she had been born in Magdala, so everyone called her Mary Magdalene. This way all her cards were on the table. When he heard her name—it was, she believed, as well known in Jerusalem as Herod's—he would know who he was dealing with, and her profession would explain why she wanted so urgently to see the Lord.

At last, graciously condescending to recognize their presence, he spoke. He had a measured voice, whose sound, devoid of dialect, seemed to be intended not for the listener's ears but the essence of his understanding. He said that he had heard that name or one like it somewhere, but didn't indicate what he meant by that.

He's devilishly well bred, Mary thought bitterly. His courteous beh[illegible]vior, which in the past would have impressed her, now go[illegible]r nerves. While she was wasting time with this scrup[illegible]newcomer, the prophet, unpredictable in his decisi[illegible]ght leave Magdala, and their tormenting quest w[illegible]rag on interminably. She introduced Asha and her [illegible]r curtly, and Asha, contrary to her custom—perhaps [illegible]out by the courtly appearance of the stranger—remained [illegible]rmal, and limited her conversation to senseless approval and negative sighs.

It was commendable, the man said, that they wanted God's son to receive them. However, he would like to know what made them think he could help them.

"Didn't you come to Magdala to kneel before him and receive from his lips the good tidings of the heavenly kingdom? If you haven't already done it, aren't you going to?"

He cast another glance at Jonathan's shop, where the sunlight glittered on the jewels, and replied uncertainly: "I think so. I think, in fact, that in some way or other I've already done it, if one casual conversation with the Savior about the renunciations expected of me can be regarded as an agreement between us, he to lead and I to follow."

"Then," said Mary eagerly, "you must have access to him."

The Judaean admitted that he had only just been converted. He believed, but of all Christ's teaching he scarcely knew by heart even the symbol of the faith. If they were relying on his influence, he wasn't the best person to bring them to the Lord. In any case the Messiah was accessible to all, even the most hardened sinners; this boundless tolerance explained the success of his movement. Mediators were unnecessary, in fact undesirable; no interpreters were needed between God and man, heaven and earth, the shepherd and his flock. They were all one body, divided temporarily and with a special aim into conflicting halves. As he talked, he seemed to be ignoring the women and repeating certain laws to himself and in himself, in order to get their real meaning clear.

Is he making fun of us, thought Mary, or of himself? The vague smile on his youthful, well-tended face allowed equally for both possibilities.

Realizing that his personal waverings didn't concern others, he said politely: "He receives all who wish to approach him, speaks to all who listen and helps all who wish to be helped."

Losing patience, Mary replied that their case was special, that they couldn't be compared with those who listened to the Messiah to kill time or who came to bicker and squabble; that Mary, Asha and her mother didn't care about hearing him, but wanted to ask something of his mercy.

"I'm afraid he won't be able to give you anything. He has nothing. He's poor as a mouse." He shrugged as if apologizing for using so humble a comparison when speaking of the Son of God. "Isn't that what the common people say about the poor?"

"So that's that," sighed Mary. He had assumed they wanted to ask Christ for money or some other earthly benefit. These exploiting idlers, these usurers, would never learn that there was spiritual as well as material treasure, and that with such mercenary ideas one doesn't get far in the New Testament.

In a certain way she now felt superior to the stranger. Thanks to his misunderstanding, she recovered a good part of the self-confidence that she had lost in the presence of his cultivated appearance. Surely she who had accompanied Christ through Judaea, Samaria and Galilee, knew more about the Son of God and his teaching than this parvenu who admitted he had known him for only a few days. Hadn't she been an eyewitness of his miracles, which the newcomer could only have heard of? Hadn't she been so close at one of them—at that most miraculous of miracles, which had raised her to her feet and drove her in pursuit of the wonder-worker—that she could say it had happened to her personally? Yet now she must implore this newcomer for a service which by the nature of things she should render to him.

Be that as it may, she told herself, you must refrain from any rash action. Therefore she chose her words carefully when she explained that their ugent need to see Christ was not for any material purpose, but for something directly affecting their souls.

"Souls?" he asked.

"Yes, souls."

"Immortal souls?"

"What else?"

The stranger's face suddenly assumed a vague expression mingling continued respect with bored irritation, adoration with blasphemy. To tell the truth, at this moment so decisive for the women, he had been more concerned with himself than with them. Insofar as he had concerned himself with them at all, it was only as a good excuse to be concerned with himself, once again without regard to his decision to embrace Christianity, to examine that continually changing relationship between his intuitive faith in Christ and his reasoned need to raise countless objections to Christ's teaching.

Soul here, soul there. Nothing without soul, nothing against soul. From soul to soul, through soul into soul. My, your, his soul; ours, yours, theirs. All the souls of the living, plus the souls of the dead from the beginning, and naturally the souls of women. As well as the souls of the newborn and the souls of those not conceived. Yes, even they have souls. The souls of beings and the souls of things, the souls of animals and their mates. The souls of stones which have fallen and smashed into myriads of little kindred souls. The souls of plants and their seeds, each after its kind. The souls of times and distances, as well as the independent soulfulness of what happens in the network of dimensions. At the very end, boundless and harmoniously formed, the soul of God. And then perhaps, he thought hesitantly, still one more soul without precursors, uniting in itself all that cargo of souls: one impossible, all-embracing, beginningless and endless, subordinate-to-nothing, primeval soul.

Conscious that such speculations were blasphemous, since they falsely reflected the divine creation of the world, Thomas (for the stranger was Melhit, son of the Sadducee leader Alkan, who was to become the apostle Thomas Didymus, known as "doubting Thomas") thought uneasily that if he persisted in his intention, he would spend the most rewarding years of his life in the exclusive selfish company of the soul, either his own or that of others imposed upon him. And if he didn't shake off the hypnotic power of the Nazarene, he would never return to selfless, insignificant things such as soulless drowsiness in a swing in the still Jerusalem afternoon; a soulless diadem in a shop; a soulless landscape unfolding with the day like a flower and not demanding close attention; the contact of lips in the street below the soulless window of a hesitant man; the hide-and-seek of children below that same soulless window; the soulless moonlight like a cold hand upon the earth without a soul; the soulless law which turns the soulless carousel of fate around the eternally raised finger of God; the soulless chance incident which hinders his sovereign legislation, soulless, soulless, soulless.

What was that woman talking about? When a whore asks for medicine she must have the clap. So why doesn't she go to a doctor?

Since you can't get anywhere with the Galileans without a knowledge of the soul, Thomas decided he must study its role in the faith. He must learn all about it: constitution, characteristics, possibilities, its worth according to the new standards ordained by the Savior. While learning, he would probably have to accede without grumbling to its tyrannical demands. Worse still, he would have to find a sincere satisfaction in that service. That was the established tenet of the faith, to which there was no concession.

Just look at them, Thomas thought, listening inattentively to Mary's explanation, no more nor less than remission of sins! She didn't explicitly admit this, she even avoided suggesting that their plea be presented as a desire for the renewal of innocence, but what else could it be? Even without tacit admission their intention was clear: to be freed of their sins, to become as newborn children, untainted and impervious to evil. In fact, he thought, was there anything indecent in their aspiration to rinse from their bellies the filth of alien delights? You help the cripple if you set him on his legs, the blind if you open his eyes, the lunatic if you restore his reason, the dead if you resurrect him. How could you help the whore unless you made her innocent again?

As for soul, in the world he had lived in it had a much more innocent meaning, a much more measured influence on men. Even in the Torah, where the people's customs reduced the soul to a rather convenient and organized drill ground for repentance, it was only one component of a complicated machine whose every cog, including the sexual organs, was of equal importance to the life of the individual and the community. Balance was respected, for it was understood as a *sine qua non* of survival both for the individual and the community. If balance were disturbed, the world would collapse: if the soul outweighed the body, the world would become a madhouse; if the body outweighed the soul, the world would slide down the rough slopes of history. In the private life of the Israelite, in his education, the soul bridled the body and the body in turn made excuses for the soul. There was a tacit agreement between them for defense before Jehovah, something like a child's plot before a strict father who pretends (when it suits him) to be simple—a sort of mutual counsel in case of sinning. If the body committed adultery, the soul was there as its excuse; if the soul sinned, it could cite the imperfections of the body. All was organized on a friendly basis. Only the doctors of the Sanhedrin had headaches about it, because they had to devise the least painful interpretation of the many prohibitions which encompassed half of life as in a vise.

But for the brotherhood in Christ, the body didn't exist. Since it continued to be there, and was created in the image of God, it had to be separated somehow from its powerful creator; also, with due respect to its distinguished ancestry, its destructive activities had to be attributed to the devil. So it turned out that, as a vengeance for original sin, the immortal soul, grumbling and complaining, had to drag with it this ugly, savage body which both stole from it time which should have been devoted to God, and led it into temptation. Since it couldn't divest itself of the body completely, the soul wrapped it in a conspiracy of silence and endured it with shame. Hating the body to which it was condemned, it abused it pitilessly, cast it before the feet of murderers and torturers, ravaged it by penances and fasts, killed it by despising it.

To be absolutely innocent, he thought—uncomfortably aware of his petitioner—means to be a saint, doesn't it, or at least to be within the domain of sanctity? Women, do you aim so high? To stand shoulder to shoulder with the Mother of God, to be in kinship with the Virgin?

Pretending to misunderstand, he said amiably:

"All right, I see you're ill and want to be healed."

Had she had more time, Mary would have explained in detail what they meant by healing and what help they expected from the Savior. But fearing lest the prophet slip away, she simply confirmed the stranger's assumptions, which were correct regarding the act itself of healing, but incorrect regarding her ultimate aim.

"You're right, sir, I wish to be healed."

Thomas turned to Asha and her mother. "What about them?"

"They do, too, sir."

"You see me, so you're not blind. You speak, so you're not dumb. You reason too well for a lunatic. If you were leprous or paralytic, it would be obvious. And you're alive. You aren't bleeding, woman, are you?"

"No," said Mary.

Asha could no longer restrain herself. "Why beat around

the bush, Magdalene? Tell the man we're whores!"

"Shut up!" said Mary.

"Harlots, whores, bitches of Sodom!"

"Shut up, I say!"

"And that before we got here, a good half of all lousy Judaea had slept with us. Maybe even this distinguished gentleman, though now he's playing the innocent!" Asha approached Thomas, who drew back quickly. "Come, sir, do us the honor of remembering which one of us you laid!"

Mary tried to stop her, but couldn't.

"Come on, you half-baked apostle, think: did you ever screw any of us? Don't look at the ground like a blushing bride. If it wasn't you or someone like you, who was it?"

"Evil spirits," said Thomas. "Demons. There are seven in such circumstances, they say. Seven for each soul."

Asha smacked her bottom: "Here are the demons! Demons—what a laugh! Men put their filth under our skin—not spirits! They think we're foul holes where they can find relief when they feel like it. You're all pigs—ungrateful pigs!"

Asha's fury subsided as suddenly as it had welled up. She sobbed silently. Standing against the wall of Jonathan's jewelry store, she looked like a rag hung out of a ground-floor window to dry.

"Now you've heard everything, my lord," said Mary Magdalene. "Under the circumstances, I don't suppose you'll take us to the Savior."

She was holding back her tears. Furious with Asha, she made up her mind to leave the other women and try to meet the Savior on her own. Consequently, her astonishment was great when the stranger said he would take them. Though he couldn't guarantee that their request would be listened to or forgiveness granted them, he hoped the Son of God would understand their suffering. So they could come after him, not beside him. Hadn't he said clearly: *after* him? A few steps behind. Where he went, they should follow.

As the wind swept away the shadows of the clouds, he strode across the square, not once turning to see if the women were following.

On the way Thomas wondered how it felt to become—suddenly and without the regular atonement—sinless, pure, purer than pure, washed in the clear river of God's forgiveness, free from earthly silt, like a faded picture dug up from moist darkness and restored according to some ideal model, made new in primal chastity and once more returned to the beginning. To start all over again. What previous knowledge of innocence had these women had? Infants at the breast couldn't know such an exceptional feeling, though they were closest to it. Their own recollections couldn't go back to the cradle and to the state of earthly sinlessness. How did sinlessness feel to those who had never experienced the absence of sin? In what way was it reflected, except in communion with a sinless God? In any case, he thought, resisting the temptation of inquiring into concepts of higher powers, it must be unusual, not to say ridiculous, for grown women to have the pure soul of a newborn child. And when you add to that their profession, their new state—if approved and granted, that is—it must be even more unusual.

As she followed him, Mary Magdalene trembled all over from the surge of feeling that the whole nightmare of following the Messiah would soon end by some liberating miracle, and that she would revert to her former state, the true undistorted life for which she had been fashioned. By a single word from the wonder-worker she would be set free. She would be opened up and cleansed thoroughly of everything that had been thrust on her by force and fatal misunderstanding. Free at last. Herself at last.

Does to be innocent mean to be empty as a vessel from which a drought has sucked up every drop of water, Thomas wondered. Empty as a body from which death has squeezed out the last breath? Uninhabited like a void? Or does it mean to be filled, overfilled, jammed tight with sinlessness, like a mule overladen with goods? Stuffed with innocence, like a turkey fattened for the gourmet banquet of God? Or like Noah's ark caulked with pitch—hermetically sealed by saintliness?

Mary rejoiced. Overcome by a desire to leap with delight, she sang and frolicked, embraced the silly little Asha and her massive fleshy mother clattering after her, and sang with them:

"O Lord, my God, I rise in the mornings for you, my soul thirsts for you, my soul longs for you in the dry, thirsty and waterless land. My voice ascends to God and I call unto him; my voice ascends to God and he will hear me. In God my soul finds peace, in God is my salvation."

Perhaps, thought Thomas, the innocence created by a miracle is no more than giving life a chance to start all over again from the beginning, from nothing. Perhaps it offers no defense against fresh vice, evil-doing, lawlessness and temptation, but only annuls all the old. It doesn't make a man a saint automatically, but exposes him to new temptation, leaving it to him to choose freely between heaven and earth, paradise and hell, good and evil.

"We thank you, O Lord, we thank you," Mary whispered. "Your holy name protects us. Your miracles tell of you.

"Praise the Lord for he is good and his mercy is forever!

"The Lord reigns; let the earth rejoice, let the multitude of islands be joyful.

"Rejoice, women, rejoice! Rejoice, you whores, rejoice!

"Sing unto the Lord a new song, for he does miracles!"

All this is damned unusual, thought Thomas, and absurd. Yet you can't shake this man off. You can't run away from him. You can't take his yoke off your neck. On the contrary, you believe in him unconditionally. You know the whole undertaking is crazy, that he himself is probably crazy, but instead of rejecting him you support this mad adventure. You're caught up in this insane dance, you know you're dancing to crazy music and you try to learn the right step as soon as possible. Yes, the right step, though it's crazy.

I'll have to take notes, he thought, keep a diary. The Gospel according to Saint Thomas, the slave of God, concerning his attachment to the Lord! Naturally, with such a viewpoint you can't count on being included in the canon, if it's ever established, that is. And yet you believe no less firmly than those who follow him. As if you were split in half, one part sane, the other crazy. When crazy you mock the sane half, and when sane you mock the crazy half. The sane one convinces the crazy one and the crazy one confounds the sane one. If only my father could hear me now! Of course he'd say I was a fool. He's always so aristocratically blunt; for him everything is so aristocratically simple. But perhaps you really are the Perfect Fool.

"Where are you going, brother in Christ?"

Before Thomas stood a Galilean in the coarse cloak of a bedawi, with a hood to shield him from the heat, his ascetic face like a lump of unslaked lime crushed into a dark, wavy frame. The white bodiless head pressed into a crumple of dark cloth. He was bony, knobbly, angular. If naked, he might have been mistaken for one of the savage disciples of John who roamed around Salim on the Aenon, eating nettles and locusts. His sparse coal-colored beard looked plucked, not shaven. He kept his hands under a robe which, open slightly at the belt, revealed a dirty undergarment. His greedy and violent eyes—the eyes of a fanatic—acquired a certain gloomy beauty from unknown and dangerous forces.

It's all over, thought Mary, it's finished. As if it had never begun. That's the end of our Lord and our salvation. She didn't even turn to see how Asha and her mother were reacting to this man's intervention. She knew they were standing there behind her as if caught red-handed in a theft, both struck dumb, both powerless to make the slightest move.

"So it's you, Jehuda," Thomas said flatly. "You startled me."

The answer of the man called Judas, or in Hebrew Jehuda, was lightning-swift, as hard as if his syllables had been hewn from a stone tablet where they were engraved for all eternity.

"He who follows the Lord with a pure heart has nothing to fear."

"I was thinking."

"He who follows the Lord with a pure heart has no need to think."

"All right," said Thomas wearily. No point in arguing with Judas ben Simon. In the three days he had spent with the Christians he had come to that conclusion. Judas was always ready with those decisive words which excluded all others, with that measure of faith against which all other measures seemed erroneous.

"I asked you where you were going, brother Thomas."

"Do I have to tell you?"

"He who follows the Lord with a pure heart has nothing to hide."

"Honored brother in Christ," said Thomas, "I really don't see why I should give you an account of my actions. But since I don't want to bicker in the street, I'll tell you that these three sick women implored me to bring them to your Teacher—mine too, now—and that I was carrying out this task so pleasing to God when you rudely stopped me. These women are in a difficult situation and any delay—including this discussion with you, dear brother—could have irreparable consequences."

"If that worries you," said Judas, "let the sin fall on my head."

"Your suffering tomorrow won't lighten their burden today."

"Do you know them, if you're so concerned?"

"Am I doing something wrong?" asked Thomas. What a stinker, he thought, what a conceited unchristian stinker!

"Only God knows if you're doing wrong, but it's obvious at a glance that as a beginner you're overzealous in the preaching of our faith. Did you have any idea what these women were suffering from, when you decided to plead for them before him who represents the unknown aims of God?"

"Evil spirits cause them to do unworthy acts with men—the same acts which under the protection of the Law and custom are called conjugal rites. But if you prefer that I use your language: these women are whores."

"Are you sure?"

"Yes."

"Quite sure? As sure as God?"

"I'm sure," said Thomas. "As sure as God."

To everyone's surprise, Judas took his hands out from under his mantle and pushed Thomas aside. As he did so, he appeared immeasurably larger than he.

"Wretch," he yelled. "Out of God's way!"

He was face to face with Mary. All the coarseness suddenly vanished from his bearing. To Thomas's complete bewilderment, he expressed the deepest idolatrous devotion toward the women whose illness only a few moments before had not interested him.

"Peace be with you, Mary of Magdala," he said, bowing low. "Peace to the dust your consecrated feet tread on, peace to the air your ever-blessed mouth breathes. Before your innocence and that of your reverend companions, I bow to the most renowned of all the miracles of the Son of God—I, Judas Iscariot, his slave and apostle."

Mary didn't say a word.

Thomas wanted to ask what sense there was in welcoming a Jerusalem harlot with the respect usually reserved for a saint, and in arrogantly reproving him for giving her the chance of a meeting with Christ, which might enable her to become one. But he gave up. Everything seemed crazy: these shivering prostitutes who dreamed of virginity in the dust of Magdala; that stupid envoy of the Savior, who while praising God, honored the rankest sin; and most of all his feeling that the apostle and the women had met before but refused to admit it.

Judas said: "Has your purity come to thank our Teacher for the sanctity he granted you in abundance? Or are you seeking fresh commands and fresh instructions for the glorification of the Almighty Creator?"

Mary was silent.

I ought to stop him, Thomas thought, but did nothing. Words won't help, but how about a blow on the head? He looked up and down the street, but there wasn't a rock. Not satisfied by his relief that there weren't any, he decided again that Judas by his inexplicable behavior was committing a crime against the faith and should be stopped. If the favorite of the Savior and the most authoritative interpreter of his faith welcomed the highest good in the blackest evil, what kind of world would result? Impossible—Judas couldn't be doing it on purpose. It was a foolish error, a passing aberration, an inexplicable misunderstanding. Such morality doesn't reflect the Christian spirit, isn't based on its dogmas, doesn't determine its future or represent its essence. It's the result of straying from the true path. In his greeting to the whores, the form had remained Christian but the marrow of the faith had been eradicated. Perhaps, Thomas thought, Judas isn't a Christian at all but the paid agent of other gods, and has wormed his way into the faith to destroy it. In that case he should be stopped at once, he thought, but he did nothing.

"Perhaps, virgin, you want to report to the Son of God what you've done with the virginity he restored to you? To make known the wounds you've licked to quench the fire consuming the lepers. To announce the names of the dying whom you've so mercifully consoled. To display the bruises your faith has earned you in your contests with infidels and Pharisees."

She still didn't answer.

"Or if you've come simply to share with us, who are unworthy of you, your joy in his presence, then once again welcome, most blessed virgin!"

Perhaps he's making fun of them, thought Thomas, appalled; perhaps he's reminding them of their sins which cry out for punishment, though they themselves yearn for forgiveness. But such puritanism must be hateful to God and disagreeable to him who was sent to help sinners, not destroy them.

Though the apostle addressed himself mostly to Mary Magdalene and only incidentally to her companions, the trouble began with Asha. The skinny girl—despite Judas's hymn of praise (hasty, malicious or ironic), we don't dare call her a virgin—stood leaning on her mother's massive shoulder as if all this had nothing to do with her. What's more, she seemed oblivious to the squabbling, as if some shadow play was being performed before her eyes, and not a dialogue of which she was the subject. However, though masked by an illusory calm, her behavior suggested that something unusual was happening in the recesses of her flesh and soul. In her catalepsy, reminiscent of the stupor of a fly warmed by the January sun, an undefined movement was beginning, at first invisible in the tangle of her entrails. She felt it like a tide of heat kindled by a hearth within her body, rising to the cold undersurface of her skin to be cooled, and then thrown back again in the hearth.

This rhythmical interchange of hot and cold currents made the girl sweat profusely one moment and shiver the next. Only when her stomach muscles began to quiver under her rags, her unwashed thighs and breasts to tremble, her nipples to sway, her head to swing from side to side, as all her limbs were set in frantic motion, did that movement become perceptible. Not a single muscle resisted its dynamic force or the rhythm of its ritual dance, which emulated copulation. All this in deathlike silence: not a sigh from Asha's lips.

Thomas took a step toward the girl, but Judas held him back. Perhaps Judas alone foresaw the catastrophe—if we may use that word for something with the elemental force of an earthquake—but knowing that he couldn't prevent it, did his best to explain it instantly as yet another fulfillment of God's power and foresight.

"The chaste Asha sees God," Judas said. "Would you hinder her in this vision, the essential purpose of her sanctity?"

No, Thomas didn't dare; he stepped back.

The twitches of Asha's quivering body become strong spasms, savage and uncoordinated, until her whole being was convulsed and she began to spin like a whip-lashed top, inscribing terrible figures in the whirling dust of the street. Her frenzied dance was accompanied by inarticulate cries forced out of her by the discordant movements of her body.

"She's talking to God," said Judas.

"She doesn't look very happy about it," said Thomas.

"Nonsense! If she weren't happy, she wouldn't be dancing. Look, brother, God's terrible and invisible face seems to be honoring those other two, also."

Indeed, Asha's mother was dancing slowly with gyrations similar to Asha's, and the nervous twitching of Mary's bare shoulders showed the same frantic movement pushing her into the orgy. Mary's whole body had expanded with the unshackled force of that movement, and she recognized, in the partial darkening of her senses and in the mad dance which had already seized Asha and her mother, the assaults of the illness that had attacked her more and more frequently. No bodily pain provoked by a wound or illness could be compared with the pain she now felt, except perhaps the pain of a dying man unable to expel his soul.

"Damn you!" screamed Asha.

"Damn you!" shrieked her mother.

"Damn you!" yelled Mary.

"These curses aren't addressed to God, are they?" asked Thomas, who by now was prepared for anything.

"Certainly not," said Judas. "After filling them with his power, God has departed and Satan has come to abuse them. These saints are putting up a good fight."

"I understand their defending themselves against the devil," said Thomas, "but why do they keep looking at us like that?"

The whirling women collided like billiard balls. Thrown off balance, they collapsed in the dust, tangled in a confused knot. They struck at one another with all their might, so that blood spouted from their wounds and reddish scraps of skin fell in the dust.

Judas felt the time ripe for yet another explanation: "I assume that by this self-punishment pleasing to God they're letting Satan know his instruments of torture can't harm them, and that his red-hot cauldrons are powerless before their sanctity. The more horrible the violence, the more the devil will be disheartened. In the end he'll go searching for more docile victims. Look!"

The women lay still in thick funnels of dust, as in white, narrow graves. Everything was motionless except their breasts, which rose and fell, raising a quivering drift of dust. Their eyelids were closed, their feet awry; from their clenched fists oozed blood mixed with pus, hairs, scraps of cloth and sweat.

"You see," said Judas, "the devil found he couldn't hurt them, so he left. They're resting now in their sinlessness like little girls in fresh diapers. It wouldn' be wise for us to disturb them, brother in Christ. So let's go find the Teacher. It's time to leave Magdala and move on to Decapolis." And he blessed the women: "Peace be with you, virgin sisters!"

Accompanied by Thomas, he went down the street into the quiet Magdala twilight.

"Will it make you angry, honored brother," said Thomas, "if I ask you something?"

"Ask. If the question isn't displeasing to God and I know the answer, I'll tell you."

"You called these women virgins and showed them the respect due to saints. Why?"

"Because they're sinless, and in their virgin innocence renew the sanctity of the Mother of God, the Virgin Mary."

"But how can they be sinless if they're sluts? How can whores be virgins?"

"God be with you, brother," Judas shouted in astonishment, "who says they're whores? They were once, but no longer."

"Just a moment!" Thomas searched for the most conciliatory words to express his disbelief. "Honored Judas, do you mean to say these women aren't notorious harlots?"

"Of course not! What can a man who follows the Lord with a pure heart say, if not the truth?"

"They're not hardened sinners?"

"No."

"When did they stop being sinners? Did the Savior restore their innocence and ransom them from their sin against the seventh commandment? I didn't see him purify them by placing his hand upon their bellies."

"It happened a few years back, during one of our visits to Jerusalem. In that sink of iniquity, in that stable of the Golden Calf, many women lived tormented by devils which drove them to seek relief in whoring. Each woman had seven devils who abused her nightly. By day there were fewer, or none at all. The Savior listened to the plea of some of these whores, including Mary of Magdala, Asha, Susanna and Joanna, the wife of Chuza, a clerk in the tetrarchy. He plugged their bellies with an iron hand, and with that same hand as if with a shovel cleansed them from the dregs of men's filth. Freed from their former sins and unable to commit fresh ones, they became models of innocence and standard-bearers of our faith."

This revelation shattered Thomas. All this time he'd been convinced these unusual women were prostitutes following the Savior to ask forgiveness of their sins and then, through personal sacrifice, to become saints. Now it turned out that they had long been saints and had broken with the devil, while Thomas himself had still been living as an infidel Sadducee, in ignorance of the gospel of the heavenly kingdom.

On the other hand, if they were no longer whores but honored and respected virgins—though Asha's vocabulary made such a transformation doubtful—why were they rushing after the prophet from Nazareth? What did they still hope from him? If they were saints akin to God in their sinlessness, why had God remained aloof from them? And what did Magdalene mean when she said that their case concerned the soul, when the sins from which they had been freed concerned the body? Why—he beat his brains as he walked beside Judas—why did these holy women run after the Son of God so savagely, so persistently, and what did they want from him?

When he asked Judas, Judas shrugged his shoulders:

"I have no way of knowing. Perhaps they want to thank him once again for their sanctity before he dies for us. Or perhaps get some special assignments for their sanctity. Who knows?"

Even so, thought Thomas, someone must know. If Judas didn't, or pretended not to, the virgins must. So Thomas told Judas he was going to visit a childhood friend, and hurried back to the crossroads where they had left the women. His alleged reason for leaving Judas was as irreligious as his real one, for both offended the infallibility of God's mysteries: the first, by scorning the Teacher's demand that believers reject parents, brothers and former friends forever; the second, by seeking to interrogate the real essence of sainthood. But Thomas took the risk.

There was no one at the crossroads but crazy Elkan, blissfully rolling in the white waves of dust, where the outlines of the three women's bodies were still visible. Luckily for his intention, but perhaps unluckily for his immortal soul, Thomas saw their tattered skirts disappearing round a corner. He caught them up at the entrance to the pillared portico of a building which exhaled an unbearable stench of decay. Hesitating to approach them on so delicate a mission, he let the most suitable moment pass. Then all the women had vanished through the gateway.

If he wanted to catch them he couldn't hesitate any longer. Cautiously pushing the gate open, he faced a spectacle which, overshadowed by a bare wall, in the half-light filtering through the gate recalled statuary showing the clash of angry Western gods with their disobedient worshippers. The three women were standing stock-still above a fourth, stretched out on her back across the lichen-covered stone threshold, dead. The skin of the dead woman was a virulent green hatched with irregular rips, as if something living beneath that skin had wanted to force its way out at any cost and in its final exit had been aided by her teeth and nails. It was also obvious that when that something did get out, it wasn't through the pores or other orifices: it had split her stomach open from within. The split ran from just below her breasts to her groin, though nothing indicated it had been made by any instrument. From that mangled trunk protruded stinking entrails that flowed down her flanks like festering spit. From her gaping mouth issued swarms of fat summer flies. There was not a shred of clothing on her. But the strangest thing of all was a large stone in the crotch of her outstretched legs. Though the body was motionless, it still seemed to breathe. Perhaps that force was still spilling out, releasing the stink of carrion which festered in the close forenoon.

The women were gazing at Susanna's corpse without compassion. Rather they looked with the terror one approaches a corpse with, not seeing in it a lost relative or friend, but oneself some bleak day in the future.

Thomas turned to Mary Magdalene: "Forgive me, Virgin of Magdala, for disturbing your prayer for the soul of this sufferer. But since I'm in a hurry to rejoin the Teacher, who is leaving this city, I must talk to you now."

Mary didn't even look at him.

"What has led me to you is perhaps a sacrilege, but I hope to be forgiven, as I've learned only recently the secrets of the faith which you and your reverend companions have known intimately for years."

There was no reply. The women gazed as if hypnotized at the mortal remains of Susanna.

"Since you're already recognized as saints and you've cast off the nature of whoredom, I just wanted to ask why you still accompany the Savior and what you expect from him. But I can see that this is neither the time nor the place to ask such a question."

He was about to withdraw when Mary replied: "There's no better time or place for you to get the answer to your question, stranger. We want to become whores again."

Thomas recoiled. "Dear blessed woman . . . !"

"I told you. We want him to make us what we were before—what his Father had made us. We want to be whores again. And don't call me 'blessed woman'!"

"I don't understand. You want to be sinners as before, yet you begged to become sinless?"

"Begged? Who begged? Asha, did you?"

"No!"

"And you?" Mary asked Asha's mother. "Did you ever want to become a virgin?"

"God save me from such an honor!"

Mary pointed to Susanna. "Or did Susanna here chase after your Christ to be healed of vice? Judas must have told you all this, or the lie wouldn't be so perfidious. The truth is, we were whoring on a grand scale and as the Book of Genesis says, we were happy earning our daily bread by the sweat of our bodies. We weren't in anybody's way till your terrible companions came along. Unfortunately for us, just then the governor of Judaea expelled all cripples from Jerusalem, and your friends lost the raw material for their wonder-working. Then Jehuda or Judas, damn him, remembered that the prophets had attributed to the future Messiah the power to drive demons out of man. Since lunatics had also been expelled, they decided that whores might be thought of as possessed, and that there was no real difference between prostitutes and madmen because madmen live in other worlds and we live in other men. I must say the Savior resisted Judas's idea. He didn't think we were worth the spiritual effort he needed for that act. But Judas was obstinate. All he cares about is prophecies and their fulfillment. Do you know what he said to me when I asked if the desert wind remembers the camel it swallows in its mad course? He said: 'The wind bloweth where it listeth and where God directs it. It riseth not to remember but to sweep away.' I'll tell you something, stranger: the wind forgets the camel it kills, but until it dies, the camel remembers the storm that killed it.

"Then Judas led the Messiah into the brothel. If we'd had any inkling of what was going to happen, we'd never have let them in. Naively, we thought we'd be dealing with Galilean peasants who weren't used to haggling, and we'd get them to loosen their purse strings. But it happened the other way around. Their purses remained unloosened and we were shut up. I've never heard so many curses shouted as when our bellies were sealed. He went away with his flock and we stayed there locked up by the invisible key of virginity. Though we could still perform the mechanical acts of lust, we couldn't provide any satisfaction with our bellies, or procure any for ourselves. Our bodies were shackled like slaves by the iron fetters of miracle. And from, let's say, the bodily viewpoint, we really did become virgins."

"I know," sighed Thomas. "It's always the problem of the soul."

"But that dirty miracle didn't affect the soul. Because it's immortal, it's associated with the eternity of God and can't be remodeled. Our body cast out sin, but our soul still clung to the vices it remembered and yearned for. The body couldn't obey the soul, and the soul was powerless before the body's incapacity. And *that* was the blessing of sanctity given us! Those spasms which attacked us in the street and made us torture one another were our sinful souls fighting with our bodies, trying to dissolve them, to tear them to pieces so they can enjoy life once again. So far our souls haven't succeeded. But Susanna's did. Look, stranger! Imprisoned in that virgin body, Susanna's lustful soul got so swollen with desire for a man that it tore its way out, the way fermenting new wine breaks open old wineskins. And what did the wretched woman get by it? She escaped from her divine prison, but lost her body; so she wanders the world without the means of enjoyment and will never find peace. I don't want to come to that, stranger! I'm still young. There must be other magic than Christ's, some other way to open me while there's still time. I've followed your Teacher hoping he'd unlock me and undo the evil he did. He must know my whorish soul and virgin body don't get along, that their struggle makes for terrible suffering. I think he'd have helped me if I'd reached him, but I never did. For months we've dragged ourselves after him all over Israel, but not once have we met him face to face. That bastard Judas was always there to prevent us. And why? So your Teacher wouldn't have any doubts about the salvation wrought by his miracles! So he wouldn't refuse to perform more miracles and so betray those bloody prophets! And Judas refuses to admit we still love vice, and insists that we act like virgins. He knows why we're running after the Messiah, but he's careful not to show it. I won't be a saint, stranger! I don't give a damn for the prophets or for agreements with God. I don't give a hoot for the salvation of the world. All I want is to be free, the way I was before this awful miracle spoiled the only blessing I ever got from nature. Since your Savior hasn't helped me, I must help myself. If I don't, I'll die like Susanna and with my last breath curse the lot of you. Now you've got an answer to all your questions—go! Go where my eyes won't ever see you again, you or any of your lousy Christian brothers!"

And Thomas left. What else could he do? To console them made no sense, and he had no solution to offer. He knew he couldn't evade the wary Judas and smuggle the women in to the Messiah, and he himself, albeit against his will, could see that their ambition was impious and anti-Christian.

When he got to the street he found a large crowd of Magdala citizens. The rumor had spread that these women, once whores, were now saints and able to work miracles themselves. Many believers among the local people had hastened to render them homage and some to beg a magic spell for themselves or their children. The crowd had formed a circle several ranks deep around the gateway. Some were kneeling, and others standing on the curbs to see the virgins better when they came out. Some were singing the hundred and thirteenth psalm, praising God who humbles himself to look at things on earth, then raises the poor out of the dust and the needy out of the dunghill.

It was too much for Thomas. He couldn't bear to witness the confrontation between those unwilling virgins and the adorers of their sanctity. He went his way quickly with downcast eyes, closed lips, and ears unable to hear anything except the twilight wind which clashed with the darkening walls of Magdala.

He was far away when the crowd awaiting the virgins sang the beginning of the hundred and fourth psalm:

"Bless the Lord, O my soul. O Lord my God, thou art very great; thou art clothed with honor and majesty. Who coverest thyself with light as with a garment: who stretchest out the heavens like a curtain."

He was still farther away when they reached the end of the psalm:

"Let the sinners be consumed out of the earth, and let the wicked be no more. Bless thou the Lord, O my soul. Praise ye the Lord."

Miracle at Bethany

> Jesus said unto her, I am the resurrection and the life: he that believeth in me shall never die.
>
> John 11:25–26

FIRST OF ALL I must rest and then find a suitable place for the pyre. I put down the hatchet and lay the corpse on the grass and sit down beside it. Wrapped in a linen cloth spotted with blood, muddied by earth and sweat, the dead man looks like a sack of potatoes brought to market. The crickets aren't chirping yet and there's plenty of time before sunrise for me to do as ordered.

I say "ordered" because as a servant I'm used to the word, but in this case I was entreated to do the good deed which has brought me to the Mount of Olives. The timing was of great importance to my master. He insisted that I not light the pyre at night lest its flame attract those who would maliciously frustrate his plans. And this time he didn't dare take any risks. He must at all costs reach the Lord. I, Hamri ben Elcanaan, his devoted servant, got an explicit order or, as I have said, an entreaty to undertake this task.

As soon as I catch my breath, I'll begin my preparations. My bones, unfortunately, aren't as strong as they once were, for I've eaten the Passover cakes sixty times already, and sixty times seen the blood of the lamb sprinkled on the doorposts of Bethany in commemoration of the Exodus. Maybe he died wasting on the cross, the dead man in the sack, but he's heavy and I had to carry him on my back, making sure no one noticed. I spent the whole day crouching in the bushes at the foot of the crosses, and all I had to eat was a thin loaf of cornbread handed me by the master's sister,

Martha. I still have to gather branches for the kindling, cut faggots and light the pyre. I'm sure I can't do all this right if I don't have a good meal first to restore my strength. I take a piece of goat cheese from inside my blouse and try to think of nothing but its taste while chewing. It's sour.

I reckon I'll need about three hours for the whole job if the day stays windless. As it is now. Only two if there's a wind. Otherwise the place is just right for what the master intends: the dense thicket of the Mount of Olives plunges downhill toward Bethany, and on the southeastern side the uninhabited wilderness of Judaea is like a blinded eye which can't see anything happening on the hill above. Around me the unbearable quiet of Elul will last only until the cry of some crane or sacred ibis challenges it. But the quiet lets me find out if anyone is still searching the thickets and rummaging through the caves to find me and the body.

Resting in the dry grass, I gaze toward Jerusalem, which from here looks like a horseshow planted in the Judaean countryside. I'd say nothing is moving in the valley of Kidron. The listless plain of Jehoshaphat is peacefully awaiting the condemnation of the archenemies of Israel, and Zion, oppressed by the heat, is wisely ignoring the weak voices which reach me like sighs of immeasurable hopelessness from Golgotha, where this afternoon a few matricides, traitors and so-called Christians were crucified. I'm sorry for the new believers—mostly poor people from the suburbs whose only joy is to imagine new gods. There's really no other way to bring them to their senses but to let them die.

And down there, as I can hear, they're dying.

All the time I'm here I'll have to listen to their terrible wailing, their screeching cries for help that are no longer addressed to men—if they ever were—but to God-the-accepter-of-sacrifices, to God-who-shortens-torments, to God-the-giver-of-refuge. Who feels like working when men are breathing their last behind your back. Except for executioners, maybe. They should at least give them a mouthful of wine mixed with mandragora, but they don't. The new governor of Judaea won't allow any relief at the place of execution. He's forbidden even the breaking of the shinbones, so that death comes more slowly and naturally.

Anyway, what can I do? I suppose I can always crush a laurel leaf and stuff it in my ears.

God of my fathers, why in my old age should I have to scramble about the mountain with a corpse on my back? All this could have been avoided; but if it couldn't have, and it was written this way, why couldn't it have been someone else? Has any prophet keeping watch over Israel ever mentioned me?

I'm sure there's never been any mention of me in the prophecies. There's been no word of my master either, though there's been plenty of talk about resurrection. Now I know we're chosen at random, not sought out so that what was written can be fulfilled. On the contrary, what was written is fulfilled just because we're at hand. And that if it wasn't us, it would be someone else.

But we happened to be at hand.

My master Lazarus and myself were having supper with a few harvesters from the estate. While the master's sister Martha was serving the food, making sure that all the laborers had enough, her younger sister Mary entered, leading a stranger by the hand. Any description of the stranger would be too mild for what I felt when I first saw him, stunted, enigmatic and aloof, hesitating at the threshold. He didn't seem strange, like a foreigner from some unknown land. On the contrary, his nationality was clear from the Jewish cut of his domed head and the generous folds of his Galilean clothing. He was strange the way some rare plant is strange to an herb seller who'd like to understand its virtues, or strange as night is to day, which borders on it but never mingles with it. He was no different from the fieldworkers watching him with curiosity as they chewed their cornbread, yet as the same time he was very different. The blood-colored fire which leaped out of the logs to greet him at the door, as if some huge saddened heart were crackling on a brazier, didn't illuminate him but cast reddish shadows over him. I'll never forget the waves of blood on his face, ebbing and flowing with the flames. It was someone meant for the executioner, or the executioner himself. Perhaps it was the stamp of the martyr that I saw on him.

Mary explained that the Galilean was a pilgrim to the Holy City asking for a night's lodging. Unfortunately, my master wasn't one to say that a few dozen paces past Bethany one could find a more comfortable inn—or one more suitable for a stranger, anyway. Instead, he invited him to be his guest.

The Galilean accepted without a sign of gratitude, as if used to such a welcome. When he took his place at the table, the laborers got up, saying they needed rest before the next day's harvesting. Out of courtesy, I had thought of leaving, too. Only later did I learn that in their superstitious hearts the laborers had recognized in him a traveler who brings misfortune. Maybe I had that same feeling. I too am of humble origin and uneducated.

One other thing should have warned us: the newcomer didn't wash his hands before eating, though vessels for the cleansing rite were at hand. In front of all of us, the guest violated this custom dating from the time of Moses. The actual rite of washing the hands up to the elbow isn't really obligatory—the master himself practiced it more from hygienic than religious reasons—but it should have aroused our doubts, for if the guest didn't observe minor laws, he wouldn't respect the laws of living and dying.

Even so, Martha saw to it that the man was hospitably entertained. Her younger sister peered bodly at the newcomer, who said nothing but chewed briskly as if he were very hungry but food meant nothing to him. I couldn't understand what Mary, a flighty girl, saw in this reserved Galilean who didn't inspire a bit of confidence. Now I realize she was the only one at that wretched supper to suspect who was sitting with us.

When the meal was over, I and my master Lazarus struck up a conversation about the cattle prices in Galilee. The guest knew nothing about that. I suspected that he didn't know a bull from a cow. Had there been any rain in the north lately? He didn't know. My master pretended not to notice the stranger's insulting ignorance, and changed the subject in the hope of finding something he could talk about. No use. He knew nothing about anything, as if he had just arrived from some other world where wheat wasn't sown and reaped, or cattle fattened and slaughtered.

The discussion died away altogether, and I and my master Lazarus took the liberty of going to bed. Before leaving, my master ordered his sisters to prepare a couch for the guest in the room where we'd been sitting.

When we went out onto the porch to breathe some of the freshness from the Mount of Olives (that same mountain where I'm now imploring fate, resting beside a corpse in a shroud), the master asked what I thought.

I hedged a bit: "Think about what?"

"About the fellow Mary brought in."

"Master, he's strange. Very strange. I'd say your sister knows more than she lets on. Did you notice how she looked at him?"

"I did. That look was improper, but otherwise I don't know what it meant. She saw something, Hamri. It was as if she saw a big hump on him."

"Your sister didn't see anything *on* him; what she saw was *in* him. Otherwise we would've seen it, too, and felt wonder or repulsion, as the case may be."

My master agreed. Expressing the wish never to see the Galilean again, he took his lamp and went to bed.

I then went to inspect the stables and outhouses, my last task of the day. I was surprised at the harsh lowing and the thrashing about of the cattle, which usually precede a storm. But for some reason I connected their uneasiness with the presence of the stranger in the house.

I tied the cattle to their mangers and tightened the knots of their ropes, then inspected the barns and went to get some sleep. Passing by the dining room I peeked in and saw a strange sight. The fire had gone out; a thin funnel of smoke was rising like incense to the ceiling. The room was bathed in hot, lead-colored shadow. Martha was busy with the dishes, while nearby those two were sitting and gazing, like two conspirators exiled from our world. The Galilean was on the bench and Mary, crouched at his feet, was looking at his face. He must have been pronouncing some fervent sermon.

That was the beginning of our misfortunes, as a result of which I now sit on the Mount of Olives rejoicing in the death of my master instead of weeping over it. I thought no evil even on the following morning, when the Galilean left without saying good-by to any of us. Martha was furious:

"Can you imagine, Hamri, I'd been slaving in the house the whole blessed day, and then all alone looked after the guest. And Mary—she was the one who dragged him in off the street—sat at his feet whispering with him. When I yelled at her for not helping, he—not she—roused himself enough to tell me that by sitting and listening to him, she was offering him greater hospitality than I did by working my fingers to the bone! 'You, woman,' he said, 'offer me food, the fruit of your hands, but your sister offers me her soul, the fruit of God's hands.' I was mad and said that if God had granted me a soul I'd give it back to him, and not to any vagabond who came knocking at my door. 'You speak truth,' he said, 'but blessed is the one who recognizes God in good time.' I just barely stopped myself from telling him that no one's soul would be enough to satisfy such a glutton, and went on washing the dishes while Mary and that ingrate talked right into the night. I don't think the two of them slept at all."

It's time I got on with my work. I must find the driest tree, with a trunk that isn't too thick (large logs burn slowly), cut it close to the root, trim off the branches and cut it into equal pieces, about six or seven feet long.

First I drag the corpse into some bushes and cover it with grass, branches and earth. I place a few rocks on the mound, so while I'm away wild animals won't desecrate it. Then I take the ax and go into the thicket. Right away I come across an olive tree which suits me, and with two cross cuts leave a blaze on it. As I go farther into the undergrowth, the cries from the execution site become less and less clear until, thanks be to the Lord of Hosts, I can't tell them from the rustling leaves or the moaning wind on the open heights.

Then I come across other dried-up olive trees contorted with age and weakened, their branches leaning against one another. I mark them with a blaze for felling, as I did the first.

Less than a month after the Galilean had spent the night at our house, the Sadducee Nicodemus visited Bethany. This distinguished member of the Sanhedrin demanded a private talk with my master. The collection of contributions for the building of a new synagogue at Jerusalem was about to begin, and I thought that the Council of the High Priest had chosen Lazarus, as the most respected and devout resident, to supervise the work in Bethany. I was not present at the conversation. My master told me about it after he had collected his thoughts and recovered his breath a bit following his first death. First, he said, they talked about conditions in the Jerusalem district, about the new governor of Judaea, about some theological squabble between the Sadducees and the Pharisees, and so, bit by bit, came to the prophet and his prophecies.

Nicodemus asked if my master believed that Isaiah would triumph and the one of whom the Judaean prophet spoke would really appear and free Israel from servitude. Lazarus said he believed that—until now, anyway—all the prophecies had been fulfilled, but that the times weren't ripe to welcome such an individual. Did my master believe, the Sadducee went on, that this being would be in blood kinship with God? My master thought that any kinship between the God of Jacob and that person would be of no significance; he would be inspired by God, and God would fill him as sweet incense fills a cheap vessel, but he himself wouldn't be God. Would he be able to perform miracles? asked Nicodemus. Would the Messiah—to give the being his generally accepted name—be able to make the sick whole, give reason to the mad or resurrect the dead? No, said my master, he didn't think so, even though the Scriptures predicted such powers. Those were only the customary, exaggerated metaphors for natural miracles. In that case, said Nicodemus—more harshly, this time—that revolutionary you gave shelter to isn't the Messiah sent by God, though he does all those things.

"Honored Nicodemus," my master replied, "I don't know of any revolutionary under my roof, and none of the unexpected guests I've offered hospitality to has ever claimed to be the Messiah. I can swear to that by the holy Ark of the Covenant, by the High Altar or any other object which Jehovah has made sacred, as you please!"

Nicodemus smiled wryly and asked to see Lazarus's two sisters. First he asked Martha whether any travelers had recently passed the night under their roof. Martha told him everything about the Galilean's visit and his utter ingratitude. A damned ingrate, said the girl: it wasn't enough for him to eat our food—but he wanted our souls as well! Then Mary yelled at her sister that the Galilean wasn't an ingrate but Joshua ben Joseph, the Son of God from Nazareth, the lamb whom the Father had sent to take our sins upon him!

"And you begrudge him the cakes you fed him!" she screamed.

My master listened with astonishment to this blasphemous confession, not daring to look Nicodemus in the eyes. "Hamri," he told me after he'd risen from the grave the first time, "I wanted the earth to open and swallow me up when that silly girl began to preach about the Son of God—meaning that beardless Galilean—and about us as if we were a bunch of dried figs, and the noble Nicodemus as if he were a clay pot to be broken on the day of the Last Judgment. Her language was that of a cowherd, not the most sought-after girl in all Bethany!"

Then my master solemnly swore that he had had no idea who Joshua ben Joseph was, or that a warrant signed by the most gracious tetrarch had been issued against him.

"I believe you," replied Nicodemus, standing up, "but it's up to you to convince the Holy Sanhedrin. Get ready, Lazarus of Bethany. We must go to Jerusalem."

It was a polite request, backed up by the spears of the Judaean national guard. My master said good-by to Martha, who was weeping and tearing her hair, and to Mary (instead of thrashing her immediately, as I would have), who in her foolishness encouraged him to become the first martyr of the new faith—a faith of which he knew nothing, except that it was preached by a callow youth and professed by a girl just as callow. Finally he said good-by to me, giving me orders for running the estate in his absence. Then, just in case, he tucked a thick woolen blanket under his arm and left with the men from Jerusalem.

We never saw him again, at least not in his first life.

I've finished blazing the tree trunks. For the most part they're twisted olives, a few cedars and one fairly stout pomegranate which I'll work into the base of the pyre. They're all within a radius of about fifty paces, so I won't waste time rolling them long distances. That'll make it easier to bring them to the spot I've chosen for the pyre. Now the hardest work begins. I must cut down all the trees I've marked.

Come on, Hamri, get going. Pretend you're slashing not at the forest but at the apostles of Jesus of Nazareth, especially at Judas Iscariot!

My master didn't return from Jerusalem on either the first day or the second. We were worried. Even Mary stopped talking of her brother as a first martyr whom we ought to adore, and thought of him as some unfortunate who must be snatched from prison. On the third day, when there was no longer any doubt about the nature of his absence, his sisters implored me to go to Jerusalem and inquire about his fate. They gave me a basket for him in which Martha had put some sheep cheese, a charcoal-broiled knuckle, a dozen or so rolls, some figs, pomegranates, dates and lemons, and a sealed flask of twenty-year-old wine, as well as two linen towels and a sponge.

When I reached the Holy City I went to Amonach's tavern to get food, and some information I didn't dare ask for publicly. The tavern, close by the Pretorium, was always packed with Roman legionaries, mercenaries or freedmen, who carried out minor jobs for the governor, and sometimes even important ones. Pilgrims stayed there, too, and merchants whose affairs required only a short stay in the city. They all sat on wooden benches or three-legged stools at dirty tables, complaining over copper cups, earthenware dishes, jugs and small bowls. They were divided into groups as if some invisible wall had cut the inn into cells where mercenaries played at dice, petty officials accepted bribes, merchants haggled and pilgrims exchanged impressions of the holy places.

My eye caught an isolated group of Jews. They were sitting together, though it was clear that they didn't know one another and feared this companionship as much as they wanted it, and that the only thing more unpleasant was the unpleasantness of being without it. There were more women than men—mainly Galilean women from the Lake of Gennesaret—but there were also visitors from Northern Judaea, the Philistine seacoast, Samaria and the regions cross the Jordan. What tied them together, whether they liked it or not, were the baskets similar to my own which the despondent women had on their laps or at their feet.

I joined them, thereby acknowledging that I was one of them though I didn't know why, except for the basket I was carrying on my arm. They accepted my arrival as something natural, though they didn't greet me in any way. I sat next to a man from Ziklag who was holding a basket in his spadelike peasant hands as tenderly as if it were an expensive ostrich egg and not a bunch of reeds. I soon realized that they were talking monotonously in threads of voices that joined in an enigmatic murmur like the rustling of leaves.

"Today they didn't take my parcel."

"Maybe he's gone."

"They tell you when they're gone."

"Not always. It depends who's at the gate. Today it was that nice young man."

"The hell he is! He kicked my ass once!"

"You must ask at the governor's office."

"This wine's terrible—camel's piss, not wine!"

"What did you bring?"

"A little cheese and beef. I don't bring rolls, they crumble them at the guardhouse. And the cheese goes bad, too."

"You should bring black bread, sun-dried. I mean it."

"Yesterday afternoon they crucified three of them, one was

from across the Jordan. Is anyone here from across the Jordan?"

"I am, but they took my basket."

"That doesn't mean a thing, my friend."

"They say that Manlius is taking a personal interest in him."

"Why should a Roman do anything for a Jew? They like us to kill one another."

"We aren't killing one another. They're killing *us*."

"I'm in the sixth month."

"No time to be pregnant. Best to have a miscarriage."

"A lot the rich care! They always find a way to get their asses out of the fire."

"My man's innocent."

"How do you know?"

"I sleep with him."

"What does the word 'Christ' mean, anyway?"

"It's all crazy. My Simon said it was all crazy, too, but he wanted to see what would happen."

"So?"

"The blind man saw."

"That's for circuses! That blind man was no more blind than you or me!"

"You really *are* blind if you don't believe in the Savior!"

A man from Ziklag asked if I was a newcomer. I told him I was, though I didn't understand why he asked. He told me all these people were looking in the Jerusalem prisons for relatives arrested for preaching the faith of the new Messiah. There was no point in listening to all these babbling women, he told me.

"I hope to get it all done right here in this tavern."

"How?"

"I've got my eye on a clerk who works in the office of the Holy Sanhedrin and comes in here now and then. I always bow to him humbly. Yesterday he noticed me. Tomorrow I'll talk to him, and if they don't crucify him in the meantime, I'll be able to get him off with a life sentence in the quarries. And who've *you* got inside?"

"My master."

"Was he a disciple, or just denounced?"

"Neither. He just gave the man a night's lodging."

"That's enough. He's for the cross."

"But my master didn't even know the fellow!"

"All the same, he's for the cross."

"What should I do?"

"Get a clean cloth to wrap the body in, and a towel for the head, so you have it handy when he's taken down," he replied crossly.

The man from Ziklag told me there were several places in the Holy City where you could ask about prisoners. Better not to though if you didn't want trouble yourself.

The prison in the cellars of the Town Council was only for minor offenders awaiting minor punishments: the cutting off of a hand, scourging, or ripping the scrotum with a wild boar's tusk. The prison in the Tower of Antonia, known as the "Roman" prison, was for serious criminals accused of activities against the state, insults to the majesty of Rome or rebellion against the Emperor. Set aside for choice tortures and a refined death, they were often ordered to make public confession with penitent disclosures of all accomplices, so that their trial at Gabbatha was very entertaining, they say, even though everyone from the judge down to the witnesses knew the accused were lying. They were very surprised to find themselves condemned to death—and not acquitted, as they'd been promised, in compensation for good behavior in front of the judges.

The third prison, under the control of the Holy Sanhedrin, was for those in trouble with the ancient faith of the fathers and its laws. The priestly leaders questioned them to substantiate the accusations, then sent them to the procurator of Judaea for judicial action. In that prison were many learned reformers and counterreformers, false prophets and counter-prophets, self-confessed messiahs, heretics, wizards, sorcerers, fortunetellers and sectarians. The man from Ziklag said they were all lucky to be together at least and to be given a chance to defend their own teachings and to attack the teachings of others before competent authorities. The cries that came from the Sanhedrin prison proved that they were taking full advantage of their opportunity. Naturally, the man from Ziklag concluded, there were also the procurator's state prisons and the reception centers outside Jerusalem where criminals were collected for transport to distant mines within the empire, but there was no point in inquiring about them; the prisoners there had all been sentenced without appeal.

My master could only be in the municipal or the Sanhedrin prison, I thought to myself, as his case had nothing to do with the Roman majesty. The municipal prison was nearer, so I went there, but they rejected my basket because according to their records Lazarus of Bethany wasn't inside.

At the Holy Sanhedrin I had better luck. They took my basket, and after slicing the fruit, crumbling the bread, cutting up the meat and tasting my twenty-year-old wine, told me that everything would reach Lazarus of Bethany in perfect order.

For two days I carried packages from Bethany to Jerusalem, but on the third the guard told me my master was now in the state prison awaiting trial. I went to the procurator's office, but there they told me my master had been sent back to the Sanhedrin.

So off I went to the gates of the Sanhedrin. The guard didn't want to take my basket, but the Sadducee Nicodemus, who happened to be there, ordered him to hand over to me the corpse of my beloved master Lazarus wrapped in a waxed cloth. I broke out wailing and howling, but only about the bitter fact of Lazarus's death, never suggesting by tone or words—I hadn't taken leave of my senses yet—that the priests had killed him. Nicodemus begged me to give his condolences to Martha and Mary, till he could express them in person. Then he told me what had happened. As I swing my ax now, cutting down trees for burning on the Mount of Olives, I remember his words, as well as what my master told me after his first resurrection.

According to the Sadducee Nicodemus, the Holy Sanhedrin questioned my master concerning Jesus the Nazarene, and after finding him guilty of preaching the Christian heresy, sent him to Pontius Pilate. Pilate refused to pass judgment and sent him back to the Sanhedrin, after which he would have been released, since Nicodemus had interceded wholeheartedly on his behalf. But on the way from the governor's offices to the Council Hall, the stupid Lazarus had slipped away from his guards, and in his flight had fallen into the hands of the mob, who stoned him to death before the Sanhedrin guards could rescue him.

According to my master, after he had been interrogated, the priestly leaders sent him to Pilate. Disgusted by all these religious squabbles, Pilate freed him from the charge and sent him back to the Sanhedrin. On the way to the Council Hall, where he expected to be set free—he never even dreamed of running away, as he was much too old for that—he was stoned by a crowd of idlers, among them minor officials from the Sanhedrin, while his guards did nothing to protect him. He breathed his last—if he remembered correctly—in a remote blind alley of the suburb. The last thing he could recall seeing was a doctor's plaque obscured by black clouds, with Aesculapius's cock within a circle of gilded Greek letters.

Anyway, I hired a mule and took my master's battered body to Bethany, where relatives and friends had gathered to mourn him. The number of mourners wouldn't have been so great had the true cause of his death been known, but I'd advised his sisters to say that Lazarus had been trampled to death by a maddened mule while returning from a visit to his friend Nicodemus. His body was indeed badly bruised, but who could tell whether by hooves or stones the brand of punishment or the brand of chance? The blood was clotted around his mouth because his entrails had been smashed to pieces. After we had washed and dressed him according to custom, and had wept for him and sung his praises and recommended him to the Almighty, we buried him in the graveyard of Bethany.

That was how my master Lazarus died the first time.

These tough old olives are giving me a lot of trouble, but they'll burn like a torch. I have a few more trunks to fell and then my job's almost over. I'm walking back to the clearing where I hid the corpse, and the cries from Golgotha are sharper, like the distant screaming of frightened birds. That's because the evening shadows are gathering around the trees and the first drops of darkness are sprinkling on the heat with their freshness. That freshness revives the crucified and they again feel at one with their bodies. It's always been like that at the place of execution: moans in the morning, delirium at noon and moans again in the evening. Death doesn't choose any special time. Sometimes madness destroys the efforts of the heart to live; it hastens the end but doesn't make it easier.

I've been thinking a lot about that. Several times, especially lately, I've lain down in the bushes and tried to understand the secret of dying on the cross. Now I know that it's in the prolongation of the agony, in hope, in the stupid stubbornness of an incurable invalid who avoids every unnecessary movement and so prolongs the end. If, God forbid, I ever find myself on the cross, I know what I'll do: I'll thrash about and scream, twist and turn, spit out my gall and struggle with death. But that'll all be a fraud, because I'll only be helping death along. But I don't believe that Hamri Elcanaan will hang upon the cross. The Sadducees and Pharisees have no reason to persecute a Jesus-hater who would hand over those Galilean rascals to vengeance. No, it won't come to that. But if it should, I can only say: "Praise the name of the Lord that until now I have remained whole between the hammer and the anvil, between the Savior and those who refuse to be saved."

On the day after my master's funeral, after we had eaten the funeral cake, I decided to discuss with Martha the expenses of the funeral and the funeral feast. Mary was crouching by the sofa just as on that evening she had crouched at the feet of the Galilean, gazing vaguely at the camel dung which was smoking in a metal brazier because the month of Elul was colder than usual.

"We'll have to sell some cattle," I said, "though the prices are anything but good."

"Can't we borrow the money?" asked Martha.

"I dreamed a dream," said Mary.

I explained to the elder sister that the lenders might refuse us credit until they saw how we got along in business without Lazarus. Of course, we might lose because of the low cattle prices, but then we'd lose just as much because of the high interest rates.

"A very strange dream," Mary went on.

"Well, if that's the case," Martha agreed, "we'll sell some cattle."

"Tomorrow," I said, "I'll drive a herd to the market in Jerusalem."

"A dream as I've never dreamed before," Mary insisted, looking at us provocatively.

Martha replied harshly that she wouldn't have dreams at night if she kept busy during the day.

"You won't speak of my dream like that when I tell you what it was."

Martha snapped at her that dreams always came from the devil.

"My dream wasn't from the devil. Since when has the devil taken such good care of the glory of God?"

To put an end to the squabble, I asked Mary to tell us her dream.

"I dreamed of a landing place on a lake cooled by a grove of pines and olives, with vines and the quivering reflections of cities. A fishing boat whose rowers' faces shone like newly minted gold pieces was about to dock. A man stood at the prow whose face I couldn't see, for he was wrapped in a shining mist as if in a soft linen towel. The man climbed onto the breakwater and blessed the people, who fell on their knees and cried out: 'Hosanna to the son of David!' The waters rose in waves and a thunderous fanfare of trumpets commanded Israel to bring the morning burnt offering, though Israel was too far away to hear that holy sound except in my dream. Then a man dressed in rich garments asked him something. Accompanied by the worshipers who thronged about him like ants, he followed the suppliant, who hurried away, turning to see if the faceless man was still there. But the faceless man was pressed by the mob, and as he touched a woman whose skin, nose and lips were bleeding, they stopped bleeding. Then the faceless man paused in front of a house where women were wailing and minstrels were singing a dirge. He raised his hand and everyone fell silent and my dream became soundless, like life under water. He went into a room where a dark girl was lying on a bier. He took her dead hand and breathed on it, saying: 'Talitha cumi.' The girl revived, the people sang a hymn of thanksgiving, the mist cleared from the face of that man and I recognized him."

"Well," I said, "who was he?"

"Jesus the Nazarene, the Son of God."

"Damn him!" Martha yelled. "Damn him! He killed my brother!"

"But he can bring him back to life," said Mary confidently. "Or why would I have dreamed such a dream?"

I agreed that it would be honorable for the Galilean to repent and mend the consequences of his visit that night. Perhaps he wasn't as bad as he appeared, but that dream showed only what he'd like to do, not what he actually could. A beautiful but useless dream.

Mary agreed that her dream was a personal message from the Galilean, and its effect upon her was beyond all doubt. He who can send dreams, she said, is able to carry them out. Dreams foreshadow events, forecast the future, they are God's signs, which it would be blasphemous to disregard. Her dream was clear: the little girl was her brother Lazarus, who'd rise from the dead, and the figure breathing on his body and saying, "Arise, Lazarus my brother," was Jesus the Nazarene, the Son of God.

"No one will breathe on my master while Hamri is alive," I shouted. "No one has ever been born twice, except on the dread Day of Judgment. And then, little dreamer, remember that he—I don't care who his father is—and my good master will stand right in the shadow of the winged seraphim and look them in the eyes, while the Galilean's sins and the burden of Lazarus's innocent life are weighed in the balance."

I went out because the girl's infatuation made me mad. That troublemaker—that demagogue who in promising a new life destroys the old one; who foretells great happiness but takes away what little we already have; and offers us fairy tales instead of well-being—must belong to one of those Maccabean bands which in the name of freedom burn down the Roman storehouses, though they know that the only freedom they'll get is freedom for the Romans to crucify at least one innocent Jew for every sack of burnt flour!

Hoping that Martha would bring her crazy sister to her senses, I got to work on preparing the animals for sale the next day, and forgot all about Mary's foolish dream.

I must find a good spot for the pyre, in some thicket out of sight yet large enough so I don't set fire to the forest. This small pine grove seems hidden enough; I'll build the fire in the clearing in the middle of it. Yes, I can cremate him here. The trees will let enough wind through to make the bier burn, but not so much that the pines nearby will catch fire, too. First I'll bring the felled trees, then cut off the branches and trim them into logs a few yards long.

That'll make a fine pyre: a fierce little volcano to consume the body forever and leave it a handful of dust. That's what we agreed. "Not one tiny bone, Hamri, not the least bit of flesh, not a rotten tooth, not a hair or a nail should remain; not even the most amorphous shape which can be touched by a finger, not a fraction of the face which can be recognized, not an organ which can be made use of."

I, Hamri son of Elcanaan, bow before Him Whose Name I Dare Not Say, the One God, unseen and almighty, and swear that this will be so.

Martha, however, didn't accomplish what I had expected from her level-headedness. On the fourth day after the death of my master, just as I returned from the cattle market, that Galilean, that phantom of the night, that man with the double face of executioner and victim—the Son of God, the Redeemer, Jesus of Nazareth—showed up. A few dusty peasants with gloomy faces came with him. They looked like millers. They were, in fact—millers who ground human flour! Don't hurry, I thought, there's no flour for you here!

I stopped them from entering the courtyard.

"Who are you not to open your gates to him who comes in the name of the Lord?" one of them asked crossly. (Now I know it was Judas ben Simon, known as Iscariot.)

"I'm the servant of the dead Lazarus. Who's here in the Lord's name?"

"The servant of the living God."

"Then we'll talk in the servants' quarter," I said, hoping to keep them out of range of Mary's adoration. "There's an old Canaanite saying: show us your servants so we can see what sort of people you are. Hasn't your god ever heard that wisdom of the people?"

Realizing that this ill-omened Galilean was a charlatan, a usurper of the glorious role of servant of God, I knew that by insulting him I didn't risk challenging his powerful employer.

"Shouldn't the servant of a dead master be dead, too," said the Galilean's chief aide, "so his master can be recognized through him?"

The threat was clear. In the Holy Scriptures it would rank as a wise maxim discussing in allegorical form the virtues of devotion, but in conversation it had the harsher aim of scaring me.

"You heard Judas," one of the Galileans whispered. "Get away from that door, or they'll be reading the Kaddish over you in no time!"

I drew back. Unfortunately, before I could do anything—I had thought of calling the fieldworkers to chase that so-called band of salvation out of Bethany—the two sisters rushed out of the house. Mary, all flushed, had eyes for no one but Jesus, who was standing quietly aside, rather aloof and—why not admit it—irresistible. Martha, avoiding my reproachful glances, behaved reverently, like a player who doesn't believe in the game but won't let the team down.

The women had tricked me, but I didn't feel I should blame myself. How could I have suspected that Mary would win over her hardheaded sister and the Galilean return to Bethany because they'd invited him? How could I have suspected that those hallucinations of a flighty eighteen-year-old—unless she'd made up the whole resurrection dream to give herself importance or stage another meeting with her prophet—would open to a murderer that very gate we'd just carried his victim through?

"Lord," Mary cried out, "if you had been here my brother wouldn't have died!"

"By all the holy names of God he wouldn't have," I said. "This Galilean would have died in his place."

"Thy brother shall rise again, Mary," said Jesus mildly.

"We know that already, young man," I said. Martha pulled me by the sleeve and the disciples looked at us like we were pig shit. "He'll be up again at the resurrection, but I don't think your meeting with him will be particularly pleasant."

"I am the resurrection and the life: he that believeth in me, though he were dead, yet shall he live. And whosoever liveth and believeth in me shall never die. Believest thou this?"

"I believe," said Mary, who groveled in the dust.

"Blah, blah, blah!" I shouted. "What's wrong with you, sisters of Lazarus? Are you out of your mind? When burying your brother, did we stuff your brains in the coffin to amuse him for all eternity? Why do you let this Galilean fool you, this man wanted by the authorities, this man the doctors of the Sanhedrin have cast their anathema on?"

"Shut up, Hamri!" Martha snapped. "Will you give my brother life?" she asked Jesus in the same dry, businesslike tone she uses to the Bethany vet when our cattle are sick.

"Where have you laid him?" he asked, like a vet who'll promise nothing until he's seen the sick animal.

"It's been four days since the Kaddish was recited over him," said Martha. "Hamri will take you to his grave."

"Not me!" I shouted. "Hamri's no informer!"

"I'll do him no harm," said Jesus.

"You can't, even if you want to!"

"I can't because I won't, brother Hamri. I am love."

"What does it cost to try, you fool?" Martha hissed in my ear. "Maybe he is God, maybe he isn't. If he is, he'll raise Lazarus from the dead and I'll believe in him. If he isn't, he won't, and I'll denounce him to the Sanhedrin. It's as simple as that, and not worth squabbling about."

That settled it. Put down by the logic of a practical housewife, I went with all that murmuring salvationist gang through the blazing sun to the Bethany graveyard. The grave was covered by a rough stone on which my master's name and the year of his death were engraved in Aramaic script.

The Galilean ordered that the stone be raised and that we withdraw twenty paces from the cavernlike tomb. We would have done this anyway, because once the volunteers had raised the stone, the stink became intolerable—so dense that it formed a haze whose shadow was like a gigantic butterfly with fleshy, massive wings. In the Elul heat the shadow dissolved into a multitude of little stinking butterflies which hovered over the graveyard. Great as our respect was for the late Lazarus, we stuffed our handkerchiefs to our noses as if weeping. The Galilean breathed toward the cave and called out:

"Lazarus, come forth!"

Nothing happened. The Galilean called again:

"Lazarus, come forth!"

Again nothing happened. The Galilean called for the third time:

"Lazarus, come forth!"

Wait—what's that? A snake in the grass, or the quivering of a bird against the leaves? No, it must be the crackling of twigs, the rolling of stones. It's coming up the Jerusalem slope; behind it I hear the wailing and screaming from Golgotha. Some wild animal from the Judaean plain? No such luck—it's people. I hear the clop of sandals on the rock, the tearing of clothes by the bushes, curses and shouts in Aramaic. God Almighty, my corpse! What if they stumble on it?

I slip into a thicket and wonder what prayer to say for protection. There are no prayers against life, there's no ceremony to preserve death, no litany against resurrection! I can invoke death, but death is here already, closed in a hempen sack, secure, won. The trouble is: how do you prevent it from escaping?

I lament with David: "I will cry unto God most high; unto

God that performeth all things for me. He shall send from heaven, and save me from the reproach of him that would swallow me up. Selah, God shall send forth his mercy and his truth. My soul is among lions; and I lie even among them that are set on fire!"

Maybe it's only slaves from the sawmills, whom the overseers are driving back to their huts. Or excursionists from Jerusalem, with baskets of mushrooms. Or fowlers visiting their traps.

No, only son of Elcanaan, they're followers of Jesus—apostles, vultures! I hear the stony voice of Simon, son of Jonah, crying out: "He isn't here!" And the commanding voice of Matthew, the publican: "Nor here, either!" I hear the doubled voice of the sons of Zebedee saying I'm not where they're looking, and Judas Iscariot shouting that he hasn't found me in the olive grove.

All I can do is pray: Adonai, make a wall around me and my corpse, an impenetrable wall like the gates of death, like the inviolability of your face. Blind my enemies who circle round me like the dancers in the Temple, and let them circle in vain about my well-wrapped corpse, for it belongs only to you, Elohim, it's yours. (That's all I can think of, Lazarus my master. I've never been good at prayer.) Look on him, Hashem, how he's been made ready for paradise—virtuous, sealed. He's dead now: take away the branches, spread out his shroud, convince yourself he's dead, dead as the damned of Sodom in your salt shaker. He'll be the deadest dead man in your mortuary, if by just moving your little finger you keep these apostolic hyenas from dragging him out of the earth. In the name of all the burnt offerings and lambs sacrificed over many years, I, Hamri, servant of Lazarus of Bethany, implore you!

Thank you in the name of my master Lazarus: the apostles are going away, their voices are sliding down the steep slope toward Jerusalem, toward the shrill cries from the place of execution, which like poisoned lances stab the golden Temple, the navel of the city of God. Their voices are rolling like beaten hoops down the rocky olive thickets, and scratched open by the brambles, die away in the sleepy murmur of

Judaea. They're off the track, the man hunt has lost its quarry, the arrow of Bethlehem has missed! The bandits have gone away and peace has descended over my corpse in the olive grove, as soft as God's palm. Now I can strike the trees with my ax again and get going with the pyre.

As I was about to say, after the angry Galilean had summoned him for the third time, my master Lazarus came out of the tomb. But it wasn't a dignified appearance of a man summoned by God, or the regal striding forth of a man triumphing over death, or the rapturous escape of a liberated man who with dazzled eyes yearns to take in every bit of the world, or even the cautious stretching of a sick man who unexpectedly walks again and tests out his legs, or the joyous leaping of a man aroused from trance. On the contrary, his coming forth was ludicrous and sad, clownish and clumsy, preceded by groaning, wriggling, coughing, snuffling, spitting, and cursing in Aramaic. Tearing his shroud and shaking off the earth, Lazarus rose in jerks like a trampled reed. He straightened up, spewing fragments moist with saliva, and fat white worms which wriggled out of his flesh. From his teeth, his eyelids, his nails fell phosphorescent scraps of putrefaction. He crawled out of the shattered tomb with bluish, I'd even say frostbitten, limbs wrapped in stinking cloths, and with a rag about his jaws which rattled and coughed out little dusty clouds. He gazed vaguely at the Jews gathered around him and said:

"My God, it stinks here!"

That was how my master Lazarus rose from the dead. After greeting his sisters, he permitted me to kiss his hand and thanked the wonder-worker for his miracle—wholeheartedly, but with delicate reproach for the stoning in Jerusalem. Then he called upon the Jews present to celebrate his return to life. He took them to his house, where he first washed, put ointment on the bruises and changed into festive clothes. Then he sat at the high table, with Jesus of Nazareth and his gloomy followers in the places of honor. Dressed in a Galilean costume of seamless weave, with fringes representing the precepts of the Law, Mary crouched at Jesus' feet as on that evening when we first met him. This time we didn't reproach her for her adoration: the young man certainly knew his job, and her dream had proved effective.

James the son of Alphaeus, one of his apostles, told me proudly that we had just seen the third successful resurrection. The other two involved the twelve-year-old daughter of the leader Jairus at Capernaum and the only child of a widow at Nain. In his toast Judas Iscariot said that the resurrection of Lazarus was the personal victory of the Messiah over the Sadducees, who didn't believe in miracles or in life beyond the grave, and for whom the return of a man from the dead was as impossible as the lighting of a fire in water. Naturally he said that the Sadducees were sinners and heedless of the Law, and that it wasn't in their interest to arise on the Day of Wrath, for they had nothing to gain except a just punishment; but the Messiah had now shown that they'd have to rise and accept their sentences, as Lazarus had proved to them. That was a great, probably a decisive, victory in the battle for the New Testament, a triumph to which the flushed apostles drank in cups of sparkling Hebron wine.

Only their leader took no part in the feast of new birth, the songs of rejoicing, and the conversations about the difference between individual risings from the dead and that universal rising at the end of time. He was alone, even though he was sitting with us and Mary's raven hair like a coverlet of black silk warmed his bony knees. He was even more isolated than my Lazarus in his coffin. More isolated and unhappy.

As for the resurrected Lazarus, he drank, lauded the New Kingdom in the presence of its founder and sang psalms of thanksgiving. He sang in a dark, hoarse bass, somewhat soured by the wine and the grave, which echoed in the hall as in a covered bronze cauldron. But he never spoke about how he'd felt when dead, as if in those four lifeless days nothing memorable had happened.

We lauded the miracle until late afternoon. Then, at Judas's warning, Jesus excused himself—another task awaited him at Tekoah—and after blessing Lazarus, the guests and the table, left accompanied by his disciples. While they were only tipsy, we were drunk. We danced around the table and then in the courtyard—vertiginous dances under the sky which murmured below the scattered clouds and a somber sun that sharpened its rays on the grindstone of the Judaean heights. After a while we no longer knew what we were doing.

With my hatchet I dig out a shallow trench three feet long and two feet wide and place across it a few cedar logs as a base for the pyre. Then I arrange the other logs crisscross and between each layer spread a covering of brittle twigs, dry grass and dung which I collected nearby.

The first thing my master Lazarus saw when he had sobered up (he told me this after his second resurrection) was the worried face of the Sadducee Nicodemus. The face was falling from a dark height, then shooting up again, like a reddish balloon with an elderly face painted on it that danced up and down with Lazarus's panting breath, which blew it out and sucked it in just as he had breathed on awakening. Finally, the balloon stopped in mid-air. It hovered over my master and split open at the spot where the mouth was, first noiselessly and then uttering the old Hebrew greeting:

"Peace be with you, Lazarus of Bethany!"

He squirmed and twisted. The round ball of Nicodemus's head shook in time with Lazarus's convulsive starts, and swung in harmony with the ceiling which rose and fell like the glow on some distant window. First he recognized the face of the Sadducee in the brownish light, and then the brownish icy space of that same cell where he had awaited the sentence of the Holy Sanhedrin. He looked for the sign with the cock of Aesculapius encircled by Greek letters to prove he was alive, and not seeing it, thought that Jesus' miracle had lasted only long enough for a banquet in his honor, and that he was once again in his coffin: dead, but this time conscious of his miserable condition. What was Nicodemus doing in his coffin? Why was he blessing him?

"Peace be with you, Lazarus of Bethany!"

His head crackled, then burst. Above his parched lips hovered a sour, smelly cloud, like wine vapor over a barrel. His cramped, doughy limbs rested on a prison bench like broken staves, and water poured on his face from a jug Nicodemus was swinging casually.

"Peace be with you, Lazarus of Bethany!"

Lazarus sat up, babbling and belching. "The wine must have been too strong, sir! I hope that in my drunken state I didn't disobey any of the two hundred and forty-eight prohibitions of Moses? Or did I?"

The Sadducee reassured him: he'd been drunk, of course, but he'd done nothing improper, nothing to merit prosecution or anathema, nothing that came within the jurisdiction of the Sanhedrin.

"That's good to hear," Lazarus said dully, "but then why am I here?"

Nicodemus wouldn't talk about it. He offered Lazarus a cup of wine from the Sanhedrin cellar. A hangover is best dispersed by what causes it. At Nicodemus's signal, a guard brought a jug and two copper cups with silver incrustations representing grapes and a vine—the symbol of Israel. Nicodemus filled the cups, offered one to Lazarus and drank a mouthful himself before continuing:

"The soldiers must have tossed you on a mule and hauled you to Jerusalem like a sack. The guests who were celebrating your resurrection are still lying in the courtyard."

Lazarus became alert. Nicodemus had used the term resurrection, which the Sadducees denied. Today—half a millennium after Socrates, when the tamed stars obediently guide merchant ships instead of regulating destiny; when nature is no longer regarded as a terrifying picturesque fairy tale, and no longer read letter by letter like the alphabet of some foreign tongue, but rather as a primer of well-being; and when anatomists, cutting up corpses in their search for the Genius of death, find only cirrhosis of the liver or stone quarries in the bladder—today, belief in rising from the grave on the Day of Judgment is a folk superstition, inspired by misunderstood Biblical allegories and nourished by traditionalist quack scientists. Which under the state means only a temporary form of the existence of a people, an unforeseen collective vengeance for the disobedience in Eden, the inappropriate creation of bipeds abandoned by God who deny the right to pronounce ultimate punishments which are reserved for heaven alone, for the day of resurrection, for the wrathful hour of settlement between the Creator and his creations. The

Pharisaic doctrine was basically against the state, whether it referred to the administration of the Roman occupation or to some future independent Judaea. For, the Sadducees contended, if our decisions aren't valid in this world, but subject to revision in a worthier world to come, how can the authority of the state be preserved, as well as the reputation of its leaders and the purpose of a civilization which would become cross-eyed, with one eye harrowing the earth and the other gaping for signs from heaven? Though only a peasant-noble, Lazarus favored the doctrine of the Sadducees and had several friends among them. The most prominent was the Most Reverend Nicodemus Bar Tara, who did him the honor of resting in his olive groves on a particularly hot afternoon of the Jerusalem summer.

Lazarus was careful not to exasperate Nicodemus. The possibility of resurrection was as important to Nicodemus as the balance of prices between Canaan wheat and plantation goods was to Lazarus; one had based his existence on the idea of the impossibility of the renewal of life, the other on the stability of agricultural prices. What's more, his bruises still hurt. Though they had nothing to do with the dogma of resurrection, he was told, they were the consequence of a misunderstanding for which he alone was to blame. Lazarus felt he should be distrustful of anything that might cause a repetition of them. Until Lazarus had experienced resurrection, he had himself stubbornly denied it. Now he couldn't deny it any longer. That rolled-away tombstone, that filthy covering whose stench was still in his nostrils, the worms he had spat out—all that couldn't be erased so simply. His death had in fact been vouched for by the physicians, who diagnosed that he'd expired from loss of blood. That he was now alive was also a fact. So between these two facts—his death under the sign of the cock of Aesculapius, and his being alive here—there must also be a fact of his resurrection in the Bethany graveyard.

"Does anyone know I'm here?" he asked.

"Your sisters, and your servant Hamri," said Nicodemus, looking at a buzzing fly choking under the filthy ceiling.

Lazarus felt that it was kind of them to have at hand a

reliable man who would accompany him to Bethany when this sluggish conversation had ended. Now they'd ask how he'd felt when dead and he wouldn't be able to answer. But Nicodemus didn't ask, he toasted him instead.

"To your health, Lazarus of Bethany!"

Lazarus bowed humbly but didn't touch his cup, which glimmered faintly on the marble bench. He was on his guard yet his face, swollen by blows, showed a certain malicious indifference.

"When I mentioned your resurrection," said the Sadducee, "I meant of course that comic little episode in the village graveyard." He peered at Lazarus with mischievous protruding eyes which looked like corns. "I meant your return from coma, which the superstitious peasants interpreted as resurrection."

So that was it: Nicodemus didn't believe he'd been dead. Unconscious, yes, but not dead. If he'd been only comatose, his resurrection could be explained in accord with the teaching which denied it. Lazarus wondered how Jesus could have counted on such a possibility when preaching at Kishon in the valley of Esdraelon, many miles from Jerusalem, while he, Lazarus, had been expiring under the sign of the cock of Aesculapius. Jesus couldn't rely on catalepsy since he didn't know the circumstances, yet had agreed to restore him to life. He must have been sure of his powers, full of faith in resurrection undertaken by some divinity of its intermediary, God himself or his Son. But he said nothing.

"You yourself know that you weren't dead."

Lazarus still didn't answer.

"You couldn't have been dead. It's impossible for anyone dead to rise again. That's contrary to nature."

Lazarus agreed that resurrection was indeed contrary to nature. That tallied with his personal pro-Sadducean convictions and he could explain what had happened only as an incomprehensible slip in natural laws.

"It's good we agree," concluded the priest cheerfully. "That simplifies the whole affair."

Lazarus felt depressed. He might have expected the priests

of the Sanhedrin to be annoyed by the miracle, but he didn't believe they'd persecute him for it. He'd only been the subject, the most minor cog in its mysterious mechanism. Any corpse in Judaea would have been equally fit to serve the Galilean's aim. He hadn't wanted that resurrection, he hadn't arranged it or taken part in it except as guinea pig, and once it had taken place he couldn't, by Jehovah, have stayed in that shithouse of a grave just so a fine doctrine shouldn't be in doubt. He recalled Judas's malicious comment that the miracle at Bethany was Christ's personal victory over the Sadducees, the triumph of the New over the Old Testament. The apostle's words showed that Lazarus couldn't be blamed for his new life, that he was only a chance weapon in the war between the Christians and their adversaries.

"Unfortunately, my dear Lazarus," Nicodemus went on, combing his Hellenic beard with his fingers, "not everyone is as reasonable as you and I. The people of Bethany, let's say—those simple-minded Jews who were present at your so-called resurrection—believe that it really took place. They believe in that lousy Christ. What do you think?"

"Yes, I'd say they believe, Most Reverend. As eyewitnesses they can't do otherwise."

The Sadducee Nicodemus put aside the goblet, huddled his knees under his blatantly white priestly garments, leaned over the resurrected man, and asked deliberately and pointedly:

"What about you?"

Later my master explained to me what he'd been thinking, but I didn't understand any of it. He was a supporter of the Sadducees and yet was serving their adversaries. He didn't believe in resurrection, yet he'd had to endure it; he knew that he'd been dead, but he also knew that he couldn't have been. He lived only so he could sincerely disavow it.

"What about you?"

He couldn't give Nicodemus an honest answer because he hadn't been an eyewitness of the miracle, only its subject; he hadn't hovered impartially above the tomb, but had thrashed about and wriggled inside it, in his moldy resting place between the foul earth, the wood and the shroud, trying to extricate himself from the hole which he thought had yawned before him during some walk through Jerusalem just as he saw the cock of Aesculapius within a circle of Greek letters.

"What about you?"

"I don't believe," he replied almost arrogantly. "I wasn't an eyewitness."

Nicodemus sighed, waved his goblet, and, shaking it as if to disperse some comic vision, smiled.

"I really ought to keep twenty paces between us because aren't you dead and I a priest who respects the Law? But all this is sheer nonsense, my dear Lazarus, sheer nonsense"—now he became serious—"like those silly stories of winged angels who dash around heaven carrying God's messages, and whose fiery eyes are the stars, or those inane tales of a paradise where men enjoy their bodily happiness in garments which can't be torn, or a hell where they bathe in their ever-flowing blood. Nonsense! But dangerous nonsense! How many idiots neglect their property on earth, hoping that in heaven they'll have better opportunities? How many don't live or die like real men because they think that death only begins where in fact it ends? They believe that you've been resurrected. How are we to disillusion them? What are we to do, Lazarus?"

Nicodemus was sincerely upset; his aged face fell, crumpled like a papyrus scroll exposed to heat, while his dry hands dangled through the slits in his fan sleeves like two pale broken flowers.

"O Lord, what will happen to Israel?" he mourned, shifting from leg to leg like a wailing woman. "What will happen to the lovely land that was promised us? Hashem, Hashem, look graciously upon the seed of Jacob!"

Though he couldn't see any connection between his resurrection and the disasters which were to befall Israel, Lazarus felt sorry for him.

"What's wrong?" he asked.

Nicodemus pulled himself together, took a sip of the wine and spoke, stressing every word as if it were of bronze to be smitten on the anvil of Lazarus's attentive ears.

"It's all your fault, Lazarus. You're alive when by all the laws of nature we believe in, you should be dead. The trouble is that whenever these idiotic countrymen of ours meet you they'll shout: 'Look at Lazarus of Bethany who lay in the grave four days—he's now up and about! Fancy that!' Or: 'Here's Lazarus who was resurrected by Jesus of Nazareth!' And we'll live to hear them say: 'The Sadducees say there's no resurrection. What about Lazarus? The Sadducees are wrong and Jesus of Nazareth is right. He really is the Son of God!' I hope we understand each other, Lazarus. Because of you, they'll lose faith in us and scorn our teaching. The prestige we need to carry out our program for the renascence of the Jewish people will be destroyed. Then there's our Biblical mission, too: through the ancestor Abraham, Adonai-Elohim chose us on the Mount of Moriah to be his envoys, the bearers of light to this world. He didn't ask that we guard his invisible face from the gaze of the godless, but that we blind them with it. He commanded us as Isaac commanded Esau: 'Take thy weapons, thy quiver and thy bow, and go out into the mountains and hunt me some game.' The world is the quarry which Jewry will place at the feet of God. You know our ideal, Lazarus. Isn't it magnificent?"

Lazarus was in full sympathy with that ideal; he believed in it in his spare time—between studying the quotations of the Alexandria market and supervising his estates. Indeed, that was an ideal world worth living for.

"If it could be fulfilled," said Nicodemus, "then the descendants of Shem, Ham and Japhet would live as brothers, the wolves would guard the sheep, the snakes sleep with the toads and the cats suckle mice. The faith of Abraham, Isaac and Jacob would become the faith of all men, and the Promised Land a land for all."

Lazarus agreed with that, also.

"Yet you cast doubt on it all with your silly resurrection," concluded Nicodemus, standing up. The Sadducee didn't sound reproachful; he merely regretted the circumstances which had turned Lazarus, once the adherent of an ideal, into its mortal enemy. "Think about it, Lazarus!"

And Nicodemus departed, leaving behind him the yellow

scent of sandalwood, the squeaking of rusty locks and the threatening reverberation of his Jeremiads.

Left to himself, Lazarus went over the whole conversation to try to find some unstitched seam in that steel-hard girdle of casuistry which linked his resurrection to the downfall of Jewry and its international mission, but the girdle woven by Nicodemus's logic remained intact. Today it was clear to everyone that he wasn't to blame, but tomorrow who would care? No one would say: "Look at Lazarus, whom they resurrected," but "Look at Lazarus, who rose from the dead!"

On his next visit to the cell, Nicodemus ordered that a Sabbath supper be served to both of them. The food which couldn't be cooked on the day of rest had been kept hot in a hay box. The Sadducee was in good humor. He showed no intention of continuing the conversation where it had been broken off. On the Sabbath it wasn't proper to talk business.

"If I ask what I'm accused of," Lazarus asked humbly, "would that be regarded as business?"

"Who said you've been accused?" said Nicodemus, twisting a fig between his fingers before taking a bite. "You aren't accused of anything. In fact, you've been brought here simply to discuss some general principles endangered by your impossible resurrection."

Nicodemus didn't go on to discuss Lazarus's resurrection. True to the ban on business discussions on the Sabbath, he turned to Jewish history and dwelt enthusiastically on examples of heroic self-sacrifice by individuals for the cause of Israel. He quoted the Holy Scriptures with great learning, especially Genesis, Exodus, Numbers, Joshua, Samuel, Judges, Kings, and Chronicles, along with the major and minor prophets. He spoke of the ancestor Abraham, who when tested by God didn't hesitate to slaughter his son—though thanks to God's mercy it didn't come to that—to acquire his favor and establish his inheritance. He spoke with respect of David, the son of Jesse, who sacrificed himself for the people, entering into unequal contest with the Philistine Goliath of Gath. He spoke of Esther, who married the foreign emperor Ahasuerus to save her scattered people from extermination.

He spoke too of the prophets who, by announcing the truth, exposed their lives to torment, but preserved the alliance between God and Abraham and all the traditions of the seed of Jacob.

Nicodemus talked. One example followed another, one picturesque tale another. Lazarus made no comment but inadvertently, to himself, compared his position with that of Abraham, David, Esther and all the other workers for the glory of the homeland. As he was leaving, the Sadducee begged Lazarus to think over what he had said.

Lazarus did. It wasn't hard to grasp what was required of him. Despite the Sabbath Nicodemus had talked business and that business meant that he, Lazarus, must find some way of erasing what that troublemaker from Galilee had done by bringing Lazarus back from the dead.

But what could he do, even if he stifled his gratitude to him who had granted him life? Perhaps he could tell everyone that he had never really died, but had felt reluctant to shame and humiliate the wonder-worker. But that wouldn't quite do it either; even if Jesus hadn't restored him to life, by raising the stone from his grave he had kept him from dying. He'd have to sell his property and settle in some other province of Canaan where no one knew him and no one could regard him as an example of the Nazarene's powers. Or go to some foreign land, to Susa where they didn't know God, or behind God's back to the Iberian peninsula.

That would indeed be a great sacrifice and in its own way worthy of the historical forebears whom Nicodemus had cited, for Lazarus loved his native land and the rich valley under the dark wing of the Mount of Olives, the plain of Jehoshaphat where, surrounded by his plantations and stud farms, he could peacefully await the judgment on the enemies of Judaea. He loved the fat, heavy aroma of Judaea; the zip of the plowshare through the rich soil; the dusty daybreak in the ravines of the eastern plateau, torn by the lowing of cattle and the tinkling of the bells of the slaves getting up. He loved the hot stench of the stables and the grinding of the winch at the well; the dark gold reflection of the Great Temple at Har

Habayt, where the unseen God resided in black stone; the piercing rams' horns; the quick thudding of the pilgrims' mules; and the lazy braying of the donkeys weighed down by their panniers. He loved every detail in that juicy, multicolored, noisy picture which like a dark decorated scroll unwrapped before him as soon as he opened his eyes at dawn and looked toward the white mirage of the Holy City. He couldn't sacrifice more than that because he didn't possess more than that.

When Nicodemus visited him for the third time, Lazarus dejectedly offered to leave Bethany. He proposed that, before leaving, he kneel in the public square and reveal the truth.

"What truth?" asked the Sadducee.

"That I was still alive when that man resurrected me."

While praising his good intentions, Nicodemus expressed serious doubts about the effects of such a sacrifice. Eyewitnesses would rather believe their eyes than Lazarus's words. How could he convince them that he had lived for four days in the grave? Without food? Without water? Without air? After the stoning had drained the blood from his veins?

"No mortal could live in such conditions," said Nicodemus.

In amazement Lazarus asked if Nicodemus suddenly believed in resurrection. If he had to have been dead in the grave and was now alive, someone must have restored him to life.

"Don't be silly!" said the Sadducee, who suddenly grew unfriendly, harsh, even blunt. "I'm speaking for those fools you'll have to convince. Your idea, Lazarus, is worthless."

"How would it be," Lazarus ventured, "if I left Bethany for a while? I have relatives at Pella in Gilead, on the far side of Sheriat el-Kebir."

He intentionally used the Arab name for Jordan; he felt that if he uttered their own glorious Hebrew name he'd be committing sacrilege, in addition to abandoning the land given him in trust by Jehovah.

"And when you return to Bethany, they'll say: 'The man who was resurrected has come back again,' or worse still, 'The man whom the Messiah resurrected has come back.' No, no, that's no good, Lazarus!"

"I could sell my properties and move to the north, let's say to Galilee."

"Only to be greeted there with: 'Look, the man who was raised from the dead has come.' "

"Should I change my name? What if I move to some other place and take a new name?"

"So they can say: 'That's the man whom the Sadducees forced to change his name after he rose from the grave.' "

Lazarus raised his battered hands to heaven. He had exhausted every possibility except his own destruction. He was tortured, crushed, drained by these interminable discussions, prolonged through the dark, unvarying, impersonal hours in the prison, discussions in which not only Nicodemus Bar Tara took part but also the priestly judges, the officials and the theologians of the Holy Sanhedrin, alternating with one another those doctors of the Holy Sciences (according to the Law, they must be without physical flaw) who came and went, only to return again, always fresh in their immaculate, braided-gold robes, golden-tongued, tireless, pigheaded, piercing as augers, insensitive as bronze, always ready for argument and persuasion. He became numb, like a wooden stake which had grown into the bench, his bottom swollen, his eyes inflamed, and his eardrums cracked, shaking his empty head from left to right, left to right, left to right, without sleep or refreshment, listening to them as they tried to convince him in the tones of worried fathers that he must die once and for all, but this time in the highest interests, or shouted at him in prophetic rage, anathematizing his cowardly betrayal of principles, his conspiracy with the revolutionary Galilean and his newly usurped life. He was a great, hopeless sinner and only by responding with the highest sacrifice could he be saved in Jehovah's all-seeing eyes.

When Nicodemus came again to interrogate him, Lazarus wept bitterly.

"O Lord, my God," he wailed like Job in the land of Uz, "why didn't they shut the doors of my mother's womb and hide sorrow from my eyes? Why didn't I die in the womb? If only I'd never lived. If only I were dead!"

"That's the idea!" shouted the Sadducee. He beamed and

clapped his hands. Those two cups with the silver symbols of Israel appeared once again. He slapped Lazarus on the back, cheered him up: now that the fateful idea had come to him at last, everything would be settled quickly and happily.

"What am I supposed to do?" asked Lazarus, still a little apprehensive.

"Nothing special," the Sadducee replied, "just die all over again."

Flatly, Lazarus refused to die. It was all very well to die the first time (it had been, it appeared, a misunderstanding), but to die once again would be intolerable, no matter what his sin. Did the noble and erudite fathers know what it was like when the lungs exploded and consciousness crumbled as if the wheels of a cart had rolled over it? He was convinced that his patriotism would find a place in all schoolbooks, that he would stand side by side with the martyrs of prophecy, and that men would say: "That was Lazarus, whom the false Messiah could not resurrect, so strong was his faith!" But he simply couldn't live through death once again. By comparison, resurrection was a nursery rhyme.

"No, Hamri," the master told me later, "the proposed redemption far exceeded my sin. The weight of sacrifice—all honor to Abraham, David and Esther—was way out of proportion to the offense of reincarnation. I refused to die, Hamri! I refused even to discuss the possibility!"

While these learned gentlemen were interrogating my master, I was lying in the next cell in the Sanhedrin prison, and they treated me well enough. On the nineteenth day of the month of Elul they took me into the courtyard where they told me that the Holy Sanhedrin would judge my master Lazarus for offenses against the faith of the fathers and that I must attend as a witness. They led me into the hall of the Supreme Court. Except for me, the seventy judges and the Av Beth Din, Daiaphas, who presided over the Council, there was no one in the hall. Naturally, there were also my master and his guards.

Though my master seemed tired, he was alert and walked with the firm step of a righteous man. His eyes avoided the real objects of the courtroom and searched in some invisible space for his favorite faces, while his bearing had in it something foolishly blissful, an abstract saintliness. He was fettered by a leaden chain and round his neck he wore the symbolic marks of his blasphemous crime, but he was escorted by only two unarmed officials of the Sanhedrin. Clearly the high priests didn't regard him as a hardened sinner; this humiliating procedure was a mere formality, though obligatory. This helped explain his self-confidence.

The first to speak was a rabbi who enumerated Lazarus's misdeeds. In a low, impersonal voice he explained that Lazarus, son of the deceased Zacchaeus of Bethany, by profession a landowner and cattle breeder, was accused before the Great State Council of the Jewish people of having given hospitality, on the seventh night of the month of Elul, to the self-appointed wonder-worker Joshua ben Joseph of Nazareth in Galilee, though he knew this man was wanted as a serious offender against the faith of the fathers; that Lazarus had embraced his heretical teachings and zealously propagated them among the local residents, among whom he enjoyed the respect due to a wise and wealthy man; that while professing an orthodox doctrine he had insinuated himself into the congregation of the Unwavering Righteous Ones, where he worked for the benefit of Joshua ben Joseph; and above all that in conspiratorial agreement with him he had staged his so-called resurrection in the Bethany graveyard with the aim of winning for the erroneous Christian teaching the greatest possible number of followers. The evidence for that accusation, said the prosecutor, consisted of sworn statements from eyewitnesses and the voluntary confession of the accused—a confession which was particularly serious because of his social standing and the perfidy with which he abused it in order to penetrate the faith of his fathers and to assist the spread of the false faith of the charlatan prophet from Galilee. Therefore, the prosecutor ended, on the basis of the indictment itself and not from mere human malice and prejudice, he recommended the accused Lazarus of Bethany for the exemplary punishment of the Holy Sanhedrin.

The indictment was drawn up to cover the most serious offenses, each of which individually involved exclusion from the religious community, public stoning and an anathema pronounced from the balcony of the Great Temple. Even so, I wasn't worried, for I knew my master was innocent; with a single word of defense he'd refute all these senseless imputations. Imagine my amazement and sorrow when I heard the first exchange between the Av Beth Din, Caiaphas, and my master:

"You've heard the list of your sins, Lazarus of Bethany," said the high priest. "Do you plead guilty?"

"Guilty, Your Reverence."

"Do you repent of the sins you've committed?"

"I do, Your Reverence."

"Tell us how it came about that you offered shelter and hospitality to that sinner from Nazareth."

"I'd professed his doctrine for a long time," Lazarus replied calmly, "and for a long time I'd believed in him as the Son of God, who brings us the mercy and forgiveness of him against whom our ancestors sinned."

"Yet you publicly adhered to the Sadducees and shared their doctrine?"

"My official adherence to the Sadducee party was a mask behind which I concealed my real activities for Christ and the Christians."

"What were those activities?"

"First, the offenses in the indictment: spreading the new faith among the Jews; informing Joshua ben Joseph of the intentions of the Sadducees concerning his person; and sheltering his persecuted adherents. But also other misdeeds which the indictment has magnanimously overlooked: regular infraction of all the sacred prohibitions; neglect of the customs and regulations of the Torah; and sowing distrust of the doctors of the Sanhedrin, who preach respect for such prohibitions and customs."

The priest who had enumerated all my master's misdeeds rose and said that this fresh revelation of offenses should be added to the list, but that he wouldn't ask for any special punishment, because the penalties already incurred exceeded the possibilities of mortal man. On the other hand, he hoped that the voluntary admissions of Lazarus of Bethany wouldn't mitigate the punishments originally demanded, though such mitigation would be of no advantage to the accused; whether condemned to the same death three, five or seven times, he could only die once.

This statement made a great impression on the court, and though I knew that my master could put forward serious objections to it, he didn't muster up courage to mention a single one. To all the questions he gave resolute and always penitent answers, as if competing with his judges in digging his own grave.

Now it was the high priest Alexander who questioned him: "On several occasions you sheltered disciples of Joshua ben Joseph under your roof?"

"I did, Your Reverence."

"And on the night of the seventh day of the month of Elul, you concealed the man himself?"

"I did, Your Reverence."

"Did you know who he was?"

"I did, Your Reverence."

"Were you aware that you were committing a crime?"

"Your Reverence, at that time I was a Christian. For me it would have been a crime not to conceal him."

"And now?"

"Now I'm no longer a Christian. I've realized my error and repent of my sins."

My master a Christian? What was he talking about? Had he been chewing mandragora? What kind of masquerade are you watching, son of Elcanaan, I thought to myself, desperately signaling him to pull himself together.

Meanwhile my master described more or less accurately how Nicodemus Bar Tara had visited him, how he had disclosed his activities to Nicodemus, how he had been arrested and interrogated, and finally how he'd been stoned in a Jerusalem alley.

"Who stoned you, Lazarus of Bethany?" asked the high

priest Annas, "since you hadn't been sentenced to stoning?"

"The people, Your Reverence."

"Why? Why did they stone you when, as you say, you were doing your duty in the service of God's justice?"

"Because without knowing it, I was serving Satan, Your Reverence. By bowing before the false prophet I insulted both God and you, his earthly servants. The people recognized that evil service in my face."

"The people recognize everyone by his face," said Caiaphas. "It's hard for the man who turns his face from the people, for he will know neither beginning nor end and his dust will be given to the winds."

"Amen," chanted the Sanhedrin.

The high priest Jochanaan began to question Lazarus: "What happened when the people's stones struck you?"

"I fell, Your Reverence. I fell, battered."

"And were you dead?"

"No, Your Reverence. Half-dead maybe, but definitely not dead."

"You say you weren't dead, Lazarus, son of Zacchaeus. Good. Then why did you allow them to bury you alive and read the prayers for the dead over you?"

Lazarus replied that, half-dead as he was, it had occurred to him that, since the news of his stoning would spread far and wide, he could use his desperate situation for the benefit of the Christian faith.

"I informed the Savior through my servant Hamri that to all intents and purposes I was dead, but really lying alive in the grave, waiting for him to 'restore' me to life. That would be the best proof that the Sadducees, who deny resurrection, are wrong. Furthermore, my so-called resurrection would confirm the divine nature of Joshua ben Joseph, because obviously such a miracle could be performed only by someone with authority over the mysteries of life and death."

I don't want anyone to think that what I've been saying is in any way a reproach, God forgive me, to Lazarus—who alone knows what they did to him, or what they forced him to say. But for the sake of truth I must tell you that the officials of the Sanhedrin, at a sign from Nicodemus, at that point took me into a nearby room and beat me almost to death. I've no idea what Bethany names I may have blurted out, or why.

"So there was no true resurrection?" said Caiaphas.

"No, Your Reverence. It was a fake."

Then the Av Beth Din solemnly concluded: "There is no resurrection from the dead, nor has there ever been, nor will there ever be from now until time immemorial."

"Amen!" chanted the Sanhedrin.

The rest of the trial, insofar as I could follow it after my beating, proceeded with incredible haste, assisted by my master. Thanks to the scope of his confessions, every other evidence became superfluous. They didn't even demand a statement from me, which would have placed me in quite a predicament, but instead expelled me into the courtyard to await the outcome of the hearing. There couldn't be much doubt about it. The Court servants soon told me that he'd been sentenced to expulsion from the community, public stoning and anathema from the balcony of the Great Temple. The sentence was to be repeated in all Jewish places of worship. All punishments must be carried out without delay, because God gets impatient if a hardened sinner is allowed to stay alive. To establish the continuity of the official and legally recorded death, the sentence was to be carried out at the very place—under the sign of the cock of Aesculapius surrounded by Greek letters—where Lazarus had given up the ghost the first time.

The procession escorting the condemned man moved along the usual route to the ill-famed valley of Hinnom. It passed through crooked little streets which echoed with the deafening hammers of the smiths, the monotonous whirring of whetstones, the resounding blows of coppersmiths' hammers; with the raucous rasp of cloth being torn in the booths of the merchants from Tyre and Sidon; with the squeaking clangor from the workshops of the glassblowers, whose uncongealed glass bubbles still wet condensed the daylight into sunny contours of varied shapes and colors; and above all the confused turmoil of the bazaar, like the gurgle of the tide through the uneven and discordant voices of the sea strand. The officials and the Sanhedrin guards were followed by a few ruffians of ferocious appearance. They were soon joined by several more. When the procession had reached the street of the potters it was accompanied by a large mob grumbling its dissatisfaction at seeing this sinner against the Torah and the Law still alive—this accomplice in a ruse devised by the evildoers of Israel to humiliate the Jewish God and his chosen representatives.

We found ourselves in that Godforsaken blind alley where Lazarus had died the first time. In the distance the cock of Aesculapius shone like a tiny sun. I wouldn't say that my master was unaware of his danger. On the other hand, he looked as if he enjoyed it and provoked it by his arrogant prophetic bearing, for his pace quickened as we came closer to the ill-omened sign.

Then the first stone, thrown by the trained hand of a soldier-slinger, hit the master. The skin split on his temple. His bare knees furrowed the ground as he raised his bony hands to heaven in an incomprehensible ecstasy, as if evoking the approving smile of the Supreme Observer. Though streaming with blood, his face was lustfully enjoying the tortures, as if he'd chosen and approved them, and as if the maddened lynchers served some hidden passion of his, and weren't the Sadducees' hirelings.

"If Lazarus lives, Israel will die!" he shouted under the hail of stones. "If Lazarus dies, Israel will live! Long live Israel!"

He breathed his last, as at the previous stoning, under the sign of the cock. He seemed much astonished as if, despite such eloquent circumstances, he hadn't expected to die.

I loaded his corpse on a mule, covered it with a borrowed blanket, and took it to Bethany. At night, stealthily, with the help of only Martha and Mary, I buried it in the same grave, in the same coffin and in the same shroud, closing the tomb with the same stone which, rolled away, was resting in the dust, and on which his name and the year of his death were written in Aramaic.

The pyre's ready at last. Not imperial, but not beggarly either. I scatter twigs on top so they'll catch the flames evenly. I dig out the corpse, prop the shroud on a few crossed poles and stretch it over the bier. I do this so the smoke won't spread over the forest and betray me. I place the bare body on the logs, with feet turned toward the Jerusalem palace of Jehovah, and quickly sprinkle inflammable tow over it.

We carried out the second burial at night, as I said, on the nineteenth of Elul. On the twenty-second of Elul, also at night, just as we'd eaten the second funeral meal, Lazarus stumbled in, wrapped in his stinking shroud. Turned toward the hearth, his face revealed grief, panic and anger. Exhausted, breathing hoarsely like a punctured bellows, he lay on the divan while I tenderly bandaged his wounds with balm. I suspected what had taken place.

"Jesus?" I asked. "Jesus the Nazarene?"

"Dog shit!" he hissed. "Filthy, leprous swine!"

And out of his twice-stoned, shattered chest burst his bitter grief over the vain sacrifice he'd made for the future of Israel, his dread fear of a third dying if the Sadducees found out, and the still more unbearable terror of a third resurrection. He feared too that those who denied resurrection would kill him a fourth time, and if that man revived him and they destroyed him again, that he'd have to die countless times as long as Jesus and Nicodemus, their followers and their followers' descendants lived, or their ideas persisted in the hearts of men, always, always, to eternity and beyond.

When he'd finally vented his fury, I asked why this second time he'd died voluntarily and to all appearances even happily. Why hadn't he resisted any sacrifice which involved having to die again? And what had they done to him to win him over, since for them his consent was not essential—they could have killed him whenever and however they chose—unless he'd been ordered to deceive the people?

"You see, Hamri," he said, breathing on the contusions caused either by beatings before death or by decomposition after it, "I did resist having to die again—not because I didn't understand the social justification of my death, but because I was afraid of dying. I'd already experienced one death and was now asked to do it again, like a student who hasn't learned his lesson. It was a hopeless situation. Then Nicodemus proposed a solution: I was to confess my guilt before the supreme religious court in such a way as to satisfy the immediate needs of Sadducean policy, and in exchange the death sentence pronounced against me wouldn't be carried out. Or rather, it would only apparently be carried out. In short, it would be a performance. I agreed. I thought the illusion would have a double benefit: the people would preserve their soul and I my head. You heard how I behaved before the court and you saw what happened after that. When I fell for the second time below that damned sign of the cock of Aesculapius, I was barely aware that they'd really killed me and that like a perfect idiot I'd died again. The torments of dying restored my senses, but it was too late. I was dead for the second time."

"What was it like?"

Lazarus didn't reply. Like an infested and discarded garment, the past no longer meant anything to him. He only cared about the future, or rather that limited part of the future concerned with his next death and resurrection. It was certain that the Sadducees wouldn't allow him to live, and that the Christians wouldn't allow him to die. He had become the magnificent battlefield of the struggle for the salvation of the world.

Then I asked him:

"And why did you involve me, master? Why did you lie?"

"Did I lie? I don't remember." Then he took my hand and said: "Hamri Elcanaan, servant and friend, tonight, on returning from the grave, I thought my situation over. It's worse than Job's because it can't improve except by death. I can't escape the Sadducees, but I might fool Jesus the Nazarene. I have a plan. I need a man devoted to me to carry it out. There's no one but you." He gripped my hand convulsively. "Promise you'll do everything I ask of you."

I promised. But that wasn't enough: he demanded that I

swear by the most terrible oaths, taking the name of the Lord in vain. Only then did he tell me what he wanted me to do.

"But master, that's mortal sin! A sin for which there's no pardon in heaven!"

"Let God be my witness that the sin will fall on my head! Whatever the punishment, it can't be worse than the torments I'm now enduring."

The crickets are chirring, the heavens grow gray like white smoke, the trees bow down their cool shadows to the earth. It's time to light the pyre. I face the Great Temple of Jerusalem, whose spires keep the birds from soiling God's residence, and in a clumsy monologue (there's no ceremony of forgiveness for the sin I'm about to commit) I try to prepare heaven for my master's surprise: his coming to it through flames in the Roman fashion, and not through the earth, as laid down for the chosen people as long as they've called themselves Hebrews.

"O Lord of Hosts," I say, bowing toward the Temple where the voice of thunder resides—the only thing by which our God becomes more or less recognizable. "O Lord, I am Hamri Elcanaan, your slave and the servant of Lazarus of Bethany, whose earthly remains, if you can recognize them, are on the wooden bier behind my back. Perhaps this isn't the right time to bother you, for the sun is setting and you're probably worn out by the prayers and praise from the places of worship where the services have only just ended. My excuse is time. The master's in a hurry and I am, too, because I'm bound by my oath only a little more than by my love of vengeance. Hear me, O Lord! I won't believe that you're a splitter of hairs as our wise priests, theologians and writers say, for they imagine you in their own likeness, according to their petty souls besieged by those six hundred and thirteen regulations and their countless legal progeny, by which our duties to one another have been ordered ever since the meeting on Mount Sinai. Even if corpses bear on the soles of their feet visible burns from fire or chill winds, drops of water or traces of muddy earth, which show the route they've taken to appear before you, I doubt if you'd notice them. I judge that your shining eye—or whatever formless thing you possess—is so gigantic that it sees nothing smaller than the sun which, reflected in it, must appear like a burning mote stirred up by the blizzard of the universe. If your eyes weren't so huge, so long-sighted that you don't notice what's right under your nose, long ago you'd have undertaken something against the Romans who oppress your people and trample down Edom, or at least you'd have halved the taxes, the only honor that we in their filthy empire still possess. Long ago you'd have seen how confused the cattle market is and noticed that gelded bullocks will soon be cheaper than circus tickets. You'd have noticed that it's better for us to sow tares than wheat, because they confiscate the wheat, but we sell the tares for setting fire to the crosses our masters crucify us on."

Restrain yourself, Hamri, I tell myself, you won't get anywhere by reproaches and complaints.

"You must know that your Son, or that being who's called your Son, is now wandering through Canaan, making our unbearable misfortunes still greater by bringing us salvation unasked. Lazarus, son of Zacchaeus, of Bethany, whom I heartily recommend to you, was one of his victims. I assume he isn't the only one. I don't know if you've heard of a certain Mesezeveilo, a mute from Jerusalem, whose tongue he loosed just in time for him to suffer because of it, or of a certain madman from Dothaim who killed himself as soon as he acquired enough reason to see what the world's really like. Of all these, my master fared the worst. Only to mock the Sadducees and prove the possibility of resurrection, which they deny, the Messiah arranged for my master to die three times in the worst of torments. Do you remember, Lord, what you said to Adam when you were angry with him about some apples from your estate? You said: 'In the sweat of thy face thou shalt eat bread, till thou return to the ground, for out of it thou wast taken: for dust thou art and unto dust thou shalt return.' Didn't you decide that every man should die only once? And wasn't that command valid even for Methuselah, who didn't have to die five times to survive for one hundred and eighty-seven years before he begat Lamech? But your little Son, your magnificent half-descendant, doesn't think that way. He thinks that man is as tough as a Samarian mule, and that he can be snuffed out as many times as is asked of him—every day, if necessary, or every blessed hour. And so, O Lord, whenever the Sadducees killed Lazarus to prove that there's no resurrection, your Son restored him to life, thereby showing that there is a resurrection, and each time his torments and fear were greater. Not even the sinless Job could have suffered as much as Lazarus. Above all, he wasn't conceited, as Job was, nor was he eager to win fame as a vampire. Naturally, neither the Sadducees nor the Messiah paid any attention to his personal wishes. They are chronic idealists: they don't care what their thousand-year-old kingdom costs, but only who establishes it and in what way. It looks like Lazarus must die and be restored to life in order to die and rise again from the grave, until all accounts are settled between them, and you, brother, know that never happens. There are no clean accounts; sometimes the balance is achieved, only to be exchanged for fresh figures and fresh misunderstandings. He had to defend his own death, to disappear forever. So he implored me and bound me by oath that the next time he died I'd burn him in the Roman manner: that's what I'm preparing to do. With pleasure. When his body isn't around any more, Jesus will have no one to raise from the dead, and the Sadducees no one to kill, unless they get hooked on some other wretch. But that'll be some other servant's problem. You see, my Lord, I know that this pyre is a mortal sin, but there's no other way. Look, your Son's disciples are scrambling all over the Mount of Olives hoping to find him and take him to their Teacher, so he can restore him to life once again, and in this very forest. Meanwhile, soldiers of the Holy Sanhedrin are prowling about to kill him yet again, if that should happen. Even so, O Name That May Not Be Spoken, your world isn't the circus at Antioch—at least, it shouldn't be. So accept the soul of my good master Lazarus of Bethany, which Hamri ben Elcanaan sends to you through the flames as if through the earth according to the Law, and don't, I beg you, make a molehill into a mountain.

He's suffered a lot. Don't increase his suffering, O Lord, but shield him from evil and from life."

I hear the shrill announcement of the rams' horns. Jerusalem is saying "Amen" to its God and I take the beastlike bellow of the sacred instruments to mean a higher approval to go on with my cremation. I kiss what's left of my master's cheek and light the pyre at all four corners so it'll blaze up quick.

Forced out by the snakelike rustling of the smoke and the darting tongues of flame, a fledging bird, bare as my own good Lazarus, rushes out. Perhaps it's his somber soul, rushing heavenward.

My master was right to fear that the Sadducees wouldn't be reconciled to his second resurrection. The very next day the soldiers of the Sanhedrin barged in. No discussion this time, no apologies or beating about the bush. They grabbed him, thrashed him with their spears and dragged him to the Holy City. With the approval of the procurator of Judaea, they nailed him to one of the Golgotha crosses, hoping that this way of dying would nullify the power of the Savior.

I spent that day in the bushes, not far from the place of execution. My master breathed slowly, evenly, seemingly unaware of the moaning that reached him from the neighboring crosses. Of all the condemned, he was the most experienced in dying—indeed, the most experienced of all men, the only one allowed by death to speak of it from personal experience.

In a nearby thicket lay two of the apostles: Matthew and Judas Iscariot were to let their Teacher know the hour of Lazarus's death, so the Savior could come and raise him up again. My efforts to get rid of them were futile.

"This isn't a question of your master," said Judas. "It's a question of the highest principle. Resurrection is possible, practicable and natural, and not impossible, impracticable and unnatural as the Sadducees claim. Besides, resurrection is indispensable if any other earthly act is to have meaning. Our New Kingdom is based on this—the good tidings we bring you. We can't allow the sufferings of a single man to affect us, when the fate of millions is at stake. You must understand."

I had to be really cunning here. I said that I understood what they were about, even though I didn't. I said I'd hand over Lazarus's body to them as soon as the guards gave it to me. The presence of scouts from the Sanhedrin helped me. I said I was afraid the Sadducee hirelings would see through our plan unless the apostles kept away from Golgotha. They agreed. It wasn't pleasant to watch my master dying; his death was the longest and most painful of them all. On the dry field of Golgotha he moaned gently for hours and his bloodshot, wide-open eyes called on me desperately, passionately, persistently. At about midday the merciful guards finally broke his legbones with ax blows. Soon after that he went.

The guards handed me the bits of bone and torn flesh which was all that was left of Lazarus. I jammed them into a sack, put it on my back, and instead of looking for the apostles left in the opposite direction.

The apostles and the mercenaries of the Sanhedrin quickly got the point and started a man hunt at once. Loyalty to my master gave me strength to escape and here I am. In the half-light of the Mount of Olives, in the fortress of its branches, I rapturously watch his body smoulder and crackle in the flames which are destroying everything that could be made alive again or killed again. I leap around the pyre. Like the Levite in the sacred dance I render the last honors to the great martyr, Lazarus of Bethany.

His body is consumed by the flames. With my ax I carefully pound his bones into a fine powder. An east wind has begun to blow, so I let it scatter the powder discreetly to the four corners of the earth.

Up there on the small, darkened height the fledgling bird, the reflection of Lazarus's soul, hovers, as if it hasn't had enough of earthly suffering. And grieves for more.

THE TIME OF DYING

But all this was done, that the scriptures of the prophets might be fulfilled.

Matthew 26:56

Death at Hinnom

> Then Judas, which had betrayed him, when he saw that he was condemned, repented himself, and brought again the thirty pieces of silver and he cast down the pieces of silver in the temple, and departed, and went and hanged himself. Then was fulfilled that which was spoken by Jeremy the prophet, saying, And they took the thirty pieces of silver, the price of him that was valued, whom they of the children of Israel did value.
>
> Matthew 27:3, 5, 9

I AM Jehuda ben Simon, known as Iscariot, and to the brothers in Christ as Judas the Stickler and Judas, Let-it-be-fulfilled, the youngest of the Twelve, but the eldest after God the Son in earthly suffering and heavenly glory, who to redeem Israel from sin betrayed the only-begotten Son of God, Jesus Christ, the vision of my eyes, the dream of my sleeping, the cry of my secret being and the beating of my heart, for thirty pieces of silver to the high priests Annas and Caiaphas to crucify him, so that the prophecy of Isaiah may be fulfilled: "He hath borne our griefs and carried our sorrows." To make sure not a single letter of the prophecy would be unfulfilled or overlooked, I took notes in Aramaic in the treasurer's account books day after day, hour after hour, of the month of Nisan of the fifteenth year of the reign of Tiberius Caesar, after we left the wilderness of Ephraim to come to Jerusalem for the Passover, inserting them among the records of expenses for daily needs, alms, clothing, food and donations from converts and unknown benefactors who will be praised and remembered until the end of time for what they brought to the Savior, his Almighty Father, and to you, my brothers still unborn.

In the name of the Father and of the Son and of the Holy Ghost. Amen.

For thirteen robes (washing)	*1 as*
For outlay for the festival of Purim (debt)	*1 drachma*
To the cripple Jehoved at the northern gate	*1 as*
For olives	*3 mites*
Expenses for the first of Nisan: total	*1½ drachmas*

The seventh day in Ephraim, the twenty-seventh day in Ephraim, the hundred and twenty-seventh day in Ephraim. What term has been set for Ephraim, O Lord? How many days must we stay in Ephraim?

Judas calls on the prophets in vain; Judas reads Isaiah, Zechariah, the Twenty-second psalm of King David in vain; the most farsighted among the farsighted strives in vain, that the Lamb of God be prepared in time for the holy slaughter.

He's silent. The Eleven are silent.

Ephraim dreams on its dry, rocky Judaean plain. The children of Jacob fatten lambs for the Passover. Here you aren't afraid that God's spying on you from his heavenly ambush. Here you don't think about the world which, laden with sin, is waiting for the cries from the place of execution that bring salvation.

Instead of holy cries of liberation, you hear God snoring. Glory to Ephraim, glory to his Son; the apostles sleep soundly.

We're into the month of Nisan and we're still in Ephraim. Passover will have ended and we'll still be in Ephraim. How much is given to that sleepy Ephraim, O Lord?

I ask you to listen. Judas hears the wailing of the prophets, the lament of Jeremiah over Israel, he sees in the red skies shame instead of wind, in the swelling clouds tears instead of spring rain. Where is the Son of God? Why doesn't he come? Why does he hesitate?

Judas speaks continually of their mission in vain, he describes in vain the glory that awaits them. A new kingdom to be conquered by the lanky shadow of the cross, by the harsh rattle with which, as in a mother's labor pains, the world is to be born again.

He's silent. The apostles are silent.

Forgetful Ephraim snores near Gilead, which doesn't know God. In its icy caverns the exiled gods burst out laughing. Great idols, little idols, Molochs and Baals, all the Golden Calves bellow for revolt. Their time is near, they can stretch out and fumble at the sleepers of Ephraim. Since there are no victims, there'll be no salvation and no danger from a monotheistic kingdom. They can pack their trunks for the return, they can apportion their spheres of worship and reveal their beastly features in the dreams of the sleepers.

If the Scriptures aren't fulfilled this Passover, we'll have to wait another year until the next one, without knowing whether, despite our waiting, he'll disregard it again. And this is the third year of waiting. Three times before Passover we've set out to visit Jerusalem, starting from Jericho, from Hebron and finally from Sephardic Lydda, and all three times we've returned dejected, for the Lord said that our time hadn't come yet. When is our time? Which year has been chosen for suffering, Jehovah?

When Judas quotes Isaiah, the Master is silent, nothing falls from his lips. When Judas reminds, reproaches, and persuades him, he's silent again, his sandal briskly furrowing the earth. When Judas implores him, he goes away silently.

Judas then turns to the apostles, those chosen by the chosen one, because they're the accomplices of his mission, sharers of his booty, heirs of his torments. Surely they'll understand. But they too are silent. They too go away. No one listens to Judas, no one bothers about Judas. Finally Matthew the Publican in a heart-to-heart chat urges me to devote myself to the common purse, to the accounts and my job as treasurer, and not to tell the Son of God what to do. He knows that himself; the Lamb knows when the spit is being set up for it.

"If my Master knows," I say, "why does he delay? Why doesn't he hurry to Jerusalem? Soon they'll begin to mix the unleavened bread, and before long the owner will look for blemishes in the sacrificial lambs, so that those with even one of the seventy-five faults will be excluded from the ritual. At that point only healthy, clean, innocent lambs without blemish can be in the sheepfold."

"We've got plenty of unblemished lambs in Judaea," replies Matthew.

"But God has had enough of their blood. Didn't Isaiah, the son of Amoz, say: 'To what purpose is the multitude of your sacrifices unto me, O Israel? saith the Lord; I am full of burnt offerings of rams, and the fat of fed beasts; and I delight not in the blood of bullocks, or of lambs, or of he goats. Bring no more vain oblations; incense is an abomination unto me.' "

The Lord of Hosts doesn't crave the blood of rams; Adonai demands his own blood, the flesh of man from his own body. He demands the death rattle of his creative breath to be sacrificed for our transgressions.

I take Peter ben Jona aside and tell him that for a long time, ever since the time of the prophecies of Isaiah, the Lord has been disgusted with the Passover as the Israelites celebrate it. He ignores my remark and instead asks humbly how much we have in the common purse. He's met a poor countryman of his and would like to help him. To hell with earthly beggars when the Lord himself has to beg in order to get a decent sacrificial victim from us! Didn't I tell you, Cephas, that heaven no longer accepts rams?

Cephas stands with widespread, thickset legs as if on massive pylons, and glares at me with pebbly eyes. That rock foundation of the Church stands there, expanding the panting cliffs of his chest, and retorts argumentatively:

"Who do you think you are, young man, to announce God's thoughts?"

"I'm Judas—Judas and no more. Everything and nothing. The youngest of the Twelve. The favorite of our Savior. The keeper of truth. The recorder of the Scriptures. The prophetic trumpet. The confidant of Him Who Is. Perhaps even the mortar of the Church, Cephas! I can answer anything, but does a stone hear?"

I leave Peter and look for the sons of Zebedee. John and

James are wrestling in a meadow. John is zealously teaching his brother the latest holds.

"It's Nisan," I say.

"One, two, three," counts John, devising a complicated grip. "Now left under right."

"It's Nisan."

"Then right under left." James groans in the clinch. "Then knee between legs."

"Soon it'll be the Feast of Unleavened Bread."

"Now hold firm, little brother!"

"The Passover of which the prophets bear witness."

"Hold fast, little brother!"

"When the Messiah must suffer to liberate us from sin."

"Hop-la, hop!"

In a gentle curve the adversary falls to the ground on his back.

"Come on, Judas, train with us! You look pale and weak."

"I don't care for the blood of bullocks, rams or lambs. I don't care for the blood of animals," I repeat, leaving the meadow. "I want my own blood, give me the blood of the New Testament, says the Lord."

Behind me, like the painful blades of knives, I hear the flashing cries of their wrestling.

From the man of Beth Horon	*4 drachmas*
From the man of Nain of Galilee	*3 drachmas*
In the purse there was altogether	*1½ drachmas*
For the tavern keeper Andronicus (debt)	*7½ drachmas*
Remaining on the second of Nisan, in all	*1 drachma*

A confidential talk with Thomas Didymus. Chattering in the shade of a fig tree. Its shadow quivers at our feet like a net of thick, dry threads. I don't beat about the bush. I speak openly, without restraint, wildly. But I'm also practical. All right, let him tell me that the world sunk in sin can wait a few more years to drag itself out of it. The total of sin doesn't lessen the chance of forgiveness, and once that's offered it's all the same if it consigns to oblivion one or a thousand crimes. But faith can't wait. Unjustified, it not only cools but turns against itself, and like a maddened scorpion caught in a snare, delivers a mortal sting to its own creations. Our faith is based wholly on Christ's suffering. We must go to Jerusalem without delay, so that in the heart of Israel and under the surveillance of the Great Temple we'll bring the prophetic images to life. Let the preaching retreat before the deed: the gesture must seal the discourse; blood must spurt from every word the speaker utters. What are words anyway? Only through the promise of Calvary can our sect, few in number and persecuted, pour forth a sea of faith. Only a downpour which obediently follows the drops can drown the godless land. The Cross is waiting. Two crossed beams reaching to the warm, maternal heavens are the bridge by which sin will be overcome.

Will Thomas, the only gentleman among us, understand the simple logic of a Galilean yokel, even if that yokel understands something of finance? After all, the world is somewhat deeper than Judas's purse. God's account is more tangled than a money-changer's.

Thomas listens, offensively patient, uninterested, unbearably courteous. As usual.

Yes, he knows Passover is drawing near. Naturally he's read Isaiah, but found no pleasure in it. Too much blood, too much self-congratulatory rhetoric about the offenses of others. No impartiality at all. The usual vanity and pettifoggery of a saint whom tradition didn't allow to sin, thus depriving him of the ability to understand. And then:

"What is it you want, Judas?"

Yes, he knows the passage I quoted, which refers to the tribe of Jacob. The blood of animals is disgusting to God. In fact, he wonders why God ever found satisfaction in these massacres. Frankly, they disgust him personally: the bleating of kids being slaughtered, the outpouring of fatty lymph and stinking blood, the steaming filth of entrails, the warm smell of dead carcasses.

What was it I wanted to ask him?

Ah yes, that prophecy. Of Isaiah, Zechariah and all the rest of that farseeing crowd. He never thought it would become so popular or be taken so seriously, so literally. For the Son of God to die on the Cross is a prerequisite for the salvation of the world. Who said that? Someone. But that's not important; let's say that it was definitely said. Better still, let's say it referred to our Savior. Unfortunately, men too exist, bodies to which these prophecies relate. Bodies are the instruments of words, the coarse weapons of fate. You can't disregard the body, just as you can't neglect an instrument. The body is the essential part of every sacrifice. The body which will thrash about nailed to that prophetic cross won't be pure abstraction, a poetic metaphor of an insatiate thirst for salvation, but rather a living man made in the image of God, an impossible skein of man-God which can't be disentangled and which unfortunately must suffer what is human, after which what is godlike will ascend to heaven.

"Yes," Thomas says, "but what do you really want?"

"Nothing," I say, "nothing."

And I go looking for James Alphaeus. I approach that bull without illusions, almost condescendingly (save me, O Lord, from the mortal sin of pride). Naturally, he doesn't understand anything, thinks I'm crazy. He even hints that the common purse should be taken from me because I'm irresponsible. Perhaps I *am* crazy. But I won't discard my madness, my madness is beautiful. If only we had more madmen! James Alphaeus is a mule. But I try. I tell him we must go to Jerusalem. He says our Teacher is thinking about it. There must be suffering there, James! The Teacher is thinking about that, too. Finally I yell:

"And you, James Alphaeus, what do you think?"

"Nothing. I don't think—I believe."

Whenever I listen to James Alphaeus, the raw simplicity of his faith

Peace be with you, brother in Christ! I didn't find you, but I found your book and leave a message for you. The innkeeper Andronicus asks if we want to prepare for the Passover at his inn, or can he let the premises to someone else. I remind you that An-

> *dronicus is a Greek and therefore uncircumcised; I don't know if that's according to the Law. Since you concern yourself with everything touching the Mosaic decrees, see about this also, or if you aren't sure, ask the most blessed Teacher. Your Matthew.*

forces me to wonder where the irresistible power of my own faith lies. What's the difference between my faith and James's? Perhaps because I know what he doesn't know: that the Teacher thinks for us, and the prophets think for the Teacher. So it's the prophets, not the Teacher, who think for us.

The innkeeper Andronicus is asking if we'll celebrate Passover at his inn? You must be joking! Andronicus isn't asking—*you* are, Matthew. Would a Greek at the height of the season solicit the guests who pay the least? Matthew doesn't want to go to the Holy City. He's afraid that a little bit of the cross he'll have to carry on his own back awaits him there. He's happy here. It's fine here for all of them except Judas. Why go from the frying pan into the fire? There are no pogroms in Ephraim. We aren't mocked by heretics who put us in strait jackets. There are no scribes, Pharisees and doctors of the Sanhedrin to ask us hypocritical questions. The Ephraimites are considerate, good-natured and trustworthy. Instead of learned sermons they prefer the Rabbi's simple little tales about a camel and the eye of a needle, about the marriage of the king's son, a child in the kingdom of heaven, a prodigal son or the poor man Lazarus—tales with a moral which will neither convert them nor obligate them, but give them satisfaction. In Ephraim we're respected, though the respect paid us recalls the curiosity aroused by some traveling band of physicians or comedians. Yes, in Ephraim Judas's purse is fuller than ever before, but what's the good of that if the soul is as barren as the valley of Hinnom because the light of my eyes, my merciful God, is constantly worried, huddled in the shade of some broken column, while the Eleven wander in the scorching byways of Ephraim and do nothing all day but wait for the night, and nothing all night but wait for the day, and so from one day and night to another.

I will, Publican. I'll talk to the Teacher. But not about the innkeeper Andronicus or holding the Passover in Ephraim. I'll talk about Jerusalem.

In the meantime I visit Andronicus and on my own authority tell him that we must regretfully refuse his cordial hospitality for Passover. He's bewildered, of course; it's clear that he'd offered us no hospitality, but now that we've rejected it he can at least offer it subsequently without doing himself any harm. Are we dissatisfied with his professional services? I reassure him: we must celebrate the Passover at Jerusalem. This makes him furious and all Matthew's tales are unmasked: did we dare go away without paying our bills, and how impudent of us to reject hospitality that had never been offered!

Matthew the publican, are you too on the devil's side?

Carried forward from second of Nisan	*1 drachma*
To the beggars (at the reading)	*5 mites*
To a poor man before the Assembly Hall	*2 paras*
On third of Nisan, total in hand	*3 mites*

Last night there was a cloudburst of warm rain. In the morning Ephraim was steaming. A sticky air hung in tatters under the eaves, where birds were stifling.

Before the window of our bedroom, two Samaritans were driving a herd of sacrificial lambs to the priest for inspection. The town crier, Zeebem, told the Ephraimites that the inspection of the Passover lambs should be made as soon as possible, and at the latest by the tenth of Nisan, to avoid crowds at the synagogue on the days just before the feast. Though faint, Zeebem's call aroused me and recalled to me the crackling of the divine voice of thunder. Was Judas so conceited in his knowledge of God's will that he couldn't even see the hurried preparations for the Passover, when animal blood would once again disgust God? Indeed, the efforts of the people to crave the mercy of God by sacrifices which would make him vomit, struck me as wretched and insulting.

Counting today, there are still twelve days to Passover: twelve days in which to arouse my brothers and lead them to Jerusalem, before it's too late and some stranger takes our crosses. I dress quickly and go into the town. I take the opportunity to chat with one of the Twelve: the gloomy, ill-tempered, fanatical Philip, who before his conversion was a washer of the dead at Bethsaida in Gennesaret. Philip listens attentively. However, my militancy is disarmed, the fire of my warnings quenched, by icy little smiles breaking out like purulent boils on his face. When at last I confess the inevitability of Jesus' suffering so that the Scriptures may be fulfilled, his smiles turn to hypocritical laughter. It isn't Philip who creates that mockery; it seems to be forged by every word I dare to pronounce: Isaiah, Zechariah, David, the Scriptures, Jehovah, Mission, Israel, World, Jerusalem, Cross, Suffering, Resurrection. My words against his smiles, my sentences against his laughter: the ice finally extinguishes the flame, without touching the embers. I stop talking.

"Judas," he says, "I've more experience with dead men than with living, so don't take it amiss if I'm outspoken. You're a damned liar, but you yourself don't know it."

He expects that after that I'll leave. But I stay. "I'm listening, Philip," I say with a shiver.

"What's all this rubbish? For whom is his suffering necessary?"

"For the world."

"Rubbish, brother. What world? It's necessary for *you*. *You* need him to suffer." (I'll hit him if he keeps on grinning.) "Judas worries a lot about the world. Yet your faith is so strong, so self-sufficient, that no world, sinful or sinless, is necessary for it." (Whatever happens, Lord, I'll hit him.) "But that granite faith has one flaw, Judas. It's always worrying about itself, fearing for itself, nourishing its flawless body. It's like a coin with two faces: when flipped, it always lands tails, but at the same time it's afraid that it may land heads and reveal to itself its own repulsive image: faithless to the faith." (Now I know I'll hit him!) "That trip to Jerusalem you weary our ears with has nothing to do with the Messiah or the world. Judas wants to see if the coin will fall tails as always, or at the very end of this hard road turn up that frightening heads. You want to convince yourself that you're right, that your blind faith hasn't been in vain. So all the prophecies must be fulfilled to the last detail. If a single detail remains unfulfilled, you're lost, for your faith and the faith of those like you can't stand holes, cracks or crannies. It's strong only when it's immaculate, when it's fresh from its wrappings."

I don't hit him. I let him go on talking.

"I don't envy you such faith, Judas—the most loyal, the most uncompromising, but also the most unyielding. If your faith falls to pieces, what'll be left of Judas?"

"I'm listening, Philip," I say, or think I say.

"If my faith betrays me, I'll keep on living with some other faith. What will *you* do?"

Now he's no longer smiling. His face is cold and pure: an expressionless mask.

"Remember, friend," he says, "if anyone succeeds in driving him to Jerusalem, it'll be you. But remember, too, that it won't be his path but yours."

I go away. Not his path but yours. I go away. *Not his but yours* accompanies me in glowing pictures where he stumbles under a gnarled black cross while with the thankful and saddened multitude I

> *Program for the fourth of Nisan. The Lord speaks in the Assembly Hall. Theme: he who believes will be saved and he who doesn't believe won't be. Warn him not to forget the phrase I composed for that speech yesterday: have faith in God, for verily I say unto you: if anyone says to this hill to throw itself into the sea, and doesn't doubt in his heart but is convinced that it will be as it is said, it will be truly as he said. Hope we can lunch with Andronicus. Healing of three to five cripples at the North Gate. Keep good order. Supper with the widow Nabaioth.*

wholeheartedly cry out: "Hosanna in the highest!" (If only I could go far away, but as I go Philip gloatingly repeats: "Not his path but yours." Going away I try to convince myself that even so it's his path and not mine, or even to a degree a common path, this time seen in pictures of the tormenting beams of the cross which we bear together, both under the same yoke of suffering.)

Suddenly the pictures vanish and I'm in front of the Assembly Hall. Sitting on the stone steps, Levi known as Thaddaeus is chattering with Cephas's brother, Andrew. I hear them call out: "Damn it, here he comes again—the old Stickler. Let's get away before he bores us to death!" So everyone's avoiding me. And I've got the nickname "Let-it-be-fulfilled."

Levi didn't have to run away. I turn suddenly into a side street for a long stroll through the suburbs of sleepy Ephraim, over which the moist sun of Nisan hangs like an unwrung rag.

And so all night. A tallow candle. Sultry.

Whose path will it be? The Only-begotten's? Judas's? Or both—a team of torment where both partners are equally indispensable? Jesus is the chosen one, while you're only the chosen of the chosen one, chosen at second hand from those who are chosen. Or perhaps—if Philip's right—a damned liar. Perhaps it really *is* my path, which the Messiah only makes use of—the path of faith trodden before the creator of the faith, a furrow plowed long before the coming of the sower. The prophets cut this furrow with the plow of their promises, paved it with the words of compassion. They marked the way with the signposts of the Testament. You, Judas, are only the maintenance man, the keeper of the path, the servant of the servant, the chosen of the chosen one. Or a damned liar?

The moon shines icy white, the frostbitten sky quivers, the stars are frozen in the arch of heaven and I'm burning. Do I have a fever?

I'm no longer Judas, one of the Twelve, the youngest of the Lord's envoys. I'm the Word, the Testament, the Scriptures. The world rests on my back. My back is the bed of sickness on which Israel awaits its healer. And what if it falls heads? It doesn't dare, it can't—the stakes are too great. And the sacrifice, isn't that still greater? Must my God, my beloved

Master, end so wretchedly? Is Judas bound to lead him to his death? Is Judas the shepherd who'll bring the sheep to the altar to redeem sin? Judas wants to, Judas must. Why, Judas, for whom? For the world, not me. Why do I, who am miserable without him, need his death? I'm not a liar, Philip, my faith isn't based on quotations but on love. Is it important whether or not a Judas believes? But the world, for its own good, must believe. In a sinful world what is love but depravity, what is glory but humiliation, what is honor but disgrace, virtue but vice, bravery but crime, mercy but the accomplice of disaster? In another world—a cleansed world—Judas too would be different.

Tomorrow morning I must see that Andronicus lets his rooms for Passover.

What was it Thomas said—that it would hurt? Naturally it'll hurt: bones will be shattered, the mushy marrow flow out, the brain pour over the hands which seize it and raise it to heaven in a vain prayer for help. And that'll last for hours—for days—without respite. That's my price: the tax of mercy. This isn't a market, Thomas! Jehovah doesn't bargain about the price of glory. This is a battle, a war where no quarter's given. A war for eternity.

Tomorrow I'll see if Andronicus has let his rooms for Passover.

That chill, fading brilliance outside. A balm of wind. I've got to go out, to lie down on the ground, rub my inflamed cheeks against the freshness of the earth, drench myself in the icy springs from the mountains of Ephraim.

My God will suffer. Of course he'll suffer. I adore him, but what do *I* mean to humanity? Does Adonai speak of humanity? Did the prophets speak of humanity, did Moses? Testament and Law, that's the beginning and the end, alpha and omega; between them there's nothing but the narrow, well-trodden path to Jerusalem and the heavenly kingdom.

O Lord my God, who's that snoring?

Can the Rabbi be a coward? But even if he is, does it matter? Salvation lies not in the manner of dying, but in death. He has to die, but it isn't written anywhere how he'll die, as a hero or a coward. Isaiah, to be sure, said: "He was oppressed, and he was afflicted, yet he opened not his mouth," but that doesn't mean he's brave. Perhaps he'll be silent through fear. Or he might scream. In any case, he's man, made in the image of God. A man will scream, but God will remain master of himself. Nor will the man by his cries shame the God in him, nor the God by remaining silent force the man to his endurance.

Outside it's like an icy sea. The chill rustling of the trees makes the walls of Ephraim shiver.

God, don't let me get sick and weak!

I love him, how I love him! But he has to die. His faith is above himself, perhaps even above God. Faith is Deeds. Deeds are above the Doer. You can't preserve both if Deeds are in the death of the Doer, and the death of the Doer creates the Deeds.

Judas, you're a damned liar!

Won't I ever forget the filthy voice of that washer of the dead? I'll tear it out of myself like a weed and burn it on the hearth of faith and say to him in the name of the Lord: Philip, you're afraid of Jerusalem!

Everyone's afraid of Jerusalem.

Judas, be firm, inexorable, cruel. The Scriptures must be fulfilled even if the world dies with its sins.

I feel better. I'm lying on the ground, stuck to it like a leaf flattened by the whirlwind.

Maybe it's no longer necessary to toss Philip's coin; maybe one shouldn't challenge fate. Couldn't it turn up heads and reveal the reverse of your faith, Judas? And what if it does fall heads, what if one word of the prophecies isn't fulfilled, what if the prophets are deceived in their visions, or at least in one of them? What'll become of you, Judas Iscariot?

Adonai! Adonai! Look down in your mercy on the servant of your servant, for his confusion is great and his torments can't be matched. Teach him what to do in this hour of uncertainty between his love and your truth, between man and God-man, Christ and the world, the Creator and his works; give a sign of approval, of compassion, of agreement, to him in whose ear the impatient prophets cry: "To Jerusalem! To Jerusalem!" Decide, Adonai, you who've conceived all this, and I'll obey.

Ephraim sleeps. The chill houses sleep. The cold wells. The cold shadows of the trees in front of the council hall. The cold murmur of the rain.

Adonai! Adonai! Answer me, You Who Are!

Voiceless, but with roars hurting my ears, words flow through me bursting like volcanoes, announcing nothing but blaring, taking on a soundless semblance of my thoughts, through whose deserted corridors my God threatens:

Anathema upon you, haughty generation! Anathema upon you, impudent spawn of the impudent dancers around the Golden Calf, who think that I destroyed the whole world by opening the sluices of heaven for forty days, and in a flash consumed Sodom and Gomorrah in a sulphurous rain, yet cannot save this world without the help of some human weakling. Wherein lies my almighty power if, for even the most insignificant detail, I have to search for helpers among those clay dolls which, for my recreation, I molded in my image, and into whose dead mouths only on the sixth day, out of pure boredom, I drove my breath? Are you listening, Jehuda?

I'm listening, Lord!

But once I spoke out, revealing to the prophets my visions and telling them of liberation, and what I promised must come to pass. It has already, since God, having thought something, by his very thought creates it, and it cannot be evaded that the world will once more be destroyed. You will take part in your salvation even as you took part in your destruction; you yourselves will build a paradise, even as you yourselves built a hell. For that reason I sent to you my only-begotten Son that you offer him to me as a sacrifice, as a pledge of peace between us. Are you listening to me, Jehuda?

I'm listening, Lord!

I've had enough of old goats upon which you unload your sins and drive them with shouts into the wilderness. The heavenly sheepfolds are full of your scapegoats, the universe is filled with the smell of that intolerable herd and the universal resting place stinks of rut. If I don't cleanse you but leave you in your sin, you'll go on sending me those repulsive beasts until I suffocate in their stink. Are you listening to me, Jehuda?

I'm listening, Lord!

Then what are you waiting for? What is the Lamb, my only-begotten Son, doing?

He's sleeping, Lord!

Let him never waken! The blood of the New Testament has grown alien to me. The child is terrified of suffering and pays no attention to his Father. Does the God who became the ally of Abraham on Mount Moriah, who led you out of Egypt and into the Promised Land, deserve to suffocate in the stench of your rutting goats while awaiting your grace and favor?

What should I do, Lord?

Lead him to Jerusalem. The rest is up to me. And I tell you verily, you'll become the rock upon which the Church of reconciliation will be built, and at your belt, instead of an empty purse, will hang the keys of the New Kingdom.

I determined to ask myself—for God was in me and spoke with my lips, and I spoke within myself, one moment filled with the angry roar of Hashem, another with the submissive whimperings of Judas—:

And what about Jesus?

For him it is written.

My inner peace bears witness that God has gone. The sign has been given to me. A new Judas rises from the earth, God's deputy who'll never again be humiliated when children call after him: Here comes Let-it-be-fulfilled. Don't weep, daughter of Zion, sweet-smelling rose in the teeth of Israel; don't wail, O chosen people, the Son of God comes to you riding an ass, and a colt the foal of an ass. Judas gives his pledge.

Ephraim sleeps. Let it sleep. God and Judas are awake.

To see if Andronicus has finally let his rooms. To find money to pay off our debt, nonpayment of which might keep us in Ephraim: 7 drachmas and some lepta. To hire a mule for the Teacher. Also a pack mule. To prepare food for the journey.

Death at Hinnom

After the sermon in the Assembly Hall, I approach him. He doesn't move, scarcely breathes; he sits on a humpbacked stone. His eyes are coated with virginal white ash; broken visions of the approaching place of execution writhe in them. Only he and I see the black outlines drawn in the sand, the ground plan of liberation: six intercrossing black lines, six primitive black strokes like six beams fallen to the bloodless face of the earth, three quickly improvised crosses.

He knows I'm here. My shadow strikes his eye as in a mirror which neither accepts nor rejects. He lives in a day which hasn't yet dawned, but whose fascinating and fearsome reflection plays under his feet, offering torment and reward mingled impartially in a bloody blend. He lives in a day which hasn't yet dawned, too strong to be brushed away by a heel erasing pictures of the future in the dust, too weak to throw the last God-man into the torturing abyss of his hour.

He knows I'm here. We permeate each other without contact, we understand each other without words, we weigh up without measures, we feel without intrusion. In that mutual interpenetration, that mutual flow of two counterpoises of the same gravitation, two forces from the same source and with the same estuary, we can feel destiny so link us that we're mercilessly divided, yet in that division devoted to the same glorious act.

There are two sacrificial victims.

Lovers and enemies who keep pace step by step through the word-by-word fulfillment of the Scriptures, Judas and Joshua are bringing the sacrifice which will free and redeem all mankind except themselves.

We love each other, between us there's an insatiable attachment, an indivisibility. We are chained to each other and nothing can break those chains without killing us both. I'm the skin of his flesh; he's the flesh of my skin. Through that common body circulate the bitter blood of the New Testament and the sweet maternal milk of the New Kingdom. Without me he's nothing, without him I'm nothing. Both are essential for the salvation of the world, as man and woman are essential for the birth of offspring.

That gives me confidence. "Rabbi, it's Nisan. Passover is coming!"

Now he questions me with eyes full of resinous, sticky apprehension, the left eye saying "so," the right eye adding "what?" and the whole severed glance fearfully indicating "So what?" But he doesn't answer and the next second again seems not to exist for the day in which he's living.

"It's time to set out for Jerusalem."

The word hit: Jerusalem. It fell like an overripe fruit. You can't just kick it away or grind it with your heel into the dung and dust of Ephraim, where the walls of a Jerusalem of tomorrow are already smudged, reduced to three faintly cut black crosses. Jerusalem. Something has to be said—I feel it. He feels it. Jerusalem. I wait for a reply, an excuse, almost a confession. Instead I receive a businesslike counterproposal:

"Why? We can prepare everything here at Ephraim." Then he makes a lame joke: "Ephraim lambs are cheaper than Jerusalem lambs, Judas!"

I give measure for measure, blow for blow: "That's why they aren't so pleasing to God, Lord!"

Time presses. The birds murmur low under the eaves over which the sun cascades, relentless as a yellow sea. I try again.

"Rabbi, the Scriptures say—"

"Ah, the Scriptures," he says with unutterable boredom.

"Isaiah prophesies—"

"Oh, Isaiah!" Then he declaims expressionlessly: "Behold the Lord's hand is not shortened, that it cannot save; neither is his ear heavy, that it cannot hear."

At first I flinch: I think he's mocking me, but he isn't. He's only thinking aloud, and his thought about the unshortened hand of God is proof that he understands and that I may have better luck this Nisan than I did in Nisan last year or the year before, when I said the same thing to him, always in a different town—Jericho, Hebron, Lydda—but always with the same miserable result. If his ear isn't heaven, then he hears the honing of the chisel trimming the cross, and the hammers preparing his last resting place.

"In that case, I'll prepare everything for the journey to Jerusalem."

Don't give me that bloody look, I think; don't scorn me until we've fulfilled all the days assigned us, please. Perhaps I'm slated for an irredeemable suffering and an incurable wound whose bandage won't be, as it will for yours, the entire healing heaven.

"You're impatient, Judas, as if you were the Son of God, not I."

I wish I were, I wish I were.

"As if Isaiah were talking about you when he said: 'He is despised and rejected of men; a man of sorrows, and acquainted with grief.' "

Would that were true.

"It's as if he were thinking of you, not me, when he prophesies: 'But he was wounded for our transgressions, he was bruised for our iniquities.' "

If only, if only.

"I'd bear that burden, Lord," I say bitterly.

"Really? And be happy?"

"I don't know, Lord! I'd carry your load. Is that happiness?"

"Any pack mule on the Judaean roads could tell you that better than the Son of God!" he replies angrily. "Now go, my friend, and leave me to my fears."

I go away. Both of us know that I'll return and he'll be waiting for me. And both of us hate that hour.

In the purse on the fifth of Nisan	*3 leptas*
From the wife of the jeweler Faltila (alms)	*1 drachma*
From the wife of the smith Misail (alms)	*1 drachma*
From the wife of the weaver Elisaph (alms)	*1 drachma*
From the wife of the carpenter Gudil (alms)	*7 leptas*
In the purse on the sixth of Nisan, total	*3 drachmas and 5 as*

"It's time, Lord!"

"Where are you rushing, Judas?"

"To Jerusalem, Lord!"

"Then go. I'm not keeping you!"
"What would I be without you, Lord?"
"Then wait, Judas!"

On the seventh of Nisan in the purse	*3 drachmas and 5 as*
From the widow Nabaioth (alms)	*1 drachma*
From Joash the butcher (alms)	*1 drachma and 5 as*
From an unknown Samaritan	*1 didrachma*
On the seventh of Nisan in the purse: total	*8 drachmas*

"Wait, Judas!"
"I've already waited for the fourth Passover, Lord!"
"Who's going to die in Jerusalem, you or me?"
"You, Lord! It's written."
"And is the time written?"
"Yes, Lord! It's said it'll be on Passover. The Son of man must suffer on the Feast of Unleavened Bread."
"On which Passover? Is it said in what year since the creation of the world?"
"No, Lord."
"In which year after Moses?"
"No, Lord."
"Then wait!"
And nothing more, not yes or no, I will or I won't, I can or I can't.

Paid for food	*4 drachmas*
For the cripples before the temple	*1½ drachmas*
For new sandals for Andrew	*1 didrachma*
Paid out: total	*7½ drachmas*
On the eighth of Nisan; balance in the purse	*5 as*

Today I persuade him to let me read him the prophet Isaiah: " 'He was oppressed, and he was afflicted, yet he opened not his mouth; he is brought as a lamb to the slaughter, and as a sheep before her shearers is dumb, so he openeth not his mouth.' "
"Go on!"

" 'He was taken from prison and from judgment; and who shall declare his generation? for he was cut off out of the land of the living; for the transgression of my people was he stricken.' "

"Go on!"

" 'And he made his grave with the wicked, and with the rich in his death; because he had done no violence, neither was any deceit in his mouth.' "

I stop.

"Go on!" he shouts.

" 'Yet it pleased the Lord to bruise him; he hath put him to grief: when thou shalt make his soul an offering for sin—' "

He interrupts me: "Do the prophets say anything more of those torments, Judas?"

"No, my Lord. But in the morning psalm King David speaks of them." I hesitate to continue with the description of his calvary, but he orders me. "This is what the king says of you: 'They gaped upon me with their mouths, as a ravening and a roaring lion. I am poured out like water, and all my bones are out of joint: my heart is like wax; it is melted in the midst of my bowels.' Shall I go on?"

"Yes!"

" 'For dogs have compassed me: the assembly of the wicked have inclosed me: they pierced my hands and my feet. I may tell all my bones: they look and stare upon me. They part my garments among them, and cast lots upon my vesture.' And he said: 'He trusted on the Lord that he would deliver him: let him deliver him, seeing he delighted in him.' "

"Judas, I hear you're hiring mules."

"Yes, Lord, I did."

"Cancel them. I'm not going to Jerusalem."

When I leave him I wonder what would have happened if I'd reminded him of yet another verse from that psalm—the words he's to pronounce on the cross: "My God, my God! Why hast thou forsaken me? why art thou so far from helping me, and from the words of my roaring?"

That night he wakens me. He sits on my bed. His face is like a shining hole drilled in the darkness, a window from which a faint glow throbs. At first he says nothing, he holds my hand and examines the days of waiting on my face at Ephraim.

I don't dare shatter the terrible peace of that meditation. Just before dawn, as in the dispersing darkness the cold flame of his silhouette is quenched, he asks me:

"What would you do in my place, Judas?"

"I'm sorry to say, Master, I'd die."

"In order to be dead?"

"I said 'die.' I didn't say I'd be dead."

He sits at the end of my couch, disheveled, shabby, old, like a shattered outcast, like an eroded island of the night in the wave of freshly glowing dawn. And he isn't thirty yet.

"Yes, I know that 'on the third day he will rise again.' On the third day I'll be carried up to heaven, but to be able to go there I have to die—what am I saying?—not die, but endure death. That's not a snap of the fingers, that's a process. Tell me, does it last a while?"

"Are you afraid, Lord?"

"I'm afraid, Judas!"

He takes my hand. Both hands are hot and sweaty, but even so we're freezing, as if our twined fingers had slipped into a cold, wet glove.

"Do you love me, Judas?"

"I do, Master."

"Then you must understand me."

In the wakening light there are no sounds. But now we both hear sparrows twittering in the trees in front of the window. It's a discouraging sound for a mortal approaching death, an irritating defiance on the part of life, of the sinful earth he's about to leave—a casual crumb of chance he's been waiting for in order to humiliate himself by asking:

"Judas, would you die for me?"

"Lord, I would, but Judas isn't worthy enough to die for you."

"But if you were, if there weren't those unbridgeable differences between my life and yours, between human and divine existences, if it were possible to brush away those ludicrous differences which humiliate men and burden gods?"

"If those differences vanished, salvation would no longer be necessary for anyone. But if it were necessary, who could say how it should be obtained?"

The sparrows chirp in the faint light of morning and the most trying minutes pass. The air becomes too clear for confessions.

"Rabbi," I say, repeating Thomas's words, "you're an instrument. One can't neglect an instrument. It's an integral part of the work, even as the body is an essential ingredient of every sacrifice. Could a craftsman without a good knife carve a real work of art?"

"A tool wears out, breaks. A craftsman's knife gets blunt and the master changes it for another."

"For a knife, Lord, for a real knife and not a cobbler's awl. Just as an awl can't be a knife to a knife, so Judas can't be God to Christ, nor Christ a man to Judas."

"Why? Aren't I a man? A woman bore me in labor, and men will kill me in torment. Isn't that proof I'm a man?"

"That's a proof you're a man, but what proof is there that I'm God? No, Lord, an awl isn't a knife."

He bends over me like a drooping flower of cloth, flesh and fear, with the rustling petals of his Galilean robe, with the pistils of his oversensitive hands, the stale perfume of the Ephraim dream and the harsh whispers through whose armor the ninth of Nisan of Judaea penetrates: the iron clashing of bolts and bars, the lazy creaking of side gates, the tinkling of bells on the necks of cattle or slaves, and the thin, birdlike cries of the water sellers.

"But it can stab, it can stab. If you die in my place, you'll become God in my place."

"A false god, Lord! I can die instead of you, but I can't fulfill the prophecies and redeem sins for which you're the sacrifice. My death would be in vain, Lord, no less than the life you'd continue to live."

"But who's heard of me, who's seen me? In all Judaea a few beggars, a few policemen, some rabbis and two or three hysterical women. And who among those who know me will be at the place of execution on the day of my earthly glory?

The prophets are dead, and the Twelve will keep silent. Who can tell Judas from Jesus on the cross?"

"You, Lord! You and I."

"So?"

"Isn't that enough?"

His aging, worn face hangs above me in the moving air, pale in the darkness, sooty in the morning outlined by the sunbeams. He doesn't miss a single flicker on my face, watches for even the tiniest support which might be revealed in its deadly immobility on the pillow. My Master waits for some sign of reprieve, some hope that he may evade his suffering or at least postpone it, and that my love will perceive some breach in the impregnable citadel of the Scriptures.

Instead, I repeat: "We should go to Jerusalem, Lord!"

He leaps up from the couch. As over a devastated countryside, the young dawn sweeps across his face. There is a real dawn from the window and a second dawn of hatred, poisonous, that grows within me like an incarnate anathema: Judas's love is bending over Judas to destroy him. O God, why don't his hands, the only hands unsoiled by original sin, tighten around my neck and end my torments? But he gives my brow the kiss of blessing and starts to go out on tiptoe saying nothing, not yes or no, I will or I won't, I can or I can't.

> *List of parables for telling: the master and his servants, the wise and foolish virgins (Watch, therefore . . .), the unjust judge and the importunate widow, the prodigal son, the king and the marriage of his son (Many are called, but few are chosen), the good Samaritan, the vineyard and the husbandmen (The first shall be last and the last shall be first). Think out a few more and link them with sermons.*

"The other evening I conversed with your Heavenly Father, Rabbi."

He regards me suspiciously. Till now it hasn't been the

custom for anyone but him to communicate with the Almighty, and while we've been here in Ephraim with Passover approaching, he himself has avoided it.

"He asked about you and wondered what his Lamb, his only-begotten Son, was doing."

He suddenly seemed smaller.

"He'll be in Jerusalem over Passover, to welcome and embrace his Son."

"He said that?"

I hesitate. God hadn't specifically said that, but had promised he'd take care of everything when we came to Jerusalem.

"Yes, Lord. He ordered you to go and leave everything to him. He'll see to everything."

No, I didn't lie. To take care of everything, God must be in Jerusalem. To tell the truth, he'd said nothing of embracing the Messiah, but that was obvious. The prophecy of the Ascension speaks of it. Now I can't hold back any longer. He listens to me greedily, waiting for something clearer and more definite, something consoling in view of his destiny at Jerusalem. How can I let this opportunity go by?

"If I understood him," I say, "he'll free you from your torments."

Hadn't he said he'd take care of everything? From such a promise you could draw any conclusions. No, Judas, you're not lying, only interpreting a divine order in your own way.

He looks at me, filled with joy. With boundless relief he lets his tense hands fall on his robe.

"Swear to it, Judas!"

I take a deep breath. "I swear, Lord!"

"All right, Judas, you win. Tomorrow we set out for Jerusalem." Then, when he's already some distance away, he turns as if remembering something, and says to me in the carefree tone of a pardoned martyr: "I hope that the Scriptures, which have paid such attention to me, haven't forgotten my friends also. When that hour comes, I'll remember this conversation and the most loyal among them."

I've won, in the name of the Lord. Judas the Stickler, Judas Let-it-be-fulfilled has won. After our talk the Rabbi says we'll celebrate the Passover in Jerusalem and orders the apostles to prepare for the journey. At last the prophecies will be fulfilled; the world will no longer wallow in sin, and even if it does, could Judas's faith seek a better confirmation for his credo?

Judas, you're a damned liar. Did I lie to Christ? I didn't. You did. I didn't, Philip. Why not, when you didn't reveal that it was the prophets who confirmed that Epiphany; God didn't say openly that what was written would take place. No, but he said he'd stay in Jerusalem and take care of everything. Naturally Judas will see to it that everything conforms to the Scriptures. Not that saving Jesus would falsify God's most important words: of course God can alter the Scriptures—they're his; Isaiah is only a go-between—by holding back the sacrifice for salvation and freeing the victim from the prescribed torments. Rubbish! What sort of a victim feels no pain? Besides, if he'd intended that, God wouldn't have said to you: "For him it is written" when you asked him: "What about Jesus?" But relax: even if you lied, you did so for the good of the world.

My comrades, my brothers in Christ, first bitterly protest, put forward objections, point out the dangers, then plead and finally, believing the Teacher's decisions irrevocable, place the whole blame for the trip to Jerusalem on me. Peter, known as Cephas, goes so far as to call me publicly a God-killer, a criminal, a shameful halter leading the lamb to slaughter.

A lot Judas cares! God is with him.

On the ninth of Nisan: in the purse	*½ drachma*
Alms on hearing the news of our departure	*8½ drachmas*
On the ninth of Nisan, in the purse	*9 drachmas*
Out of that, paid:	*9 drachmas*
For the hire of a pack mule	*2 drachmas*
Debt to the innkeeper Andronicus	*7 drachmas*
Remaining in the purse: total	*0*

About noon on the ninth of Nisan we leave Ephraim. It's the Sabbath, but the Messiah doesn't honor the ancient rules forbidding travel on the seventh day.

So there you are—the times of Ephraim are over, our days

are numbered, the sleepers have been wakened. The prophets rejoice, Isaiah applauds his vision's fulfillment. And you, Israel, rejoice: the heel is raised from Edom. Rejoice, Zion, rose of fragrance: the Redeemer comes to you!

Now I must relate an incident which took place on the road from Bethel to Jerusalem. In itself the incident isn't worth recording, for it leaves a bad impression of the Eleven, and it might be better if it were hushed up. However, it was of such importance to me that with a clear conscience I'll set aside all the reasons against recording it, well aware that the advantage will outweigh any harm done. Besides, if Judas is pure of heart, the core of true faith, then what's good for Judas is also good for the faith.

We were traveling by night. Above us the sooty shadow of the mountain of Ephraim clashed with the moonlight. The moon was like a window looking into some other shining world, a world freed from darkness, a world of eternal daylight. Far away, among the thistles and desert weeds, slunk the yelping silhouette of a jackal.

The Teacher, alone and full of cares, was marching at the head of our column, and we dragged along behind him, in no way militant or alert, but plunged in thought and seeing in our minds visions of the suffering which awaited him in Jerusalem. Then Peter said that if all went as it should we'd be without a leader, so the Teacher must choose from among the twelve of us, the first Christians, a legal, earthly successor, a hand to receive from him the torch of divine truth. For Peter there was no doubt that only he had such a capable hand, but it became apparent at once that he was alone in this opinion. The apostles acknowledged that Peter was the first and oldest convert among them, but denied that senility was a suitable recommendation. The first opposition candidate was Matthew the Publican, who referred to his experience in affairs of state: assessing the dues to be paid at the Capernaum toll booth. As it spread, the faith would come more and more into contact with the state and its laws; who could cope better than a former civil servant?

Thomas Didymus expressed his disagreement with such a

simplification and misunderstanding of Jesus's heritage. First and foremost, his honored brothers in Christ hadn't chosen a just criterion for the appointment of a successor. Though Matthew had judged correctly about the development of the faith, he'd done so from a false premise; the criterion could only be the courtesy, education and social virtues of the future leader. He'd have to come from higher social circles than the Messiah himself or any of us eleven. The faith would also touch the hearts of the higher classes; it would be disastrous if it were interpreted in the ungrammatical peasant dialect of Galilee, and embodied in some stuttering oaf who picked his nose and relieved himself wherever he happened to be. Instead of becoming universal, the Church would remain the refuge of the destitute and finally become—he was sure of it—a den of unrest, violence and revolution. Since it was clear that Thomas alone answered such qualifications, my brothers rejected his comments also, for wasn't it said that it was easier for a camel to pass through the eye of a needle than for a rich man to enter the kingdom of heaven? Then the sons of Zebedee, James and John, pestered the Teacher to choose them, praising their wrestlers' muscles with which—for want of better methods—the faith could most quickly be driven into the bones of the unbelievers.

I alone remained silent, calmly awaiting what the Lord would say.

And he said that his successor would be the one among us who could drink from the bitter cup which he would drain, and who agreed to be baptized with the same painful baptism as himself.

"Let my successor step forward."

The apostles didn't move. To become his successor, did one first have to die? Then how could one take over the succession, claim the inherited right and enjoy the inherited goods?

Then I, Judas, stepped forward.

"I was waiting for you, most loyal among the loyal," he said. Putting his hand on my hair, he handed over to me his earthly succession in front of the others, who were reddening from shame and envy. "You'll drain the cup which I shall drink from, and be baptized with my baptism."

"Rejoice, Judas!"

"Rejoice, loyal Judas!"

"Rejoice, the Lord's successor!"

We're at Bethany. Morning. Above the village rises the stony tent of the Mount of Olives. The towers of Zion, those incomparable darlings and brides of Solomon, advance toward heaven, which changes its paling shadows with the blazing reflections of the Great Temple. The ram's horn announces to Judaea that the first dawn sacrifice has been offered to God. We pray, turning toward God's palace. The Messiah doesn't pray. He stares at Jerusalem. With the expressionless eyes of a loophole, Jerusalem returns its gaze to its emperor, the Son of David, the Son of God. Those glances don't express amazement, don't assess like strangers, don't bargain like merchants. For a long time the outcome of that Passover meeting has been known, described, worked out in every detail. Nothing can be added or subtracted, nothing changed in that meeting of executioner and victim, butcher and lamb. The muddy walls of Zion's fragrant rose slowly unfold their petals with impatient scenes of the future, already formed. In the lukewarm Jerusalem mists the three crosses in the Ephraim sand, the six black strokes like six crossed black beams, are sketched once again. He can't learn from Jerusalem anything he doesn't know already from the prophets: Jerusalem expects nothing from him except what has been formally promised by the prophets.

The Bethany graveyard. Unpleasant memories flood over us: the late Lazarus, Hamri, the rush after the corpse, uphill and downhill on the Mount of Olives. The Teacher urges us to go to the graveyard. Maybe we'll even find Lazarus in his grave, maybe after we left Bethany in shame the vile Hamri put his master in his resting place again. No use: the battlefield of our defeat is empty. The upturned stone lies on the edge of a gaping, mocking hole. There'll be no compensating triumph, at least not through Lazarus. By his own resurrection the Messiah must prove who's right, he or the Sadducees. But it would have been good to enter Jerusalem arm in arm with the dead Lazarus.

Bethany. Supper in the house of Simon the hunchback.

Mary, sister of the late Lazarus, washes Jesus' feet with precious ointment of spikenard, then dries them with her hair. For such expensive oil we could get three hundred grosh, and our purse is empty. What will we have to prepare for Passover? In any case there's nothing in the Scriptures about such an ointment. A stupid waste of time and money.

Bethphage. We find lodgings at Bethphage, about ten stades from Jerusalem, which we'll enter tomorrow, the eleventh day of Nisan, at about noon.

From Simon the hunchback (*alms*)	*3 drachmas*
From an unknown man of Bethany (*alms*)	*2 drachmas*
From an unknown man of Bethphage (*alms*)	*2 drachmas*
From Mary, daughter of Zacchaeus, on loan	*5 drachmas*
In the purse on the eleventh of Nisan, total	*12 drachmas*

Noon. The Rabbi gives the signal for departure. I protest, reminding him that the Son of God can't enter the Holy City on foot. The prophecies are precise and unambiguous on that point. I quote Zechariah:

" 'Rejoice greatly, O daughter of Zion; shout, O daughter of Jerusalem: behold, thy King cometh unto thee: he is just, and having salvation; lowly, and riding upon an ass, and upon a colt the foal of an ass.' "

Naturally the apostles grumble. Where are we to find donkeys? They accuse me of airs and graces and splitting hairs. I'm not splitting hairs. The only thing of importance to me is that the Scriptures be fulfilled, for if even a single letter isn't fulfilled, it'll be as if nothing were. So I persuade the Teacher to send the sons of Zebedee into the villages to find an ass and a colt the foal of an ass. They come back quickly, leading in a halter two mules, one female, one male, both limping from overwork. I explode: isn't there in all Bethphage a single decent donkey on which the Son of God can enter his capital? The sons of Boanerges say the local people show no understanding. They'd had trouble getting even these mules; if I didn't like it, why didn't I go myself? Then they tell their story: when they'd asked for donkeys for the Lord, the people of Bethphage asked for money. They had none. They offered their blessing instead, but the godless peasants spat on that blessing, saying they couldn't ride on it. And who was this most important gentleman who couldn't hire two donkeys? When referred to the Scriptures, they said they couldn't read. On their way back the two apostles had come across these nags; to avoid arguments with the owner, they took them without asking. What did it matter if the Savior entered Jerusalem on a donkey, a cow, a buffalo, a mule or a goat, so long as he entered and the essence of the prophecy was fulfilled?

The Teacher is ready to give way. He has no sense of the finesse of a prophecy (I remember our argument about the healing of a leper woman at Jabneel after leaving Hazor, and not upon entering Capernaum, as it was written) but I remain unyielding. Judas can't allow his painstaking work to be frustrated because of a donkey shortage or our own clumsiness.

I went personally to Bethphage and found what we needed: a she-ass and its foal. The owners raised no question about the loan of them, which the Lord, at some time or another, would repay a hundredfold. The animals were in poor condition; their skin was cracked like dried mud and they lacked the dignity required, but at least they were donkeys, not mules.

The actual entry into Jerusalem also required certain arrangements. The Scriptures (the One Hundred Eighteenth Psalm) foresaw that the people of Jerusalem would enthusiastically greet their Savior and Redeemer: "The voice of rejoicing and salvation is in the tabernacles of the righteous. I will praise thee: for thou hast heard me and art my salvation. Blessed be he that cometh in the name of the Lord." But in the present state of things, we couldn't expect that prophecy to be fulfilled of itself. As soon as the Lord—not without a certain delicate urging on our part—had mounted his donkey, a few apostles at my order ran to the city gates, spread their robes over the cobblestones, waved branches of palm and shouted as was written:

"Hosanna to the Son of David! Alal! Alal!"

"Blessed is he that cometh in the name of the Lord!"

"Hosanna in the highest!"

"King of the Jews, Our Redeemer!"

"Long live Jesus the Nazarene!"

As we entered Jerusalem many of the citizens, who didn't know what it was all about, joined in with the apostles. They liked to make a commotion in the streets, so that the expression of public respect—even though our procession couldn't overly inspire them—fulfilled David's prophecy beyond anything we dared to expect.

As we had planned, before evening the gentle Teacher drove out of the Temple porch the money-changers and sellers of sacrificial doves, who'd turned the place of worship into a den of thieves. Then he healed a few cripples, and managed to hold his own against the priests and theologians. That was Jerusalem on that day, which was only the first.

Unfortunately, the expulsion of the money-changers from the Temple made no impression on the public—even though I'd planned it down to the last detail—except that I had to pay a fine of two drachmas for disturbing the public order. The healing of the two paralyzed cripples made a greater impression, but unfortunately they were from the interior and the people of Jerusalem didn't know them, so that rumors spread that they were stooges of the wonder-worker with whom he staged this comedy in all the towns. As for the argument with the priests, such learned squabbles were so common in the city that yet another one couldn't excite the Judaeans.

I don't lose hope. This is only the first day in Jerusalem. If we still haven't met the godless at whose hands our Lord is destined to be slain, it's only because the time hasn't come yet, the Passover lamb hasn't yet been killed. In the meantime, relying on the iron book of prophecy, we do our best to make trouble.

Program for the twelfth of Nisan. Morning: healing of cripples before the Great Temple, immediately after divine service (must find some local cripples, if possible a blind man); sermon in front of the Tower of Antonia in which he should violently attack the Pharisees (parable of the vineyard, the husbandman and his servants); against the Sadducees, a sermon on resurrection in front of the Council Hall; anathema on all the godless, delivered in the square before Herod's palace (as many oaths, curses, insults as possible!). Afternoon: ride on donkeyback through Acra and the Lower City (apostles, mingling with the crowd, to shout: Long live Jesus of Nazareth, King of the Jews! We expect much from that). Evening: await the outcome.

In front of the Council Hall, while the Teacher's delivering his sermon on resurrection (not the best theme for a settlement of accounts with the Sadducees in view of our failure with Lazarus), I check out the effect on his listeners. I'm not satisfied: the reaction's pretty flabby. There's no doubt that the theologians are annoyed at the self-proclaimed Savior, but they're still not ready to do him physical evil to the extent that answers our needs. They just laugh at him and seldom contradict him. Most often they're indifferent. This way we'll never get anywhere. We've got to do something more definite—something to force them to a crime.

I sample public opinion. I wander through the remote side streets, the bazaars, the markets. I go into places of worship, craftsmen's shops, warehouses. I loaf about in the waiting rooms of government offices. No one knows about the Lord. Yes, one or two have noticed him riding on his donkey, and think that pranksters have been playing a joke on some little Galilean peasant. The young fellow looked wretched and more like a laborer for hire than a king. Was he really all there?

I talk with a middle-aged potter who heard his sermon in front of the Antonia Tower. A good sermon, beyond a doubt, but a little messy, the words badly arranged. Then too, it's not good for a speaker to get heated when someone contradicts him. He'd heard him swear, and Moses forbade oaths.

A cartwright from Tekoah asks me who this Galilean is. I say he's the son of David. Which David? David the municipal clerk, or David ben Tara from Acra? Or the wheelwright from the Upper City? No, I explain: King David. The man from Tekoah takes my answer as a bad joke. Did I think him a fool? That David lived more than ten centuries ago! How could this thirty-year-old be his son?

The situation is alarming. The day after tomorrow is Passover, the seven days' cleansing in memory of the Exodus: the time the prophets ordained for the suffering of the Son of God; Passover and Shevuoth (Pentecost), in memory of the wanderings in Sinai and that glorious day when Moses, illumined by the fiery presence of He Who Is, brought down from the mountain the Tablets of the Law. Unfortunately, for the moment nothing indicates that it'll come to suffering. The people are in a peaceful, holiday mood, the priests don't feel threatened, and the Romans regard a Galilean carpenter's pretensions to the Jewish throne as a part of that Israelite obsession with glory which lets them hold the country in subjection. As long as he speaks only against his compatriots, the Romans won't intervene. To them, in any case, it's comic, even appealing, that this people—ragged down-and-outs, lazy farm workers, unskilled stock breeders, cripples, prophets, wonder-workers, fanatics—have wasted half a century bickering about the essence of its impotent, invisible and never mentionable God, and wasted the other half quarreling about how to serve him. However, if it comes to riots, they'll order their legionaries to scourge him and expel him from the city.

O Lord in heaven, is it really possible that something so terrible, so humiliating, could happen? Can it be that from all my labor a colossal burst of laughter is born? No, Jerusalem mustn't be transformed into Ephraim; the time of Jerusalem isn't a time for sleeping but for suffering, for consecrating the New Kingdom. The Scriptures shall be fulfilled. Judas swears to Him Who Is that everything written in the books of Truth shall be fulfilled.

Sermons, sermons, sermons. Words, words, words. Rides

on donkeyback. Hosanna to the Son of David. Alleluia! More sermons. Woe upon you, scribes and Pharisees, hypocrites! Woe upon you, blind leaders of the blind! More rides on a donkey dropping with fatigue. More sermons, pledges, anathemas, oaths. Serpents, generation of vipers! Woe to you, Jerusalem, who kills the prophets! Harangue before the palace of the procurator (the legionaries don't know a word of Aramaic!), harangue in Acra, harangue in the Lower City, harangue in the street of the potters' guild, in the alley of the tinkers, in the booths of the clothmakers and weavers. Sermons, sermons, sermons. Words, words, words.

And from all that—nothing!

> *Thirteenth of Nisan. Program. The Lord will announce before the Council Hall that he's the Son of God and King of the Jews. That he can destroy the Temple and raise it again in three days. He'll make the same announcement at Bezetha, in the Suburb and other places. Speeches will be written for him to excite the fury of the Herodians and the suspicions of the Romans.*

I spend the whole sleepless night before Passover beating my brains. What's going to happen? Why doesn't God accept his lamb, the sacrifice he wanted? Where have we gone wrong? I go over every detail of our journey here from Ephraim and compare it with the prophecies. I know perfectly well: "If a single word is not fulfilled, it is as if nothing has been fulfilled." Everything's in order, we've taken it all into account. So where's the break in the link between prophecy and actuality? Isaiah, Zechariah, Amos, Jeremiah, all the prophets should be satisfied. David, too! Psalm Twenty-two, Psalm Forty-one . . .

Psalm Forty-one!

How could I have overlooked it? How could I have left out the psalm which alone makes clear the way to Calvary? In furious haste I skim through the squared characters of the papyrus scrolls to make sure the forty-first is the right one:

The Third Psalm, when he fled from Absalom? Not that.

To the chief musician on eight strings? Not that. Psalm Twenty-two, Twenty-five, Twenty-six or -seven? Not those. A psalm of David? The consecration of the Temple? When he pretends to be crazy before Abimilech? Not that either. To the chief musician Iditun? The Forty-first? *That's it!*

I read out as quickly as I can:

" 'YEA, MINE OWN FAMILIAR FRIEND, IN WHOM I TRUSTED, WHICH DID EAT OF MY BREAD, HATH LIFTED UP HIS HEEL AGAINST ME.' "

Silence.

The Eleven stand before me: Andrew, son of Simon, and his brother Peter, known as Cephas; James and John, the sons of Zebedee; Bartholomew alias Nathaniel; James Alphaeus and Levi known as Thaddaeus; the former washer of the dead, Philip of Bethsaida; Matthew nicknamed the Publican; Simon the Canaanite; and the eleventh, Thomas. Their rigid bodies form an impenetrable barrier of scorn and disbelief. Their faces are turned to me like smooth, tough shields of tanned leather.

The first to recover is Cephas: "Recite that psalm again, Judas, word for word."

"That was the Forty-first Psalm, ninth verse, between 'Shall rise up no more' and 'But thou, O Lord, be merciful unto me.' It reads: 'Yea, mine own familiar friend, in whom I trusted, which did eat of my bread, hath lifted up his heel against me.' "

"And how do you interpret it?"

"First of all, my brothers in Christ, you should know that the Forty-first Psalm, because of which I summoned you, isn't the only one which prophesies betrayal—more accurately, commands it—as a direct cause of the Savior's torments, though in it that thought is expressed the most concisely and irrevocably. The Fifty-fifth Psalm also speaks eloquently of it, but it's not so concise, though more definite about the group where the betrayer should be sought. 'For it was not an enemy that reproached me; then I would have hid myself from him: But it was thou, a man mine equal, my guide, and mine acquaintance. We took sweet counsel together.' The prophet Obadiah gives striking evidence of that betrayer: 'All the men of thy confederacy have brought thee even to the border: the men that were at peace with thee have deceived thee, and prevailed against thee; they that eat thy bread have laid a wound under thee.' There can be no doubt of the meaning of those prophecies. Even the fact that this evening the festival begins and nothing has happened forces us to ask if we've disregarded some detail of the prophecies, some little word. For if a single word isn't fulfilled, then it's as if nothing's fulfilled. This is the highest, I'd say the only, essential Law of the faith. Delving through the Holy Scriptures last night, I had the good luck, with the aid of the Almighty, to find a prophetic passage whose nonfulfillment even by a hair might hurl the world into eternal hell. Look, my brothers in Christ: 'Mine own familiar friend'—that is to say one of his most intimate company; 'in whom I trusted, which did eat of my bread'—a paraphrase that only strengthens the original decree for the betrayer, especially if by the term 'bread' one understands the faith which has nourished us; 'hath lifted up his heel against me'—provokes, therefore, his suffering.

"The Fifty-fifth Psalm, though more roundabout, goes even more deeply into the personality of the betrayer when it says that he who rose against the Lord was 'Thou, a man mine equal, my guide, and mine acquantaance,' for to whom would our most gentle Teacher compare himself if not to us, his first, and you could even say his only, followers up to the present? If we penetrate the sense of the verse, 'We took sweet counsel together,' we'll see that it could only mean us, the Twelve, to whom the Lord has entrusted all his earthly aims and with whom he rejoices in their fulfillment. Finally, strip away the husk of Obadiah's prophecy, and the destiny written for him will be completely clear: 'All the men of thy confederacy have brought thee even to the border' can only mean the frontier between life and death, the blade of suffering, the sharpest edge of the martyr's agony which makes essential the reverse side of every sacred sacrifice. 'That were at peace with thee' again speaks of us, for in this sacred moment only we share the same faith with the Savior. Finally, 'they that eat thy bread have laid a wound under thee' must mean the same as the conclusion of the Forty-first Psalm: he'll betray you, catch you in the snare of fate, open to you the gates of suffering. Taken as a whole, brothers, all these prophecies in a similar manner describe the pattern of the Savior's downfall and determine our role in it. One of us twelve, who is as our Master is, who shares the joy of his mysteries, will raise his heel against him, set a snare for him and betray him to the high priests and the godless, so they can crucify him and the Holy Scriptures be fulfilled. I add that this betrayal must be paid for, by those who profit by it, with thirty pieces of silver, so the prophecy of Zechariah is fulfilled: 'And I said unto them, If ye think good, give me my price; and if not, forbear. So they weighed for my price thirty pieces of silver.' "

The impression that my interpretation leaves on the Eleven is devastating, but the authority and inevitability of the Scriptures are such that no one openly denies it. At Ephraim they might still have contradicted me; if it's written that the Son of God must suffer on Passover (when could a lamb suffer except at the holy slaughter?), nowhere is it written on which Passover. Now, when it's already begun and we're in Jerusalem, it's too late to go back.

Simon the Canaanite tries anyway: besides the Twelve there are a few other men who can be said to share our faith and await the New Kingdom, men familiar with the Lord and who occasionally break bread with him. Joseph of Arimathaea, for example, a man of high standing who attached himself to us since Bethel. And a silly boy, a certain Stephen or Stefanus, who because of his fickle youth answered best to the role of innocent betrayer. Simon adds that the Scriptures don't specify the sex of the betrayer. Doesn't a horde of women always follow the Savior, carried away by his fiery discourses? Why shouldn't the betrayer be sought among them? What about Lazarus's sister Mary, already so steeped in the faith that she could be considered the first woman apostle? Or Salome? How many times has the Lord broken bread with Lazarus's other sister, Martha?

I reply: "Simon, the Scriptures say the betrayer will be one who 'is even as I am' and not 'might be.' I know this burden is the most terrible demand of the prophecy, perhaps even heavier than the Savior's, but we don't dare transfer it to the unauthorized, for if this one little word of the Scriptures is neglected, it can invalidate everything fulfilled earlier."

Andrew tries to look at the matter from an opposite viewpoint. He says: "Obadiah orders: 'All the men of thy confederacy have brought thee even to the border,' and not just one of them. According to that, we must all betray. In any case that would be fairer."

"That's correct," I say, "but haven't we already done it? Haven't we all brought him to the frontiers of death, all of us together? But only one must drive him to his death. The psalms say: 'It was thou, a man mine equal' and 'my guide and my acquaintance' and 'mine own familiar friend.' Not you, not men, but 'thou' and 'a man.' Let any one of you eleven decide. We haven't much time till nightfall."

"We're twelve, Judas," Philip comments, "twelve and not eleven. Or have you forgotten how to count, you who have charge of the purse?"

Imperceptibly we draw away from one another and the bulwark of faith cracks into twelve isolated units; each one breaks of itself, fears for itself, denies for itself.

I turn to Peter's brother: "Andrew, will you betray the Son of God and earn eternal fame?"

Andrew bows his head and is silent. His faith is weak and his soul too ordinary to grasp the greatness of the opportunity he refuses.

"Peter?"

"Peter is too humble to divide the salvation of the world with God."

Old good-for-nothing!

I put the same question to the sons of Zebedee. James replies: "With pleasure, Judas, but there are two of us and in the Scriptures it speaks of one betrayer. We can't both betray, nor can we split up in betrayal."

Philip grins. It's that same repulsive smile of comprehension he disarmed me with in Ephraim when we had our talk before the departure for Jerusalem.

"I'm sorry, Judas. I revere the Scriptures, but to me the Teacher is more important than the teaching."

"Matthew?"

"God keep me from it!"

"Simon?"

"Why me, when there are others? How about that Stephen?"

I don't bother to ask James Alphaeus. He's so thickheaded I couldn't send him to the well, let alone to the Sanhedrin and the high priests.

"Thomas?"

Thomas speaks slowly, in that sophisticated dialect of the Jerusalem high schools. He's one of those men, I'm convinced, who if told the world had come to an end, would ask calmly: "By what means?" He understands the necessity of upholding the prophecies, though he wonders that so vulgar a crime must serve as the cornerstone of the New Kingdom. If the betrayer succeeded he wouldn't scorn the man who'd taken such a task upon himself. But he couldn't personally accept that task, for even if he managed not to scorn another, he wouldn't spare himself. He's aware that he's depriving himself of the greatest holiness, but with regret refuses to become a scoundrel for idealistic reasons.

I might have expected that. Aristocratic swine! He wants to be pure in faith, but refuses to dirty his hands for the sake of it. How he'll be smashed when we're all numbered, when the earthen pots are broken at the end of the world!

I turn toward Levi Thaddaeus, but he's nowhere to be seen: the rat has simply vanished. There is still Bartholomew.

"Bartholomew, in your time you've been a robber and a murderer. Will you betray the Son of God and in this way earn release from the everlasting fire?"

"I don't dare, Judas, I'm afraid! What'll happen afterward to the man who betrays the only Son of the heavenly Father?"

"What are you afraid of? The betrayer is as inevitable as the betrayed, and was prophesied together with him. Without the one, you can't have the other. As an instrument in the world's salvation, you'll be under the protection of the prophets who announced your task. If Jesus sits at the right hand of the Father, you'll be seated on the left, for betrayer and betrayed are the two faces of the great work of redemption."

"In that case," Philip remarks sarcastically, "why don't you betray him? Besides general indications, doesn't the psalm give a brief description of the betrayer in phrases like 'mine own familiar friend' and 'in whom I trusted,' which could only refer to you, the Lord's favorite? Surely you're the one with whom he 'took sweet counsel together' and who was 'a man mine equal? Aren't you Judas the Guardian of Truth, Judas Let-it-be-fulfilled? So take this command of the Scriptures on your own back and don't load it on the backs of others like a coward."

We stand facing each other like the two banks of a river which have no chance of ever meeting and which, by virtue of that separation, make possible the flowing of the water: Judas on the one side and the Eleven on the other. Alien, distant, inaccessible. Then I say:

"Let the Lord decide."

> *On the fourteenth day of Nisan don't forget: by the well at Bezetha a water carrier will be drawing water, the Lord says, go after him and he'll lead you to a host at whose house we'll prepare for Passover. Then prepare some bitter herbs, parsley in salted water, and unleavened loaves (Mitzva cakes) for the seder. Be sure there's no leaven in them. Since the blood of lambs and goats is displeasing to God, there must be no Passover killing and no smearing of the doorposts with the bloodstained hyssop. In any case, won't the Savior himself be the lamb which tonight we'll place before his Father?*

Before evening the Teacher called me to discuss how we'd celebrate Passover. I took advantage of this opportunity to tell him what I'd found in the books of the prophets and the psalms of David concerning his sufferings. He was surprised, not to say pleased. He took a lively interest in the details of the prophecies, asked questions and discussed them. He was particularly struck by the Forty-first Psalm; I had to repeat it to him several times so he could learn it by heart. Then I had to admit that not one of the Twelve was willing to betray him; so the prophecies could be fulfilled without delay, I'd proposed that he himself choose the betrayer.

He smiled. Since we'd gone to Ephraim, this was the first smile to thaw his gloomy, sealed face. That smile was wry, unpleasant, bitter; an inward smirk which scarcely moved the skin about his lips and eyes and chilled everything it touched.

"All right," he said. "Now leave me."

We prepared for Passover at a modest tavern at Bezetha. We wanted to be as close as possible to the Sheep Gate, through which the road goes to Bethany and our lodging in the house of Simon the leper. The rented room was as narrow as a tunnel and scarcely lit by torches which burned along the walls in brackets of twisted rams' horns. The table had no cloth. On its darkened pine stood dishes of green herbs, unleavened leaves in seder bowls and goblets for wine with thirteen earthenware pitchers.

We sat in our usual places, the Teacher in the place of honor, I on his right and Simon Peter on his left. The other apostles sat around the table in no special order, except that on this occasion, in contrast to others, they sat as far as possible from the Teacher to avoid the slightest chance of being chosen. We were all as tense as bowstrings, not because of reverence for the ceremony, but because of this choice. It was this terrible uncertainty, not scornful disregard of the customs, that made us sit at the table instead of standing around it, our loins girded, our sandals on the feet and staff in hand, eating in fear and haste, remembering the evil days of Egypt.

He hesitated. As if intentionally delaying his choice, as if to torture us. Though he'd never been scrupulous in carrying out the Old Testament ritual—it was on that very heedlessness of the past that he'd founded his New Testament future—he now carried out all the customary ritual with unbearable slowness, not overlooking a single one of the Passover rules or the ceremonies required by the Law. Moreover, he gave to the ancient Levitical rituals, such as the breaking of the loaf, a new significance, based on the terrible fate hovering over him that night. Even though he'd always said he hadn't come to destroy the Law or the prophets and was eager to fulfill the rites as accurately as possible, he'd subtly distorted them, adapting them to his own ends without altering their outward form. He'd brought a fresh spirit into the ancient ritual. This reassured the traditionalists and the religious pedants, giving them the illusion that by accepting the spirit of the New Testament they in no way transgressed against the Old. But from then on, the Passover would no longer be a thanksgiving for liberation from slavery under the Pharaohs. In any case, why should the Jewish slaves and convicts be grateful to Jehovah, since with his aid they'd exchanged one slave driver for another, falling from Egyptian into Roman slavery? No, the man-God had something quite different in mind. Only that morning—besides worrying about that psalm of David—I'd worked out the procedure for all the communion details—with new significance, naturally—which he had only to repeat now carefully.

First he blessed the bread, repeating the ritual laid down, but after it had been broken into twelve parts, he gave one to each of us and so established his Holy Eucharist, saying:

"Take, eat. This is my body."

Then he took the goblet of wine, and after praying over it gave it to us to drink from. While the cup was being passed around the table, he said:

"Drink ye all of it, for this is my blood of the New Testament, which is shed for many for the remission of sins."

This was the right moment for him to tell us on whom his choice had fallen, but instead he began to tell how, when the hour of his suffering should come, we'd abandon him and flee in all directions.

I couldn't bear the uncertainty any longer.

"Lord"—I interrupted him just as he was comparing himself to the first vine and Jehovah to the husbandman—"I apologize for disturbing so fine and moral a sermon, but it's getting late and we beg you to finish what you have to do, so he whom you choose can do his work. Later you can go on with your parable."

"Ah, yes, that psalm: 'which did eat of my bread, hath lifted up his heel against me.' "

"Yes, Rabbi, that psalm."

"Must I be the one to do it?"

"Who else, Lord? It's your suffering. It's right that you hold all the threads in your hands."

"Very well," he said, sighing, "then I say to you that one of you will betray me."

Hurry, in the name of God, I thought, we've told you all that ourselves. But who, *who?*

"Who, Lord?"

"He to whom, dipping it in the dish, I shall give a morsel."

DIPPING A MORSEL IN THE DISH FILLED WITH THE JUICES OF THE HERBS, HE GAVE IT TO ME.

And he said to me:

"What you are going to do, do quickly."

I stand up. He smiles at me with a tiny tight smile which only I can see, and it's because of me that he smiles. I stand up. The Eleven stare at me, seeing only a man who rises to his feet; they don't recognize in me the twelfth fraction of the new dispensation. They look at me with loathing and respect, expressing neither emotion audibly. I stand up. I feel I should defend myself, shout, howl or give elaborate thanks for this honor, but I say nothing while the air whistles from my lungs, expelled by the gravestone of my brothers' glances, and his invisible smile like a mocking epitaph engraved on that same stone. I'm both ashamed and proud.

Without saying anything, I go out. At the door his mellifluous voice reaches me:

"As you see, Judas, the Son of man goes where it was written he should go and as you wished him to, but 'WOE UNTO THAT MAN BY WHOM THE SON OF MAN IS BETRAYED; IT HAD BEEN GOOD FOR THAT MAN IF HE HAD NOT BEEN BORN.' "

Jerusalem on the night of the fourteenth of Nisan.

Why me, Lord, why was I chosen? Why pluck only Judas from the meadow of the faith?

All Jerusalem glorifies the Exodus. Only Judas, the first man to taste the holy sacrament, deputy and chosen of the Chosen One, wanders like a mad dog with its tail between its legs through the empty city, through the crisscross flickerings of oil lamps, braziers, candles and torches from the Jerusalem houses. According to custom, men will remain inside those houses until the morning, protected by the blood-besprinkled thresholds and doorposts from which the hot lambs' blood drips, reassured and in all probability self-deceived by the idea that Jehovah enjoys breathing such rank incense, and singing hymns of thanksgiving. On all sides, in all directions, from above and below, the festival outcries are heard. In all this humming, echoing and singing sea of gratitude down the deserted byways of Zion, nowhere is there a single man passing by, nowhere a single cripple dozing, wrapped in his mendicant's rug, and nowhere a single drunk wallowing in the ditch, for even they have found company with someone somewhere. Only Judas, like a vulture soaring over Moriah, goes toward the Council Hall and all the time farther and farther from it, crushed by the locked houses, each a little fortress tonight, squeezed by the nasal, hoarse, piercing, hissing yells of the Holy City, barricaded in this desolate night of Passover against the memory of Pharaoh's mercenaries, whose gigantic phantoms—armed with cudgels, pikes and spears bearing tiny heads of baby Jews impaled on them—are still looking for the terrified children of Israel.

Why not Peter? Or Philip? Or Thomas? Why the favorite of the Most Beloved? Because he loves you. Because he wishes to share his Task with you alone, to live with you alone in his Task for time immemorial.

If he really loved me, he wouldn't force me to carry out the filthy obverse of his Task and keep its pure face for himself. He wouldn't send me to collect the excrement of the great sacrifice. The Task will look two-faced to the world to come. Will it be able to tell Judas from Christ, the redeeming crime from the redeeming sacrifice?

The greasy smell of roast meat, the many-voiced singing, the chomping jaws behind shuttered windows, the hum of devout chatter, the gurgling of wine, the faces smirched with ashes from the hearth. No one dares to go out till tomorrow. That's the Law. The gigantic phantoms of the Egyptians with axes and mallets watch at the corners of the streets. That's history.

This is your night, Judas! Your night in deserted Jerusalem!

What if he really hates me? What if the dipped morsel that he gave me is a revenge? Why should he seek revenge on him who spread the Kingdom beneath his feet? Because the coming to Jerusalem was my idea. My doing, and of course that of the prophets.

All right, Judas, he said, I'll go to Jerusalem. And he also said: Hope that the Scriptures, which have paid such attention to me, haven't forgotten *you*. Oh, don't worry, they haven't. I'm already in the Scriptures, pilloried by prophecy, walled in by fate.

What am I to do, Lord, what am I to do? To be fulfilled or not to be fulfilled?

The flabby artisan guzzles the herbs, wallows in the dish, stuffs himself in honor of the liberation, he whose peasant ancestors were kept alive by heavenly manna and the lichen of Sinai.

Philip says I'm a damned liar. I'm not a liar. How could I be a liar? I don't have a tongue of my own: what I say comes from the Scriptures.

Didn't you yearn secretly to be chosen? You conceited bastard, didn't you think that you alone were worthy of that sacrifice which is greater even than his—worthy of that holy crime which is greater than any virtue, more excellent than purity itself; because he'll give his mortal body as redemption for sin, but you'll give your immortal soul?

I didn't yearn for it. For who kept watch over him, sleepless, while he slept? Judas. Who nourished him? Who, standing in front of him, saved him from stoning at Timnath? Judas. Who reminded him of every word of the prophecies so God wouldn't reject him? Judas.

You paid less attention to him than to his Task. Like it or not, to preserve the Creation you must guard the Creator also.

How base he is, and how I love him! How evil he is, and how I worship him!

Deserted byways, deserted squares, deserted doorways, deserted Jerusalem, all full to the brim with Judas, with his footsteps and the echoes of their echo which reverberate from the peeling walls to wander through the night. On the shining curtain of the sky Judas's shadows quiver.

In the Council Hall the high priests celebrate the Passover. Annas and Caiaphas and the whole Sanhedrin are there. I must go to them and say: Here's Christ, give me my thirty pieces of silver. Here are fifty. No, I only want thirty, the appointed price.

Never.

You're afraid of being scorned, Judas. Are you afraid your name'll be thrown on a dunghill like carrion whereas his, washed clean by purity, will cleanse every mouth that utters it? Unjust, isn't it, Judas? Cruel!

And who'll be able to scorn me? Who dares look down upon the divine instrument? If it weren't for me, there'd be no salvation. I'm the Savior, not he. He's an ordinary sacrifice—a lamb like any other, a little blood which spouts from the cross.

O, get thee behind me, Satan!

At the unspread table, the family guzzles fast. That's the Law. One must eat quickly, because at any minute God's summons to the Exodus may come. The bundles have already been prepared, and on Jehovah's advice the valuables of the Egyptians have been despoiled. That's a fair, albeit compulsory, wage for forced labor. Payment for Pithom and Rameses, beneath whose towers the bones of Israel rot. Eat, hurry, stuff yourselves! Soon enough God will call you all into the wilderness.

"Hear, O Israel," Jerusalem sings. Streets dark as the tunnels of a molehill roar with praises.

Suddenly I'm standing before the Council Hall and the sentry taps me on the shoulder:

"What is it, young man? What are you looking for out there on this holy night?"

What am I looking for? Decision? Consolation? Truth? God? Salvation?

"Why aren't you eating your lamb?"

Oh, I'm eating soldier, I'm eating, I'm gulping down mouthfuls! I'm butchering my Christ, my only lamb.

I turn and run and the soldier laughs. His laughter runs after me, catches me, hits me in the face and gashes it with the sharpened nails of mockery.

Farther, Judas, still farther from your fate! Run, fly, find or dig some hole, you louse, coward, bastard! Fuck it all! The world, faith, God and the prophets. Get into your hole and don't peep out of it. It'll be nice for you in there, in your little hole: you'll be pure as the sea air, innocent as a corpse.

I'm in front of a hovel watching the shadows, now fused, now parted, as they hastily chew the bones of the lamb. The bones crackle. The teeth grind. Hurry, Jerusalem, till God announces that he'll lead you out of slavery.

And my lamb? He sits at the table and waits. He smiles.

It's time, Judas! Time for what? Betrayal. I can't, Lord, I can't! You must, Judas! The Scriptures must be fulfilled. You know that. One way or another.

Then better this way than any other. You've been chosen, you can't change that. At long last you drove him to Jerusalem. You drove him to provoke the priests and the Pharisees; that row with the money-changers in the Temple was your idea. He used your words when he scourged them, saying: Generation of vipers, whores and whoremongers, lawless, sinful idlers! Remember how briskly you stepped forward when one was sought to drink with Jesus the cup which had been poured for him, and to be baptized with the baptism prepared for him. Here's the cup of shame. Drink! Here's the juicy—the overjuicy—morsel from the table, from God's own dish. Swallow it!

That damned singing! And your faith? Is it really a crime? Faith knows nothing of crimes, it knows only of failures. And your love? Faith doesn't know love, it knows only means.

Your immortal soul? Faith knows nothing of souls, it knows only immortal deeds. That damned singing! When will it stop?

The singing stops.

The anointed priest Caiaphas looks me up and down with the pale, faded eyes of an old man. He must be eighty at least. Behind him, in high priest's garb, stands the lean, spry Annas, his loins girded, a traveler's staff in his hand (in memory of the haste in which the first Passover in Egypt was eaten). At the table a few members of the Holy Sanhedrin are chewing the bones and ladling out the lamb's tripes. Only the Sadducee Nicodemus hears my offer.

"Who is this Nazarene?" Caiaphas asks Annas.

Annas shrugs: he's never heard the name. Joshua ben Joseph? A very common name in Galilee. Meanwhile, the priest Ohozius reminds the Most Reverend Caiaphas of the case of a certain blind man, Bartimaeus son of Timaeus. That was long ago. A man with a similar name restored his sight. For unknown reasons Bartimaeus gouged out his eyes soon after, but the miracle had lasted a while. Caiaphas can't remember. Annas can't remember either.

Perhaps there's still hope for Judas. I think. Perhaps the whole thing will collapse of itself. I hate my own thinking because I know that the price of Judas's salvation is the downfall of the world and the defeat of the faith founded on its redemption.

Nicodemus gives His Reverence Caiaphas some scanty information about Christ. A Galilean. A peasant, indeed a peasant artisan. A wonder-worker. A poor speaker. To some extent an intriguer. Basically, rather naive. Nicodemus doesn't recommend punitive measures. Perhaps a good scourging and as a final resort, expulsion from the city.

"Your Reverence," I intervene, "I must contradict the most honorable Nicodemus. This man thinks he's the child of God."

"We're all children of God, young man," replies Caiaphas.

"But he thinks he's the only one."

The priests stop gnawing their bones.

"And that he's a king!"

"A king! And where's his kingdom?"

"In heaven, master!"

"Pretty far away," mutters Annas.

I beg them to accept my betrayal, I beg them not to: these two passionate prayers course through me like opposing waves of the same stormy sea.

"He breaks the Law, master!"

Caiaphas says sorrowfully: "Young man, a good half of this ill-mannered people do just that."

"He performs miracles."

The priests return to their meal.

"On the Sabbath," I add humbly, hoping this will annoy the theologians, but it doesn't. In the end I lose control:

"May His Reverence pardon my free speech, but this Nazarene says publicly that the Holy Sanhedrin is a bunch of swine, that you're the head swine and Their Reverences here the pigs of lawlessness!"

"Ohozius"—Caiaphas turns to one of those at the table—"give this young man a few guards to bring that blasphemer here."

Judas fulfills what is written. "If you think it good, give me my price. If not, forbear," I say, repeating what was written for me.

They weigh out my reward: forty pieces of silver. I take only thirty. Then I lead the hirelings of the Sanhedrin to the tavern. It's empty, wax dripping from the candle which is nearing its end, darkening the room and its table covered with bread crumbs, overturned goblets and leaves from herbs. The innkeeper tells me that the Lord has gone to Gethsemane.

Jerusalem is still singing. The roofs of the houses, straining toward heaven, sing; the towers of Zion, pale against the darkness, sing; the cobbles, the ramparts and the bloodied thresholds of the houses howl. Jerusalem is devouring its sacrifice. But only now Judas is rushing to slaughter his.

I wade across the brook of Kidron and lead the Sanhedrin hirelings through Gethsemane, hampered by the spectral mists of dawn. We pass close to the apostles. They are sleeping wrapped in their mantles. They don't know what's happening or don't want to know. They snore while Christ and I, two zealous workers, continue our task of saving the world. He's nowhere to be found. Has he run away? We search the paths, the soldiers thrust their spears into the bushes, looking for the lost lamb.

Now I hear curious murmuring. A sob reaches me from a clearing where the dark is fading. The Rabbi is lying prone, and praying:

"O my Father, if it be possible, let this cup pass from me."

Silence. Heaven doesn't answer. Jerusalem is no longer humming with song. The celebrants are preparing to cross their bloodstained thresholds at the first light.

"O my Father," he repeats feverishly, "if it be possible, let this cup pass from me."

No reply. Or is there? Silence. It's the answer to both of us, the irrevocable answer to our cowardice. To his cry for mercy and to my shame. God wants his true sacrifice. He's tired of the blood of lambs, kids, bullocks. Don't waver, Judas, or your Passover will have gone. He's lost all manliness, crouched there on the earth, which darkens in contrast to the clear, mute peace of the skies.

I approach him. He rises quickly, but when he sees no one behind me, his face in the dawn becomes thankful, perhaps seeing in my return without an executioner the answer from his Father. The last kiss—my kiss of farewell, his kiss of gratitude born of misunderstanding—and all is over. One more word of the Scriptures is no longer just a word. Face to face, yet infinitely separated, we make up the two halves of the work of salvation.

Then both at once, with no time to think, we hear the steps of the Sanhedrin guards approaching, swinging their lanterns filled with the dawn of the new day, the day of suffering.

Fourteenth of Nisan. In the purse: total	*12 drachmas*
Rent of rooms for Passover	*3 drachmas*
Six kilos of greens, half an ephah of flour	*4 drachmas*

Unleavened loaves	*1½ drachmas*
Cutlery (hire)	*½ drachma*
Candles, lanterns, torches	*1 drachma*
Expenses on the first day of Passover	*10 drachmas*
Income on the first day of Passover	*30 pieces of silver*
Fifteenth of Nisan. In the purse: total	*30 pieces of silver and 1 didrachma*

There's nothing left in Judas. Nothing left in Judas Guardian of Truth, nothing in Judas Let-it-be-fulfilled. Judas the Stickler is empty, drained. Is there anything in Judas the Betrayer, in Judas the Savior? Is there anything in the new Judas, now that the old has passed away?

There isn't. Neither shame nor pride; neither panic nor arrogant self-confidence; neither grief nor cruel indifference; there's no past, but no future either. No more Scriptures, but where's the compensating freedom? Neither faith nor lack of faith; neither authority nor lack of it; neither triumph nor defeat. There's nothing in Judas. Not even an emptiness, but less than that: nothing. Less than indifference: nothing. Less than absence: nothing. Less than nothing: nothing.

Last night Jerusalem was empty and Judas full; now Jerusalem's full again and Judas's empty. Last night I filled, I glutted, the deserted streets; now I pass through those same streets, but being nothing I don't fill them. Look at the blood dried on the thresholds which the sleepless citizens of Jerusalem step over at dawn to fill the Holy City, which at that same moment I leave empty. The fresh cheek of the day rests on the dark blood of the lambs, as the children of Israel push their way through my absence, through my stifling nonexistence, the rustle of nothing, while they clamor in the deserted corridors at my voicelessness and echo heedlessly amid the uninhabited walls of Judas's deed.

Faces pass that are dried and slack from prayers and vigils; faces moist as if drawn from a well; faces like mildew on old wood, like worn coins, grease drippings, tangled balls of wool; faces drowsy from communion, belching from too much unleavened bread. The clarity of daylight dispels the visions of Pharaoh's mercenaries with raised pikes. I see faces yellow, blue, red, black, green, gray, gold and orange: tiny masks in the dense smoke of the incense which I, unfulfilled and drained, recognize down to the last senseless detail. There goes a smith, black as coal, taking his family for a morning walk; a Levite, spawn of Aaron's rod, speeding to the Temple before the first wail of the holy ram's horn; a cripple dragging himself on his calloused stumps among the crisscross footsteps of the citizens; a veteran of the Tenth Legion leaning heavily on his javelin, who dreams of his bestial saturnalia in December among the worthless Oriental mobs, unhappy and lonely, but unhappy as a master and lonely as a despot; a little whore who rubs herself against me, hating Passover because it's celebrated in the family circle, and who tries hysterically to find compensation for her forced abstinence in the bearlike grip of some soldier of Herod's; and street kids bloated from green herbs, whose noisy cries break on the impenetrable wall of holiday walkers.

Through Judas, as through the empty corridors of salvation, stream the countless processions of the redeemed.

Here I am again before the Council Hall. Here are the heavy gates through which an apostle went in and a betrayer came out. Here's the guard. Naturally, not the same one as last night, and doubled besides. Inside they're judging Our Lord.

"Are you the Son of God?"

"Thou sayest it."

"Are you the King of the Jews?"

"Thou sayest it."

"A breaker of the Law?"

"Thou sayest it."

"A wonder-worker?"

"Thou sayest it."

"A wonder-worker on the Sabbath?"

"Thou sayest it."

In the courtyard of a butcher's shop opposite, the Eleven are awaiting the outcome of the trial. I approach them, but they move away in silence, maintaining the distance laid down by Moses for intercourse with lepers and excommunicates. Seven paces from Judas.

Seven paces from the sacrifice? Seven paces from the Savior? Wasn't all that agreed among you, you sons of bitches? What am I but your long arm, your spellbinding tongue, the body of your thoughts? Why these seven paces of damnation, you sons of bitches?

"Cephas?" Silence. "Thomas?" Silence. "Philip?" Silence. "James Alphaeus?" (Blockhead of the Lord, have I reached the point of turning to you?) Silence.

Sons of bitches! Bastards! Filthy bastards!

At last Cephas begins to speak. But he's careful not to lessen the seven paces' distance. He speaks without looking at anything, for I'm nothing and can't be looked at. As if from an unbridgeable distance, he turns toward that somebody /nobody who exists only temporarily, thanks to his attention and his merciful voice.

"O Judas, our glory, hero of the faith!"

The Eleven sing melodiously: "Alleluia! Alleluia! Glory to Judas in the highest!"

"O Judas, first among the first, greatest among the great, savior among the saved!"

The Eleven respond: "Alleluia! Alleluia! Glory to Judas in the highest!"

"We humbly bow to your sacrifice, made for the redemption of sin!"

Then why those seven paces? Why in this apotheosis—because that's what it is: humility before a divinity in recognition of a superhuman deed—why that glance aimed at nothing? It's as if that glance doesn't search for God but takes it for granted that he's here, evident to devout eyes, and that he's mounting into the skies so that all Jerusalem, if it weren't drunk, could see him rising above the roofs, the synagogues and ramparts like the bloody reflection of a humble Galilean who in the muddy courtyard of a Zion butcher still hesitates to accept the highest distinction. Why those closed faces? They're featureless, without expression. In the penetrating, revealing, treacherous sun of Nisan there are eleven dead worshipers, eleven sacks of dead flesh.

Isn't Judas a greater god than Jesus? I offered more, sacrificed more, suffered more than Jesus. I'm more of a man, so aren't I more of a god? More of a god and therefore more of a man? Aren't I He Who Is, and Jesus only what I wanted him to be? The prophets prophesied through me, and wasn't every one of their messages—he didn't even bother to read them—uttered by Judas's voice? He didn't know a single prophecy, not even those which personally concerned him. Who brought him to Jerusalem? Judas. Who set him on a donkey? Judas. Who produced those cries of "Hosanna to the Son of David! Hosanna in the highest!"? Judas. Who prepared the Jerusalem sermons? Judas. Who prepared the last Passover? Judas. Finally, who sold him for thirty pieces of silver, so the Scriptures could be fulfilled? Judas. Everything that was done was done by Judas. My Lord didn't move a finger. All that he'll do now is rise from the dead after three days and ascend to heaven. Maybe he won't be able to do even that by himself. Maybe Judas will end up doing it for him.

Now I understand the behavior of the Eleven. The seven Mosaic paces aren't inspired by fear but respect; it's a withdrawal not from scorn but adoration. The Old Testament has become the New.

Suddenly Cephas breaks the solemn mood and goes on in a businesslike manner:

"They subjected Our Lord—as you yourself know, since you betrayed him—to interrogation in the Great Council, then escorted him to the procurator, Pilate. We don't know what happened in the governor's palace—they're judging him now—but you can be sure they'll condemn him, if only to fulfill the Scriptures. You who've always attached such importance to the prophets—and I hope you still do—know how the prediction runs. The Lord, together with two thieves, will be crucified; on the third day he'll rise from the dead, and as announced to us in a vision, will ascend to heaven. Then redemption will take place, what has to be will be and every letter of the Scriptures will have been fulfilled. Except the one referring to you, Judas Iscariot!"

All right, when I die I'll take my place at the Lord's table, on the left side of the Rabbi, as the inseparable third of the

Holy Trinity of the Savior: Judas, Jehovah, Joshua, JJJ. What besides respect can I look for here on earth?

And I say: "Let's not exaggerate, Cephas! The Scriptures said of me only that I'd raise my heel against the Lord with whom I was even as he was, and that for thirty pieces of silver I'd betray him to those who don't know God. Nothing more!"

But Cephas insists: "That's only part of the prophecy relating to you. When he chose you for evil, didn't the Lord say: 'The Son of man goeth as it is written of him: but woe unto that man by whom the Son of man is betrayed! It had been good for that man if he had not been born'?"

I burst out: "Jesus isn't a prophet! Jesus himself is only a work of a prophet."

I want to say my work, Judas's work, but remain silent. The Deed is above the Doer and outside him, as warmth is outside the flame. The Creation is more important than the Creator, the Teaching more important than the Teacher, Salvation more important than the Savior.

"Allow me to contradict you, Judas! He who's prophesied is unchangeable, made ready before he began, and acquires the right to prophesy, to make others unchangeable and ready even before they've begun to get ready. Born from the Scriptures, he gives birth to them again; he gives birth to a new Scripture. The Lord has come out of the Old Testament as its last word. From him will come the New Testament, in which you, Judas, will be the first word."

"What more do you want of me?"

Peter Cephas hesitates to explain. Leaning against a wall, James Alphaeus drowses, reliving the Last Supper; Philip smirks with that sleepy Ephraim smile; the sons of Zebedee look at me murderously with the staring eyes of boxers in the ring; and the coward Bartholomew is, as always, surprised, and with the astonishment of a man who doesn't know what it's all about, is already thinking up excuses to avoid involvement.

Then Peter Cephas speaks:

"Judas, we want you to repent, and to give back to the priests the thirty pieces of silver so that with them they can buy the potter's field and use it as a graveyard for strangers, and it'll be called Aceldama, the field of blood. We want you to fulfill that 'Woe unto that man by whom the Son of man is betrayed,' we want you to die. I think it would be best if you went outside the town and quietly hanged yourself."

"That's not possible!" I scream, but all that can be heard is a hoarse whisper, like the rubbing of paper on paper. "Why should I hang myself? How am I to blame? I've only fulfilled the Scriptures."

Peter speaks again: "We all know that, Judas. Haven't we bowed our heads before your magnificent sacrifice? But if the prophecy isn't carried out and you don't kill yourself, no one will believe in the power and truth of him whom you followed. Men will ask what sort of a wretched God lets them go unpunished who betray him, put him to death and disregard his orders. How then do we maintain the faith? On what do we found our Church?"

That's your own thinking, Judas—your vocabulary. Your truth which you now listen to like a schoolboy: the Deed is above the Doer, the Creation above the Creator, may the Scriptures be fulfilled even if the world comes to an end. That's you talking to yourself.

"This is what the prophecies say of you," Peter goes on, "the Hundred and Ninth Psalm of David. To the chief musician: 'When he shall be judged, let him be condemned: and let his prayer become sin.' "

Judas doesn't dare pray. They judge him without appeal. The crime is before the criminal, the evildoer before the evil deed. Sons of bitches!

" 'Let his days be few; and let another take his office.' "

Peter, you son of a bitch! You're the one who'll get it!

" 'Let the extortioner catch all that he hath; and let the strangers spoil his labor.' "

Do these bastards want to take my Deed from me? To pollute my sacrifice, so they can get fat on my torments and feed like lice on my boundless faith?

" 'Let there be none to extend mercy unto him; neither let there be any to favor his fatherless children.' "

Judas has no one whom mercy will benefit. No one except

himself. No one except himself, you sons of bitches! Somewhere will there be a kiss even for Judas? Despite the prophecies, despite the Scriptures?

" 'Let his posterity be cut off; and in the generation following let their name be blotted out.' "

From apotheosis to anathema, from glory to curses—a short while ago greater than God, now less than Satan! Where's truth, you bastards, or are there two truths? Both true—two inimically true truths, one within the other, contradictory in the same world, at the same place, at the same time, ready to be accomplished with equal truthfulness?

" 'Let the iniquity of his fathers be remembered with the Lord; and let not the sin of his mother be blotted out.' "

You can save the whole world, your own mother can't. You've thought it out nicely: Judas can make a saint of a stinking Magdala prostitute fresh out of a brothel, but he can't expiate the sin in which his own mother bore him! Must Judas blush for whores? For bitches? For bastards?

" 'Because that he remembered not to shew mercy, but persecuted the poor and needy man, that he might even slay the broken in heart. As he loved cursing, so let it come unto him: as he delighted not in blessing, so let it be far from him.' "

Didn't I remember to show mercy? Is it a small thing to save the world? Isn't that mercy?

That's Scripture. Prophecy saved the world.

Naturally, but at Judas's expense.

I drove the poor and look where it got me. And in my own heart don't I seek death? Answer, you bastards! Howl, you dogs!

" 'As he clothed himself with cursing like as with his garment, so let it come into his bowels like water, and like oil into his bones. Let it be unto him as the garment which covereth him, and for a girdle wherewith he is girded.' "

And the Eleven sing in unison: "Amen. Accursed be thou, Judas Iscariot!"

Once again a lightning-swift turmoil of faces. A torrent, a flood, a waterfall of faces overwhelming Judas, violet flowers of faces blossom around me, berries of faces burst open, colliding with one another in a bestial swirl of greasy skin, seamless robes, heavy Nazarene beards and shepherds' staves with which the children of Jacob hurriedly pace their way through the wilderness of Sinai. As if I'm fleeing through my own dream, running faster and faster, fleeing but not getting anywhere, not even managing to move, while the roar of the Jerusalem crowd explodes around me, farther and farther from truth, farther from destiny, from the Hundred and Ninth Psalm, from the apostles glued to the fence of a butcher's courtyard.

> *On the fifteenth of Nisan prepare towels and a clean shroud for the burial of our Lord, Jesus Christ. An oka of myrrh and aloes to anoint the body. Consult about that with the women, especially Salome and Mary Cleophas. Also find a grave in which to bury him. Refer to Joseph of Arimathaea, but so as to*

Why am I writing all this? What concern is it of mine? Why should I still carry out my duties when I'm damned and outcast?

Let the Eleven worry about that. Let that worthless Cephas worry about the burial. And wasn't Philip a washer of the dead at Bethsaida? You, Judas, worry about your own affairs. Hurry, look for a strong tree and a well-plaited rope and a stone on which you'll climb toward heaven to put your head in the noose. Letter by letter, word by word, fulfill your end; repent, throw the pices of silver at the feet of the priests, go outside the city and hang yourself on the first strong tree you come across, hang yourself facing Jerusalem, the abode of God and the endless eastern sky.

Come on, Judas!

The world is waiting: you owe it only this. You won't feel safe in your salvation as long as you're alive. You won't believe until, hanging there, you see your guts split open.

Come on, Judas!

Hang yourself, split open your guts for the world—not for

your mother, but for those harlots of the Caesarea docks who vomit fish heads on the sailors, for that Jerusalem trash; not for your own mother, but for Caiaphas and his whore of a mother, for Annas and his whore of a mother, for all the mothers of the world except your own dear little mother, who bore Judas.

Come on, Judas!

Hang yourself, burst your guts so the prophecy will be fulfilled. Split open for the faith and the Church. Don't wipe the spit of scorn off your face. Burst on the gallows like a dry gourd in the frost.

Come on, Judas!

The aedile of Jerusalem keeps the way open; the procession from Gabbatha winds nearer. First came a squad of drunken legionaries from the procurator's guard and then, swaying above the throng of Jerusalem sightseers, those six black beams in the semblance of three bare crosses. They're taking My Lord to Golgotha. The robbers who'll hang on his right and left—so the Scriptures will be justified—bear their crosses firmly enough. But the Lord is bent under his. He staggers along the narrow corridor of the Jerusalem onlookers, lurching from side to side as far as the soft walls of flesh, while the long arms of the cross drag along the cobbles and at times strike the knees of the spectators. They swear and kick the cross away, forcing the condemned man from one side to the other of the passage. He falls, borne down by his last resting place—the position will soon be reversed—then rises to his knees which are visible, thin as spikes, under his bloodstained rags. Then he falls again, hitting the earth with his battered body, while the Sanhedrin guards, unable to strike his head ringed by thorns, beat with their staves on the cross.

A man beside me whipers hoarsely: "Come on, speak! 'Forgive them, Lord, for they know not what they do.' Come on, speak, King of the Jews! Barabbas has said his piece. Say yours!"

He rises again and goes on struggling toward the Silchem Gate, rebounding from the walls of the Jerusalem onlookers as if from a stretched bowstring. And there, at the exit from the city, an unknown man takes the Lord's place, bearing the cross on his own weak back.

If this unknown old man can bear another's cross, though not forced to do so, why can't Judas bear his own predicted one? At the Day of Judgment will some anonymous Jew be greater than Judas? Will it be said of Judas: "So then because thou art lukewarm, and neither cold nor hot, I will spue thee out of my mouth"? Redemption is your work, the fruit of your labors, the reward of your sufferings. You can't withhold it now, even if you don't believe in it any more. But you *do* believe and won't die unconsoled, complaining that your birth was futile.

And so, directly after divine service, while the summons of the ram's horn is still dying away in the narrow streets, I go to the Temple and return the thirty pieces of silver to the elders of the priests. They won't take them. So I throw them on the stone floor; the random money rolls clinking on the floor of his Father's house. Before I leave, I warn them they must use that money to buy the field, make of it a graveyard for strangers and call it Aceldama.

Then I go looking for a rope. Since the shops are closed, I beg the apostles to get me one. Always maintaining those seven paces of distance, they refuse—except for friendly advice—to take any part in my hanging. The Scriptures say nothing of their cooperation.

I buy a rope several yards long from some Samaritan caravan leader, who takes it off his mule for two of my remaining drachmas. It's only fair that Judas's rope be paid for out of the common purse. I try its strength, then pay. So I'll hang myself with a halter. Or a yoke. Besides, don't I and the Samaritan mule have a common destiny: on our backs we bear the burden of others!

Now to choose a place. The prophecies are no help. They don't say the creator of the Passion should himself suffer. In this, Judas has complete freedom: he can die wherever he likes.

The only thing asked of me is that I die outside Jerusalem.

Does that mean I'm given time to travel the whole world over to find an appropriate place? Must Judas search for his grave from the Pillars of Hercules to the Hyrcanian Sea, from icy Scandia to the bottomless pits of the black South, and find it nowhere, before the grave finds him? But Judas isn't a rat. He remembers Ephraim:

"And is the time written?"

"Yes, Lord! It's said that it'll be on Passover. The Son of man must suffer on the Feast of Unleavened Bread."

"On which Passover? Is it said? In what year since the creation of the world?"

"No, Lord."

"In which year after Moses?"

"No, Lord."

"Then wait!"

Couldn't I too ask what time was written for me? I could tell them to wait, for my time hasn't come yet.

You brought the Lord to the City; bring yourself to the Tree.

Only three places outside Jerusalem come to mind: the valley of Hinnom, the valley of Jehoshaphat, and Golgotha. At Golgotha the sacrifice and the sacrifice of the sacrifice would hang side by side: Jesus on the cross, Judas on the tree. What a spectacle! The Obverse and the Reverse of salvation in the same place: the united Deed in the same hour of revelation, before the prophesied adoration of the Obverse erases every expression and the loathsomeness of the Reverse is still more deeply incised. And there'll be lots of people there—those who love to look on suffering. They bring their lunch, spread out their rugs on the grass and watch. Sometimes they vomit, but that's a risk they have to take. Sometimes the soldiers drive them away and they go away without protest and come back again on the other side. They'll always be there. They recognize in suffering an alien exploit which they themselves aren't capable of—an exploit they accept without thought. They laugh if they're reminded of the simulated deaths in traveling circuses, or if they're threatened by the outpouring of semen flowing not from enjoyment but pain, or if they mourn over others' crosses or over their own, real as those at which they stare, branded on their shoulders where everyone bears the scars of humiliation, lies, pain, the agony of forgiveness and the pain of repentance. Even so, they are at the executions, laughing, holding back their tears, disgusted, angry, indifferent, at the place of execution and not at home, at the crosses and not at table, looking at the monstrous face of death not of childbirth (though in the case of the Lord there's precious little difference between death and birth, for one is born also in agony). They don't know who's dying or whose torments they'll tell about in lively stories at tomorrow's supper. Sometimes they even lay bets: who'll go first, and whose shinbones the impatient soldiers will have to break. Golgotha. The public. This housewife whose milk is boiling over at home but who is watching life boil over at the place of execution. That vendor of mead, dates, sweet grape juice, wine and refreshing water. Those hordes of little boys playing hide-and-seek among the legs, the crosses and the bushes. Those cripples pleased that at last they are witnessing a greater misfortune than their own. No, Lord, Golgotha isn't the graveyard for Judas.

The valley of Jehoshaphat is more in accord with the Scriptures. In that fertile—overfertile—plain, the Lord will judge the enemies of Israel. But I'm not an enemy of Israel. I'm its Savior. So what business do I have in that waiting room of the Last Judgment?

There remains the valley of Hinnom. Tradition has it that the gates of hell are in that dry, barren wasteland, but even so the land is all sold and the leading Jerusalem artisans have their fields there. A few fertile properties in the vicinity of hell. It would be right if I hanged myself in that very field the priests will buy as a graveyard for guests. Aren't I a guest in Jerusalem, a foreigner in my own land? Unredeemed in my own redemption? The prophets didn't think about Judas's grave—the dogs will take care of his bones—but if they'd thought about it they'd certainly have chosen Aceldama, his rich reward. Even destiny has its own destiny, its own limits. Perhaps some casual, imprudent prediction creates a whole century.

Come on, Judas, get to the valley of Hinnom.

The way to the valley of Hinnom leads through the Upper City. The way to death leads past the brothel. At the window of that house of shame Mary Magdalene appears. Yes, Mary also is my work to some extent. She waves a thin, transparent hand. I don't turn. The Lord has done his work with her.

"Rabbi," I said, "you've made the paralyzed walk, the blind see, the mute speak; you've cleansed the unclean and brought the dead back to life. Transform the Magdalene, the whore from the Upper City, into a saint, for it's written: he keeps company with publicans, harlots and sinners. Shut her up like a grave. Lord, bar her to all men, prevent her from opening herself, no matter how many knock at the door of her chastity."

You went in. I went in with you. You paid, though in fact I paid for you out of the common purse. You talked with the pimp from Sarepta, who offered you first a Syrian girl, an ordinary bamboo reed, describing her ventral skill as if it were his own, and then a barrel of a Numidian whom he claimed was a real *perpetum mobile*. You wanted a Jewish girl, Mary of Magdala. You had to wait, for she was busy. When your turn came, you went upstairs and I, yearning for a fresh miracle, went with you. You looked for the Magdalene's room. The numbers were like the holy psalms, one, two, three, four, seven, eight, in that overheated passage that smelled of dirty bedclothes and the sour stink of spittoons; the walls, scrawled all over with genitals, resounded from creaking beds and coarse tendernesses. You went in and I stayed outside. As always: I prepare everything, then you go in alone. Everything took place behind those doors, in the iron ring of the keyhole as in an iron trap; the edge of the bed with a shabby wool coverlet, the chapped soles of the Lord's feet, and the thighs of the Magdalene shining in the half-light of the lantern on the wall. That night you closed her and I peered through the keyhole. As always.

Farewell, Jerusalem. Farewell, padlocked maiden of Magdala.

Hail, Hinnom, Judas's open bed, his last pillow.

Hinnom is a flat desolation over which some foolish bird

swoops, casting its shadow on the earth. Far to the right, by the Kidron valley, a tree is withering. Judas's tree, carefully tended and reserved for him. There's nothing in that harsh plain between me and my tree, between the two innocent tools of prophecy. O, my innocent little tree! Do you know the man who hurries toward you in the moonlight to throw himself into your embrace? You've survived long enough to bear Judas. Indeed, the tree only follows its wise destiny. Even a tree can't escape what's written. A boulder rolls where it's been written it should roll. Water runs to where the mainstream waits for it, and light is drawn toward the sunset. "The thing that hath been," says the Preacher, "is that which shall be; and that which is done is that which shall be done: and there is no new thing under the sun." Why live, O man? Rather pore over your Bible, read the prophets, sing the psalter! Why? Isaiah will take care of how you live. Zechariah has prepared your death. Joel has numbered your torments. Amos pushes you one way, Obadiah another. You'll go this way, for Ezekiel wants it; you won't reach where you're going, because in this or that chapter or verse Daniel expressly forbids it. When you sneeze, skim the pages of the prophet Malachi and you'll find: "And then he sneezed."

As for my tree: it'll wither as soon as I hang myself. After that it's no longer important and can die. There's no difference in freedom between me and my tree. It has grown only so I can hang myself on it, and I was born only so I can hang on it.

Now the earth will quake and announce the Savior's death. In fact, it's quaking now. That's how it's written. Under a clear sky—unexpected, unless a man knows the Old Testament by heart—a thick scum of storm is gathering. About a dozen flashes of lightning, for that too is written. It's over quickly, for it isn't a natural storm. The night again becomes clear and reveals the valley of Hinnom. Naturally, my tree still stands. Not a single thunderbolt dares strike it. That isn't written.

Shit.

What'll happen if Judas doesn't hang himself? Despite

Isaiah and Ezekiel and Zechariah. To spite Jeremiah. If he just spits on all this, leaves the tree and returns to Jerusalem?

And the Deed? The salvation of the world? "If a single word be not fulfilled, then it will be as if nothing has been fulfilled."

The earth has quaked. The world was saved when the Savior died. My hanging is a totally unnecessary ritual. What use is it to anyone?

Don't blaspheme, Judas! Remember: Let's go to Jerusalem, Lord. It will hurt, I'm afraid. It's written, Lord, that you'll suffer at Jerusalem. It will hurt, I'm afraid. By these torments, O Lord, you'll redeem original sin. It will hurt, I'm afraid.

If Christ's death has meaning, Judas's has none. Judas's death is a whim.

If you don't hang yourself, the Church will crumble. It will hurt, I'm afraid. If you don't hang yourself, who'll believe in justice? It will hurt, I'm afraid. If you don't hang yourself, on what will the power of your Teacher be based? It will hurt, I'm afraid.

I touch my loyal tree. Its bark is coarse and wrinkled. It's grown old waiting for me. But I don't believe that it longs to wither. Even a tree strives to live on.

Lord, come to Jerusalem. Mount the donkey, Lord. Curse the Sadducees, O Lord. Come, Lord, heal this one. Resurrect that one. Finally, Lord, bear your cross.

What will happen if this tree of mine and I remain two unfulfilled little words of prophecy, if we outwit the Scriptures?

My jealous God from Ephraim appears and his thundering roars through me: To the tree, Judas, to the tree! I beg him to let this cup pass from me—a full-voiced wail through this unbearable noise—because I don't want to die at thirty (And my earthly Son, how old was he on the cross?) because I haven't lived a single day fully (And how many full days did he live through?), and I won't die because of some crazy prophet and his sick visions. Judas, to the tree! roars God, his powerful shout penetrating the forest of my complaints.

(To the tree, Judas, to the tree!)

I can't, Lord!

(How could he?)

He had an aim beyond death and mine was in his suffering. Now what's left of my life doesn't belong to any son of a bitch of a prophet, to any lousy word of prophecy, but to Judas, unwritten, unforetold, ruled by chance, free (To the tree, Judas, to the tree!), and I've the right to do with myself what I like, to hang myself or not, for I'm no longer in the Deed which by that earthquake a short while ago you handed over complete into my hands.

(To the tree, Judas, to the tree!)

I take the rope from under my cloak, make a noose, tie a triple knot, throw the rope up in the tree and tie it firmly to a branch. I make sure I've got a stone to stand on, fix it in the earth so it won't shift, test the rope to see if it'll bear me,

> *Jerusalem, sixteenth day of Nisan. Yesterday Jesus Christ was buried. On Friday evening, so as not to desecrate the Sabbath by a burial. Joseph of Arimathaea buried him.*

then go back to Jerusalem.

While I was fussing with my tree, a few of the faithful buried the Savior. They buried him immediately after the earthquake with which the earth said farewell to the Son of God—or maybe Satan, bursting with bile, said farewell to humanity. Did men feel any change—that lightening of heart a sleeper feels when the nightmare leaves him, or that freedom when persistent pain suddenly passes away? I didn't feel any freedom, but I'm excluded from salvation. I and my mother. And my children, if I had any. The people of Jerusalem whom I meet in the street don't seem sinless to me, no more than yesterday when they were languishing under centuries of guilt. In no way purer. In no way more conscious of the redemption which overtook them unnoticed last night when they were sitting at supper or chattering around the brazier where hot dung was smoking.

Now they can begin all over again. They can eat the forbidden fruit, be tricked by the serpent. Cain can kill Abel again. They can whore with Sodom. Some future Jacob can deceive some future Esau. Joseph's brothers can push him in the well again. They can again dance around the golden calf, or something else just as glittering which looks like a god. The world is once more empty and clean as a sheet of paper, on which I'm the only blot. Something which hasn't been wiped away and in its isolation unites the Old Testament with the New.

In the street of the potters I meet Cephas. He looks at me as if the ghost of Judas walks Jerusalem, since according to the detailed plan of the prophet the real Judas is hanged. Of course Cephas knows I haven't hanged myself. With ill-feigned astonishment he wants only to express disapproval. Why are you wavering, Judas? Because I don't feel like dying, Peter. No better reason.

I know you're all spying on me. Do you think that I didn't see the sons of Zebedee crouching in the stone quarry above the valley of Hinnom and how they watched me all night? I'd like to have seen their ugly snouts when I chose the tree, tied the noose, brought the stone on which I'd stand, then left and returned to Jerusalem!

Even in the city they don't let me out of their sight. Does that scum expect me to hang myself only to please them, to please those crazy prophets who up till now have served me blindly? Let them spy on me. Let them wait! What do I care?

I drag behind me those two dense shadows. I spread them about me whenever I move, I cast them whenever I stop to take a breath. If I go forward I meet John; if I turn back, James. If I turn to the right, James; if to the left, John. There's no street without them, no place where their flat, expressionless boxers' faces aren't waiting.

This afternoon I'll leave Jerusalem. Unfortunately it's the Sabbath and the caravan for Sidon which I want to join won't move until after sunset. That's the Law. I've no time for the Law, no time to wait. Didn't my Lord perform miracles on the Sabbath? Why shouldn't Judas flee on the Sabbath? If the seventh day is good for rest, it's good for salvation, too.

James, John, James. John, James, John. What do they

want? No one speaks to me. They only dog my footsteps. Persistently, calmly, like robbers. I don't see the others. I'd like to have all eleven under my eyes. Maybe then I could find out what they intend to do. They're thinking about me, that's clear. The proof of it is this overpowering, stifling heat surging within me. But what will they do? And when?

I'll be all right if I can just get out of Jerusalem. I'll go to Gevura. Why do you use the words of faith if you no longer possess it, Judas? Say: I'll go to Rome, where there's always work for foreigners. No, I'll say: I'm going to Gevura, I'm going to Kochba. Not one of those damned prophecies can take away my faith. They talk of my dying, but they don't say how I'll do it. They're only concerned with my flesh—to see it hang. Which prophet cares if Judas dies as a believer or godless? Of course I'll go to Rome. I'll get a ship at Caesarea.

At the Northern Gate, where the road to Silchem passes, Bartholomew and James Alphaeus are mounting guard.

In Rome there are more Jews than in Jerusalem; I'll found a new Church there. To proclaim the truth about the Holy Trinity: Judas-Jehovah-Joshua, JJJ. I'll restore faith in the holy crime of betrayal, in its natural outcome. I'll create in glory a place for the true sacrifice instead of the legend of the lamb. I'll announce my own truth, which until now has used a foreign tongue. I'll choose disciples, revise the Old Testament, clean up the Law, write the True Gospel.

I go back to the Jericho road. Philip and Levi known as Thaddaeus are waiting for me there.

I'll leave everything else untouched; the lie about the Passion, the lie about the sacrifice and the lie about Judas. I'll go not to destroy the New Testament but fulfill it. I swear it, Lord; just let me get out of Jerusalem. I'll preserve the faith. For the Deed is greater than the Doer, the Creation is above the Creator.

At the Hebron Gate, Andrew son of Simon and Matthew the Publican are waiting.

Only the Jaffa road remains open to me. I'll get a ship at Jaffa. No you won't, Judas. Cephas and Simon the Canaanite guard the Western Gate.

Jerusalem is shut in, it tightens round me like the fingers of a dying man. Once again the prophecies are gathering, the Hundred and Ninth psalm, Zechariah, Isaiah. The noose of the Scriptures tightens round Judas's throat.

If only day would last! As long as the streets are crowded, nothing can happen. Their eyes—what can they do to me? James's eyes, John's eyes. Sluggish, without concentration, as if created only to rest on me. But when Jerusalem is closed, when the gates now open are closed, leaving the streets to the silent dogs, what will it be like for me then?

The east is shadowed by darkness; black spots break out on the aged and pitted face of the day.

I could place myself under the protection of the procurator and seek refuge in the Tower of Antonia. Those two legionaries, even if they're off duty, won't refuse to escort me to the governor's office. But the Romans won't understand what I want and they don't speak a word of Aramaic. For a while they look at me with interest—Jerusalem is jammed with all kinds of eccentrics, my dear Rufus—then pass on in step, without turning.

Come on, Judas—after them! Hold it, Judas! What sort of safety can those two soldiers give you? Can the soldiers of earth be more powerful than the warriors of heaven, and in what language can they communicate? Can the hunted bear take refuge in a fox's den?

I must knock at another door, batter it down. Jerusalem is full of doors—knock at every one, hammer at them. Don't lock yourself up, Jerusalem, don't leave me in the streets with the dogs. I'm Judas, your Savior! Wasn't it said: "Knock and it shall be opened unto you"? It was, but you're deaf, you sleep! I'm the one who thought of that–Jesus only said it.

Dusk, James and John attack suddenly and together: three equal ingredients of the night. The door—the wooden heart of Jerusalem—remains locked. The howling of the dogs in the open space by the slaughterhouse shatters the peace of our footsteps. The second door, the third door. Not a door opens, not a single window. The eyes of Jerusalem are blind. Help me, Jerusalem! Doors like the frozen faces of hatred. Night and Cephas. Help Judas, friends! Merciless brothers! Levi,

James Alphaeus and the night. Run, Judas! Knock, shout, howl! Doors don't hear. I am he who advised: "Knock." Here is a hole in the darkness. That too is a door. Who knocks? Judas. Which Judas? There is only one Judas! I know only Jehuda ben Gomara and that isn't his voice. Night and Bartholomew in the night. Arms stretched out like grappling irons, white streaks in the slag of blackness. There's no Jerusalem, only endless closed walls which swiftly spin around. Doors without eyes, doors without shame, nameless doors. Philip, night and Philip! Knock, Judas! "Knock and it shall be opened unto you." One more door. Which door? Again, night with its company: Cephas, Philip, James, Andrew, Simon the Canaanite, John, the other James, Matthew, Levi, Bartholomew. Only Thomas is absent. Ten closed men and not one open door. Damn you, Jerusalem! Damn you, Israel! Disobedience has cost you centuries. Let ingratitude cost you eternity!

"Sir, these men are persecuting me!"

The sentry in front of the Sanhedrin is bored. Perhaps he'll take my cause to heart—a heart bored only at night.

"Our friend's joking, soldier," says Cephas, smiling.

The sentry too smiles, as far as his dignity allows.

"They'll kill me!"

"You can see he's joking." Simon the Canaanite takes me gently by the arm. "You've had too much to drink, my friend. Come along and heave it up."

"I'm Judas, who betrayed Christ!"

"Really?" says the sentry.

"They're forcing me to kill myself, so the Scriptures will be fulfilled!"

The sentry's had enough. The sons of Zebedee take me by the arms, and the soldier helps them, pushing my arm under John's: anyone can get drunk at a festival!

"Shove his head under water," the soldier calls out. They drag me over the cobbles, my knees striking the stones as if I were bearing a cross. My cross is the four intertwined arms of the sons of Zebedee: four iron beams. Will someone bear my cross, some unknown passer-by?

Judas breaks free. Someone else must have done it—not me. I know nothing about it. Jerusalem races about me, the walls whistle, the doors flash lightning. Magdalene! Magdalene! Which of the gloomy sidestreets leads to the little virgin from Magdala?

Night. Cephas again. Simon. James. Where's John? Magdalene, my little Magdalene, you who lie at the window whoring with the light, my little sealed-up Magdalene! The doors of the brothel are always open—even for Judas!

The greasy Syrian opens them. A thin man sneaks behind me. He walks as if his legs are broken. They drag him yelping from the threshold. He points at the windows, where blue wicks dimly light up thick white sins. They drive him away, shouting: "Get out, Elkan, don't bother the gentleman coming here in peace!" Can there be peace for Judas?

"Mary Magdalene, where's the little Magdalene? But first shut the door, you bastard!"

"Frankly, I wouldn't advise it. On the other hand, I recommend—"

"I want Magdalene!"

"I've got good reasons for offering you another girl."

"Magdalene isn't busy, is she?"

"No, not at all, but that's what—"

"Shut the door, you son of a bitch!"

Until now I'd wanted all doors open; now I want them shut.

He goes on about Magdalene, but I'm not listening. The rotting stairs, the sour smell of lust, the freshly whitewashed walls, on whose yellowing moisture eloquent drawings stand out, and the numbers of the rooms.

The girl is lying down, the little virgin. She recognizes me at once. "Judas? Where's that other one?"

"What other one?"

"That swine you brought here to drive the devils out of me."

"Oh, he suffered. I mean, he's dead."

"How does that help me?"

"Mary, they're after me."

"He came here like any respectable guest. He wasn't old."

"They're hounding me—shut the window."

"Outside it was pretty cool. I undressed, but he sat there with his clothes on and just looking at me, as if he expected me to take off my skin and expose my insides to satisfy him."

"Mary, they'll kill me."

"Yes, my darling, I hear you. Make yourself comfortable!"

"That Syrian down there, is he reliable?"

"Come on, take your things off and let me tell you everything. Anyway, it's all your fault. You brought him here."

"Mary, has this house got a back door?"

"Ever since he was here that time, I've felt I was a thousand years old. I can't give pleasure to anyone."

"Can we be overheard here?"

"Don't worry, everyone minds their own business."

"For God's sake, Mary!"

"He locked me up. They keep me here as a decoration till they see if I'm suddenly opened again."

"Mary, they'll kill me if they find me here."

"I'm padlocked, so maybe you'll unlock me."

"They'll kill me, woman!"

"Come on, get undressed, my little Judas."

"I'm doomed."

"I'm a whore forced to be a saint."

"Mary!"

"Take your clothes off, you bastard!"

"Mary, little Mary!"

"Out with it!"

"Mary!"

"That's more like it!"

"Who's that knocking downstairs?"

She is sighing now.

"Is that Cephas I hear?"

"Lord, how lovely it used to be!"

"Someone's coming in downstairs!"

"There's nobody—I know it."

Is that Alphaeus's voice—Philip's—under the window?

Mary Magdalene stands by the bed, naked. Her slashing glances strike me. Then she puts on a gown and goes out without looking back.

Judas, you've got to die! Come what may, the Scriptures must be fulfilled.

A whore must become a saint, the dumb must talk, the blind must see, the mad regain their reason. The dead must live again; the living Judas must die. That's how it's written.

You're dead, Judaea, my country, tended by dead hands, watered by dead mouths, warmed by a dead sun. Your chill breezes are dead. The dead winds cool you, dead rains weep for you. O land of my fathers and my children, dead fathers and dead, unborn children, you're the valley of Hinnom without a single tree except to serve as a gallows, without a single stone except for the neck of a drowning man, without a scent except of poison, without a breath except the death rattle, without a refuge except the grave. O my only land, my land of

(HERE ENDS THE ACCOUNT BOOK OF JUDAS ISCARIOT)

Cephas had posted them shrewdly. Andrew and Matthew kept guard in front of the main entrance. Because of the Roman night patrols, they left Bartholomew and Simon the Canaanite to keep watch in the street. James and Levi called Thaddaeus were to guard the back door. Philip patrolled under the windows. Mary Magdalene took the sons of Zebedee upstairs, led by Cephas. The crazy Elkan slipped in with them, tenderly carrying some goat droppings as a gift for the beautiful girl from Magdala; only now, thanks to the crush at the door, did he find a chance to give them to her.

Judas was lying on the crumpled bed with his account book beside him. He lay with closed eyes, motionless, without a word. His hand dangled from the bed, touching the bare floor. The sons of Zebedee had no trouble in setting him on his feet. Only after his first steps did they have to support him. At the door he stopped and unbuckled the purse from his belt, then gently thrust it into the woman's hands. The purse was empty, but somehow it was holy: it had once contained the thirty pieces of silver. The whore was not underpaid, though she was no longer a whore but a saint.

They took him outside. The Syrian bowed deeply, telling them that when they were in a better mood they should come again, for his girls were the most passionate in all Jerusalem and his prices the most reasonable.

Outside it was still night, but they all knew the way to Hinnom. In any case, since they were all together, the valley of the dead didn't seem so terrible: a trifle desolate, nothing more. James and John led him, holding his arms. The rest followed looking like drunken companions curing their hang-overs by a walk before going home.

At last they came to the tree still fresh in expectation of its burden; to the stone still resting on the slope, and to the rope still hanging blackly from a branch as if from heaven itself. The tiny lights in the sky, were they the eyes of winged angels?

The sons of Zebedee placed him on the stone, and Cephas placed the noose about his neck. But before one of them kicked away the stone, Judas came to his senses:

"Don't forget the Scriptures, brothers in Christ," he said. " 'On the third day he will rise again.' That's tonight."

When he died—very quickly, as it happened—the earth didn't quake. It was dead before he was.

Death at Moriah

Now the chief priests, and elders, and all the council, sought false witness against Jesus, to put him to death; but found none: yea, though many false witnesses came, yet found they none. At the last came two false witnesses.

Matthew 26:59, 60

UNTIL A few years before, Varlaam of Ramathaim, which in Latin is called Arimathaea, had no special troubles in his life except his legs which were paralyzed from birth, yet they, though useless, helped him more than they hindered him. As he watched his brothers Justin and Arimai, plowing, digging and harrowing the barren land of the Lamechs, then once a month, on the Hebron road where Varlaam begged, driving two lanky potbellied mules to sell their meager load of grains, mutton fat and puny fruit in the David Square, Varlaam became convinced that his useless legs were a gift from Jehovah and a sign of the special benevolence of heaven. It must have been that his parents, otherwise lazy and worthless, had done something pleasing to God: perhaps they'd stripped a Roman usurer dozing on the threshold of some lordly mansion, or, unwilling to allow someone else's bull to stray unprofitably, had taken it into their own herd, thus fulfilling one of Moses' ambiguous recommendations. In any case, divine thanks had fallen upon the legs of their son just conceived, and being heavy, had broken them for ever.

For a long time Varlaam's parents were unaware they'd been blessed, seeing in Varlaam's paralyzed legs the usual laziness inherited from their forebears. Later, when it was recognized as God's mercy, there were endless family discussions about Varlaam's future. Scolding him for lying all day long on his reed mat, his father suggested that he become a prophet. By that he didn't mean a prophet like Jeremiah, who'd scattered threatening declamations all over the place. He didn't advise him to call everybody and his uncle rogues, sinners and blasphemers, or to curse every nation or their kings, or to describe with enjoyment the torments they'd be condemned to on the Day of Judgment. No, he had in mind those more lucrative prophecies which please everybody and merely picture beforehand those marvelous dreams men always have of their future.

His brothers considered him too backward to imagine such pleasant visions. They tried to get him to weave baskets, boxes and cradles of reeds which they could sell in the Jerusalem market. In this way he could contribute to the household expenses without leaving the parental home. Instead, humbly following the divine mercy which had deprived him of the use of his legs, he chose to become a beggar. That profession wasn't as profitable as being a tax official, priest or artisan, but it was traditional in the Promised Land, where many leaders had once been beggars, not to speak of the beggars who'd once been leaders.

Varlaam didn't become one of those modern beggars who seek to add to the alms they receive by some silly occupation like blowing into reed flutes or charming desert snakes. They think that by such work they're commending themselves to God, but in fact they provoke his anger, for such superfluous undertakings belittle God's blessings showered in so many forms: blindness, deafness, frenzy, leprosy, etc. One such was his nearest neighbor and blood brother, Enoch, son of Enoch. While begging he blew wholeheartedly into a reed pierced with holes, thus depriving his benefactors of the pleasing feeling that they were giving him alms for no reward.

None of that was important. The important thing was that Varlaam's happiness vanished like a doe in the mountains, and his joy withered like a grape in the vineyards of Engedi.

Everything began on the first sabbath of the month of Kislev in Amonach's tavern. A certain Moabite on his way from Rabat of Moab to Zarpat said that the people of Jerusalem would soon have the chance of getting to know a remarkable being. He could give no further details, except that he spoke in riddles which he later resolved and that he was continually threatening some future kingdom. This news didn't disturb Varlaam in the least. In every kingdom except that of the beggars themselves, beggars were a necessity, so that men might have someone to do good deeds to and fulfill the countless regulations of Moses. He was confident of his ability to find a place for himself in this new kingdom, whatever it was like.

Attaching no significance to the Moabite's tale, Varlaam by the diligent use of his elbows reached the road, where he meant to sleep somewhere in the shade of the willows and fig trees. As soon as he saw him, his blood brother Enoch asked what was new in town. Varlaam replied that he'd heard nothing worth repeating.

"The peasants from Bethphage say that the prophet Elias, whom they call the Thunderer, is coming to visit us."

"Forget those prophets, Enoch," said Varlaam irritably. "They never have a penny. They give only blessings and who can live off that?"

"The peasants from Bethphage say that he's coming riding on an ass, and with a colt the foal of an ass."

"Naturally. Prophets always ride on asses. If there weren't asses to carry them, there wouldn't be prophets to prophesy."

"The peasants from Bethphage say that this man makes the lame whole, cleanses the unclean and forgives sinners their sins."

"You must be fed up earning your bread lying down."

"No, I'm not. I don't earn as much as you do, Varlaam, son of Lamech."

"Then stop blowing that bloody reed, Enoch, son of Enoch! Don't mock God and don't meddle with jobs set aside for unbelievers. Do the work Hashem meant for you. Whine, beg, scrounge!"

Though he distrusted Enoch's reliability as a messenger, Varlaam was scared. He was scared because he was the descendant of that Lamech who, as Noah's servant, chose to drown lying down, whereas if he'd run to the ark of gopher-wood he'd have been saved. He trembled terribly because of all his five thousand seven hundred lame forebears, reckoning from the creation of the world, whose beggars' staffs had tapped from Patiala in India to Lutetia of the Secuani, from dry Pannonia to blood-red Thebes. Since in him all the tribe of Lamech was frightened, he quivered as if he had the desert fever. And he prayed:

"Surely, O Lord of Hosts, you won't let some red-hot revolutionary interfere with my sacred legs. Surely you won't let him stick legs under me the way a cuckoo lays its eggs—legs which Adam himself would have rejected, if he'd known that they'd take him out of Eden? Surely you won't let new kingdoms be gained or conquered, and mine destroyed? Surely you won't kill me by salvation, as Nimrod killed the deer with his arrows in the desert of Zif?"

Tortured by fever, that night Varlaam dreamed a terrible dream. In his dream the prophet had already arrived in Jerusalem and made all the cripples whole. Varlaam alone remained crippled, for he'd hidden among the graves. Peering out at the last remnants of the legion of the maimed, he was seen by one of the prophet's followers. This man sent a posse after him and shouted that they'd catch him and make him whole. So he hired a fast-footed Nubian to take him on his back and in this way tried to escape the posse.

"Seize the last of the wretches!" shouted the prophet's deputy, running after him.

"Seize the last of the wretches!" his followers repeated, trying to drive Varlaam into a blind alley.

"Seize the last of the wretches!" howled the cripples who'd been made whole, and who joined the posse.

"Seize the last of the wretches!" screamed the people, preparing an ambush.

But Varlaam's black, an animal of the primeval forest tamed in the conquering forays of the mighty Tiberius, thinking that the procurator's messengers were drafting volunteers for the next war, fled at redoubled speed, revealing how he'd managed to survive all preceding wars.

Then in his dream his pursuers shouted to him to stop,

saying he should surrender to salvation without fear because it wouldn't hurt in the least. Besides, it had to be done one way or another, so there wouldn't be a single man unsaved in the world to spoil the harmony of the new kingdom.

Though he didn't feel he was moving at all, he was fleeing not from one prophet but from a whole flock of prophets and prophetesses, messiahs, miracle-workers, greater and lesser gods—some as large as David's House and others as small as a grain of millet; some lanky as spears and some rounded like a buffalo's balls; some hairy, some beardless; some naked, some in rags; some alone, some with armies and banners—all of whom rushed after him, caught him and threw him to the ground, and showered upon him marvels and gifts and benefits and mercies terrible to see and even worse to endure, each setting him to rights in his own way. Since there was such a multitude of them and each healed him in the name of the kingdom which was the best, they left him a hideous monster with ten pairs of arms and legs, not to mention other multiplied senses and countless changes in body. There Varlaam's dream broke off, to be continued in some unknown stone quarry—unbearable for one of the sons of Lamech—where he saw himself laboring with a dozen others, and then awoke groaning horribly.

He was awakened by a great uproar. He found himself lying on his beggar's reed mat, while above him there shone good-humoredly, like the sun among dark clouds, the face of a stranger. At first Varlaam paid no attention to him. Then with wonder he saw his blood brother Enoch, crippled till yesterday, hopping and skipping about with agility, and saying to the stranger:

"This is my blood brother, Lord! Have mercy upon him also, so he can eternally glorify your name!"

And the man, misinterpreting Varlaam's fear, said:

"Don't be afraid, my son, your sins have been forgiven you. Come, get up, take your bed and walk!"

And Varlaam, son of Lamech, stood without stumbling, picked up his bed and, paying no attention to anyone, ran home. And those who saw this with their own eyes wondered greatly and believed that the man who'd done it had come in the name of the Lord, and was his only-begotten Son who'd release them from sin and every kind of misfortune, and would bring them purified into the embrace of heaven.

Some years had passed since then. During that time the blood brothers Varlaam and Enoch heard nothing of the man who'd given them sound instead of crippled limbs. How could they? A great part of the year they passed in the stone quarries of Ephraim, far from Jerusalem, where for a pittance —not as much as a beggar's alms—they sweated from the black morning to the still blacker evening.

So their legs had brought them no good, and as they lifted each stone to place it on another's back, they imagined that they were lifting the enemy who'd healed them, imagined that they lifted him high, cast him against the rock and heard him break into fragments.

Varlaam had good reason to be furious with Enoch also. Enoch had been healed first, and not foreseeing the full extent of the miracle, had begged the prophet to work a similar miracle on his sleeping blood brother. If it hadn't been for Enoch, Varlaam would still be lying in the cool shade of a tree, begging alms which would make men better than they'd been before. That he didn't reproach him was due to Enoch's penitent attitude and the hatred he cherished for the prophet —a hatred Varlaam couldn't match.

Twice every year, in the course of the quarrying season, the blood brothers were linked to a single yoke and with the other stone carriers brought the hewn stone to Jerusalem, which the procurator used for public buildings and the construction of the ruler's house. Having no plans for the future except to be afraid of it, and no obligations toward the past except to regret it, they took advantage of their stay in the Holy City to squander all their savings, carrying out that brief task with the indifference of men locked in the narrow circle of monotonous everyday life.

Thus in the month of Nisan in the fifteenth year of the reign of the Caesar Tiberius Claudius Nero (whom the divine

Augustus had adopted), the blood brothers found themselves again in Jerusalem. When they'd unloaded their stone in the open space surrounded by a palisade near the south wall—after which they were free until ordered back to the quarries—they went as usual to Amonach's tavern to meet men who shared a similar fate. All were onetime cripples whom that same prophet had healed. To one he'd restored this and to another that, but to no one had he given a better turn of fortune—quite the contrary. If God hadn't created nature and become identified with it, it might be said that nature itself had protested against the violence wrought on its creations. A common misfortune united former beggars and they met from time to time to recall the past, as old schoolmates or members of the same regiment hold reunions.

Among them were a former mute from Jezreel named Jututun; a former blind man, Naum, from the Naphthali plain; a former madman, Zebulon, whose origin nobody knew, though he appeared to be a foreigner; and even a former corpse who, on the excuse that he was under an evil spell, refused to give any informaton about himself.

Brought together by misfortune, they drank without measure, and when a sistrum player came in from the streets, they called him over to their table and after some false starts began, one by one, to sing of their sufferings.

God of Vengeance, God of Vengeance, come!
When he sits in judgment, let the guilty one stand
before him,
May his prayer be sin.
May his days be short
Let another seize his power.
Let his debtors take all that he has.
Let him never find anyone to love him
Or show mercy to his children.
Let the misdeeds of his ancestors come before God
And let his mother's sin never be forgiven.
God of Vengeance, God of Vengeance, appear!
Because he has persecuted the poor and the crippled

And with joy in his heart has sought out death.
He who loves cursing, let it strike him
And let the curse envelop him like a garment.
May the curse enter him like water
And like oil enter his bones.
God of Vengeance, God of Vengeance, come!

When their singing was over, a thin man with huge limbs and harsh features came over to their table. He asked if the evil man whom they'd been cursing was Joshua son of Joseph, from Nazareth in Galilee, who proclaimed himself the Son of God.

And the former cripples answered that it was.

"In that case," said the stranger, "I'm pleased to tell you a piece of news at which you'll all rejoice. The evildoer has been put in prison, accused of breaking the laws of God and man, of claiming to be King of Israel and the Son of God, of prophesying falsely and spreading a false gospel of some heavenly kingdom."

With joyful cries they expressed satisfaction that God had at last heard their prayers and broken his heavy staff over the head of their enemy. Varlaam and Enoch were especially exhilarated; grateful for the best news ever to come their way, they asked the stranger to join in the celebration.

The stranger laughed enigmatically. He understood their eagerness to celebrate this blessing, but couldn't in any way improve it, he said. It wasn't yet time to rejoice. It would only increase their disappointment if the trial came to nothing.

The former cripples grew alarmed. Was the stranger playing a joke on them? Hadn't he himself said that the false prophet was in prison, awaiting trial for actions meriting the pain of death? So how could they be disappointed by the outcome of the proceedings against him?

"To be accused," said the stranger impatiently, "doesn't mean one will be sentenced. Evidence is needed to support such an accusation and assure the credibility of the judgment pronounced. Didn't Moses say repeatedly in the Law that one witness isn't enough to convict a man of any evil or sin, but that the matter is established by the witness of two or three? So for Moses one witness wasn't enough, yet you'd condemn this man without any witnesses at all. Blasphemers! Don't you know the Sanhedrin passes judgment according to the Torah, which is according to Moses, according to God himself? The charges against this man are serious but unsupported; they lack soul. The soul of an accusation lies in proof. Therefore the Sanhedrin is looking for witnesses among the people who can confirm the Nazarene's guilt. So far it's had little success. A few witnesses have been found, but they can only testify about what this prophet preached, not what he did. Since words don't have the force of deeds, the prophet may get a light sentence in proportion to the proven sin of his tongue, but disproportionate to the evil which he seems to have done you. So why are you so joyful? On the other hand, my friends, though there's no reason to rejoice, there's no reason for grief either. Your affair, if I may call it that, isn't hopeless. Find witnesses who'll give evidence about Jesus' unnatural activities. Those whom the prophet healed are of special importance, since their healing broke the laws of God which reserve miracles for heaven alone, and the laws of man which disavow them. I conclude from your songs that you're just the right people to do this, since you can testify about his deeds and show the priests your legs, tongues, eyes and other results of his miracles. This way you can contribute actively to the prophet's misfortunes, not just take pleasure in them."

Filled with confidence, the former cripples asked at once where they should go to testify about the guilt of Jesus of Nazareth.

"To the offices of the Holy Sanhedrin."

In some strange half-hearted way the stranger seemed both disgusted and pleased. Standing at the door through which the beggars were hurrying out, Varlaam asked him:

"Tell me, friend, are you a Sanhedrin official?"

"No," the man replied sullenly, "I'm Judas, son of Simon, whom they call Iscariot." And he withdrew into the shadows by the darkened wall of the tavern, where he sobbed bitterly: "Is there anything else Judas must do so the prophecies will be fulfilled, the Scriptures justified and the world saved? O Lord Almighty, have pity on me and tell me that at last the seventh day, the day of rest, has also come for Judas!"

At the offices of the Sanhedrin, the cripples were registered in the list of witnesses against the prophet from Nazareth. Varlaam and Enoch were especially enthusiastic. Neither doubted that their evidence would be taken into consideration, for all the officials of the Supreme Court had known them as cripples, whereas now they appeared before the court as healthy men.

When summoned, they were led through a forecourt crammed with cripples waiting to give evidence, and from there into the Council Hall. For the first time in several years, they saw the odious prophet. He was standing between two guards, his hands bound by a rope. Welts and bruises made his gray skin grayer, as if he'd been rolling in ashes. One of his eyes was closed; across the other hung a lock of dirty, sweaty hair. He was dressed in rags which flapped about his legs, revealing emaciated thighs and thin calves. Otherwise he appeared dignified.

The high priest asked Varlaam and Enoch if they recognized the prisoner before them. They knew him very well, to their misfortune, they replied. Then the high priest asked the arrested man if he knew the witnesses, and he replied that he didn't remember them. This was called the confrontation. Then the priests asked Varlaam and Enoch where they'd known the accused; they answered that they'd met him on the Hebron road as he was coming from Bethphage riding on an ass. They asked the accused if he'd come by that road, riding on the aforesaid animal. And he replied: "Thou sayest it!" Then they asked the witnesses if they'd tried to meet the accused or if he'd come to them unannounced. Competing with one another, the former cripples replied that the accused had approached them of his own will while they had been lying peacefully on their beggars' mats. Then they asked the accused if this was true.

"Thou sayest it! For it is not the sheep which go to the shepherd, but the shepherd who visits his flock."

Then they asked the witnesses what the accused had done to them, and they replied angrily that he'd made them whole.

"And before that you were cripples?" the priests asked.

"We were, we were, reverend fathers!"

And when they asked the accused if this was true, he replied: "Thou sayest it! If there was a miracle then it was I who performed it, for who other could do so except the Son of God?"

At that blasphemy they raised their hands to heaven and cried out: "Sentence him! Sentence him!" and "Death! Death!" and "Anathema! Anathema!"

Then they let Varlaam and Enoch go. As they were leaving the Council Hall, thinking joyously that they'd avenged themselves, the accused man turned to them and said:

"Today you've done my Father a great service and you've merited the eternal gratitude of men. Go in peace!"

They marveled, thinking the fellow must be crazy, since he didn't realize their evidence would lead him to the place of execution. As they boasted to the cripples in the forecourt of what they'd done, it occurred to them that the prophet had gone crazy from fear of death when he'd thanked them so wholeheartedly.

"So you two testified there was a miracle and he worked it?" asked an old man named Bartimaeus, son of Timaeus. Instead of eyes, he had two cold blue holes.

"We did, old fellow," replied Varlaam and Enoch proudly. "Do you think we should have defended him?"

"And you?" The old man turned to the other cripples, "What evidence did you give?"

"The same as these two. We told how he healed us. We said he'd worked a miracle on us."

"Listen, old fool," said Varlaam, "if that fellow had healed you, too—as I see he didn't—you'd be singing a different tune. Since it was us and not you that he did it to, it's natural that we wanted revenge. Our souls won't be at peace till he's hanging on the cross."

"Unless he himself wishes it," said the old man.

"Who ever wanted to hang on a cross?"

"Then why did he thank you instead of reproaching you?"

"That's right," Varlaam acknowledged uneasily, "he did just that. We figure he's out of his mind."

The old man turned to the other witnesses: "And you, what did he say to you?"

"The same as to them. That we'd done his Father a service and could go in peace. He must be crazy."

"Not *him!*" screamed the old man wildly. "You're crazy! You've all done something insane!"

Enoch was offended: "Didn't we honestly help to convict him?"

"And because of that you've given him peace! You stupid fools, don't you know who he is and why he came into this world?"

"To save it from sin, old man."

"How?"

"That we don't know," the former cripples replied in chorus.

"Of course not! You don't know anything! If you'd known, you wouldn't have done what you did. According to the prophecies the Messiah must redeem human sins by his death. If there's no death, there's no redemption, and if there's no crime, there's no death. And there's no crime without witnesses. If it hadn't been for you who testified, his death wouldn't take place. Nor the redemption of the world. That's why he thanked you, imbeciles—if it weren't for you, he'd still be wandering about Israel a tramp, a cheat and a false prophet. Instead of harming him, you've brought him to God's bosom. Instead of unmasking the plot, you've taken part in it like sheep. Damn you all, damn you a thousand times!"

With these words Bartimaeus, son of Timaeus, the blind man from Jericho, left the forecourt of the Council Hall.

The trial was over and the forecourt quickly emptied. Suddenly, bewildered attendants rushed to the priestly leaders to recount an improbable happening: the corpse of Varlaam, son of Lamech, had been found in one of the rooms. He'd hanged himself from the hook on which the Temple servants hung the sheep slaughtered for the burnt sacrifices.

As for Enoch, son of Enoch, he went on working in the

quarries of Ephraim. Every spring in the month of Nisan, and every autumn in the month of Tishri, on his strong shoulders he brought the hewn stone to Jerusalem.

After all, one has to do something for a living.

Death at Gabbatha

> But ye have a custom, that I should release unto you one at the passover: will ye therefore that I release unto you the King of the Jews? Then cried they all again, saying, Not this man, but Barabbas. Now Barabbas was a robber.
>
> John 18:39–40

RUSTY, worn as a silver didrachma rubbed by the thumbs and bitten by the teeth of merchants, Barabbas ben Tahat, an outlaw from the desert of Moab, a slave from the Jewish bank of the Jordan, stood in the Jerusalem prison, waiting for the supervisor Tiron to carry out the decree of the procurator and free the man of the people's choice. The smith had already broken the fetters on his legs and with difficulty Barabbas had been able to beg his leg-irons from him, to take them to Kir Moab as a gift to his sons. The children would surely be delighted with this traditional souvenir from God's city.

Like all poor men, he was particular about his clothes. His limbs—darkened as if struck by lightning, the oracle of fate—protruded from a sack of undressed sheepskin, and in his hand he held a square piece of leather, a meager reminder of his town hat. From time to time he'd put on the leather and move closer to the guard's shield to view in it that wrinkled remnant of his robber's dignity, which the rats at the Tiberias mills had been chewing for fifteen years. Then he spat and turned humbly to the legionary:

"Soldier,"—the guard stepped back and brandished his spear—"do you think the supervisor will show up soon?"

"The supervisor will come in his own good time," the Roman said. "And you, Barabbas, shut up!"

"I will, but I've been waiting for him ever since morning."

Barabbas fell silent, listening to the harsh grinding of the millstone which echoed from the mill or from his memory. He couldn't tell which, since for a long time he'd been inhaling the thin, stifling stink of flour, like the prick of a needle in his nostrils; even his chapped skin smelled of it.

Then for the third time since daybreak he heard the mob before the Council Hall shouting: "Crucify him! Crucify him!"

"Soldier," he said pensively, "for years past my humble ears have taken pleasure in that Israelite catchword. Why not adopt it as a greeting? Herod the Tetrarch, may his western gods protect him, could issue a decree."

"Shut up, Barabbas," said the soldier, yawning.

"All right, only let it be known that the son of Tahat likes Jewish folk customs."

As he was saying this Barabbas glanced through the square opening, in the courtyard of the prison, which glittered in the sun as if anointed with olive oil. There were three chestnut trees in front of the flour store and from them hung huge flabby leaves, like gigantic, yellow scales of dandruff, swinging to and fro. Only one of them, hanging vertically, was doing its best to twist around its own stem. Being a gentle soul, Barabbas gave thanks for the approaching storm; a downpour was the only way heaven could pay tribute to the one who'd be crucified that day at Golgotha in place of the Moabite.

And you, how will you pay tribute? Even if one doubted that Joshua ben Joseph, whom certain harebrained bigots called the Messiah, had saved all men, it was certain that, by getting Barabbas out of his troubles, he'd at least saved the most unfortunate of them. But the Moabite didn't have time to think of the sufferer whose sentence had been pronounced by the prophets, and which the Sanhedrin had merely confirmed. He had his own troubles. Those troubles, naturally, wouldn't exist if the procurator of Judaea hadn't pardoned him on Passover. Though the zeal of a savior, the Nazarene god-man, had taken from Barabbas precious years when he'd have prepared for the day of final settlement, cheered on by leaden whips, he didn't blame Christ. But he wasn't grateful to him either, and when freed had no intention, as was expected, of vanishing into the hills of Abarim more swiftly than the tempest when it retreats into the thickets above the Dead Sea. For no one knew about Barabbas's mysterious adventure: neither the Savior, who was worried only if he'd be enthroned on the left or right side of God the Father; nor Pilate, who was pressing from the Jews, as from overripe grapes, the pension for his old age; nor the Pharisees, concerned about the color of the rod with which Moses divided the sea between Egypt and Canaan; nor the people, who reckoned only in battles. That secret was all he had, and it gnawed at him vengefully like a worm gnawing at the state flour in the prison.

No, by heaven, it wouldn't be enough to stand before Lucius Caius Tiron and announce:

"Thousand times most gracious sir, I feel profound satisfaction that for all this time, for all the fifteen years I've spent in Caesar's mills, I've cheated you wherever I was, and judging by the fact that you trusted me, I have now at our leave-taking—which I hope will be eternal as hell—the right to conclude that your wisdom is enough perhaps for some lazy slave, but quite insufficient for the supervisor of a state prison."

That's good, Barabbas, only son of Tahat, that's good, but a trifle monotonous. You rattle like an empty pot, and heaven only knows if you'll manage to pour out all the insults nourished over all these years, before they throw you out of the office. Nothing can happen to me, Barabbas thought, as long as I'm protected by Passover and the procurator's promise to exchange me for that crazy reformer from Nazareth. But they might halt him when he got to "the right to conclude," or even earlier at "profound satisfaction," for what satisfaction could he seek other than what he could squeeze out of all those innocent hearts from Idumaea to Phoenicia. Suddenly and painfully he realized how little fifteen years of suffering was on which to base the rest of his life; he'd turn the millstones eagerly and with enthusiasm for yet another fifteen years, if he could be sure that in that time he'd polish his sentence, finding for it those true, unique, hitherto unspoken and unimagined words. He said dejectedly:

"As far as Barabbas is concerned, he has plenty of time."

"Shut up then," snapped the soldier. "Can't you see I'm thinking?"

Barabbas envied the young warrior of the Tenth Legion. He felt a veneration for literacy, acknowledging his own painful inability in the field of such importance to him. This veneration was recent, arising from the dead end of his sentence, from the humiliating inability to imagine, elaborate and put into words the ill-humor he felt toward the supervisor Tiron. The pardoned man grieved: if I were only as educated as these Romans, what a sentence it would be! With only a little schooling, it could be a longer, more important, clearer and more fervent curse from which the Jews, the Idumaeans, his own Moabites, and even the conceited sons of the Tiber bitch—not to mention the ragged naives of the western wildernesses—would imbibe hope, till it went to their heads like the new wine of the Samaria vineyards. Only educated men, he concluded, should be sent to concentration camps; only sages and prophets who could pour out farewell sentences—if ever it came to farewell—endless, wise, golden-mouthed sentences, as deadly as the salty sweat of the slaves over their millstones.

"I revere wisdom," Barabbas confessed humbly.

Unquestionably, the Messiah was reasonably well educated, but his glorious saying after the judgment, which had enchanted Barabbas, was neither endless nor wise, still less golden-tongued. In Barabbas's opinion it was silly, and so, without trying to recall it, he'd limited himself to exchanging experiences of suffering with the popular wonder-worker, whose entertaining of crowds at village fairs the new prisoners had mentioned. What had the prophet from Nazareth meant to say to his judges?

Was it: You're blessed because by killing a man you create a God?

No, that wasn't it.

Was it: What's your judgment to me—I can't be killed?

No, that wasn't it.

Or: If you spare me, I'll work for you and perform miracles?

No, it wasn't that either.

Barabbas looked at the bare courtyard where the wind stirred the tiny shadows of the leaves. A stray sunbeam was wasted on the wall of the mill.

Though he couldn't remember the Nazarene's sentence, he knew it was unusual, dry and short. It had to be short. Both short and incomprehensible. It was well known that he'd been talking all his life, while over that same time Barabbas had uttered scarcely a hundred words, of which half were prayers and half oaths—in fact, prayerful oaths which in his formal approaches to God gave the impression of friendly directness. Therefore the Moabite had to hurry, had to say everything now which he'd failed to say in so long.

But God of my Fathers, what am I to say?

Barabbas, you desert ox, you cow fed on henbane, you were aware of the faults of your sentence when they were taking the yoke from your neck; while you were packing up your rags in the storeroom; and when the warder was frisking you (cautiously, as if touching weapons, though no one could take anything away from the imperial mills except the grinding of millstones, the whistling of whips and the undertow of a lifetime of curses) in the registry where your name on the waxen tablets had been replaced by that of the wonder-worker. And here you are, waiting to insult Lucius Caius Tiron with four words for every year of suffering, each one taking vengeance for a season and sixty words for fifteen years. In fact there are more than sixty words in the sentence. The extra ones are in revenge for the ills which, till the end of the year, the supervisor Tiron might have inflicted on you, if the procurator's decree hadn't forestalled him.

Besides the striking faults which in the course of a mere fifteen years couldn't easily have been avoided, his sentence also had some indisputable qualities: dignity of expression, because a pickpocket from the aristocratic suburbs of Alexandria had helped him choose his words; daring ideas, thanks to the timely counsels of Jochanaan, a con man from Baal-Harmon; and some cool official terms provided by Somna, a three-time murderer from the plain of Sharon, till he won the long-avoided and unenthusiastically awaited honor of being smeared with tar, wrapped in tow and ignited so as to illuminate a puppet-theater performance for the children of the Roman garrison.

Hesitantly, with the pride of an unrecognized artist, Barabbas thought of the labor he'd expended during fifteen tormenting years on those sixty-odd words, reckoning even the two-letter words.

That spring in Sivan, when he'd been hewing stone in the Ephraim quarries, as much as a whole month had passed without his even touching his sentence. Heavy as the weight on the neck of a drowning man, it had rested on the very foothills of his numbed memory. But with every ore-bearing rock he'd lifted to take it to a place from which, at the very next moment, he must take it back to where he'd got it, without any hope of its remaining there, he also lifted the chilled body of his sentence until it rolled over again, and, crushing all before it, always became different and, he hoped, more perfect.

He believed in it, as the Nazarene believed in his. Yet the advantage was on the side of Barabbas, for he still hadn't uttered his, had done nothing irreparable, nothing which for a mere trifle would waste the labor of years. The conceited prophet had never doubted his own paltry concept, had never thought that compassion for one's enemies—yes, his sentence had begun with compassion or something like it—undermined a healthy instinct for revenge as a balance, a balance which had assured him his worshipers. Barabbas, however, since he'd spent all his life with animals—or with slaves who in speech didn't differ much from horned cattle—had begun to have serious doubts. Not vain enough to sustain a feeling of omnipotence with only a few syllables of his sentence, he enjoyed working on it as on the stone of Ephraim which promised ore, or liked to just think about it until he knew it by heart. But he'd never heard it spoken. It was dead: a bodiless living shadow dumb to him, yet mutely and passionately recalled, and impatiently milling about in his mind.

Standing in the pitch-dark catacomb of the Jerusalem prison, Barabbas ben Tahat remembered how he'd had to resort to bribery. To Joel, the idiot accused by the Pharisees of desecrating the synagogue, he'd relinquished his portion of oatmeal—a hard but necessary renunciation—and in exchange this madman fettered to him by a safety chain had declaimed aloud the sentence of salvation. They'd had to be wary because the supervisors, undersupervisors and head supervisors sneaked in among them in silent sandals. To stifle Joel's clucking, whistling voice, Barabbas had crushed the Ephraim rock with a vigor which only superhuman efforts could inspire. This astounding outburst ensured that of every score of lashes intended for the team as a whole, Barabbas's back received at least fifteen. The economical Romans didn't allow convicts to distinguish themselves by either malingering or overworking: just as they suspected the apathetic slave of stealing from the state by slacking, so they suspected the enterprising slave of hoping for a pardon (rarely granted) which would rob the empire of years of forced labor.

Either because Joel uttered it without real conviction, without understanding and in the peasant dialect of the northern provinces, or because the sentence really was incomplete, sterile and insignificant, Barabbas, when he first heard it, was overcome by shame: it was blasphemous that the most eloquent declaration of his life sounded like a knot of phlegm dragged from the stuttering lips of an ignoramus. The synagogue must have felt humiliated in just this very way when Joel, devoted to some private god, in a compulsion of religious fervor, and hoping for some divine gift in return, had sacrificed his meager excrement, the only currency he had. When pronounced by him, the sentence had seemed slimy as a leper's spit in the Pool of Siloam. Listening to it, Barabbas had imagined rotting fruit falling to the ground on the Abarim plateau.

"Most gracious sir, I'm pleased that all this time I've been deceiving you while you trusted me, so I doubt that you're the man for this job."

He'd been unable to resist the temptation to strangle Joel with the chain that linked them in brotherhood. He'd hoped the next season to be fettered to some more intelligent slave, or to some cunning city vagabond who didn't mispronounce verbs or refer to the state penitentiary as "this filthy clink." Better still, he might be fettered to some golden-throated actor sentenced for insults to the Roman majesty—though his tongue, the instrument of his crime, would probably have been torn out by the city executioner before the condemned man ever reached the camp.

Unfortunately, nothing had come of all this. They'd thrown his partner's corpse to the guard dogs and chained him to a brutish Numidian who didn't know a word of Aramaic. Barabbas hadn't lost patience—he had all his life before him—and undertook to teach the black a language from which he could draw words for his magnificent thought. They'd been getting on quite well when suddenly the pupil breathed his last, unable to fulfill the daily quota of stone to be quarried between sunrise and sunset. Before he gave up the ghost, the Numidian actually spoke a sentence—not Barabbas's but his own—in a language understood by no one living.

"I can wait, soldier," Barabbas said meekly. "I can even wait all day."

"Then wait," said the ill-humored legionary. "That's all you can do!"

"And all night, as well. It makes no difference to me!"

Then, for the fourth time since daybreak, the mob passed in front of the Council Hall, yelling war songs from the struggle against the Philistines, and chanting: "To the cross with the King of the Jews!" Their turmoil mingled with the harsh whirring of the millstones turning in the cellar.

Barabbas paid no attention to either. He devoted himself entirely to his coming farewell to the supervisor Tiron. Dejectedly, he had to admit that the older his phrases of farewell, the more clumsy and bloodless they seemed.

Death at Gabbatha

For Barabbas there was only one life: strong food, healthy sleep, and roads filled with careless merchants—a way of life which the more literate had succeeded in transforming into the jewels of idleness: jewels they'd bequeathed to him as the God-given Law of his forefathers, that Law which from the most ancient times had managed to survive all disastrous wars and all predatory occupiers with their usurping gods, taxes and customs. Under the sizzling skies of the caravan routes, that Law had found the narrow pass into Barabbas's robber heart, which, inexperienced in the higher spheres of politics, couldn't resist the beauty of the prophetic visions, the divine inspiration by which they were revealed and the fervent agitators who under the protection of the desert dunes had spread them on both sides of the Jordan. He could scarcely recall those wonderful words which mysterious speakers had aimed at him as the simoon whirled sand in the eyes of the camel drivers on the Judaean uplands. Freedom, for example. Freedom was one of them; another was Final Settlement or Revenge—he wasn't quite sure which—and the Romans were mentioned and the Lord God not forgotten: words with which, from time to time, his mother either lulled him to sleep or frightened him. Finally, if he wasn't mistaken, there'd been talk of the Return of someone or something. These words, otherwise without any practical sense, had shaken him like an earthquake licking the skies of Moab with the foaming tongues of the Dead Sea, and he—God forgive him!—after muttering a few prayers for absolution, had raised his hand against an agent of the tetrarch who, disguised as a cowherd sitting beside the caravan fire, had praised the occupiers from the west. Carefully, so as not to spoil his clothes which could be sold, Barabbas had broken his spine, stripped him and buried him in the sand, first with his head turned to the west, for Barabbas was vengeful, but then with his head turned to the east, for he was even more devout.

When later he found himself in prison, enveloped in the sweaty smoke of flour—in the merry-go-round of the mill where slaves smelling of carrion walked in circles like shining ghosts in hot wind—if he wanted to avoid collapsing, he recalled again the words which he had learned from the Jewish agitators, and undertook to change these provocations of misfortune into accomplices of his salvation. He arranged them all until he obtained a sentence, the mother sentence of all those that followed: a formula which didn't disappoint him but didn't excite him either.

"The Lord will take his revenge on the Romans and will return to us our freedom."

Something about this didn't quite fit. The Lord bewildered Barabbas, for if he was personally obliged to settle accounts with the occupiers, why should the Moabite do his job for him, and if salvation was not exclusively a divine undertaking, why was his name called upon unless to lead the naive robber on with ingenuous guarantees? In this first crisis it became clear to Barabbas that his program must be personal, not national—still less Jehovah's—and that it must express his own personal opinion concerning the origin of evil.

Through no fault of his own or the Greeks, he became a philosopher who pondered the swiftest and most effective salvation for a convict awaiting the death of a draft horse. He was helped in this by his complete nonenthusiasm for turning the millstone, and his repulsion at the certainty that he would turn it until he died. He was still well preserved; there was no prospect that his life would end in the foreseeable future. He still had to make countless circles around the central pier of the mill, to whose handle he was chained, and still had to grind countless sacks of wheat until he died some night, like a worn-out waterwheel horse. Thinking over his position, he felt some self-respect at having strangled his partner Joel. By granting him salvation, he had swiped from the Roman masters two strong, submissive, long-lasting arms.

From that mother sentence—as he called the first one—he threw out all general and impractical expressions: "freedom," which he couldn't conceive of; "the Lord," whom he didn't believe in; "the Romans," whom he feared; and "return," which he got rid of from superstition. In any case, deprived of all historical knowledge—he knew nothing about David,

Solomon and the other kings of Israel—how could he have any idea of a past so worthy that one might want it to return? Of all the words, he retained only "revenge," and from it began his grandiose task.

The first problem he had to face was how—if circumstances were favorable and he obtained an amnesty—he could bring great evil upon the supervisor Tiron. To reach a solution, he studied carefully the nature of the supervisor's calling. After strenuous investigations—some of which ended with a scourging and others with several days without food—he found that every supervisor, and therefore every undersupervisor, believed himself to be all-seeing, ever-present, undeceivable: in a word, God in a simpler and more efficient form. He decided that he must let one of them—if possible, the most conceited—know that this was delusion. So Barabbas constructed a new sentence which, unlike his first, owed wholly to his own ability and took the form of a modest confession: "Most gracious sir, I've cheated you." Then, to make it more insulting: "Most gracious sir, I've cheated you all the time." To tell the truth, "all the time" wasn't such an exceptional advance, though it made the sentence longer and the insult endless, as if these ten little letters—ten lightning shocks for his hitherto useless voice—stretched his sentence to eternity.

No, Tiron, it's not a matter of some innocent, short-lived lie, a single hour's shirking or some crust stolen from the stores. I must provoke the unbearable thought that behind the slave Barabbas ben Tahat lurk months and years stolen from your stinking empire, and mountains of loaves filched from your thieving legionaries!

Barabbas didn't remember why the supervisor had punished him that summer by adding three more pounds of lead to his fetters, but as a counterblow he'd added to the sentence some private emotion of his own. At that time it had sounded magnificent enough:

"Most gracious sir, I'm pleased that I've cheated you all the time."

After his striking success in refining his passions, the sentence suffered no serious changes except in tiny details which he added or subtracted, more out of his habit of playing with it than for any need to lengthen or embellish it. In place of "all" he'd at first put "the entire," then added "this." Then, disgusted, he threw out both of these and replaced the original "all." Next, bewildered by the number of variants and combinations, he'd added "this" again, so the tortured phrase read "all this time."

The following winter Barabbas had decided to omit the honorifics from his greeting. This occurred to him when, after three months' confinement, he crawled out of the sweatbox: the place where disobedient slaves, or those suspected of disobedience in the absence of the supervisor, were kept, without any possibility of sitting, lying down or standing. But he'd become aware of his bias and in the spring—when memories of the sweatbox had evaporated under the heavy scent of grasses breathed in from the tales of newly arrived convicts—he reflected coolly and restored the "Most gracious sir." He justified this by telling himself that without the honorifics his sentence would seem lame in its ridicule, more of an excuse than a mockery.

Be careful, Barabbas, son of Tahat. That treacherous Roman is capable of any malice; the cruelest at his disposal is that he won't understand you—the terrifying innocence of a tyrant!—and will fail to grasp the mockery in the exaggerated honorifics. To be quite sure, he exchanged "Most gracious sir" for "Thousand times most gracious sir," a form of address which the protocol of the Palatine reserved only for Caesars. Knowing that in this parvenu state every nitwit, from a supervisor of slaves to a rheumatic veteran, had the hope and real chance of being lifted up on the shields of the Pretorians to become an autocrat, Barabbas wasn't afraid that the astonished Tiron would cut him short before he reached the insult at the end.

The following winter, some time around Hannukah in the month of Kislev, he almost wavered when Somna—to some extent his collaborator—expressed the fear that the sentence was too short and that Tiron wouldn't take any notice of it;

he would need some time to realize that a slave was addressing him and still longer to reconcile himself to such audacity. Overwhelmed by these two emotions, would he realize what was being said to him?

"Do you know what that scoundrel will say to you, Barabbas?" Somna said. "He'll say: 'The procurator has pardoned you, Moabite dog, but if we ever meet again, Tiron will crucify you, but only when you've been reduced to such a state that you'll beg him for death!' And do you know what you'll do, Barabbas? So as not to meet him again even in a dream, you'll flee to your Abarim and spend the rest of your life on one leg like a heron. And do you know why? So you won't fall asleep. That's how your vengeance will end!"

Discouraged, Barabbas admitted Somna was right if one viewed the affair from the supervisor's viewpoint. Viewed from his own, everything looked quite different and the sentence was its own justification.

"I admit that my sentence is as short as one of God's commandments at Horeb, but I can't hold Tiron in front of me for a lifetime while I explain what I think personally of him, his bloody emperor and his people. Even so, my sentence as it now stands gives me hope that it'll contain words which I'll never be able to pronounce and others which don't even exist yet. Somna my friend, can anyone utter a curse without drawing a breath which would last until his death, and not draw it as easily as one breathes in the freshness of the morning?"

Somna agreed that such an anathema was out of the question, that only a powerful god could exhaust all his words in a single thunderous outpour of bile.

That winter Barabbas almost abandoned his task, and without an aim very nearly died. The next winter revived him with the blood which Tiron's cat-o'-nine-tails drew from him. The following winter he forgot all about the project, feeling only fatigue. But the winter after that the sentence was again resurrected, for by some miracle he was still alive, and for that very reason had to find a better explanation than his endurance or Roman compassion.

Standing in the pitch-black catacombs of the Jerusalem prison, Barabbas watched with envy the hundred-year-old slave Laban, who was conceived under the millstone and could expect to breathe his last upon it. Clinking the fetters forged in the time of Pompey the Great, Laban was pushing a rubbish cart across the prison yard, spearing the dry leaves with a pointed stick and piling them neatly in the cart. If I had time like old Laban, he reflected, I could think of something unheard-of since the time of Exodus. If by some good fortune the procurator's pardon were an administrative error, or if the fickle mob changed its mind and asked that the Nazarene be freed, then he'd compose the most eloquent and telling oath in the world. Or at least he'd have a chance of composing it, and if he didn't he could only blame his own lack of skill.

Hating Christ because, interested only in his own mission, he'd snatched precious time from him, Barabbas sang his own words to the age-old cowherd's song which David had used to bridle Saul's rages, and in so doing Barabbas stirred up his own.

The legionary said he hadn't heard a sweeter hymn in years.

Just then a squad of the procurator's guard emerged from the peristyle, escorting the Nazarene wonder-worker to the place of execution. The self-styled King of the Jews was almost naked, and bloody as a sheep whose slaughter has been botched by amateur butchers.

Barabbas started. Why not ask advice from Christ? He was under an obligation to give it to him. If it hadn't been for Christ, Barabbas would be turning the millstone for countless more years and have endless chances to perfect his vengeance. The Nazarene could well relinquish to him his farewell sentence, which in any case would no longer be of use to him.

"Lord," he called out, "what was it you said to me recently?"

With the vague glance of a nearsighted man, Jesus looked at this hairy fellow in rags. Thinking him some unbearably sanctimonious follower, indifferent to the true faith, who was exploiting his last chance to wheedle some heavenly advantage, he replied gruffly: "I don't know," and started to move on.

But Barabbas wouldn't let him. He grabbed the Nazarene by the arm:

"Tell me, Lord! Help me so I too can say it and deserve your kingdom!"

Jesus replied dully: "Let me pass, good man. Can't you see I don't remember?"

"I'm not a good man," said the Moabite. "I'm the robber Barabbas!"

He stepped toward the condemned man who, backing against the wall in self-defense, threw pleading glances now at his unknown assailant and now at the doors, behind which growled the crowd in front of the Council Hall.

"Answer!" said the Moabite.

"I don't know," whispered the Nazarene.

The legionaries laughed heartily. One offered a short spear to Barabbas, who grabbed it by the blade and used the handle to beat the Nazarene.

"I don't know!"

He defended himself more out of distraction than defiance. "I know nothing!" he wailed, then fell.

Disgusted now by the sight—a bungling squabble between two unevenly matched wretches—the soldiers kicked the Moabite into a corner and led the condemned man away—gently, even tenderly—to the common task which awaited them.

Barabbas emerged from the corner, and wiping his bleeding palms on the wall, said to the guard:

"I'll wait."

He had a naïve belief in the consistency of Roman heartlessness, consoling himself that there was plenty of it for all peoples and all lands. But years had passed and he still hadn't forged his sentence, he lacked even a premonition of its outline. For three winters he'd turned the millstone in the company of an apathetic mule, and in all that time had only decided on a few more additions to the sentence. He'd spent the next season in confirming these additions, and the one after that investigating their grammatical form. First he'd put "greatly" in front of "I'm satisfied," then decided on the skillful strengthening of "all the fifteen years." This, he thought, gave his curse a precision previously lacking.

After a few unbearable months of drought—which also had their good side: the pestilence from which his colleagues died, so that he changed his partners more often and lived a more intense social life—Barabbas was horrified to find that he'd overlooked a crucial fact: Caesar's mills, his place of work, were nowhere mentioned! "All this time, all the fifteen years" combined nicely with "I've spent in Caesar's mills," and another decisive part of the insult, "I've deceived you wherever I was," was completed by "and judging by the fact that you trusted me," so that with this and one or two other minor changes, the sentence read:

"Thousand times most gracious sir, I'm greatly satisfied that for all this time, for all the fifteen years I've spent in Caesar's mills, I've deceived you, and judging by the fact that you trusted me, I have the right to conclude that you're not cut out for this job."

Up to the unexpected amnesty, the only changes he allowed himself were when "I'm greatly satisfied" was altered to the more distinguished, almost patrician "I feel profound satisfaction"—a gift from Jochanaan, the con man from Baal-Harmon; and when "deceived" was changed to the more impudent "I've cheated you wherever I was." He'd now learned that, among the Romans, bums and idlers without apparent reason became Caesars while losing nothing of their former character, even as Caesars became bums and idlers while still retaining all the vices of their former honors. He exploited this fact by recalling the proverbial laziness of slaves in the conclusion of his sentence:

"Thousand times most gracious sir, I feel profound satisfaction that for all this time, for all the fifteen years I've spent in Caesar's mills, I've cheated you wherever I was, and judging by the fact that you trusted me, I have now at our leave-taking—which I hope will be eternal as hell—the right to conclude that your wisdom is enough perhaps for some lazy slave, but quite insufficient for the supervisor of a state prison."

As the sentence got better and better, juicier and juicier, you, Barabbas, got thinner and thinner, uglier and uglier. But it—not you—was the most important thing. It was the best part of you, Barabbas, your only immortal relic, your only descendant.

Barabbas looked at the sundial at the end of the courtyard, that round stone face which changed its expression every five minutes. Just a little longer, he swore, and I'll have finished this disgusting sentence. O God of my Fathers, give me just another fragment of time, just a chip of eternity which you'll scarcely even miss, you who are so overrich and spendthrift, and which—you selfish and invisible usurer—you'll never use for anything of profit to men. You gave me fifteen years of torture, spare me now one little hour.

And Barabbas thought more quickly than he'd ever thought before: "profound satisfaction" goes out; "spent in Caesar's mills" goes out—they're sties for swine, not work-shops for men! Because of the freshly acquired "sties" he restored "spent," and instead of "I've cheated you wherever I was" chose the effective peasant expression of his homeland, "I've made an ass of you."

Barabbas thought more quickly than he'd ever thought before: I won't exaggerate with "Thousand times most gracious sir," and I'll say "I'm overjoyed" instead of that fruity "I feel profound satisfaction." I won't complicate things with "for all this time," but I'll say vulgarly and accurately "for all these fifteen years." And I'll be damned if I'll say "judging by the fact that you trusted me, I have now at our leave-taking —which I hope will be eternal as hell," because I'll do my best, dear Tiron, to make sure that we meet again. And even if I die here waiting for you, Tiron, fixed in your memory forever will be the mocking smile of Barabbas, son of Tahat, the robber from Moab, the slave from the Judaean side of the Jordan.

And Barabbas thought quickly, more quickly than he'd ever thought before: I'll stand before Lucius Caius Tiron and I'll say: "Gracious sir, I'm overjoyed"—and how!—"that for all my fifteen years in this pigsty I've made a fool of you, and now at our leave-taking I think that your common sense is good enough for a slave but insufficient for a master."

Barabbas spits on your aid, Savior of the world. He can get on without it. He'll stand before the supervisor Tiron and say to his face: "You know, Caius, I feel great because in your own pigsty I've been leading you by the nose for fifteen years."

No, by Adonai, you'll say: "Listen, you Roman son of a bitch, you leprous bastard . . . !"

By Adonai and all my sufferings, I'll tell him: "You . . . you . . . Roman son of a bitch . . . !"

"Go on in, Barabbas," said the legionary. "The noble supervisor has come."

Barabbas went into the supervisor's office, repeating the only thought left to him after the destruction of all the other thoughts in the world. When he came out—he'd been in there only a very short time—the soldier asked him how he liked Marius Lentulus, the new supervisor of the prison.

Saying nothing, the son of Tahat went out into God's city, dragging one leg after the other as if they didn't belong to him. Now he remembered the sentence he'd begged for from Jesus the Nazarene: "Lord, forgive them for they know not what they do." But what good was that to him now? There wasn't a thought in this world which could restore him to life.

An hour later a muleteer discovered the robber's corpse in the gutter; a horseman had ridden him down and was already far away on the road to Hebron.

Death at Golgotha

> And as they led him away, they laid hold upon one Simon, a Cyrenian, coming out of the country, and on him they laid the cross, that he might bear it after Jesus.
>
> Luke 23:26

WHAT HE EXPERIENCED that day was surely death.

Death in the shape of four pains, sharp as thorns, driven through his tendons into the wood, and he was crucified on the four-branched pain as if he were on a hot beach looking at the sun which, like the fiery tow hurled from a Balearic sling, fell from the heavens above Golgotha. A thin chill like the palm of a hand dipped in water passed across his eyes and was then dispersed in the heat. On the bushes and stubble the shadows dried like black laundry. To the southeast, from the cliffs on the hill of Zion, Jerusalem rose against the new God, to whom after so many offenses black Friday had come at last.

To his left, a knotty voice was cursing in Philistine; to his right, the breathing of the crucified man sounded like the undertow of the tide on a sandy shoal. Below the soles of his feet, in the cleft of shadow the dice rattled in the helmets of the procurator's guards, and distant, very distant, almost hopelessly remote silhouettes crouched and wailed in the aloe thickets. Only above the crosses all was quiet; above the three crosses the heavens were empty without the birds which the summer pestilence had long ago destroyed.

The place of execution sizzled in the sunlight. Death was well illumined, quite clear through the heat haze in which the three crosses quivered like three spits.

Death didn't hurt just his hands and feet crushed by the iron nails; death pinched him between the thighs because there, wrapped in cheap cloth, was the wooden wedge supporting his body. This fifth emissary of death was also the most unbearable; comic and insulting, it didn't belong seriously to dying, except that it humiliated him and transformed the torso of the condemned man into a huge, stabbing blister.

Would his God come, he thought as he listened to those crude men from the west quarreling over his clothes. He knew they weren't grabbing them because of the value of those stained and bloody rags, but because, like the lock of a dead man's hair or a piece of tooth, they brought luck, especially if the executed man was important. It really gave him pleasure that they thought him important and that his relics, hung about the neck as amulets, could ward off illnesses, the evil eye and the whims of destiny. He snickered maliciously. "O God, forgive them for they know what they do!"

Those Roman fools didn't really know what they were doing and would only grasp it when it was too late and the crosses were set out for them also, an endless row of spits for the orgy of heaven. He felt a flash of rapture that he wasn't the only one deluded, but it passed quickly; it was a stupid exploit to deceive others by his own death.

From the cross, as if from an observation post, he could see the roof of the Cyrenian's house, a tiny fist with node-like red tiles. What was Temna doing now? Lying on the sheets sprinkled with scented waters, before calling on a friend from Acra to sort out over supper the most recent Jerusalem scandals? Asking herself why her Simon was late for lunch? Or was she supervising the servants cleaning the silver with ash from copper vessels? But what's the use of thinking in such stifling heat?

Would God come as he had promised? Or, rather, would *his* God come? He hadn't promised anything, of course, but he had to turn up sooner or later.

But God didn't come and it was late in the afternoon and the guards were snoring in the meager shade of his still body. God hadn't come and yet he'd believed him, Rufus had sworn in his name and Israel had amused itself greatly with his miracles, for whatever the Pharisees babbled in the synagogues and old men in the market place, they were more miraculous than the neck-breaking feats of the Babylonian magicians, more miraculous than the tricks of the Temple charlatans in the land of Khem, more than the titillating miracles of Astarte's maidens, more miraculous even than the miracles of Moses.

As for the wonder-worker himself, he was self-taught. His miracles were new and original. Whether they were of any value wasn't decisive, because one doesn't really expect miracles to help, only to change. One doesn't expect the greatest of miracles to distort the present, but rather to clear the way for the future. They'd finally convinced him. Totally. The water from Cana of Galilee had gone to his head. He knew that the stone vessels for the ritual ablutions contained nothing but rainwater, nothing but slush. Even that knowledge though hadn't been enough to keep him sober. He and the rest of the wedding guests had sung psalms and popular songs, whereas Rufus, devout and toadying even when drunk, had drawn crosses with his fingernail on the thigh of a girl from Cana. Only a powerful God could have performed something so incredible. Or perhaps some dextrous innkeeper.

And God had left him to perish in his name.

Who were you, you stupid ass, to deserve his attention? Worm among worms, son among sons, the chosen among the chosen and, by Hashem, a fool among fools. You've trotted through places of worship, run messages to all the crossroads of Judaea from Ziklag to Dan and from Jericho to Joppa, pursuing the swift, false shadow of God, which fled away like a mirage before the thirsty wanderer. Into Judas's goatskin bag you've dropped the silver pieces earned by your sweat—that bag which finally held the thirty pieces of silver, drops of the most precious sweat of death which the world has ever smelled—all this, instead of getting good and drunk and—leaving Rufus to go on chasing that elusive divine shadow—you yourself, simply and painlessly achieve your place in heaven: the best possible, since it would be yours alone, and if you got bored with it for any reason you could wash it away with a single jar of rainwater. Clothed in rags, you knocked on every door; kept company with lepers and whores; and lived with the dead and the possessed, alongside herds of swine that were ready to accept their demons from anyone willing to send them there. They stoned you, spat on you, and chased you with sticks like a mongrel bitch with a can tied about its neck sniffing the trail of some canine divinity. You didn't wear bells around your neck, but rattled your rebellious truths as if you did. You were disloyal to your own flesh and blood so that the new kingdom should come. You scorned the testament of the fathers so that the kingdom should come. You even slandered your neighbors—you who could have had anything on earth. The new kingdom hasn't come and even if it had, you'd never have noticed it in your frenzied rush.

What new kingdom? Instead of the new kingdom, the old crucifixes are erected. As for equality before God, that amounts to dying with criminals; between an incestuous thug and a murderer to be exact, and there's no difference between them in the manner of dying.

God slipped away into his heavenly cellar and you, old fool, are stretched on the cross like a wild boar being skinned in a dirty Byblos butcher shop, while Peter is being chased by the godless all over Jerusalem, and the sons of Zebedee are being beaten under the walls of Zion with wet canes, belts and reeds!

And there's no God among us as he'd promised. He's weaseled out and skipped, hasn't he?

Where's the truth announced to us on the Mount? Where's the kingdom conquered for us? Where's the open Book of Life we were called upon to peep in? Where's "to the right" and "to the left" of the Father, when there's no Father and my bloody glance crawls across the desolate Judaean plain over which the ravens fall like black bolts of lightning.

What is truth when I'm dying?

Where is truth when I'm dying?

What truth can survive, untouched, and outlive my death?

Death at Golgotha

Is my cross at least within the reach of heaven, which according to the prophecies awaits us with open arms? Ah, sweet-spoken whore! Ah, divine whore, why was I chosen to die? Ah, prophetic whore, ah, manger-born whore, is this your heavenly bliss?

And that merciless sun which scales off as if to devour his dried slough as soon as he's dead in order to scorch the survivors with its fresh, cold brilliance, those red-hot scales which cling to his wounds, that dead air which sticks in his throat like a bone, that thorn's blossom in the eyeballs, those boiling geysers in his ears, those winged nails which tear at his testicles. God, is this possible?

Everything had for him the fresh face of a shadow. Three kneeling dromedaries on the Silchem road were three dirty spots in the sand, three insignificant humped shadows in the flood of heat. The winged, living shadows of the vultures cruising over Golgotha, always in one place like a wheel stuck in the mud. The brittle, fragile, dusty shadow of the thorns; the slender shadow of the javelin leaning against the cross; the pointed shadow of the cross itself stretched along the earth; the earthen hot shadow of an odd rock; the rounded shadow of the helmets; the flat, level shadow of the jugs of vinegar which shone below his nailed feet; the transparent, holy shadow of his garments as they are passed from hand to hand, the shadow of a sigh, the bodiless, windswept shadow of dying which lay silent between the arrowlike crucifixes.

What day is it?

Is it Friday? The last day of suffering before the Sabbath rest, the last day of life before the eternal Sabbath? Black Friday before White Saturday?

He was thin, emaciated, ill. He hoped slyly that he wouldn't hang long like some of those bumpkins who took their time dying, three days and nights, bleating like billy goats on the skinners' hooks. They won't break my ankles, he thought, glancing sarcastically at that bear of a Philistine stretched out on his cross, wrapped in a sheepskin, strong, tough as Moses' rock. The rod would strike a long time on his chest before the water of his dog's life poured out. That one, I swear, will have time to get used to his death, while you, wretch, will fulfill the prophecy, not to prove this or that prophet right, but because you'll give up the ghost before there's need to break your shinbones.

There were three of them on the crosses that Friday. Each on his own cross as if in his own cradle. Perhaps there is only one death, Father of my fathers, but when it attacks me, then it's mine alone; it's not Zachary's who hangs on my right, nor the Bear's who hangs on my left. Finally, you ass, you've got something which is yours alone and which you mustn't share with the most gracious Caesar. Anyway, what would a tithe of your death look like tossed into the sacrificial bowl of Jehovah's Temple, the first fruits of your dying given as an offering? What would a tithe of your death look like in the imperial treasury, and how would the imperial treasurer test its purity and weight? How would the customs officer bite your death, test with his teeth the tithe of your death when you pay him your toll? How would it be if you supported your family by your death? And Temna, could she dress herself in your expensive dying?

That idea cheered him a little. He'd have liked to share it with his neighbors, but decided not to.

And God is nowhere!

Nowhere!

Nowhere!

Your God has run away!

It sounded like a Galilean marriage joke, he thought.

"I thirst," he said.

The centurion with the reddish fuzz on his chin stuck a sponge on the tip of his spear, dipped it in vinegar and offered it to the man on the cross. He sucked at it avidly, then spat in disgust a yellow fluid on the Roman's rusty snout. He enjoyed the curses of the soldier, who didn't dare touch him (it was strictly forbidden to interfere with a death sentence) and withdrew angrily into the shade of Zachary's cross.

To hell with that whining Zachary, who was constantly pestering him with prayers:

"Remember me, O Lord, when thou comest into thy kingdom!"

What could that mean?

"Idiot!" he screamed.

"He's calling Elias," a woman in the crowd explained confidently.

He hadn't called anyone except his God who'd deserted him at the crucial moment, he'd called him softly, with sweet words, as if luring a bird into a trap suspended under the burning sky. Who needs that obnoxious Elias? He was in no mood for company anyway.

It's four o'clock and God isn't here. No sign of him. And very likely he won't be. God's in no hurry, nothing's hurting him, no iron nails poking through his hands and feet, no wooden wedge under his balls, no crown of thorns digging into his temples, no live coals of the flaming sun burning his eyes, no bloody spit boiling under his tongue.

On Sunday you were supposed to go to the wedding of Rufus's friend. Not likely that you'll go. On Sunday, if all goes well, you'll be dead. Anointed with cheap oil and wrapped in stone. Stone will be cool at least. No more roasting in this brutal sun. You'll be resting on your bier with your wounds covered. The professional mourners, led by pipes and double flutes, will extoll your virtues and achievements (no mention of those that brought you to the high cross above Zion), and Temna, ripping her garments, will wail "Oy, Ahib!" and "Oy, Adon!" But Rufus will go to the wedding. That swine doesn't give a damn about his father. If only none of us gave a damn about our fathers, earthly or heavenly. Heavenly, especially. Adonai, he cursed, can't you see how your Chosen One has led me by the nose? And how from a carver of wood he's turned into a carver of men?

Zachary and the Bear said they should talk to make the time pass more quickly.

"What are you thinking, Son of God?" he asked.

"I'm not the Son of God," he replied.

Then why did you bear the cross, why did you run

I didn't run

you did You were scared that the cross and redemption might pass you by

but the procession by great good luck
what lousy luck
got jammed in the Gate of Justice in the middle of the north wall like a divine seal on the last page of the history of sin as a sign of the ultimate end as a prophetic brand which will never be moved forward or backward nor will it ever be erased
the spit of Israel what brand and seal's that
the mob red blue yellow white green black amid the merry-go-round of color only one man bewildered and caught in the act like a child
was it you
who'll be able to tell us apart when all differences are wiped away and canceled among us and when I hang here for both
you hang for God and you hang for man
I hang for myself in place of God and man
it's hard for me and would have been harder if I'd had to bear the world as I bore the cross knowing what no one knew and fulfilling what no one was asked to fulfill
if I'd known how I'd end how I'd die if I'd known this pain this thundering in my limbs and lightning in my eyeballs
but that cross wasn't mine
I knew nothing and it wasn't heavy for me and simply didn't belong to me just as the burden he carries for a master doesn't belong to the porter
I had to lug it along as far as Golgotha and that for me was all its weight and torment for a while
though Temna'll never forgive me for running away from her bed
I must think clearly
crosses are beds for men and beds for gods
either way his death is
my death
the spit and the hare embracing one another
what am I here and who am I here
look I bear the cross with no effort and it doesn't worry me that the longer crossbar which has slipped from my shoulder drags across the cobbles and splinters a fine thick cross any-

way for a fine thick torture from which future generations will grow fat

and I peek between the longer and the shorter arm and see his thin hairy legs disappearing among many strange legs

and there were so very many

in strange clothing red yellow blue white green black

at six o'clock the skies grew gray as the belly of a sick man perhaps my God is coming with a belly gray with anger but instead night fell

with strange unstable voices and strange mercies until I lost sight of him as he wiped his sweaty face with our neighbor Veronica's scarf

so Temna my little dove it was too late to throw off the cross it weighed me down as if it were my own and made to my measure

how it hurts how it hurts

but I'll think clearly and with dignity

think of what since there's no way back and my God's nowhere

there's a lovely shade there the roof of my house and the red tiles over you and you dream in that shade and my moan is so near your windows that you can touch it with your finger dip your little finger in wine and offer it to the moan to lick

O God O God why have you forsaken me

plug along carry your weight for you've arrived in time after a whole life of searching in time to meet with God with truth and with you who are the most important truth

and all these years do you know what that means all these years will remain empty like shallow footsteps in living sand

At seven o'clock he heard breathing which couldn't have come from his companions. Perhaps my God of Hosts is returning, he thought, distraught by the murmur of the crowd. Instead of God, a wind blew from the hill of Zion and refreshed him enough to feel all the pain.

how that wedge under my balls hurts and that lie in my breast

I want to think straight

how many hours to death to God to vengeance to mother

give me back the palm of my hand Temna which lies forgotten on you lost in you I need it to defend myself these palms are pierced and limp and give me back my accidental deaths preserved in you if you remember them to introduce them to this painful death really painful and unite them with this death which hates me because it's not mine but I grabbed it I pulled it by the hair and begged it to be mine and now I want to return it only I have no one to return it to there's no God among the red blue yellow white green black clothes or among the hairy legs to scoop it up from the dusty altar of the dust for what will the omniscient prophets who crave fulfillment say what Jeremiah Isaiah Amos and the children of Israel who wait for him to die for them but know nothing of me and what will Jehovah say when I come before him without proof that I did anything of what was ordained on this earth and all that work and torment for what

squandered otherwise I could probably have sat on the right hand if I could be sure that there's someone on whose right hand I could sit give me water and not the truth give me water men Romans mother mine I don't want vinegar you son of a bitch and Rufus my son why didn't you look at the bearer of the cross as the procession passed through the Gate of Justice your father that was and not the father of the world or of Jerusalem or of Israel but your own father crushed under the weight of another's cross don't believe my son don't believe anyone I can't think of anything but water give me that water I didn't want to become God how can he who is deceived be a God he who lugged the cross for another like a donkey caught by the roadside and harnessed to a robber's cart go away Temna how it hurts when I call God is that Lazarus hanging about my neck and aren't I the one the blind first saw the deaf heard the paralyzed followed the lepers embraced the dumb greeted why didn't they prophesy of me and say take this cross bear it to Golgotha and then all is fulfilled according to the Scriptures I'm not the Word Temna I'm the Sin give me water for those who call a lie a lie I'm the only lie and all else is truth there's no lie where there's no faith my pain is greater than the world Romans give me water vinegar even if you don't know what you're doing the torments'll come tomorrow and I could have died on the cool grass in a bed of moist cold leaves in the shadow of icy branches holding my Temna by the hand and not under these dry Hebrew Latin and Greek inscriptions O God be damned you've forsaken me water I beg you vinegar I beg you brothers and let there be a miracle as at Cana when water became wine vinegar water which gives pleasure as it cools and heals

When he came to, he heard a dry rustling and thought cheerfully: Perhaps my God is weeping? Instead, rain fell and washed the blood from him, prepared him for new suffering.

Why are those women in the bushes crying? What if I sent them for God? But where's God now? Who can find God at the time of death? Couldn't I send them for Temna? They're so far away they can barely see me. How would I send them anyway? Who can get these women, Salome and Mary Cleophas, to give up this sight; before their eyes the Savior of the world is dying, before their eyes—so they hope—he's unrolled the mysterious unique process of the universal redemption of sin, and they believe that with every breath of my death rattle a stain of the filth of original sin is being washed from them.

Oh, you mother-fuckers, he swore, shaking his thorn-crowned head, ah, Mediterranean worms, Egyptian lice, Sodom and Gomorrah, the victor's wreath swayed like a pendulum, this way and that, the dumbest of all the dumb sons of Israel whom that old mongrel Moses led into the land of Canaan! What's your God doing now? Where's your God now?

Out of the corner of his eye he saw the inscription above his head, in Hebrew, Latin and Greek:

JESUS OF NAZARETH, KING OF THE JEWS

"Eli, Eli, lama sabachthani!" he sobbed.

Which means: "My God, my God, why hast thou forsaken me!"

"Let me die in peace, you son of a bitch," bellowed the

Bear. "If you're the Son of God, get down from your cross and help us to get down, too. If you aren't, shut up!"

"I'm not the Son of God."

"Bear, you Philistine nitwit," Zachary said, "until everything is over you don't know a thing." Turning to him who was dying between them, he added: "Remember me when you get home, Son of God!"

"I'm not the Son of God."

"Whoever you are, remember me when you get home."

"Then he'd better hurry," said the Bear. "He'll kick off before he gets there. He's just barely hanging."

How true, he thought, I *am* just barely hanging. To spite my neighbors. My God.

"We've been sentenced just like him," said Zachary, "but we've done evil and he hasn't."

And the Bear replied: "I robbed five merchants. Wish it'd been six. You just had fun with your mother, Zachary! But this bastard, here, he wanted to steal from all men and sleep with all women! He aimed high; let him carry his own cross!"

"This isn't my cross," he said.

"Then get down from it, Son of God!"

"I'm not the Son of God," he went on apathetically, "and I never thought I was. I did no evil except now and then I was unfaithful to Temna, and in my spare time I read the Ionian philosophers. But I was stupid, and that's an evil for which I deserve the cross."

He no longer felt any pain; it had died away on his skin like a faint itch. He no longer groaned, vomited or ground his teeth. His dying eyes saw a tremendous storm gathering. When the earth quaked for the first time, lightly as if shivering in the frost, he thought it was the footsteps of his God hurrying to help him. The brilliant shadow of a star melted on the helmet of a guard who pricked him with a knife to check if he was alive. In the smoke of the torches his face looked like an open wound. From the Mount of Olives came the roar of the forest. In a black ball in the center of which rose the place of execution bristling with three crucifixes, everything was suddenly clear: the black outlines of Jerusalem, the black mass of the Judaean hills, the black mantle of heaven torn by lightning, the Romans on the black sand, and in the midst of it all, the white suffocating smoke of the three torches stuck in the black rock at the foot of the crosses.

Everything was clear to him now, but he whispered anyway, to keep the record straight:

"Eli, Eli, lama sabachthani?"

"Don't wail," said the Bear kindly. "Get down from that cross if you're the Son of God! Come on, leap down, Jesus of Nazareth, King of the Jews!"

"I'm not Jesus the Nazarene, you Philistine ox, and I'm no king. Can't you tell God from man, the teacher from the disciple, the king from his subject, the sensible man from a fool? I'm Simon of Cyrene," he said wearily.

"I was on my way back from the fields when the Messiah met me, when they were taking him to the terrible place. Me, Simon the Cyrenian. I was greedy for the new kingdom and I begged to carry his cross, to ease his burden and save my soul. He didn't refuse. He never refused those in misfortune. I took up his cross and while I was exalting his name and singing of his kingdom, the Son of God vanished in the crowd. You Romans," he said, spitting on the centurion's helmet, "didn't see him. Drunk as skunks, you crucified me instead of Christ.

"I deliver my secret into your hands, captain!"

O bright sun, he thought—lucidly, all of a sudden, and so knew he was dying. Here on Golgotha there's been a glorious misunderstanding between heaven and earth. You're a burdened worm, Simon, but a worm which through its suffering will drag the whole world by the nose. Wasn't it written that the world would be saved? For that to happen, it was essential that Joshua, son of Joseph, and not Simon, son of Eliezer, die on the cross: not the Cyrenian but the Nazarene. So everything has been in vain—miracles, prophets, parables, sacrifices, deprivations. The world wasn't saved, original sin wasn't washed away. Simon thought maliciously of the men who'd live according to that error, with the illusion which he, though unintentionally, would weave by his death rattle. How can man replace God, and how can man in return for sacrifice put a beetle in place of a bull, tares in place of wheat, rainwater in place of oil? He felt he'd like to push all their faces in: robbers, guards, Christ's proud mother who at this moment ceased to be the Virgin, Christ who at this moment ceased to be the God-man, Jerusalem, Israel and the whole universe.

"You aren't saved! You aren't saved! You aren't saved!"

But in that effort he died, and as he breathed his last he didn't know whether the storm had already begun or the Philistine was mocking him.

It was both.

As they took Simon the Cyrenian down from the cross, the captain said:

"This was a righteous man."

Fearing lest the procurator of Judaea, sensitive to the truth, might punish him because he'd killed an innocent man and let a guilty one go free, he had a herald announce that Jesus, known as Christ, had breathed his last.

On Sunday, Christ appeared to Mary Cleophas—certainly not, as is thought, to Mary Magdalene—and after confirming his teaching in the hearts of Simon Peter, of unbelieving Thomas and all his other disciples, and after issuing detailed instructions for the spreading of the gospel of the kingdom of heaven, he fled into the distant Pontic lands.

And nothing more was heard of him for a long time.

Writings from an Unbound Europe

■

The Victory

HENRYK GRYNBERG

The Tango Player

CHRISTOPH HEIN

The Houses of Belgrade

The Time of Miracles

BORISLAV PEKIĆ

Fording the Stream of Consciousness

In the Jaws of Life and Other Stories

DUBRAVKA UGREŠIĆ